BROKEN FRENCH

TASHA BOYD

Natasha Boyd, LLC

BROKEN

french

For all of you still here to love again.

Content edit: Judy-Roth.com

Proofread: karinaasti.com

Cover Design: hearttocover.com

Cover image © Erin Gianni

First Print Edition April 2021

ISBN 978-1-7369979-0-1

CHAPTER ONE

JOSIE
Charleston, SC, USA

I pulled a pillow over my head to block out the sound of an early alarm beeping incessantly through the thin wall in our downtown Charleston apartment. When the sound didn't stop, I flung the pillow off my head and blinked my eyes open. "Tabitha!" I huffed on a moan. "Why?"

There was no answer, but the clinks and bangs of antique pipes running water to the shower down the hall in our only bathroom answered for her. Tabs must have forgotten to turn off her alarm clock. It was a good thing I was getting up early anyway. Today would be a turning point for me. I felt for my phone and squinted at the screen. It was way earlier than I'd normally get up, but there were two missed calls from my mother. She was as anxious about my presentation today as I was, and she'd transferred that agitation to me without even trying. No amount of "I got this, Ma," could stop her motherly worrying.

I padded through to our tiny kitchen and sighed with relief to see Tabs had started the coffee before showering. I'd call my mother back as soon as I could think straight.

The water in the shower turned off and while I poured coffee, there were the sounds of makeup bag rummaging, and then the hairdryer. She must have a fancy client meeting today. Something dropped, and she hissed a curse. I poured a second cup and knocked on the door. "Seven a.m. wake up? Who's the client?"

The door opened and she poked her face out, brown skin shining and vibrant. "Coffee? Josie, you goddess."

"You're welcome." I leaned on the doorjamb as she took the cup.

"My girl in France quit yesterday. She was supposed to start in three days. I have a video conference call with the family in a couple of hours. Well, the dad. He's a single dad. Filthy rich. A filthy rich Frenchman who probably wants his money back." She grimaced.

"So, you're dolling yourself up to get him to what? Change his mind? Ask you out?"

"Hey!" she protested with a grin. "To look professional, of course."

I smiled. "Okay." It was no secret that Tabitha, in running her own agency providing exclusive, highly vetted nannies to the rich and famous, was hoping that one day she'd find her own happily-ever-after. A single dad would definitely fit the bill. She wanted a successful business and then a family, in that order. She'd accomplished the first within several years of us graduating college.

"Stop, Josie." She rolled her eyes good-naturedly. "I was hoping to find him another nanny, but I've exhausted all my available people and it's so last minute. I'm about to let him and his daughter down. I'll ask Meredith if she knows of anyone when she wakes up. Anyway, I'll be out soon."

"Good. I also need to look professional today."

"You always do." She turned to the mirror to finish her eyeliner as she talked. "You're going to do great. You know you're going to get this promotion. You've put in the time and the work, and from what you've shared with me, you always have the best designs. I don't know what historic Charleston would do without you looking out for its aesthetic."

"Ha ha."

"I'm serious! It actually came up in conversation yesterday. I meant to tell you. I was at the bank and some big wig was congratulating them on renovating while enhancing the historical elements and the bank manager mentioned your firm. So you can guess I immediately jumped in and told them your name and how you were the architect to watch."

"You didn't!"

"Of course I did. No point in letting that old lecherous boss of yours get all the credit when it's your designs getting him the praise."

"That's what being a part of a prestigious firm is about. It's a team effort. Besides, my immediate boss is a sweetheart, it's the other partner, Mr. Tate, who holds the lecherous distinction." I'd adored that project. Most of our projects these days were new construction though.

She snapped open a case holding the fake eyelashes she always wore for video conferencing. "And that's another reason you need your name on the team door. So you can start changing the work-place culture."

"We're only as good as the work we *all* put forward," I said, parroting the company motto. "And name on the door? Hold your horses. I'm trying to make senior associate, not buy in to partner. It will be a while until I can afford that."

"I know, love. Student loans will kill us all. But seriously, you are the best young architect they have. You can't tell me that frat boy nephew of Mr. Tate's has one ounce of your talent."

I took a sip of coffee to hide my grimace at her accurate assessment of our most recent hire, Jason. "I don't like to speak ill of people. Anyway, hurry up, glamor puss. I need to shower."

She tutted before dabbing some gloss on her lips and giving herself a side-to-side preen in the mirror.

"You look great," I said.

She came out the doorway and pointed at me. "And you'll have your name on that masthead before long. But in the meantime, after you get this promotion, maybe we can all move to that new building by the marina and finally have a view."

Our main picture window looked over a cobblestone alley and faced the brick side of the next row of homes. It was a beautiful brick wall as brick walls went. Antique, built hundreds of years ago, and adorned with earthquake medallions. But it was still a wall. A view could be nice.

I grinned. "Thanks for the pep rally. And I'm all for a view, but don't sell me on a view of boats, you know how much I hate boats."

Tabs closed the door to her bedroom but not before poking her head back out. "You hate *being* on a boat. Looking at boats is not the same thing."

"Fine," I conceded with a laugh.

I showered quickly, tying my hair out of the way, glad I'd had the foresight to wash and blow it out the day before.

Meredith, Tabitha, and I had moved in together after college. I'd still had a year of architecture grad school, but Tabitha was already earning a decent income from the agency she'd started out of her dorm room, and Meredith had just started at a small investment firm courtesy of her family connections. We'd lucked out when we'd found this apartment on the top floor of a converted row house in downtown Charleston. It was in the historic district. I *loved* the historic district. There were some of the best restaurants in the South on our doorstep, architecture to admire, and history to steep in. And girls' night with some dancing and a couple of martinis was never more than a few steps away. But we were definitely cramped and still all sharing one bathroom. Almost four years later and the other two could afford more, but

I'd been paying off student loans, with plans to then save every nickel in order to one day buy in as a partner at my firm. I was determined to be the youngest partner in the city. Before then though, I had a promotion and pay raise to negotiate. After that, I might consider moving.

I still worked at the same firm that had sponsored my architecture residency right out of college. Meredith and Tabitha had tried to get me to shop around. They said it was my aversion to change. But I called it being unfailingly loyal.

I finished up in the bathroom in record time and realized when I came out that Meredith still wasn't up. She'd had bad cramps the night before, so she was probably exhausted. I poured a cup of coffee for her into an insulated camping mug, added her favorite vanilla creamer, and tiptoed into her room. She was a lump of pale pink duvet topped with streaky, dyed blonde hair poking out the top. I put the cup on her bedside table for when she woke up.

Within twenty minutes I'd done my makeup and run a flat iron over my waves to combat the Charleston humidity. I dressed in a navy pencil skirt, blue linen blouse, and stuffed my most comfortable pair of heels into my bag. I hated the archaic dress code at work that women *had* to wear skirts. It was ludicrous in this day and age. Especially when we went to job sites. But working at such a highly respected firm made me keep my mouth shut.

I took my bag and roll tubes full of my latest plans into the kitchen so I could make breakfast. The sun had finally come up, and golden rays of it slanted through the alley outside and through the window across our worn slip-covered sofa.

"Hey, let's do a girls' night tonight." Tabitha looked over the top of her laptop. "I haven't been out for ever. Invite Barbara from your office. We can celebrate your promotion and me surviving that call. Oh, wait. Didn't Mer want to set you up with a new guy from her office?"

I gave a small eye roll. "Yeah. Jed or something."

"His name is Jed? No. Way too *'dude bro'* for you."

I laughed. "You can't judge someone on their name."

"*I* can. And I will. You wouldn't date someone named Adolf, would you? Anyway," she barreled on as she often did, waving a hand elaborately in the air. "You need to be with someone who sounds foreign and exotic. Josephine and ... Xavier. I like that." She pronounced it—Zav-ee-yeah.

"Who the heck is Xavier?" I asked, pouring some granola and yoghurt into a bowl.

"The filthy rich Frenchman I have a call with today. That name is ... ahhh. I'm not saying *him*, obviously, but a name *like* that. Though, wow, he's hot. You're named after a queen. Your guy's name should be just as awesome. Just saying."

I shook my head with a grin. "You're hilarious. I believe she was an empress, not a queen. But the name obsession is better than when you were obsessed with matching everyone's Chinese horoscopes in college."

"Hey, that's a real thing."

Tabs ducked into her room and I called my mother back.

"Ma."

"Josephine. I thought you were going to forget to call me before you left for work." Her voice was a mix of relief and accusation with a healthy side of guilt-tripping. Ah, mothers.

I took a deep breath. "Nope. Just trying to get showered and dressed. I'll call you as soon as I get out of the meeting."

"I'm so proud of you, Josephine. If I don't say it enough, I just want you to know it. After Nicolas—" her voice hitched. "Well, I'm so thankful our family name will be prestigious once again. Your father, God rest his soul, is so proud of you. I know it."

"Thank you. And Mom, I'm not making partner yet. That's a few years away. No pressure or anything. "

"You know I don't mean it like that."

"I know." And I did.

"Good luck, my darling."

"Thanks. I love you, Ma."

We hung up, and I gobbled down granola, brushed my teeth, applied lip gloss, and headed out.

The streets were just waking up. Street sweepers were finishing their shifts, and garbage trucks tipped last night's bottles and trash from the alleys behind all the bars and restaurants.

I stopped in at my favorite coffee shop, Armand's, and ordered an espresso with a shot of cream. It was served in a tiny paper cup, and it was just the bolt of energy I needed before a day like today. I swung onto East Bay Street, taking a hit of the marsh and sea breeze coming in off the water, and passed by Rainbow Row, the colorful historic townhomes that faced the Charleston Historic Foundation building and the Charleston Yacht Club. I waved at the French lady, Sylvie, who worked at the yacht showroom on King Street as she passed me on the opposite side of the road. Most mornings I ran into her at Armand's, and we sometimes exchanged small talk.

Finally, I arrived at the plate glass doors of *Donovan and Tate, FAIA, CPBD, NSPE,* one of Charleston's most prestigious architecture firms. With my hand on the stainless steel bar that served as a door handle, I paused and thought of my conversation with my mom. Without her believing in me as hard as she did, I doubt I would have made it this far this soon. It helped that I felt as though I was doing this for my father. Hopefully one day, there'd be another name on the door plate. Mine. I'd been so happy to be granted an interview after my graduate degree, and even more overwhelmed to have been offered a position at such a prestigious firm to complete my three-year residency requirement to get licensed that I'd jumped aboard and never looked back. I'd always loved architecture, ever since my dad would take me on long walks on Sundays around the city and point out all the various details people used that evoked the feel of this influence or that.

I'd also been relieved to have Mr. Donovan instead of Mr. Tate as the partner overseeing my residency requirement. It seemed it was an unspoken understanding that it was best if Mr. Tate didn't mentor young, impressionable women. Mr. Donovan, I knew, had my back. He respected my work and often made sure my contributions weren't overlooked. However, a small niggling feeling had been bothering me for weeks about Mister Tate's nephew, Jason, who'd joined the firm just last year after moving down from Virginia. No. Jason didn't have near my experience with historical ordinances and designs. He was always submitting brash glass and concrete monstrosities better suited for big city tenements than the genteel low-profile look Charleston was desperately trying to save. I was the better designer and I had more experience, and after they saw my designs today, it would be a no-brainer to make me the Senior Associate.

My phone dinged. It was Meredith.

> *Sorry I missed you this morning. Heard about girl's night tonight. I'm in. We'll celebrate your promotion. You've got this! HUGS*

I took a deep breath and pushed open the door to my office building with confidence.

CHAPTER TWO

Barbara, my friend and Donovan and Tate's longtime assistant, greeted me formally since she sat right outside both partners' offices. "I'm afraid Mr. Donovan couldn't come in today. Martha was taken into the hospital."

Mr. Donovan's sweet wife who I absolutely adored had struggled with several cardiac incidents over the last year. "Oh no." I frowned. "Is she ... is it serious?"

"I'm not sure." Barbara grimaced. "Mr. Tate is doing your review," she said with forced positivity.

My heart sank further. "Oh. Are you sure?" I whispered. "I mean, I can just wait. We can reschedule." I'd rather not be promoted today than have to have my review and associate presentation with Mr. Tate.

"He's already expecting you in his office."

I swallowed, then blew out a breath to steady myself. "All right. Thanks, Barb. Oh, I forgot, girls night tonight after work?"

She made an exaggerated sad face. "Sorry, Jeff has a thing tonight. Have one for me?"

"Sure thing." I turned on my heel.

she called, and I turned back. She lowered her voice. your guns. You deserve this."

smile broke through the tense muscles of my face. "Thank ou."

I arrived at the open doorway of Mr. Tate's office. His nephew Jason, my co-worker, was in there. Conversation stopped abruptly.

"Am I interrupting?" I asked

Mr. Tate stood. He always wore pastel colored button down shirts tucked into his suit pants, or into pressed and pleated khaki's on Fridays, and seersucker suits on Sundays for church. Today, he wore a mint green shirt that clashed with his slightly ruddy cheeks and fleshy jowls. "Jason and I were just catching up."

Jason smirked at me then turned back to his uncle as he stood. "Yeah. So glad you were able to come by and meet the new commissioner," he said to his uncle. "You two hit it off. See you for our eight a.m. tee off tomorrow?"

"See you there."

Jason, blond hair slicked back, passed me. "Josie."

"Jason," I returned, my expression as bland as I could make it in the face of his supercilious smirk.

I shut the door behind him. I didn't like being in a closed room with Mr. Tate either, but I hated the thought Jason might listen in. I ran through the words I'd just heard. "The commissioner?" I asked.

"The PPS commissioner," he answered and gestured for me to sit, not at one of the chairs at his desk but in the seating area where he had a low couch. Low couches were the enemy of skirts. I lowered myself gingerly and angled my legs to the side.

Mr. Tate couldn't help himself, his gaze still slithered down my legs to my shoes and back to my thighs and then quickly to my face.

"The PPS?" I pressed.

"Planning, Preservation, and Sustainability."

"Oh," I said. "I haven't met the new commissioner." I had adored the woman, Carole, who'd been in the position before. She'd worked for the mayor's office and the zoning department for thirty years. She and I definitely saw eye-to-eye on curtailing some of the more egregious development plans greedy investors had for our small coastal city.

"He went to school with Jason's father, my brother. Same fraternity. He's Jason's godfather. Good to have contacts in the city government when you're trying to get things approved, am I right?"

"Sure. Though, there shouldn't be a problem with any approval since we all stick to the historic and preservation guidelines, right?"

"Of course, of course. But you never know."

My eyebrows had pinched together, and I made the effort to relax them. Mr. Tate had fingers in a lot of pies, and I had an inkling he was one to err on the cheaper and uglier side of design if it meant a small kick back for him from a supplier. I had no proof of that obviously. But call it a gut feeling. I had a lot of gut feelings about Mr. Tate. And the way he came to sit next to me on the couch rather than take one of the chairs didn't help.

"Well." I forced a bright smile and brought out my plans. "Here are my designs for the exterior of the proposed East Bay Street Hotel. I think you'll see that even though it might be slightly more costly, we'll make up for it in other ways, and it will have no trouble being approved by—"

"The hotel has already been approved." He waved his hand dismissively at my rolls, and surprise and dread hit me square in the belly. "The commissioner already saw Jason's plans at dinner last night," he went on.

"Jason's plans?"

"This hotel will be a huge coup for the commissioner in his new role. It will bring in lots of construction jobs for the city. They're salivating."

"But—"

"Look, honey." He leaned forward and almost put a hand on my knee, stopping himself just in time.

I stiffened at both the aborted action and his condescending address. His words played over in my head. If they'd already approved Jason's designs, did that mean I was off the project?

"I know you get your panties in a wad over the historical fancy-schmancy stuff."

My mouth dropped open, but he continued. "And I get it, I really do. This is Charleston. But we also need to show the world we're a modern city. We can accomplish that with a few flourishes and detailing to keep the history buffs happy, but at the end of the day we're a business. The developers are a business. And the builders are a business. The cheaper and quicker we can get things built the better off we'll all be."

"The better off *you'll* be. Not the city," I snapped, then immediately dug my teeth into my lip. I shouldn't be speaking to my boss this way. My palms were damp with panic. "I'm sorry. I ..." I looked down at the roll tubes at my feet containing my vision for another unneeded Charleston boutique hotel that was heartbreakingly being built on a site that had once held a residence built by a freed slave. The lost building in question had arguably been built by the first African American architect and had been lived in by the legendary Eliza Lucas Pinckney who'd freed him from slavery. The residence had been destroyed by fire and a subsequent hurricane over a hundred years ago. Sadly, an archeological dig had been held up in municipal haggling, but I'd designed a facade to go with the interior that would pay homage to all those elements. I'd worked on it for months and months. "So to confirm, you don't even want to see what I've drawn up. You're going to go with Jason's exteriors?" I asked, my heart slowly cracking. Months and months of research and hard work and the only person who'd probably see it would be the janitor.

His hand went for my shoulder and I jerked back.

"Look, honey," he said, and I felt a shudder roll through me. "I know you're a good architect. And I know you've been with us some time, and Donovan, well, he has a soft spot for you. But you have to know that I'll be giving the promotion to Jason. I mean, *I* started this firm. It's going to stay in the family. Jason will be Senior Associate, and in time, he'll be partner. And then it will be Tate and Tate. Donovan is fixing to retire. And look, I'm not saying you don't have a position here. It's great, fantastic even, to have a female architect on board. And you're easy on the eyes. *Great* to put in front of clients. And talented, of course." He smiled magnanimously, believing he'd given me a sincere compliment. Then his eyes turned somber again. "But even if it wasn't a family decision, which it is, I assure you, I don't know how you could have thought you'd ever really make it to the top in the company and have your name on the door. Not in Charleston."

"Wh-what... why?"

"Nobody has forgotten Nicolas de La Costa."

I was cold, my skin prickly, as all my blood seemed to drain away from head to toe. *God.* "You know I didn't have anything to do with my stepfather's business—"

"That's good to know," he said as if it was news to him. "Regardless. You know Charleston. A small city with an extremely long memory. Of course, we value you here. And I'm sorry that Jason got this project, but there'll be others. You'll have a job here as long as you want it."

"But not a career."

"What?"

"You said I'll have a job here, but not a career." My voice warbled slightly as I tried to rein in my devastation. "You'll never promote me, and I have no way to move up." And after losing the opportunity to work on the East Bay Street project, that seemed insignificant. But damn it. My job. I really needed that promotion. I had to get a grip and focus on what was important. History was being lost. It was more important than my job in the grand scheme of things. I could appeal. As a citizen of the city—

Mr. Tate leaned forward again. "Oh, Josie," he said, tilting his head slightly. "It's not as bad as all that." His finger reached out and then before I knew it his whole hand was on my knee. His hot, clammy, chubby hand.

I froze.

He squeezed gently, his face genial. Comforting, even. "I'm not saying you could *never* be promoted. At least to Senior Associate. Loyalty and dedication to the team is always appreciated. And rewarded." Another squeeze. My stomach churned. "Just not ... today."

I lurched to my feet, and his hand slid off my knee. "Don't touch me again."

"Now, now," said Mr. Tate, palms up. "We'll have none of that nonsense. I was just comforting you. I know you're disappointed about being passed over."

My breath seesawed in and out of my chest, my heart pounded in my throat. I couldn't stay here another second. My chest cinched up tight, and I blinked to try to mitigate the stinging in my nose and eyes that preceded tears of anger and frustration. I dug my fingernails into my palms, my balled-up fists. "I can't stay here."

"Sorry?"

"I quit."

There was a long silence.

"Well, there's no need to be hasty," Tate said, looking surprised.

"I quit," I repeated, though my voice shook.

"Right. Well. If you're sure." He held out his hand.

Numb, I reached out and without thinking, shook it.

Mr. Tate pursed his lips. "Actually, I need your badge and secure ID."

"Oh." I blinked and then fumbled the clip off the buttonhole of my jacket with trembling hands and handed it over. Immediately, I wished I'd thrown it in his bland, jowly face.

"You can leave your roll tubes here too. Your designs belong to us."

I looked down to where they lay at my feet and felt a surge of tears rising up the back of my throat and nose. Not here, I told myself.

"Anything else you need from your desk?"

I shook my head, not trusting myself to speak any more. *Holy shit.* What had I just done?

"Well, if there is, I'll ask Barbara to pack it up." He gestured to the door. "Bye, Josie. Good luck."

I took a breath and lifted my chin. I'd done the only thing I could do. I was a damn good architect. And if they didn't see it, someone else would. I had contacts. I had some meager savings and could temporarily defer my loan payments. I could get a reference from any number of previous clients *and* Mr. Donovan. I couldn't protect East Bay Street, but at least I had my pride. Feeling only a fraction of a percent better after my rationalizing, I turned to the door, then stopped. "Mr. Tate?"

He looked up as he rounded his desk, a placid look on his face like the last ten minutes hadn't even phased him. "Yes?"

"Fuck you very much," I said sweetly and spun on my heel and walked out, putting an extra sway in my step.

CHAPTER THREE

XAVIER
Valbonne, Provence, France

The afternoon sun slanted across the wooden farm table, bleached and worn from decades of use on the sunny patio. The scent of lavender from the fields in the valley wafted across the lawn, mingling with honeysuckle.

"Can I get you anything before I leave?" The gruff voice of Martine, our longtime housekeeper and sometime child minder, roused me from where I'd been in a semi-meditative state after my pre-lunch laps in the pool.

I glanced to the spread of lunch waiting for my daughter to join me. In years past, when my wife was alive, this table had been filled with friends, acquaintances, and extended family almost every week. These days it was a party if Evan, my bodyguard and best friend, joined us.

"*Non, merci,*" I thanked her. "Just send Dauphine down when she's changed out of her swimsuit." A wet towel was still on the chair next to me from where Dauphine had abandoned it. She'd spent the morning in the pool begging me to join her while I took calls and tried to organize childcare. I adored spending time with her, but it was impossible when she was out of school for the summer and I still had a business to run. Of course, in a month or so business would be slower. It was almost August, and practically everyone would be on vacation for *les grandes vacances*. But for now it would be tricky to manage without help.

"Any luck?" Martine pressed, glancing down at my laptop. "I'm sorry I have to leave before you found a replacement nanny."

"I have a call with the American agency this afternoon. Hopefully they'll have someone else for us."

"Keep me informed. I can try to shorten my trip if necessary."

I waved my hand. "No, no. You must go and see your family. It's not your fault our summer *au pair* fell through at the last moment." She'd very unprofessionally cancelled her contract three days before arriving. "The American agency will have someone else, I'm sure of it. They've always come through for us in the past."

She gave a brief nod. "*D'accord*," she said, looking unconvinced.

If it wasn't for knowing that Martine's sister had been diagnosed with cancer, I'd insist she stay until I had someone else lined up. But Martine disliked coming on the boat, always butting heads with our chef, and I wanted us to head out on my yacht for at least a month. It was time we did something together, Dauphine and I, that didn't involve rattling around this big old house with all its memories. If I wasn't working on one of the biggest deals of my business life, I'd suggest we go overseas somewhere and reset.

"*J'arrive!*" Dauphine spun out the door. Her lanky ten-year old body was dressed in a t-shirt and denim shorts, her hair unbrushed.

"And I'm leaving," responded Martine and pulled her into a tight hug. Then she set her at arm's length. "You be good for your papa, you hear? I will see you in two months. Try not to get sunburned, brush your hair and teeth, and don't forget to keep up with your reading. Less *YouTube*, more words. Okay?"

I stood and gave Martine a kiss on each cheek. She'd been a Godsend after Arriette died two years ago, filling as much of a motherly role as she could in our household. Not that my late wife had been an exceptional mother, I hated to admit, but Martine was a female presence at least when my mother couldn't be around.

Dauphine and I sat and ate the *Pain Bagnat* sandwiches and drank our sparkling drinks. Orangina for her and Perrier for me.

"Do you have more work again, Papa?" Dauphine asked when she'd exhausted all her topics of chatter.

"*Mon chou*, I always have work. I'm the boss. My work is never done."

She folded her arms. "I'm bored."

"Only boring people get bored." I shrugged.

She slitted her eyes. "I'm not boring!"

"I know."

"Hmm," she griped. "So what should I do? I'm bored of swimming, and you won't let me be on a screen. You know I could learn something on a screen."

"Like what?"

She gnawed her lip. "Like ... baking?"

I inwardly cringed, knowing that would lead to her wanting to cook something, and with no Martine here to supervise, that was an impossibility.

"How about drawing?"

"That's boring."

I raised my eyebrows, unwilling to be pulled into a disagreement over that particular hobby. She loved to draw. "What about coding your own video game?"

Her head cocked to the side. Her nose, slightly pink and peeling, was dotted with tiny freckles. I needed to be better about sunscreen.

"Truly?" she asked.

"Yes. Find a YouTube video about basic coding and see if you can make a game we can play against each other." I pushed back from the table and stood, leaning down to kiss her forehead. "Or draw," I suggested again, knowing that's what she would probably pick. "Now, I have to get on a call to America. Please take our plates inside on your way."

After she'd left, I poured another water just as a movement caught my eye. Looking up, I saw Evan striding toward me, having come around the side of the house.

"Christ. You'll give a man a heart attack sneaking up like that," I said, switching to English as I sat back down.

He grinned, eyes hidden behind reflective Ray-Bans. "For your own safety, you should be more observant."

"I employ you for that, asshole."

We clasped hands like an arm wrestle in the air across the table, then let go and he sat.

"*On est prêt?*" I asked him, switching back to French.

"We're ready," Evan confirmed. "The boat's all stocked up and the crew is waiting." His accent in French was atrocious. Normally I ribbed him, but today I let it go.

"Did you have any luck finding a nanny?"

"I have a call in twenty minutes. Hopefully we'll have an American on a plane by tomorrow night."

"Amazing what enough money will buy. Dauphine will love that. She loves all those American shows."

I grimaced. "Banal teenage humor. She's beginning to talk like she's ten going on seventeen. But at least she's improving her English."

"I hope you find someone. I have the itinerary planned for all the meetings you gave me, and you'll be spending a lot of day times off the boat." Evan shifted. "I, uh, took the liberty of speaking to Jorge."

I opened my mouth at the mention of my mother's private

secretary, but Evan spoke over me. "Just as a precaution. Your mother will be in Monaco for most of the month, but in a few weeks she'll be in the *Cap Ferrat* house. Jorge says she's been talking about reaching out and asking if Dauphine can visit for longer than just the occasional weekend."

"Did he now?"

I leaned back in my chair, spreading my legs and resting my arms on each arm. "And I don't suppose you then happened to mention we'd be on the boat and in the area?"

Evan had perfected the art of non-expression. "I may have mentioned it."

We stared at each other.

At least, *I* stared at his sunglasses through my sunglasses, giving him the stink eye. For all I knew he was taking a quick power nap.

"Fine," I ground out after a moment. "Did I mention how much of a nuisance you are?"

"Not that I recall. You should tell me again." Then he broke out his stupid Tom Cruise smile.

I tutted in disgust, which only made him laugh.

After a second, he sobered. "You have to see your mother more often. She misses you. You can't just let her be a grand-mother to Dauphine and not be a mother to you."

"I'm not avoiding her. I've just been busy." That was the truth. I adored my mother, and she'd been wonderful since Arriette had passed. But lately, she was nagging me about moving on romanti-cally, and I was tired of her little comments and constant plans to set me up. So yes, I'd been avoiding her.

"The second part I can attest to. But listen, X. Let her help. She's got no one to fuss over, let her do what mother's do best. Let her fuss over you as well as Dauphine."

I felt like he was going to say more. "What?"

"Just ..." He shrugged. "You could use a vacation."

My hand swept around. "My life is a vacation. Didn't you hear?

Ritzy mansions, mega yachts, fast cars, and faster women. It's been in all the papers," I added, a bitter tone entering my voice. The paparazzi had been relentless since Arriette died, trying to misconstrue everything I did. "Apparently I'm still a tragic prince in mourning. And ready to crash and burn."

"X—"

"They're not wrong. Look around. This *is* my mansion. Have you looked in the garage lately? And wait, aren't we about to leave on my yacht?"

"Well, they are wrong about the fast women. *Any* woman. That's what I mean about taking a vacation." He lowered his voice. "I mean take a vacation from being a dad just for a few days. Even a week. And, I don't know, maybe go on a date?"

I barked out a laugh. "Jesus. As if it wasn't bad enough from my mother. And just who the hell would you suppose I'd do that with? Any woman I've even had a business meeting with has ended up splashed in the papers. Who would want that? Oh wait, can't you see I have women waiting in the wings?" I gestured around the large and empty manicured yard. "Far more than I can handle."

At that moment, Gérard, my ancient, toothless gardener, who I seemed to have inherited with the property came over the rise. I guess he thought I was waving hello because he raised a hand in greeting.

Evan pressed his lips closed in what looked like a bid to bite back another laugh. One of pity, probably. "Your mother said she's tried to introdu—"

"No."

"There are services—"

"I don't need a hooker," I snapped.

"Not a hooker—"

"Nor an escort."

"My French must really be rusty." He switched to English. "I meant *dating* services, asshole. Discreet *dating services* for high net worth individuals."

"Oh. So you'd like me to date someone who is *specifically* looking for a rich man?"

Evan let out a pained sigh. "Never mind."

"Just drop it, okay?"

"It's dropped."

"Good."

"Great."

We sat in silence.

"Well," Evan said eventually, "I guess I'll just go. Boat has to leave the marina promptly at 5 a.m. on Tuesday if we're going to keep the security protocols in place around your itinerary. You need to be on there by Monday night. Whether or not we have an *au pair* by then."

"Yes, boss," I said.

"Cute."

I looked at my watch. "I have a call."

The chair scraped as he pushed it back and stood. "Great chat." He headed across the yard to talk to Gérard. I knew he personally spoke to everyone who worked on the estate and made sure they knew to look out for potential trespassers and tele-lenses in trees. He'd also be taking over as my driver, since I was giving most of the rest of the staff time off.

I poured another glass of sparkling water and took my laptop over to the shaded loggia where we had the outdoor living room. I went through my security protocols to open my laptop and found the email from The Tabitha MacKenzie Agency in Charleston, South Carolina and clicked the meeting link.

My own image came up on the screen. My dark hair needed a trim. My eyes and the circles under them showed the strain. Not even the exercise and sunshine could erase the fact I'd been working around the clock the last few weeks with my team in *Sophia Antipolis* to get our latest innovation packaged up for presentation to investors. And several times a week Dauphine still awoke with night terrors. Maybe Evan was right about taking a vacation. Not to go on a date—God knew, my libido had dipped to nothing—but simply to fucking sleep.

After a few seconds my image shrank to the corner and Tabitha Mackenzie's friendly face filled the screen.

"Monsieur Pascale," she greeted.

"Xavier, please," I responded. "How are you?"

She grimaced. "Doing all right. I'm so sorry about the previous nanny. I'd never have referred you if I'd thought the agency would be unreliable. I got your email request, and I've tried ..." She looked down and seemed to have misplaced something. "Hold on. I left your file in the other room."

She moved away from the screen, leaving the view of an architecturally elegant, but minimally decorated, high-ceilinged living room. There was sound of a heavy door opening and latching closed. And then suddenly a red high-heeled shoe shot past the screen and hit the wall.

My eyes widened.

"Mother-fucker," came a woman's voice off-screen.

Another high heel sailed past. "Tabs?" the voice called. "You still home? Goddamn assholes," the voice raged. There was a rustling and then, "Stupid, irritating, uncomfortable, anti-feminist contraption." A bit of white lace catapulted into view and then landed on the chair back. "Ah. That's better."

A bra. My mouth dropped open.

Suddenly a figure followed the voice—curves encased in a tight pencil skirt and lush auburn hair spilling down her back.

My stomach bottomed out. And she was turning toward the screen as she re-buttoned her blouse.

Shit.

She had no idea she had an audience.

As if woken from a stupor, my hand shot out and slapped my laptop closed.

A beat of silence passed. Then another.

Breath burst through my lips in a harsh exhale, and I blinked. Belatedly, I realized my heart was pounding like I'd been reacting to an erotic movie.

I guess my libido wasn't dead after all.

Holy shit.

I busted out a snort of laughter.

Who the hell was that? Whoever it was hadn't realized I'd been witness to the whole thing.

She'd be mortified if she realized.

Tabitha Mackenzie would be embarrassed too. It wasn't exactly the professional and discreet image the agency prided itself on.

Whoever that woman had been, she oozed unconscious and fiery sex-appeal. I reached for my glass of water. My mouth felt dry all of a sudden.

I'd give it a few minutes then reconnect and pretend I lost the connection as soon as Ms. Mackenzie left to go get her file.

CHAPTER FOUR

JOSIE

Tabitha snapped her laptop shut and whipped her headset off. "Damn. That was brutal. And he hurts to look at."

"That hot, huh?"

"You have no idea. But a grumpy son of a gun." She eyed me from across the room where I now sat in my comfiest sweatpants, a clay mask on my face, digging into a pint of Ben & Jerry's Triple Caramel Chunk. "So, you want to tell me what the heck you're doing home?"

I lifted a shoulder and dug up another spoonful. "I quit."

"You told me that already. I guess I'm asking you to elaborate since you came home having a meltdown, and I had to get back on the call."

"Yeah, about interrupting your call. I'm *so* sorry."

"*I'm* sorry I couldn't drop everything to be a shoulder." She gave an amused grimace. "Thank God his connection went down. He would have gotten an earful and an eyeful."

The tips of my ears grew hot. I wasn't *entirely* sure he hadn't at least seen or heard something. I'd been having a pretty epic melt-down and basically stripping out of my work clothes before I'd realized Tabs' computer was open on the table. It was disconnected when I turned around. And he'd called back and hadn't said a word. I had to just hope and pray that was the truth.

"So, what did you tell him?" I asked.

"Don't change the subject. We can talk about the sad, hot, Frenchie later. First spill."

"Sad? Why?"

She shook her head. "Nope."

"Fine." I planted the spoon into the leftover ice cream and set it on the table—I was starting to feel mildly ill from how much I'd eaten anyway. I brought Tabitha up to speed on the events that had transpired that morning.

When I was done, she sat with her mouth hanging open. "I knew it," she burst out. "The old boys club continues alive and well. Obviously you're going to file a complaint."

"To who? Barbara? Mr. Donovan's assistant? There's no Human Resources department in a company that small."

"The newspaper then."

"Tabs, no."

"Josie. This is egregious!"

"I know, okay?" Tears pricked my eyes. "I know it is. It's disgusting and unjust. But I can't put my name out there by going to the news. You know I can't. It would destroy what little amnesia people have developed about my stepfather. It would kill my mother to have all that trotted out again. I have no recourse. None."

Tabitha crossed her arms and began pacing the living room. "There has to be something."

"Look. Tabs. I'm raw. Just let me process this. Let me break the news to my mom. And then I'll try and see what comes next for me." And how the hell I'd pay off my student loans now. I let my head fall back.

She stopped and came over, plopping on the sofa next to me. "You're right. I'm sorry. I'm just mad on your behalf."

"I know. And I love you for it."

"Have you told Meredith yet? Wait. No, don't. I'll do it. She needs to get out of work early. We need an emergency girlfriend session. Girls night is starting at," she glanced at her watch. "How about four o'clock? You better eat something better than ice cream so we can drink. Coz we need to drink to strategize revenge."

"Can we table revenge and simply strategize about where I might get another highly respected job doing what I spent eight years training for?" My heart thumped heavily. It felt suddenly as though I was letting my father down. And my mother. And not just myself. Had I done the right thing? I was going to need to apply to a bunch of firms as soon as possible.

"Fine. We'll throw some ideas around. But then we are going to come up with a way to castrate those assholes."

———

"A bag of dicks," said Meredith calmly, her hazel eyes focused on not spilling a drop of her Pear Blossom Martini as she brought it to her mouth.

I felt my eyebrows rise as I set down my Gin and Elderflower Tonic. "I'm sorry, what? It sounded like you said bag of d—"

"Dicks. I did. So, there's this service and you can anonymously go on and type in your nemesis' name and address. Then a few days later, they get a package in the mail. All mysterious. They open it up and it's like a literal huge bag of edible dicks. So many dicks, they'll go on for days. And they're gummi right, so like do they eat them? But there are so many of them. Do they give them away? Throw them away in shame? And," she chortled, "if you're extra salty you can add glitter to the package."

Tabitha hissed. "Glitter."

"Glitter." Meredith nodded sagely.

"Oh em gee," Tabitha crowed. "That's genius. Send them to the office, Josie."

I thought of sweet and lovely Barbara opening the office mail. "Er, that'd be a no."

"No, no, no," Meredith said. "You always have to send it to their home address. That way they have to open it in front of their family and explain to them what they've done to deserve a bag of dicks." She took another sip of martini as Tabs and I caught each other's expression in a knowing and horrified expression.

"Tell me you haven't sent a bag of dicks and not told us," I directed at Meredith.

"To a married man," Tabitha added.

Meredith hid her face back in her martini. "I didn't know he was married, okay? Hence the bag of dicks."

"Oh, honey." I winced. "I'm sorry."

"I was so ashamed, you guys. I didn't want to tell you. I felt like such an idiot. And no one knew we'd hooked up, so I tried to just forget about it."

"Who was it?" Tabitha asked. "You haven't talked about anyone since that lovely guy from Cincinnati who was here— oooooh." We both grimaced. "Yikes. I'm sorry."

"How did you find out? I thought you guys just fizzled because of the distance? And I didn't realize you'd … you know, done the deed before he left."

"I shouldn't have. Ugh. Warning bells were sounding and I just ignored them. But yeah, I found his social media profile. Not only is he married to the most gorgeous woman, who's a pediatric surgeon by the way, but they have twin boys who are so freaking cute. Ugh. Why are men such evil creatures?"

"They aren't all evil creatures," I defended, and then thought of my stepfather and what he'd done to my mother and by extension to me. "Not that I have a lot of good male influences to call on ... but they have to be out there. Good men. Kind men."

"Kind is sooo sexy," Meredith said wistfully. "Men who are kind, who read, love animals, love kids, and bring their women tea in bed."

Tabitha raised her glass. "And always make sure she comes first."

I raised my glass to Tabitha, and Meredith joined in. "I'll drink to that."

"I bet the Frenchie is kind," Tabitha said.

"The sad, hot, Frenchman?" I clarified.

"One and the same."

"But he's, like, a squillionaire," said Meredith. "So that makes me think he might not be so good at the make-sure-she-comes-first thing. My theory is that men who are hot and rich don't have to try as hard to keep their women happy. They're entitled and used to getting what they want without working for it. Case in point, Cincinnati Man. Deliciously handsome. Loaded. Gorgeous wife and kids that he doesn't appreciate. And he's still out there expecting more. And I can tell you, I definitely did not come first. Or at all for that matter."

"Nooo," Tabitha breathed in shock. "That's criminal."

Meredith slapped the table. "And that's why I sent him a—"

"Bag of dicks!" we all screeched in unison as we busted out into hysterics.

After our laughter had died down and we ordered another round of drinks, I gave a happy sigh. "I really needed this, guys. Thank you."

"I needed it too," said Tabs. "I hate letting clients down. It made the whole day feel shitty. Especially on top of what happened to you. But I've honestly reached out to every contact I have, and no one is available at such short notice to go nanny for this family. It would be a plum job for the right person. He offered to triple the normal rate. I've even reached out to other agencies I trust, wanting to give them the lead. But there's no one. And people who haven't already got summer placements are either looking for short-term weekender gigs to fit around other stuff they have going on or full-on long-term contracts. No one who I can stake the reputation of my agency on is available right now for six to eight weeks."

The server dropped off our drinks and a basket of tortilla chips. Clearly, we looked as though we might need to soak up some alcohol.

"But we live in Charleston," Meredith said. "It's a college town. And this is a summer job. Surely there's someone."

"You'd think. But I can't just pluck a random college student. Even with a background check they might be crazy or try and sleep with the dad. I can't risk it. He has the most gorgeous little girl too. And they've been through a lot. His wife died a couple of years ago, and no way, I can't risk sending the wrong person."

"*You* could do it," I suggested.

Tabs shook her head. "Ha! I wish. My days of nannying are over. And you know my sister is getting married next month, I have to go home to Aiken for the whole lead up. I'm taking a much-needed break from my business."

Meredith slapped her palm on the table, making us both jump. "Josie could do it."

"Do what?"

"Go to France and nanny for the sad, hot, Frenchie."

My belly disappeared down to my feet. And then I barked out a laugh. "No way."

Tabitha turned her head and stared at me, her brown eyes suddenly glittering with hope and excitement, like I was a fat trout at last light.

"No. No, no, no. Don't look at me like that." I shook my head. "She was joking."

"No, I wasn't," Meredith chirped.

"Shh," I hissed at her. "Are you crazy?"

Meredith popped a tortilla chip into her mouth. "Nope. I'm a genius."

"Tabitha. It's the drink talking," I reasoned. "I have student loans. Rent to pay. I need to get my resume vamped up and out to other firms."

Tabitha dragged her eyes off me to Meredith. "You *are* a genius, Mer."

"No, she's not," I whined. "She's dumb."

"That was low, Marin, but I'll let it slide." Meredith popped another chip in her mouth like it was popcorn and she was settled in for the entertainment. "And please, let's not forget, Josie, that your Pinterest board is covered in Frenchy French things."

"That's only because of my dad's family heritage." And mine, obviously. Meredith was right though, I had a whole board dedicated to all things French. Little old medieval towns, cobbled streets, old farmhouses, fancy chateaux, cafes, vignettes of French farm tables piled high with baguettes and fruit with sunshine spilling in from some old thrown back pale blue antique shutters. Okay, so for someone who'd never been, I could qualify as interested in going. But it was a bucket list item. It would happen *some* day. Not tomorrow for goodness' sake.

"Please," Tabitha pleaded. "Literally no one else is available on such short notice. It will be awesome, I promise."

"Hold on, hold on," I said. "Aren't you getting a little carried away here? I'm an architect, not a qualified child minder. I don't know the first thing about being a nanny and watching kids. I don't even think I *like* kids—"

"That's because you've only met my brother's kids and they're little shitheads," Meredith explained gravely.

I pointed at her. "That's a true story. But I'm being serious."

Tabs suddenly grabbed my pointing hand. The look in her

brown eyes turned her into a puppy. At the shelter. On Christmas Eve.

"Oh, no. Tabs." I shook my head side to side. "Don't give me the eyes."

"You'd be doing me a massive favor," Tabs pressed. "Saving my ass and helping my business. I'd really like that commission. It's great money for you too. Especially while you look for another job. And I know you. I *trust* you. You're responsible and loyal. I know this family. They need a good person. A nice person. They've been through a lot. Think of it as doing a really good deed for several people at once."

Meredith leaned forward and took my other hand. "You need a fresh start. A place to lick your wounds and figure out your next steps. Somewhere you can't wallow. You can send your resume out from France just as easily as from here."

That was true at least. The thought of waking up every day realizing my dream had just been flushed into the sewer and I was going to have to dig around down there and pull it out and try to get the stench off was almost too much to think about right now. I'd worked so freaking hard. For so many years. I was fucking exhausted if I was being truthful. And worse, I realized, I'd been running without moving forward for quite some time. That was why this promotion mirage today had hurt all the more. Never mind the sleaze factor. That was just topping on the shit pie.

"What have you got to lose?" asked Meredith.

Nothing, I answered mentally.

I needed to leap off the edge and trust the universe.

It was France. Somewhere I'd always wanted to go. Somewhere I thought I'd go with my dad one day. He would want me to go.

But there was no way I could be that impulsive.

Could I? That wasn't me.

The idea grew and grew in my chest—a bubble of nerves, but

mostly excitement, until I found I could hardly breathe. "Hell, yes," I suddenly burst out. "I'm going to France!"

"Please, Josie, I—wait, what?" Tabitha blinked twice and a cloud parted across her face. "Josephine Marin, did you just say, yes?"

"Yes," I confirmed and felt my heart rate triple. I wasn't an impulsive person and yet today, I'd upped and quit a job without thinking it through and now I was agreeing to—"Wait. I'm not saying yes, *yet*," I backtracked in a panic. "But *hypothetically*, where would a nanny be going *exactly*?" I'd seen pictures of the industrial areas around the cities. This guy was a billionaire. Which meant he probably needed a nanny while he worked. What if he lived high up in a penthouse in an ugly city, and I never got to experience the France of my dreams? "And I need straight truth right now. Am I going to be nannying next to a smokestack? And are you sending someone to childmind the demon spawn? Is that why no one else will take the job?"

She gave a smirk. "South of France, no and no. They are an amazing family. At least they seemed to be when Arriette—Mrs. Pascale—was alive."

My heart rate wasn't slowing down. South of France? I'd taken French in school and always meant to do a refresher. I'd thought I had plenty of time. What if I couldn't speak to anyone? And what about nannying experience? Was I really going to do this? I grabbed my gin and took three hearty gulps.

Meredith seemed to realize I was freaking out. "Hey there. Breathe," she demanded.

"I—I don't have enough experience, do I?"

"You babysat tons growing up," Meredith assured me, then frowned. "Didn't you?"

"I have an in at the YMCA," Tabs cut in before I could answer. "I'll get you in tomorrow's Child and Adult CPR and First Aid class. No problem. You need that anyway to be covered under my company's insurance policy."

"Insurance policy? Like if something happens to the child on my watch?" The magnitude of responsibility was growing bigger. "Oh my God, I can't breathe. What did I just do? How old is the kid again?"

Tabitha was now stroking my hand like I was a wild horse about to bolt. "You're not as qualified as some of my girls. Actually, at all. I'm going to tell Xavier Pascale you're not normally a nanny. But that you're good with kids. He just needs *someone* he can trust. Dauphine is ten. She's hardly a baby. It will be a walk in the park. A walk in paradise even. I'll tell him I'm staking my reputation on you. That I trust you. And I do."

I swallowed.

In through the nose, out through the mouth. In through the nose. Out through the mouth.

"Josie," Mer cooed softly. "Tabs was so desperate, I almost quit the bank and took the job myself. But with what happened to you today, I believe it was divine intervention. If you hate it, call us and we'll figure something out. But give yourself a chance, Josie. Go grab a slice of paradise and get some perspective. Work on your resume from there. Shit, go look at a shit ton of European Architecture."

Chills raced over my skin at that. "It really is an architectural mecca. So many influences. So much history. I never thought I'd have a chance to go for years at least."

Meredith nodded. "And it doesn't hurt that you'll get to look upon Xavier Pascale's face every day," she said dreamily. "Have you Googled him? You should." She fanned herself.

"Mer," Tabitha snapped. "She can't see him like that. She *can't*. He's off-limits."

"Fine."

"I'm *serious*. This is my business."

"Yes, yes. When was just looking a crime?"

"It's fine, Tabs. You can trust me." I slid my eyes to Meredith with a cheeky smirk. "I've never been attracted to the family man type."

Meredith gasped with feigned drama. "Again. Low blow, Marin. I'm keeping score."

"You do that. But you'll have to do it from across the ocean." I grabbed a chip and a chance. "Coz I'm going to France, baby!"

CHAPTER FIVE

My neck ached as I straightened it and blinked my eyes open. I flexed my jaw. Ouch. My hand rubbed at the offending area. I was leaning my head against the glass of the train window, and the pressure was now spreading into a dull headache. Having only fallen asleep half an hour before landing, I'd been a zombie getting through customs and finding the train station. Somehow, I'd found a place that sold baguette sandwiches and fallen upon one like a woman possessed before passing out on the train to Nice. I wiped at some drool on my chin.

"*Nous arrivons dans trente minutes,*" the man across from me said gruffly, punctuating the sentence with a jab of his chin in the direction of the window.

I turned to look where he pointed and gasped, my mouth dropping open. "Wow," I mumbled under my breath.

There was nothing but blue at the edge of the tumbling rocks of the shoreline. The sky, and the incredible blue of the Mediterranean Sea, stretched as far as I could see. It was the kind of blue that was hard to tell someone about. Definitely the kind you didn't need an Instagram filter for. It was vivid, deep, bold, vibrant shades from bright turquoise to midnight ink, almost cartoon-like in its color palette. The ocean gave way to the sky that stretched away into another endless cerulean dream. My chest grew tight, and I sighed, almost brought to tears. I was in France!

"*Alors. C'est beau, non?*"

I looked back at the man, trying to process what he'd said with my tired brain and high school French. *Beau.* It's beautiful?

"Um, uh, *oui.*"

He grunted, clearly unimpressed with my conversational skills. "*Vous êtes américaine?*"

American?

"*Oui,*" I answered.

"*Bienvenue.*"

He shook out his paper with a welcoming smile and went back to reading. My cell phone buzzed with a text. I'd been lucky to get on the train Wi-Fi because I didn't have an international data plan. I hadn't had a chance before I left.

Mer: *Hey, you get to Nice yet?*

Still on train, I typed. *Getting there in about 30.* Double clicking away from messages, I opened the email application. Then I searched Meredith's name. There was a thread to me from Meredith and Tabitha, outlining the details. A driver would pick me up at Nice Ville Train station. I would be taken to the family home in Valbonne before we boarded the yacht the day after tomorrow. Wait. A yacht?

OMG, I typed to Meredith. *Tabitha didn't mention I was babysitting on a boat. I hate boats! WTF?*

Mer: *She didn't know until after you left. I know you hate boats. But do you hate yachts? French yachts?*

Same thing.

Mer: Er, no. Not the same thing.

Same

Mer: Not.

Same.

Mer: Not.

Ugh!

Mer: You have to let me know if he's as hot IRL.

Who? I typed, being deliberately obtuse.

Mer: The pope.

*I do believe we went over this. And please don't stress
      Tabs out.*

*Mer: I know, Tabs would freak. But you can look, right?
      NOT that I'm endorsing you lusting after your boss,
      but it can't hurt to have a beautiful work
      environment. And I don't mean the Mediterranean.
      Wait, I can never spell that. Two r's or two t's.*

Seriously?

*Mer: I know. I know. Also, maybe he's too pretty for you?
      Like, too perfect, you know?*

*Stop. Can we stop talking about him? I don't want you
      putting ideas in my head.*

*Mer: You haven't Googled him yet, have you? Stop the
fucking train and do it RIGHT NOW.*

*Mer: Girl. Do it. Unrelated, we should have gotten you
laid before you left. How long has it been anyway?*

Stop! I rolled my eyes.

*Mer: You need to be prepared. Thank me later. Did you
pack your vibrator at least?*

I shook my head, biting back a laugh. A link came through
text. Clearly Meredith didn't trust me to follow her orders.

Outside the train window, the mesmerizing view of the
Mediterranean was starting to disappear as the tracks wove into
the outskirts of Nice. I looked back at my phone. My thumb
hovered for about two seconds before descending.

The page loaded slowly, revealing Xavier Pascale.

I swallowed heavily.

Hollllly shit.

Screw Meredith and Tabitha right now. And Mr. Tate. And
everyone who'd played a part in me being here.

Oh, *Xavier Maxim Pascale* was hot all right. No, not hot. He
was breathtaking—beautiful in a kind of magazine-ad-that-you-
can't-turn-the-page-from kind of way. Rugged and icy in his glare.
But with suntanned skin and lazy, glossy dark hair swept off his
face. He couldn't be more than thirty-five. Not an old man, then.
I don't know why I'd thought a widowed French billionaire
needing a nanny for his kids might be older, but I had. I clicked
through to a news story about him.

In this photo, he was standing on a sidewalk in front of a
flashy looking hotel entrance, hands in his navy shorts, athletic
legs disappearing into those sock-less moccasin things European
men could get away with wearing. He was next to an even more

flashy looking car. I squinted. A Maserati. Matte black if I was guessing. On the main Google page was image after image of him being spied on—candids taken of him through windshields, from between potted palms, and through restaurant windows. Poor guy. People seemed obsessed with him.

The article itself was taken from the French version of a tabloid site. He was basically a French Kardashian. There was an article that included another, older photo of him with a dark-haired and sleek gazelle of a woman. The epitome of French chic. I blew out a long slow breath and clicked away from the article, I wouldn't understand the French text anyway, and went back to my email.

I scrolled past the logistics of my pick up to Tabitha's message.

Hi Josie -

Thank you sooo much for doing this. I've worked for this family before. Sadly though, I think I told you, it was when Monsieur Pascal's wife Arriette was alive. Such a terrible tragedy. Their daughter, Dauphine, is scrumptious! She'll be around ten years old now, I think. I can't imagine how sad it's been for her to lose her mother. Apparently, it's still tough two years later.

Normally, I'd take you out to lunch to have a frank discussion about the family. But it was all a little crazy yesterday, I have to email it all to you.

Okay, standard rules apply for the girls I position - I'm just pasting these in. I know you and know this won't be a problem. But I have to cover my ass.

1)Follow the family's rules for care, don't make up your own (mealtimes, bedtimes, routines etc).

2)No friends (romantic or otherwise) on an employer's premises without written consent from employer. (Best idea is to email employer and cc me, and then we have it in writing.

Actually, best of all idea is just to avoid visitors for the length of the contract.)

3)No smoking, drinking alcohol, or drug taking.

4)No fraternizing in any romantic capacity with any of the employer's family, friends, or acquaintances. You should mostly be invisible.

5)No using cell phone except during personal time or expressly to be in touch with employer if out with child(ren). He'll probably give you a local phone.

You are allowed two days off per week. Actually, a work week in France is maximum forty hours, but you can make the arrangement with your employer.

In your case, since it's mostly going to be on a yacht (sorry! I just found out. I feel awful. You'll be okay, right?), I imagine you'll have to work it out with Monsieur Pascale. I'll check in with you at the end of the first week, third week, and then your final (sixth week) to see if they want to extend to eight. If anything comes up in the meantime, please don't hesitate to call.

Best of luck for the best job in the world—being a guardian angel to a small soul!

Tabs xo

I blew out the long breath I'd been holding as I read most of the email. I loved the invisible part. Invisible was exactly what I needed. But was it possible to be invisible when you were going to be sharing a tiny space, like a boat? And what about if we all ventured off the boat? I had a horrible feeling that came with a shit ton of very close scrutiny. Remembering how traumatizing it had been when *my* family had been in the news, I gave a shudder.

Mer: *Ok. Your lack of response tells me you are freaking out. Trust me, Josie. It's going to be fine. Just keep your head down, and watch the kid, and six weeks will be over before you know it.*

. . .

I breathed out. My best friend knew me well.

And then what? I typed.

Mer: *Then we'll figure out your next step. Together. Love you*

Love you too.

I closed the apps on my phone to save battery life and gathered my things as we pulled into the train station.

What had I been thinking? There should be a rule to never make life altering decisions after a traumatic day followed by three gin cocktails.

This job had disaster written all over it.

CHAPTER SIX

I stepped off the train and walked through one of the ornate green double doors into the *Nice Ville* train station. The building was old and gorgeous, the main vestibule only about the size of a basketball court, but with ornate details on the walls and a roof dome of paneled glass that spoke of a bygone era. I stopped, and stared upwards, not realizing I'd come to a complete standstill with my mouth open until someone bumped into me with a muttered grunt.

"S-sorry." Nervousness pinched my belly, and I made my feet move. I wasn't sure if I was expecting someone holding a sign, but as I looked left and right, trying to stay out of the way of the stream of passengers coming after me, I saw no one who looked like they were here for me.

Someone jostled into me again. *"Excusez-moi."*

"Sorry," I muttered and headed toward a small stand that sold newspapers, candy, and cigarettes so I could get out of the way. I should at least buy a bottle of water while I waited and figured out my next move in case no one showed up. I pursed my lips together and dug in my purse for my sunglasses and slipped them on my face. I pointed to a bottle of water and handed over some of my Euros I'd managed to get out of an ATM at the Paris airport.

The sound of small feet running caught my attention. A small girl, dressed in a pink dress and Mary Jane shoes, and tangled honey-colored hair floating wild about her face flew around the corner of the newsstand and stopped dead when she saw me.

I squatted and pushed my sunglasses up to my hair, frowning. "Are you okay?"

"Dauphine!" A man's voice boomed across the station, the sound panicked.

"Dauphine!" The man rushed past, then whirled as he saw us. He dropped to a crouch, yanking the small girl into his arms. He held her tight, his head falling into her shoulder like he was inhaling her desperately.

Oh my God. It was *him*. Xavier whatever. *Monsieur* Pascale. I could tell from the brief flash of his face before I was confronted with that incredible thick dark hair. And of course, the name of his daughter suddenly clicked into place. Expensive denim stretched tight over his strong thighs, and his white linen shirt and navy blazer, that screamed custom-made, dressed a torso that didn't seem to have an ounce of expendable fat.

I stood slowly and stepped backward to give them some space.

My hands itched to drop my sunglasses back over my eyes as protection, but I resisted.

After Monsieur Pascale had given his daughter enough of a hug, he set her at arm's length and gave her a shake, his face thunderous, and his mouth sputtering all sorts of things I didn't understand. I figured he'd thought he lost his daughter and now his fear was catching up. Christ, the man was attractive. Far more attractive than the French tabloid link Mer had sent me had managed to capture. His presence alone was like a vortex.

I made myself step back farther as the little girl pointed at me.

But then the world slowed down. In the time it took for his eyes to trek slowly upward, from my feet to my face, I lived eons. I had moments where I wondered if I should step forward and introduce myself and moments where I wished I'd evaporate back onto the train before we locked eyes. Before I could decide to introduce myself, his eyes locked with mine, and the world snapped back into real time.

I felt the attraction like a punch in my solar plexus.

A tiny breath huffed out of me.

Shit.

There was nothing soft about him. His blue eyes darkened and his jaw tensed. His features were hard and angular, but slightly imperfect, in a way that took them from pretty and perfect to dangerously sexy. He was elegant with a sharp and jagged edge that made him lethal. In a flash, the look in his eyes—whatever it had been when he first looked at me—was gone. In fact, his whole mood seemed to travel at light-speed from desperate relief at his daughter's safety, to annoyance, to whatever it was he'd thought when he looked at me, and then to some kind of cold control that swept over him. All in a matter of seconds. It was actually impressive.

My throat closed as I tried to swallow under his scrutiny. I wondered what he was a billionaire of. I could imagine peons and minions quaking and quailing under this stare.

I dragged my gaze from him to his daughter who stared at me curiously. "H-hello," I stammered.

Her father watched me from his crouched position. He must have thighs of steel to crouch that long.

I stepped forward, holding out my hand, and looked her father square in the eye.

"Nice to meet you, I'm Josie Marin."

Monsieur Pascale unfolded his body with the lithe grace of a panther until he stood, towering over me. He took my hand in a brief perfunctory shake, dropping it as quickly as it began.

His eyes assessed me coolly. "Xavier Pascale," he announced.

"This is my daughter, Dauphine." His accent was like a drizzle of rich chocolate sauce that made me want to lick my lips.

I glanced down at Dauphine and held out my hand. "Nice to meet you."

She shook it. "*Vous parlez Francais?*"

Shaking my head, I adopted what I hoped was an apologetic look. "Not very well, no." I understood she was asking me if I spoke French, but beyond anything more than these basic questions I knew I'd be clueless. At least until my high school French clicked back into place, and even then, I knew I'd be woefully inadequate.

She smiled. "*Bon.*"

Good?

She fired something in rapid French up to her father, and then walked away. I expected her father to go immediately after her again based on the scare he'd just had, but Xavier Pascale didn't move. And he didn't strike me as someone who simply followed without good reason.

Dauphine walked up to a man hovering ten feet away from us. He was about my age with dark blond hair, wearing light colored but official looking pants and blazer, and an earpiece. He reached for Dauphine's hand. In his other, he held a sign dangling by his side that had my name written on it. I must not have seen him. He shot me a warm and welcoming smile.

I nervously returned it.

The man in front of me hadn't moved when I looked back at him. He studied me with a startling intensity. Nothing about it was warm and inviting. In fact, it was more like an arctic breeze. I guess this was the interview, then. In the train station. I hoped he'd buy my fare home, otherwise I was shit out of luck. But that was becoming the theme of my life.

"You are not what I expected," he said, his voice deep and accented, articulating each word.

You either, buddy. I frowned. "In what way?"

His gaze swept over me, and he muttered something in French I didn't understand.

My arms instinctively crossed over my chest, and I bristled.

Seemingly coming to his senses he shook his head. "*Désolé*. I'm ... sorry. *Merci* ... uh. Thank you for coming with much on short ..."

"On short notice?"

"Short notice." He nodded, though he didn't seem very thankful. More annoyed and perturbed by my presence. "I apologize. My English is normally better. I studied for a time in Britain after all."

"Of course," I said. "My French is normally worse."

He frowned.

"I was joking. I haven't tried my rusty high school French yet. And I may not have as much experience as most, but if you give me the rules, I'm good at following them."

I gave in to a smile I couldn't seem to hold in.

His brows instantly knitted together as if in offense.

No smiling, then. Got it.

"Well," I said, trying to stay bright. "It's nice to meet you and Dauphine. Please let me know if there are any activities you would like me to do with her while she is in my care. School work, reading, mathematics," I listed. He didn't appear to be listening to my words even though he still studied me. "Though all that would have to be in English," I pressed on. "Or we could just have fun," I added when I still got no response.

He inhaled sharply through his nose, and his eyes snapped away from me and to his watch. "*On y va*," he growled and turned and strode away. "Let's go."

Okay then. No joking either.

He snapped a finger at the other man who seemed to understand what a snap of fingers meant because he darted forward to grab my suitcase. Dauphine marched behind her father, arms folded and her head high.

It seemed I'd gotten off on the wrong foot with all of them. And worse, I wondered how I was going to get over my gut deep attraction to my new boss. Although, I guessed if he continued being a dismissive asshole, it might not be that hard. I clutched my water bottle and followed them outside.

CHAPTER SEVEN

Evan, our driver, introduced himself to me then loaded my bag into the trunk of a dark late model Mercedes. "Sorry we were late. Were you waiting long?" he asked in a British accent. A sense of relief at knowing there was a true English speaker to help me find my footing here was a massive relief.

"No, I'd just gotten off the train."

"This really all you have?" He motioned to my bag with a smile, revealing cute dimples.

I shrugged, pinching my t-shirt away from my body to let air in against my skin. "It's hot here, I figured I didn't need jeans and sweaters."

"Evan," Monsieur Pascale reprimanded loudly from the passenger door that was still open, one long denim-clad leg idling on the asphalt.

Evan hurriedly closed the trunk and went to open the back door for me on the other side of the car. "Normally quite a friendly chap," he whispered to me, his eyes rolling. "Must have accidentally sat on a carrot."

I snorted a laugh at the ridiculous assessment as the door

opened but quickly swallowed it and climbed in. The door closed and Evan got in the driver's seat in front of me.

My boss drew his leg in the passenger side and slammed his door closed. His shoulders seemed rigid beneath his linen blazer, and the cool and roomy interior of the car suddenly felt stifling like his presence took up four seats. The white of his starched collar glowed against the tanned skin of his neck. I might even say he was flushed, but what did I know? It was probably the heat. We rode in silence from the train station.

Dauphine sat in the back seat with me, her arms still folded. She watched me curiously, but as soon as I met her eyes she lifted her chin and looked away, pretending to be uninterested, only for her eyes to wander back seconds later. If only I knew how to get along with kids, I could open conversation. What had Tabitha and Meredith been thinking convincing me to take this job?

I looked at the rearview mirror to share a look with Evan but based on my angle was instantly snared in a set of ice blue eyes belonging to my new boss. Flustered, I looked away

The car purred through the unfamiliar streets. I tried to focus on the town outside the windows.

This was a mistake.

This was a mistake.

This was a huge mistake.

Scratch that.

I'd make the best of the fact I'd always *wanted* to come to the South of France. I closed my eyes and imagined visiting small little villages and strolling weekly markets. I'd sit, sipping a café on a small and charming town square shooing off little sparrows hopping around on the cobblestones, waiting for the crumbs of my croissant. Perhaps I'd be listening to the church bells to tell the time and then walk over to the churchyard and read the tombstones, imagining times long past.

I wouldn't let a grumpy boss ruin France for me. Besides,

Tabitha had called him grumpy, sure, but she'd also called him sad. Grieving. I'd try to give him the benefit of the doubt.

I opened my eyes, feeling calmer, and tried to watch the city go by, but soon it was just highway and buildings that had seen better days. The ocean was nowhere to be seen.

A throat cleared from the passenger seat. Mr. Pascale's shoulders seemed to go down as if he was forcing them to relax. I glanced up and caught his gaze again. God, his eyes were really quite arresting.

"Was your flight pleasant?" he asked, breaking the silence, and then cleared his throat again. He must hate uncomfortable silences as much as I did.

"Uh, yes. Thank you."

"And the train?" he asked.

I frowned. "It was fine. Thank you." Silence stretched. "I appreciate you coming to pick me up," I added.

"It was on the way."

"On the way?"

"To my yacht."

I thought Tabs had said we were going to their home first. Clearly, we were headed straight to the boat. "Um. I thought we were going to your home first." God, I thought I'd have a day to at least get my nerve up to get on a boat. Great.

"The plans changed," he said.

There was another long silence, and I was suddenly swamped with a sense of homesickness.

My eyes stung, and I gritted my teeth. I was damned if this frozen ice prince would make me cry on my first day. Tiredness and jet lag, that's all it was. Plus, I hadn't really processed the fact my career had just evaporated.

So we all sat quietly. Uncomfortably.

Dauphine pulled out a tablet, and my blinks became longer. The car ride was smooth and lulling. The air was cool. The stress of the last few days caught up with me, and despite my nap in the train, I closed my eyes.

The motion of the car woke me. After an hour or so, we'd left the highway and meandered down toward the coast. Again, the arresting sight of the Mediterranean Sea caused me to temporarily hold my breath when I saw it. I rubbed the sleep from my eyes. What a view to wake up to.

"Do you have a boyfriend?" Dauphine asked from beside me.

Turning to her with surprise, I saw nothing but a new curiosity on her face. "No," I whispered and shook my head.

She frowned. "Why not?"

"Uh—"

Blue eyes flashed across the rearview mirror. My boss was listening. If there was any chance my new boss had seen my initial reaction to him, it might be a good thing to casually mention I was off the market. Oh, how I wished I could say yes. Maybe I should make one up? Lying about having a boyfriend was just a boundary. Women did it all the time. I had girlfriends who'd put a ring on their wedding finger for girls night out so as not to be harassed in some of the clubs we liked to go to. I called a frantic emergency meeting in my head. Use a real ex? That cheating stockbroker I dated a year ago? Who else?

Crap. The moment had passed.

"But have you had a boyfriend?"

"Yes. Of course."

Dauphine clapped. "He's American?"

I nodded.

"What does he do, this American boyfriend? Is he a movie star?"

A laugh burst out of me. Did all foreigners only think of movie stars when they thought of America? "No. He was a financial jour-nalist." Okay, so that was the ex, *ex*-boyfriend's job. A stockbroker who wrote opinion editorials. Who'd dumped me when he realized I was never going to talk about my stepfather.

"What is this, *Finansh* ...?" she tried to pronounce with a frown.

"Financial journalist. I'm afraid you might think it's quite boring."

"What is the word boring?"

"*Pénible*," Monsieur Pascale offered from the front seat, clueing me to the fact he was, indeed, paying attention. He was holding the phone to his ear as he flipped through some papers on his lap. But it clearly didn't take his attention off what I was sharing with his daughter.

"Ahh," said Dauphine, nodding gravely. "*Continuez.*"

I swallowed a smile. "He writes about the stock market for the newspaper. Do you know what the stock market is?"

Dauphine bristled. "Yes. Of course. Papa talks about that too and makes me so ... boring." Her eyes rolled slightly.

I chuckled and also heard a soft snort from the front seat.

"Bored," I corrected with a smile. "You are bored, not boring."

She scowled, and then seemed to get it, and let out a small giggle.

"But your English is very good," I assured her.

"Papa says I am only allowed to watch TV and YouTube in English." She gave a dramatic sigh. "So yes, it is quite good. Better than the girls at my school," she added without a hint of arrogance.

I noted she didn't refer to them as friends. "What do you like to watch?" I asked as the car went around what felt like the seventeenth roundabout. My empty stomach tipped nauseously, and I reached for the overhead handle.

"On TV I like Disney Channel."

I searched the recesses of my mind. "Zack and Cody?" I chanced.

"*Oui!* I love them." She looked at me with renewed interest.

"Why is he not your boyfriend anymore?"

Yikes. This girl. "Um—"

"Did you love him? Your boyfriend?"

"Dauphine," her father snapped from the front.

I sucked my lips between my teeth to avoid laughing.

Dauphine folded her arms over her chest again but didn't press me and we all lapsed into silence again. I caught her eyes, and making sure no one but her could see me, I mouthed, "No."

She gasped in delight and then snickered. And we both looked away innocently.

Outside the window, the scenery became more enchanting with every moment. I'd never seen blue quite like the inky indigo of the bay in front of us, ringed with turquoise and sparkling in the sun. There were only a few boats anchored in the bay, but it was hard to imagine they were owned by individuals. They could double as an elite cruise ship enterprise. I hadn't thought much about the vessel I would be staying on, beyond the fact I hated the isolation and claustrophobia of boats. Add to it the fear of falling overboard, or drifting in a large expanse of sea with no land in sight, and they just weren't a vehicle I spent much precious mental bandwidth thinking about. But now my pulse began picking up its pace. I tried slow breathing exercises.

Fifteen minutes later, the Mercedes slowed to a roll over cobblestone streets and came out between a small row of clothing boutiques on one side and what looked like the *Hermes* flagship store to my right.

"What town is this?" I asked.

"St. Tropez," Evan responded.

We glided slowly through throngs of holiday makers gawking at the yachts lined, stern-to, along the quay. They towered like hulking monoliths, glaringly white with gleaming metal and sparkling glass. It was an almost gross, but breathtaking, display of the mega wealthy trying to one up each other. If the port in St. Tropez was anything like the coveted berths in downtown

Charleston, these spots alone would pay for the national debt of several small countries. Below almost every name was the word Valletta. I'd have to ask about that. To our right, cafes and restaurants had appropriated some of the street for their tables. Waiters in white shirts and aprons darted around holding trays aloft. I sucked in a joyous breath. I was here.

Dauphine was chattering away to Evan and her father in incomprehensible French. It seemed she was excited. We slowed to a stop in front of a gate arm, guarded by what I assumed was a policeman, complete with an AK-47 slung around his neck. I swallowed. The gate arm rose, and we surged forward down a long private quay with much larger boats than any we'd passed until we stopped next to a gangplank made of teak wood and steel.

I ducked my head to look out the window and gulped at the sight.

No one made a move to get out.

Evan made a quick phone call.

The boat wasn't exactly like the others, rather it was a shining marine navy on the hull with several white layers stacked above. It wasn't the biggest of the boats on the private quays, but my apartment in downtown Charleston could probably fit into the square footage of one level twice over. The name of the boat *Sirena* gleamed silver in the sun.

My view of the yacht partially disappeared behind the torso of a strongly-built man with a bald head and dressed in a white uniform consisting of a short sleeve button down and slacks. The Mr. Clean lookalike wore a name badge that read *Paco*. He had an earpiece in his ear similar to Evan's and approached us down the gangplank, looking left and right. Then he spoke to his wrist and approached the passenger side. As he opened Monsieur Pascale's door, Evan opened the driver's side door, got out, and immediately opened mine.

I looked up at him.

"Just nip onto the boat, I'll grab your things." He looked past me. "Dauphine slip out this side too please. Hurry."

My pulse rocketed at his all business manner, so different to the affable fellow who'd loaded my luggage.

I clambered out and then took Dauphine's hand and helped her out. She let go, pushed past me, and ran up the gangway.

"*Attention, Dauphine!*" Monsieur Pascale cautioned after her.

She leaped onto the boat and disappeared inside two dark gray glass doors.

I followed her route, my eyes glued to my running shoes, making sure I didn't misstep and holding the warm metal railing. It swayed, and I almost lost my digested baguette. I wasn't able to cross any expanse of water without holding on for dear life. God, why had I agreed to this again? What if I got seasick and vomited for six straight weeks? I didn't think I got seasick, but I hadn't had much experience to find out. This nausea, at least, was probably just nerves.

An attractive woman, also dressed in a white uniform, perhaps a bit older than me, with an athletic physique and blonde hair slicked back into a tight bun, had emerged from inside and now reached for my hand to help me.

Grabbing on to her gratefully, I stepped off the gangplank on to the spacious boat deck.

"I'm Andrea, the chief steward. You're the new *au pair*, right?" Were all his employees British?

"I am." I held out my hand. "Josephine Marin."

"Miss Marin, lovely to meet you."

"Actually, call me Josie, please. Long journey, my mouth isn't connected to my brain right now. "

"I'm sure." Andrea looked past me with a smile. "Monsieur Pascale. *Bienvenue. Welcome.* Any problems?" Her eyes scanned out to the port where Paco and Evan took luggage out of the Mercedes.

I turned.

Xavier Pascale nodded to Andrea and to me. "No. It seems we avoided them," he said in perfect accented English. "Please show Miss Marin to one of the staterooms on deck two."

"Avoided who?" I began, but Andrea was responding to her boss.

"No problem, sir," she said. "We have taken the liberty of moving you to the master stateroom now that the nanny is here."

"No," he said quickly. "I'll stay on deck two as well. For now." Wait, all three of us would be next door to each other? How many rooms were there? I hoped to goodness I had a window or I would have a massive panic attack.

Andrea bobbed her head. "As you wish. Apologies. I should have checked first."

Monsieur Pascale immediately took a set of stairs up to another deck and disappeared.

"Come along," Andrea said after she introduced me to Paco, the captain. "I'll get you settled and then get you up to date on the care and feeding of Dauphine Pascale and what's required of you."

CHAPTER EIGHT

As we walked through the interior of the boat, my gaze bounced all around. The huge windows on both sides offset the darker nature of the mahogany and modern brass fittings and fixtures. The built-in sofas were cozy, luxurious, off-white, with a scattering of throw pillows that seemed to pull color from the art. There was a huge twelve-seater dining table.

"The paintings ..." I stammered. "I mean, are they real? Surely not at sea?" I couldn't help but blurt as I followed Andrea. The carpet looked lush and soft despite being a tightly knitted weave. It was probably some sort of marine-grade fiber meant to withstand the realities of life at sea while looking like it could protect the precious toes of the one percent.

Andrea slowed. "Most of them are high end reproductions of the art the Pascales have at their estate in Valbonne. And they're protected. It's a fine film covering them that allows for the natural colors to show through but protects the canvas from mildew and the paint from ultraviolet rays. Everything is protected. The fabrics are stain proof. Of course, with a child on board and the odd inebriated guest, one has to take precautions." She turned to me fully while stepping backward. "You drink?"

"Uh, I won't be an inebriated guest if that's what you mean?"

She grinned. "Nah. Didn't mean anything by it. We keep the drinking for *terra firma* and keep it extremely low key." She turned back around and began down a set of stairs, dipping her head to the side even though she'd have easily cleared the space. "But when you have a night off, you should come out with us. The crew, I mean. Most nights you'll probably eat with Dauphine and Mr. Pascale."

I climbed down after her. My chest immediately tightened in the smaller, darker space. I forced myself to breathe slowly. I could do this. I *had* to do this.

"It depends on Mr. P's schedule." She opened the latch on a lacquered wooden door to her right. "This is you. Dauphine is to your left. And temporarily Mr. P. is ..." She nodded ahead toward the cabin opposite mine and her voice lowered. "He'll be in there. Since Mrs. Pascale passed away, Dauphine has sometimes had trouble sleeping. Nightmares. Mr. P likes to be close to his daughter. I guess until you settle in, he'll want to stay close by."

Poor little girl. "Understandable. So, is it okay to ask? What happened to Mrs. Pascale? And why the security concern when we got to the port?" I stepped in through the wooden door to what was to be my cabin. There was a small—oh my God, tiny—window. But the room was more spacious than I'd imagined. The bed was queen-sized and covered in luxurious white bedding and pale pink and gray throw cushions. I drew a deep breath.

"Are you okay?" Andrea asked as she noticed my breathing.

"Never done well in confined spaces," I admitted and tried to force a grin. "Nor on boats. But I'm guessing exposure therapy is my only choice right now."

She widened her eyes. "Just be glad you aren't in crew quarters stacked like a sardine on a bunk in which you can't sit fully upright. And you have your own head."

"Head?"

"Bathroom."

"Sorry," I said. "I didn't mean to sound ungrateful."

She rested a hand on my arm. "You didn't. Relax. And I'll have to tell you the story of Mrs. P when we get our night off if it coincides. But my hope is Mr. P will tell you himself when he goes over what's expected of you."

I nodded. "Can I ask though, how long has it been since she died?"

Andrea glanced over her shoulder toward the door and back to me. "Just shy of two years. That's really all I can say. But the family—what's left of it—they need healing. And this attempt to get back out to sea and spend some time together is part of it. I'm sure you know how the press treats Mr. P, like some sort of tragic prince. That makes Dauphine the poor little lonely heiress. It also makes her a target for unscrupulous types. You'll be her nanny, but also you'll never let her out of your sight."

A chill skidded over my arms. "You mean she's a target for, like, kidnapping?"

Andrea nodded.

"Yikes. That's a little above my pay grade, don't you think?"

"You just have to be another set of eyes and another hand to hold when you all are out and about. Evan was in the Royal Marines and has undertaken bodyguard training." Her eyes flashed as she said it, and it occurred to me Andrea might have a crush on the affable driver who was clearly a lot more than he looked.

"So he has lots of different roles here," I said, impressed.

"He's paid well for it, trust me. And we all go above and beyond and do whatever it takes to keep things running smoothly. We really respect Monsieur Pascale." I didn't mistake the advice for me in her simple statement. But I'd never been one to do the bare minimum or shirk responsibility. It was probably why I'd gotten so far ahead at work before I'd crashed into my glass ceiling.

"And I guess we're all hoping that with you here, Dauphine

may be a little less lonely, and maybe Mr. P will start to relax a little bit. It's been bleak, I'll tell you. It'll be a bit different from your last gig, I'm sure."

I bit my lip. "This is my first one actually. I mean, like this," I hurried on at her surprised look, not wanting to paint myself as completely clueless on my first day. "I'm not super experienced." I swallowed.

"Ahh. Well. And on a boat no less."

"Yeah."

She smiled and I relaxed. "Well, the crew's a good bunch. Just a skeleton crew for a boat this size though since it's only you three. But give a shout if you need help. It'll be me, Evan, who's first mate but also triples as security and deck hand, Rod who you'll meet is an extra deck hand and fills in as steward when we're thin, Paco the captain, and Andre the chef. On other boats I'm normally one of three or four women. At least I get my bunk room to myself since I worked here. If you need anything, from a soft drink to sunscreen while you're finding your way, I'm your gal. If you need a tender ride to shore, Evan's your guy. Anything I should tell chef to avoid for you?"

"No." I shook my head. "I eat almost everything. Where's Dauphine?" I asked, remembering the reason I was on this boat.

"Probably up on the bridge with Paco. She loves to go see him first thing."

"The bridge?"

"Boat term. It's where the captain drives the vessel—wheel, radar, sonar, satellite. All the gadgets that keep this beauty running. Paco has a cabin on the bridge level too."

I rubbed my palms on my shorts and looked around. "Do I have time to unpack?"

Andrea walked toward the head of the bed where a built-in wooden shelf ran the width of the room and held two bolted down bedside lamps. "There's an intercom here," she said, pointing out a brass inlay with a button and slats like on a speaker.

"Kind of old school, and we try not to use it unless there's an emergency. But we'll get you equipped with your own cell phone. How about you unpack, relax, shower, and I'll buzz you when Mister P is ready to meet with you to go over Dauphine's care. I'll keep her with me for the meantime, and she can help the chef prep for dinner."

I smiled with gratitude. "That'd be great. Thank you."

"Don't nap if you can help it. Jet lag will kill you if you do. Oh, and the Wi-Fi code is in the drawer," she said. "I'll leave you to it. I'll buzz you when Mr. P is ready for you."

With a smile, she headed out, and as soon as she clicked the door closed, I went to the window and figured out how to slip it open. Inhaling the briny and oily air of the port, I sucked it in deeply through the four-inch gap. I'd never had textbook claustrophobia, and I was sure it wouldn't be crippling, but it didn't mean I wasn't going to need to have a window or door cracked with the promise of fresh air. I'd have to ask what the rules were about keeping the windows open. Last thing I needed was for sea water to lap in with a big wave. I bent my neck to glance down and saw my cabin window was pretty close to the greenish and oil-swirled surface of the water. That wasn't creepy.

My phone buzzed from somewhere, and I dug around in my purse.

Meredith.

Instead of texting, I opened my settings and found the Wi-Fi, and then dialed her number through a Wi-Fi calling app.

She answered on the third ring.

"Jos, you made it?"

"I did. I'm on the boat. I say boat, but a better descriptor would be cruise ship."

"Oh my God. Is it lush? I bet it's amazing. Do they have a crew? Of course they do."

I smiled. "They do."

"I'm imagining you on the cast of *Below Deck*. Is there a mad genius chef?"

"Don't know yet."

"And are the deck hands cute?"

I thought of Evan. "Yes, the one I've met is. His name is Evan and no, before you ask, he's not my type." I'd felt nothing in the way of attraction to Evan. Certainly not in the wake of the gut punch attraction I'd felt to the one person I shouldn't even look at like that—my new boss. "God." I flopped back on the bed. "So much has happened in two days. I can't believe I'm on the other side of the Atlantic. How's my mom? Did you call her?" I'd asked Meredith and Tabs to check in with her periodically. I hated that I'd had to leave in such a hurry. She'd been shocked when I told her I quit. Even after I explained why, she didn't seem to understand the choice I'd made. I assured her my trip was just temporary—a paid gig while I found another job and got my career back on track, but all I could see on her face was shock and disappointment. I hadn't even had the heart to tell her how Tate had mentioned my stepfather, Nicolas.

"Your mom is fine. I called her last night, and I explained everything in more detail. Told her you were helping Tabitha out."

"She comes from a different generation. Women didn't quit over handsy bosses or lack of career growth in her day. She thinks I'm a snowflake."

"No, she doesn't. She's just a mom worried about her daughter being on the other side of the world."

I cringed. "Was this a good idea?"

"Stop it, Josie. Yes. It was a good idea. The fricking best idea any of us have had, period. You're a lucky bitch, you know that?"

"You're right. If I'm a snowflake about anything, it's that I'm currently sitting on a yacht in the south of France with a hot, widowed billionaire and complaining about it."

"Took the words right out of my mouth."

"On that note, you realize he's a complete paparazzi magnet? What if someone is curious enough about the new nanny to dig up my family history? That would kill my mom, if things came to light again."

"You're out of context," she soothed. "In another country. And it happened so long ago. There's no way anyone will recognize you. Also, you're essentially *the help*. No one pays *the help* any attention. You're practically invisible."

I thought of *Monsieur Pascale's* intense scrutiny when he met me and didn't feel like I was invisible to him at all. More like someone he disapproved of. And he didn't even know me.

"And even if they did," Meredith went on, "would any French people care about an obscure financial crime in Charleston? No offense."

I didn't have the energy to correct her that my stepfather's clients weren't limited to America. "I don't think my new boss likes me," I said, trying to change the subject. "I felt like a microbe under a microscope. Do I not look like a normal nanny?" I sat up.

Meredith laughed. "He probably just thinks you're hot."

"Shut it, Mer!" I squeaked and heard Tabs say something in the background.

"What did Tabs say?"

"She told me to shut it too. Dang, I was just joking. Maybe he was having a bad day. Hey," she directed at something Tabitha said again.

"Maybe he was," I said, thinking even Evan had said he was normally friendlier.

"Tabs wants a turn," Meredith said. "I love you and miss you, bitch face. Here she is."

"Love you too, bye."

"Hey, Josie," Tabs greeted me. "You get there safely?"

"Yep. All tucked into my watery coffin," I half joked. "Hey, do you know anything about what happened to his wife?"

"Actually, I don't. And I haven't done too much looking into it. There's not much online. What were you told?"

"Nothing yet. But I'm supposed to meet with him in a bit, maybe he'll at least give me the lay of the land. At least as far as what his daughter has been told. On that note. I better get myself together. I just hope I can make you proud."

"Don't be silly. Of course you will. And I know you'll have a good time."

"So good to talk to you both. Have fun at your sister's wedding, Tabs. Hug Mer for me. And tell her please don't forget about me stranded out here."

"Ha. Stranded?" Meredith had clearly wrestled the mouthpiece closer to her. "Hardly. I'm here for you any time."

"Love you, Mer. Love you, Tabs."

"We love you more."

We all hung up and I lay back on the soft bed with a grin, then I rolled off the bed and began unpacking into the dresser. The drawers had a twisty latch thing so they locked when closed. I imagined it was in case of turbulent waters. I shuddered at the thought of being trapped in this room during rough weather. Closing my eyes, I took a deep breath and tried to stay on task.

As I entered the bathroom and caught site of the mirror, I practically jumped out of my own skin.

Shit. Jet lag and a fluorescent white office tan were a rough combo. I was pale with tiredness, my under eyes looking bruised, and my light freckles more pronounced. It felt like a stranger staring back at me. Figuring out the shower took a moment, but it was blissful to step under the hot spray and quickly wash my hair and shave my legs. I imagined the boat had to store fresh water on board so I didn't dally too long.

I jumped as I heard a beep and a static crackle. Andrea's voice came through the intercom. I'd left the bathroom door open so I didn't miss it. "Hey, Josie."

I scampered out the shower, grabbing a large white fluffy towel on the way. I pressed the button. "Yes, I'm here."

"Monsieur Pascale will see you up on the top deck in about ten minutes."

"Ok. Thank you. I'll be there. *Over*." I released the button and cringed.

Andrea's disembodied chuckle came through. "This isn't girl scout camp on walkie talkies, *ten four*."

"Sorry." I laughed as I sent the message back.

Then I quickly towel-dried and wrapped my hair up. "Damn it," I muttered. What did I wear to impress professionally but not look like I'm trying too hard? I settled on a pair of white shorts, unfortunately a tad shorter than I'd like, but not indecent, and a navy and white striped three-quarter sleeve shirt. Totally nautical. I looked the part. And frankly, I'd had to work with what I had when packing.

I dragged a comb through my dark hair that was even darker when wet and slicked it back to a low bun. The dark hair and pale skin made my gray-green eyes stand out more. Grabbing my make-up bag, I put on moisturizer, under eye concealer so I didn't look ghoulish, and lip balm, then stared at myself in the mirror. "You can do this," I whispered to myself. "You are capable of anything."

I took a deep breath and headed out of my room to find my way upstairs.

CHAPTER NINE

I followed the reverse route of the one I'd come down with Andrea.

One level up was the main living area we'd walked into upon arriving on the boat. No one was around, but a delicious smell of grilled fish and garlic wafted from somewhere, and my stomach grumbled. It had been a long time since that baguette on the train. I turned to the stairwell and continued up, holding onto the brass handrail. Outside the windows, the sun was low in the sky and gleaming off all the other boats bobbing in rows. The third deck was a smaller sitting room with three steps to the bridge where I saw the captain, Paco, pouring over some large unrolled maps.

I knocked lightly on the highly varnished wood paneling on the wall next to me, and he looked up. "Hi," I said. "I didn't realize people still used paper maps to navigate."

His swarthy face split into a grin, revealing perfectly straight, though tobacco stained, teeth. "Ah, yes, but I am also a treasure hunter. Old charts are the way to find the old bays and caves." His English was good, but his accent was hard to place.

My eyebrows rose. "Really?"

"Yep. If you're lucky you'll see old annotations and symbols. Dauphine likes to come up here and look over the charts and let me know where she thinks treasure might be." His kindly eyes crinkled up as he smiled. "Is everything to your liking in your cabin?"

"Yes, thank you. More than comfortable. Am I allowed to keep the window open?"

"As long as the weather is good and we are anchored, I see no problem with that. We have air-conditioning though."

"It's more that I need to be connected to a wide-open space. Fresh air."

"Ah." He nodded with understanding, then his eyes flicked to the ceiling. "He's waiting for you."

I gave the captain a casual salute and turned toward the stairs.

As my head emerged on the top level, the evening breeze cooled my damp hair. My attention was immediately captured by a sparkling turquoise plunge pool glowing with underwater lighting in the twilight. Wow. A pool on a boat. The sounds of chatter, music, and clinking silverware drifted from the port-side restaurants. The smells were heavenly—garlic, charcoal, baking bread. I dragged my eyes toward the presence I could feel to my left, and the skin on my neck tingled.

Xavier Pascale sat at the teak table, leaning back on a matching chair, watching me. His face was expressionless, his blue eyes—glowing with the last of the setting sun hitting his face—were intent. He wore his white linen shirt from earlier and had changed from jeans into a pair of navy shorts and canvas white-soled boat shoes. His toned legs were tanned and sprinkled with dark hair and crossed at the ankles. An arm, the sleeves of his white shirt rolled up to reveal corded forearms, was slung casually over the backrest of the chair next to him.

My stomach muscles clenched of their own accord, my ovaries jerking like racehorses in a starting block. I swallowed hard. Being attracted to my boss to this extent was going to be very, very dangerous. It was just lust, I told myself sternly, and pressed two fingers against the pulse on my wrist as if I could force my heart to slow down. And given one of the reasons I'd just dropkicked my career, also really ironic that I'd think my boss was hot. I just hoped I didn't make a fool of myself.

He had papers and a phone spread in front of him, but the other end of the table was set with three dinner places.

"What are you thinking so hard about?" His voice broke the silence between us. It was gravelly yet smooth, like a bed of wet pebbles.

"Hi," I managed, clearing my throat and feeling as if I'd been caught ogling.

My belly gurgled again.

His brows furrowed.

"That I'm very, very hungry," I answered with a half-truth, smiling with embarrassment. "It's been a while since I ate."

He didn't respond, and I wasn't sure if I'd somehow stumbled into a cultural faux pas.

"Okay, well, um, also I'd like to know what you expect of me as Dauphine's nanny."

He inhaled through his nose, and then slipped his arm off the chair next to him and sat forward in a slow and deliberate movement. "Take a seat." He gestured to a chair opposite him.

Obediently, I pulled it out and sat.

Several seconds passed as he perused the papers in his hand. My eyes were drawn to the long fingers and short clean nails of his hand that held the pages, then to his wrists. He wore a wide band stainless steel watch that glowed silver against his tanned skin sprinkled with dark hair. The scent of him danced elusively as I inhaled the sea air permeated with all the smells of the port. I breathed again deeply, trying to catch the thread of something that brought to mind worn leather, eucalyptus, and bad decisions. Was that what an honest-to-God pheromone smelled like?

He set the stack down, and I caught sight of my name amid

upside down typed French. Then he leaned forward and clasped his fingers together. Blue eyes drilled me. "Why are you here?"

"Uh." I blinked, my mouth drying. "To nanny for Dauphine."

"Why?"

I didn't feel like telling him I'd quit my job. It could make me seem flighty or temperamental. And frankly I didn't want to relive the awkward experience. "I needed a change of scene. And you needed a nanny. It seems combined circumstance brought me here."

His eyes flickered, and I imagined he'd expected the standard *because I love children so much* response.

Emboldened, I went on. "I haven't worked for Tabitha's agency before, and I am sure you've had more experienced nannies for Dauphine than I. But I am honest, I work hard, and I *really* need this job. If you want a better reason than that, then I don't have one." Holding his gaze, I tried hard not to let the forcefield of it cower me. The intensity level he emitted felt as though I was staring into the sun.

"You are attracted to me," he stated.

A rush of heat hurtled up my neck to my cheeks as my mind stumbled to deal with the shock of his forthrightness. God, had I been that obvious? After only a handful of interactions? My family and friends always laughed that I wore my emotions on my face too easily. I tried to formulate a denial, but I wasn't fast enough.

"I'm not interested," he said dismissively before I could even form a response.

The heat that had come from embarrassment quickly seared to irritation. *The arrogance!* "Excuse me?"

"I said, I'm not interested. You are here for Dauphine and only her."

My blood pressure rose as the tips of my ears burned. "I'm well aware of that fact," I managed through stiff lips.

"Good. Then we understand each other." He looked back at

his papers as if the conversation was boring him. "'Unless you think it will be a problem?"

My blood pounded in my ears. "And just because you're attractive, doesn't mean I want to—that I would ..." I stammered.

He looked up, an eyebrow raised.

Great. Now, I'd just confirmed I found him attractive. I wanted the boat to swallow me up.

Under the table my fists clenched tightly. I willed my embarrassment into something useful. I was reminded of just two days ago when I'd also sat with a boss who only saw women as sexualized Barbie dolls. Did this guy think all women wanted to jump him? Gross.

"Will it be a problem?" he asked again, calmly.

I'd fucking had enough. "No. It won't," I snapped icily, attraction utterly cooled. What a jerk. "I'm offended that you think so little of me, and you've only just met me. I'm doing a good friend a massive favor by taking this position. I wasn't even aware you existed until two days ago. So if you could give me a tiny bit of credit, I'd appreciate it."

"I find that hard to believe." He snorted. "That you didn't know I existed. You wouldn't be the first trying to get to me through my daughter. I'm just making sure you understand."

My mouth dropped open at his sheer level of arrogance. "Oh my God." My chair screeched as I pushed back from the table, and I leaned forward on my hands, pushing my face close to his. His pupils flared, almost eclipsing the blue of his eyes.

"You might be a king in your part of the world," I growled, realizing that tiredness and hunger were getting the better of me, but unable to stop myself. "But I've had bigger problems on the other side of the ocean in my own world than to waste my time reading gossip magazines and daydreaming about marrying a rich prince. I don't give a continental how important you think you are. For me, you are a means to an end. A job. Nothing more." My mind screamed at me to shut up. "I'm sorry. I've had a really

shitty few days. I'm hungry. I'm tired. And I fucking hate boats."
So, if he was done with his misguided misogyny, I guessed I
should go pack up my things and email Tabitha that this did not
work out because my boss was an entitled, sexist, arrogant
asshole. I wanted to help her out with this job, but not so much
that I'd stand for being made to feel like a gold-digging piece of
trash. "I don't think this is going to work out. Good luck. You and
Dauphine probably need to spend more time together anyway.
You don't need me for that. For the second time in three days, I
quit." I pushed back from the table and turned on my heel
quickly, making my way back down the way I'd come. My heart
thundered in my throat.

Paco looked up, surprised, as I hurried past without a word.
Tears of impotent rage streaked my cheeks before I was even
halfway back to my cabin. God, why did being angry and embarrassed always make me cry? I flew down the next set of steps and
hit a brick wall of a chest.

"Whoa," the wall rumbled. *Evan.* I tried to push past but
hands gripped my upper arms gently but firmly. "Hey. You all
right, love?"

I shook my head. "Let me go, please?"

"What happened?"

"Please, can you drive me back to the train station in the
morning? I just quit."

His eyes bugged out. "You what? What happened?" Then his
forehead drew down sharply. "Did something happen? He didn't
..." Evan shook his head like he couldn't believe the question he
was asking. Then the look of utter disbelief warred with a sudden
heroic chivalry on his face. "He didn't like ... do anything to you,
did he?"

"God, no," I assured. "No. He implied some things. Accused
me of being here to get to him. Using Dauphine to get to him."

"Oh."

"Oh?"

Evan shrugged with a small grimace. "It wouldn't be the first time. You can understand, he's a bit of a target."

"Ugh. Why would anyone want to be with that entitled, arrogant ass?" God, his personality had literally just made him the most unattractive man I'd ever come across. "There's not enough money in the world." I'd pretty much probably told him that too by quitting.

Evan threw back his head and barked out a laugh.

"It's not funny."

"It kind of is. Did you tell him that?"

I folded my arms. "Along those lines. Now, can you get me off this boat or what?"

"Nope."

"No?" I cried. "I just lost my temper at my boss and quit. I have to leave the building. Like *now*. You're security, help me box up my shit and escort me the hell out of here. Now." Especially as I began to suspect I may have slightly overreacted. "He'd fire me for how I reacted if I hadn't already quit."

Evan laughed harder, his face crinkling and his eyes tearing up. "This ... this is perfect."

I stomped my foot. "Okay, move. I need to pack. I'll find my own way back."

He moved but didn't stop laughing.

I glared at him as I passed. "What pray tell is 'perfect' about this situation?"

He shook his head. "Nothing you'd understand. Just, uh, I'll tell Andrea you aren't eating with Mister P."

"You do that." I was really hungry, though. "Any chance of making myself a sandwich or something without getting in the chef's way?"

"Impossible. I'll have something brought to you or you can wait until about midnight when Chef is out of the kitchen. But I don't recommend it. He's totally OCD and counts the grains of rice left over."

"Wow. Okay." I swallowed. "I don't want to ... rock the boat, so to speak."

Evan erupted in a new round of laughter, mumbling something about how I killed him.

"Perhaps I'll just quickly pack and get off the boat and get something in town," I continued and headed into my room. I would have slammed the door on his craziness if it didn't mean it would set off all my claustrophobic alarms to be closed inside the cabin while my heart was pounding. I stared at the bed and let out a big sigh. I'd miss being able to sleep a night on that comfy bed after being crammed into a tiny airplane seat all night. I'd just unpacked and now I was leaving. I'd have to call Tabs and break the news. A heavy dose of guilt thudded in my belly. I hated I was letting her down already. But it couldn't be helped now. God knew where I'd stay in town while I tried to get home. But I'd figure it out. I grabbed my bag I'd stashed under the side table shelf, then turned to the dresser.

"You know you can't leave, right?" Evan said from the doorway, finally sobering.

I scowled at him. "Excuse me?"

"You can't leave. We don't allow anyone on or off the boat twelve hours before we move. As his security detail, I have to advise you that you are required to stay put."

I stared at him for any hint that he wasn't serious. "You're joking."

He shook his head. "Nope."

"I can't leave?"

"Affirmative. Not tonight, anyway."

"So, you'll keep me against my will? I'm a prisoner?" I opened a drawer and pulled out pajamas, bras, and underwear, dumping them onto the bed.

Evan's eyes stayed on me. "I wouldn't call it that."

I folded my arms. "What would you call it?"

"A chance to cool off. And a contracted employment period."

"For a jerk?" Who I just totally went off on?

"I guess if you see him that way, then yes. But something tells me that won't last long."

"Have I told you how much I fucking hate boats?" I looked around before catching his eye again. "I don't care how luxurious it is."

His attention seemed to go somewhere, then his wrist came up to his mouth. "Yes, she is."

I frowned and realized his attention had gone to his earpiece. "I'm what?" I asked.

Evan cleared his throat and stepped out of the doorway to my room.

In his place, and in no way less of a virile and commanding presence, appeared the object of my outrage—Xavier Pascale.

CHAPTER TEN

I unfolded my arms, glaring at the looming figure in the doorway of my cabin. Xavier Pascale's sheer presence could shrink a room into a fraction of its size.

His eyes raked over me and settled on the suitcase I'd set on the bed between us. Behind him a small face with wide eyes appeared then ducked away. I had no doubt she'd be listening to every word. At the sight of Dauphine, I felt another twinge of guilt. Crap. I ground down the thought. I didn't even *know* these people.

"Can I help you?" I asked, embarrassment crawling over my skin.

"I ... I would like you to take dinner with me and Dauphine. Have." He shook his head. "*Have* dinner."

"Why?" I cocked my head to the side.

"You need to eat. And also, you did not stay to hear the rest of the details about taking care of my daughter."

"I quit. Remember?"

"And I do not accept."

I barked out a confused laugh. "You don't accept?"

"No." He didn't return my amusement. After a beat, he looked at the heavy watch on his wrist. "Dinner will be served in five minutes," he said impassively. "I will see you at the table."

Then he turned and, unlatching the cabin door where it was being held open against the wall, closed it behind him. I had a feeling he'd felt like slamming it.

Well. Me too.

"Ugh!" I picked up a swimsuit, wadded it up and threw it at the closed door with all my might. The weightless scrap of material made it only a few feet before wafting impotently onto the bed.

Pinching the bridge of my nose, I took a deep breath. If he was still willing to employ me after my outburst upstairs, I guessed I should hear him out. Especially since I had nowhere to go tonight. He wouldn't apologize, that much I knew. Then again, why apologize? He'd stated a fact—I *was* attracted to him. *Had been*, I quickly corrected myself. It was upsetting that he'd accused me of using Dauphine to get to him, but both he and Evan mentioned it had happened before.

I cringed. Poor Dauphine. I hoped she was none the wiser. I exhaled the air I'd been holding, not feeling better at all. I was usually much better at handling my emotions in tough situations. Hell, I could be unjustly sidelined in my dream architectural position while holding my head up high as had happened just days ago. But Xavier Pascale had turned me into a raw bundle of emotions. I felt so very, very human and weak. It was exhaustion, I reasoned. Emotional and physical.

I picked up the clothes on the bed and returned them to the dresser. Then I zipped up my empty suitcase and re-stowed it under the table.

Opening the door, I jumped when I saw Dauphine waiting in her doorway to my left. She smiled shyly at me.

"Hi," I said.

"*Bonsoir. Allons-y?*"

I shrugged. "Sure, let's go. You lead the way," I said.

She danced past me in bare feet and the same dress she'd been wearing earlier. "What games do you like?" she asked over her shoulder as we made our way up the inside of the yacht.

"Games? Like board games?"

"Hide and seek?"

"Actually, that's a game I *never* play."

She swung around to face me, a challenge in her eyes. "*Non? Pourquoi?*"

"Because I don't like small cramped spaces. And all the best hiding places are like that. So I'm not a very good player."

Her brow furrowed, reminding me of a certain caustic Frenchman upstairs. There was no mistaking Dauphine as his daughter. Then her expression smoothed out. "Then I will win all the times. We *must* play!"

I chuckled. "Nope. I would love to, I promise. But I won't. We can play other games."

Her lips pursed off to the side of her mouth as if I was a problem to solve.

"Come on, princess. Let's go upstairs. I'm ready to eat my own hand."

"What does this mean?"

"It's a joke."

"Hmm."

"Race you." I took off ahead of her.

She squealed behind me. "*Non!*"

We sailed past the bridge, Captain Paco nowhere to be found. I pounded up the last few steps with a laugh. Behind me Dauphine yelled, "*Attention!*"

As our heads emerged on the upper deck, I was thankful her yelled warning was unneeded since no one had been on the stairs at the same time.

Night had settled fast.

I bent over for a moment to catch my breath as Dauphine

joined me, giggling. A glow came from the table. There were two hurricane jars enclosing a candle each on the table.

Andrea was standing over Mr. Pascale at the head of the table, one hand behind her back and the other pouring him a glass of pale pink wine. She gave me a quirked eyebrow.

Mr. Pascale looked less than pleased.

"Papa," exclaimed Dauphine and rapid fired French at him.

He let out an uncomfortable chuckle, and his shoulders relaxed a notch.

A strong smell of buttery garlic wafted toward me, and my mouth flooded with saliva.

I caught my boss's hooded eyes as they moved to me from his daughter. I pulled out the chair to his left with Dauphine to his right.

The plate in front of Dauphine had prosciutto-wrapped melon artfully placed on it. It was one of my favorite dishes with its salty-sweet flavor.

Dauphine clapped her hands together when she saw it.

"*San Daniele di Parma avec melon.* Chef made it specially for you, love," Andrea told her with a smile, then she turned to us. "And for you both, we have *Moules Mariniere*, followed by *Loup de Mer* with *haricots verts* and *petites patates.*"

Mr. Pascale shifted toward me. "The direct translation is Wolf of the Sea, it's a type of—"

"Sea bass. Special to the Mediterranean." I trailed off as I realized how I'd rudely cut him off. Nervously, I turned to Andrea and was actually thankful for my mother and stepfather's craving for keeping up with the foodie-Jones's in Charleston, which was known for its great food. "Thank you. And mussels to start?" I wanted Monsieur Pascale to realize that he hadn't employed some clueless, provincial pushover. I was intelligent and knowledgeable, and for some reason, I needed him to know it.

Andrea nodded at me. "Yes, that's right. Can I pour you water or a soft drink?"

"Water is fine. Thank you."

"No wine?" Mr. Pascale asked, a dark eyebrow arching.

I glanced at my wine glass winking in the candlelight, and the bottle of seriously refreshing looking chilled wine. I'd bet it was delicious. I wasn't supposed to drink on the job. Then again, I'd quit this job. I was hardly a lush, but I enjoyed a glass with dinner.

"That would be lovely, actually," I said with a lift of my shoulders. "Thank you, Andrea. I quit today, so I don't think it really matters, does it?"

"Um." She glanced between me and Mr. Pascale.

He sat back and eyed me with a look of puzzlement. But as I stared back I also saw reluctant admiration at calling his bluff.

"You see," I turned back to Andrea, "Mr. Pascale is negotiating with me to see if I'll stay. And we definitely haven't discussed whether or not I can have a glass of wine with dinner." In my head, I willed Andrea not to be offended by the way I was acting. I wanted to tell her I quit because he'd insulted me. I'd have to explain and apologize later. But frankly, having made the decision that I was willing to leave, it was easier to stick to my principles.

Andrea filled my wine glass. "Thank you," I told her meaningfully.

"*Non, Papa*. She must stay," Dauphine pleaded, her gaze also darting between us. *Thank you, Dauphine.*

Mr. Pascale patted his daughter's hand. "*Prends ton dîner.*"

Dauphine dove into her plate, and I smiled at her enthusiasm and obedience.

Andrea pulled the lid off a bowl on the table and revealed black-shelled mussels swimming in a creamy sauce, sprinkled with fresh green herbs. Then she set down a breadbasket of cut baguette. "I'll let Chef know to begin the next course," she directed at her boss, and then melted away and down the stairs.

"*Moules?*" he asked.

I dragged my gaze to his. "No, thank you."

"You are hungry, no? Why not?"

How could I explain to him that while I loved cream and shallots and garlic sauce—who wouldn't?—I couldn't bring myself to eat a tiny orange vagina? I'd blame Meredith for the rest of my life for pointing that out to me when I was thirteen. Now I couldn't ever unsee it. "I'll have some bread and sauce. Thank you."

He nodded and passed me the breadbasket before helping himself to the fragrant mussels.

I tore off a hunk of the crusty, warm, soft-centered bread, almost swooning with delight at the feel of it in my fingertips. Why couldn't America make great bread?

Monsieur Pascale had a piece of bread too and dunked it into the sauce in the shared bowl between us. I followed suit, trying to ignore the intimacy of sharing a bowl together and allowing a second for maximum absorption. Then I slipped the piece between my lips and groaned as the flavors exploded across my tongue. I couldn't hold in my sound of appreciation. My senses melted into the rich, creamy, garlicky flavor. Even my shoulders sank into them.

I hastily prepared another. And another.

Suddenly feeling self-conscious, I looked up to find his eyes on me, his body stiff, his mouth working slowly as he ate his helping.

"You need a spoon just to drink the sauce," I said to cut the strange tension. "It's so delicious."

He held up a mussel shell and then dipped it into the bowl like a spoon, allowing a healthy portion of broth to flood into it. Then he raised it to his mouth and drank. As he pulled the shell away, his lips glistened and he licked them.

I clenched my thighs together and wrenched my gaze to his daughter.

Dauphine was finishing up her melon and prosciutto. "Was it good, Dauphine?"

She looked up. "*Oui.*"

"Do you eat dinner with your papa every evening?" I pounced

on a topic.

"This summer, yes. When he does not have a business dinner." She rolled her eyes, making me smile. "I like it, but only when I get food good for me to eat. Sometimes Papa makes me try things I already know I do not like."

"Have you ever been surprised?" I exchanged a quick glance with her father, seeing his eyebrow twitch.

She sat back and folded her arms. "This is a trick?"

I lifted a shoulder. "I'm interested in the answer. Do you know that once upon a time, I hated prosciutto? True story. I cried too. My mother was making me try it and I was so mad. I took the first bite with tears running down my face and a headache from crying so hard." I widened my eyes for effect and Dauphine giggled. "The ham was salty and chewy just like I'd known it would be," I went on. "And I ran to the trash can and spat it out."

Dauphine gasped.

I dared not look at her father. "I got in sooo much trouble. I was sent to my room with no more food. I was very hungry and so tired from my tantrum that I fell fast asleep. I woke up when the house was quiet and snuck downstairs and found the leftover prosciutto in the refrigerator and finished it all."

Dauphine stared at me with a look of shock before bursting into a delighted laugh.

"But I don't recommend raiding Chef's fridge," I went on before she got any ideas. "Evan tells me he's fierce about his food."

There was a masculine snort from my right.

I looked up. Mr. Pascale was actually smiling. It was devastating. Like clouds parting to reveal the sun. My breath caught, and I swallowed and looked back to the little girl. "So, the moral of the story is *you never know unless you try*."

Her father said something to her in French that sounded like it could be a similar phrase. She glanced at me warily, as if it had been a trick after all. "Papa tells me that lesson sometimes."

"Wise man." I lifted a shoulder. "It's not just food either. I didn't like horseback riding until I tried it. Horses scared me."

"I love horseback riding!" she exclaimed then frowned. "But yes. Horses can be scary. They are so big."

"Exactly," I said.

"What else?"

"What else did I think I hated that I'm glad I tried?"

She nodded.

I looked up at the night sky as if deep in thought. "Hmm. Let's see. Licorice, avocado, karate—"

"You can do karate?"

"Of course. A girl must learn self-defense."

Her large eyes grew rounder.

"It's true," her father said, then he turned back to me. "What about boats?" he asked, eyes steady on mine as he took a sip of rosé. I realized I hadn't touched mine yet. "Are you glad you tried boats?"

I narrowed my eyes at him. Was he ... *teasing* me?

"You don't like boats?" Dauphine gasped. "Even Papa's boat? But it's the best boat!"

I laughed at how incensed she was. "Is it? I wouldn't know. I have never been on another because, well, I don't like them."

"But now you do," she stated as if it was decided. She wiggled in her seat, and then huffed out a breath. "Uh. *Je vais aux toilettes. Excusez-moi.*" She pushed back her chair and darted down the stairs, leaving me and Mr. Pascale alone over an extremely romantic-looking candlelit dinner.

On a yacht.

In the South of France.

But it felt more like being left inside the leopard cage at feeding time.

This time I did reach for my wine and took a healthy sip as blue-eyes-turned-navy glittered in the near dark.

CHAPTER ELEVEN

"You said you do not have much experience as a nanny," Mr. Pascale asked, clearly cutting to the interview we never had as soon as his daughter had left the upper deck. "I looked at the resume Tabitha Mackenzie sent. You worked at an architectural firm?"

As uncomfortable as I was to talk about my career, the wound so fresh, it was better than the weird tension that had suddenly bloomed out of nowhere as soon as we were alone. My shoulders relaxed, and I realized how tense I'd been. "Yes."

"In what capacity?" he asked, lifting his wine glass.

"As an architect."

His glass stopped midair.

Inside, I did a victory high five and a couple of backflips. Take that, you arrogant, gorgeous, piece of work. Being an architect is hard work. It takes years of study. Both math and creativity and a boatload of patience and attention to detail.

His head cocked to the side, his eyes studying me.

I waited, silently gloating. Though I hoped that didn't show.

"You're a little overqualified, *non?*"

That was it? That was what he had to say? Irritation rumbled through me, and my ego got a bruised backside.

"*Alors*, you will not even try a mussel after that talk you gave my daughter?" Mr. Pascale asked, reaching for one of the remaining shells.

And so we were done with me and my career. I took a slow sip of wine, letting the aromatic and rich liquid slide over my tongue.

He was baiting me and I was ... enjoying it?

There were three mussels left swimming in the bowl. It had been an appetizer, so there'd been just enough for both of us to have some without ruining our appetites completely, but I was abstaining. "You can have those," I said. The bread was finished anyway.

"You don't want the broth?"

"I don't have a spoon."

"If you have just one *moule*, you can use the shell as a spoon."

"Or you could give me one of *your* shells."

"Ahh. But where's the adventure in that?"

Maybe he did have a lighter side after all. This couldn't be flirting, could it? Not after the awful start to the evening. And not since he was my boss.

I lifted a shoulder.

"Is it the flavor? The—how do you say—the texture?" he questioned, using a fork to spear his bounty from the shell. "With all this sauce, you could eat anything." He swirled it around in the bowl for maximum flavor before bringing it to his mouth.

"It's not the flavor or texture, it's what it looks like."

He paused and looked down, studying the morsel on the end of his fork, his brow furrowed.

Then his confusion gave way to surprise, and he erupted into laughter. Moments later, the laughter still hadn't subsided and his fork clattered to his plate. He pushed back from the table, a hand on his chest as his shoulders shook, and he lost himself in hysterics.

It was contagious, though I tried really hard to hold it in. But the sight of this carefully controlled serious man, losing his shit like a twelve-year-old boy in biology class, just busted me up, and before long I was laughing too. Especially when his eyes started to water, and he gasped, "*Mon dieu.*"

There was a noise from the stairwell, and I turned to see a group of shocked faces. Andrea, Evan, and even Paco's head peeped over the top of the stairwell.

Another face appeared that I didn't recognize, maybe the chef. And then Dauphine wiggled her way through them.

"What is funny?" she demanded.

I shared a look with her father. There was no way we could tell them. It was beyond childish. And for some reason, it set us both off again.

Dauphine stomped her foot. "Papa!"

"Sorry," I managed, trying to sober.

"*Je suis desolé,*" Monsieur Pascale said at the same time, also apologizing.

Grabbing my napkin, I dried my eyes.

Evan and Paco had disappeared downstairs, but not before they both looked from one to the other of us in utter bafflement and speculation.

Looking at us both warily, Dauphine took her seat, but she was an extremely subdued version of the girl who had left the table minutes earlier. Her father's mouth kept twitching as he reined in his humor, but his eyes briefly seared me with intensity. It was gone so fast I thought I'd imagined it.

Andrea and the chef brought the main course to the table. Sea bass for the grown-ups and spaghetti for Dauphine. After a brief introduction to Chef, he left too. When Andrea went to top up my wine glass, I stopped her with a small hand motion and smile. "Thank you, but I think I should only have one when I'm working."

Across the table, I felt rather than saw Xavier Pascale's

shoulder relax. He wanted me to stay. And I surprised myself by wanting to stay too. And I'd allowed him not to have to apologize or beg me. I hoped he appreciated it because I wasn't normally in the habit of giving men free passes to be arrogant buttheads. But of course, he'd also overlooked me losing my temper earlier.

After Andrea left, we ate our meal in silence for a while. The sea bass was melt-in-my-mouth delicious, slightly salty and bursting with delicately herbed flavor. And by the time we were done, I was stuffed and happy. The grueling exhaustion of travel and ebbing adrenaline dragged at my muscles.

"What time do you normally go to bed?" I asked Dauphine.

"Eleven," she said at the same time her father said, "Nine o'clock."

She pouted and I smiled. Her father rolled his eyes. "And only because it is summertime. On special occasions perhaps ten."

"Come on," I said after checking my wrist watch. "I'll help you get ready and tuck you in. Do you have animals you sleep with?"

"*Des animaux?*"

"Yes, like teddy bears?"

"Of course."

"Maybe you can introduce them to me. My favorite growing up was a stuffed snow leopard my great aunt from New York City gave me. I miss that cat terribly."

I held out my hand while her mind was distracted with trying to unpack all the elements I'd just told her. I helped her out of her chair.

"Say good night to your papa."

She let go of me and threw her arms around his neck. "*Bonne nuit, Papa.*"

"*Bonne nuit, mon ange.*" He stroked her curls, and eyes closed, pressed a hard kiss to her head where it was tucked under his chin. *His angel.*

I reached for my plate and glass.

"You may leave it," Mr. Pascale said.

Then Dauphine grabbed my hand again and tugged me toward the stairs. "Good night," I said to her father.

"One more question, Miss Marin?"

I turned back. "Yes?"

"Do you like them now? Boats?" he clarified and cast a hand around him.

Cocking my head to the side, I pretended to ponder. "I'm still deciding."

He raised his glass with a smirk.

I turned and went downstairs with his daughter, hating how my pulse seemed to be ticking in my throat, and that sea bass was doing a tap dance in my belly. *Careful*, I told myself.

In her cabin, Dauphine showed me her favorite pajamas and began introducing me to her stuffed animals.

"Do these travel with you between the boat and home?"

"Yes. But I have more. Papa said I cannot bring them all here." Her shoulders sank.

"Hey, that's okay. You need some to remain at home to look after your bedroom there."

"But they get lonely."

"Are you kidding? They are having a party every night."

"I'm not a baby, I know my toys are not having a party."

"But they have feelings. You told me they get lonely. If they get lonely, they can just as easily be happy."

She humphed. "Being happy is not as easy as being sad. That's what my *maman* used to tell me. She said she tried very hard to be happy all the time, but sometimes it was too difficult."

God. My chest ached. I really needed to know what had happened to her mother. "It's true that some people have a harder time being happy than others," I said carefully, reaching for her toothbrush. "Just like some people get headaches more than other people."

She took the toothbrush from my hand and added toothpaste.

"I'm going to count to sixty. You have to brush your teeth for that long."

Her head tilted. "*Pourquoi?*"

"Because that's how long it takes not to miss any of your teeth and get all the germs out. You need to brush them all. Otherwise one tooth might feel like you don't like him as much."

Her eyes sparkled in amusement and she tucked the brush in her mouth.

"One, two, three, four ..." I began. By thirty, she was spitting and sighing in annoyance. I laughed. "Continue."

She rolled her eyes, but when she was finished and rinsed and had done her business while I turned down her bed, she was humming. Running and leaping, she landed square in the middle of the bed.

"Okay, time for introductions. Who is this?" I asked, picking up a lanky brown monkey.

"*Mon Chi Chi.*"

"*Mon Chi Chi?*" I asked, looking the monkey in the eyes. Then I shook its limp arm. "*Enchantée,*" I said, remembering the French greeting.

Dauphine giggled. "This is Pépé, Arnaud, Céleste, and Babar." She presented them to me one by one until we'd gone through about twenty toys from monkeys to mermaids and an entire elephant family. Finally, she got to the last one. A bear with blue peacoat, a red hat, and Wellington boots.

"I know this character," I said. "It's Paddington. How do you do, Paddington? Who gave you this one?" I asked her.

"Evan. *Il est beau, non?*"

"Very handsome," I agreed, so grateful that my high school French had started coming back to me for these little phrases here and there.

"I love the coat," she said. "It is very ... *stylish?* I wish I have more clothes for him."

"No Barbies? You can dress those."

Her nose turned up. "No. I do not like." Then she let out a big yawn.

I'd have loved to discuss our mutual dislike of Barbies, but it was getting late. I patted the pillow behind her, encouraging her to scoot down. She complied, grabbing Paddington, and I tucked the fluffy duvet around her. The boat rocked ever so gently, the waves tiny in the protected port. She yawned again.

"Were you laughing at me?" she asked sleepily. "Upstairs when I come back from *les toilettes*."

"No," I answered, surprised. "Why would you think that?"

She picked at the stitching on Paddington. "It happens at my school sometimes. When I leave the classroom, the girls they laugh loudly. And when I come back in, they stop."

My breath stuttered as emotion flood me unexpectedly. I blinked and slowly exhaled. Reaching out, I brushed the silky hair off her forehead. My mind went blank at how to comfort her.

"I think it is because of my name. Dauphine. Nobody has this name."

I cocked my head. "What does Dauphine mean?"

"I do not know the word in English."

"It sounds like Dolphin to me. And who wouldn't want to be named after a Dolphin." Still, I slipped my phone out of my back pocket and translated Dauphine. There was no translation, so I typed, "what is a dauphine in France?" "Ahh," I said as the answer loaded. "So you are the female heir to the French Royal Throne." Actually, not really that far from the truth if the tabloids were to be believed. At least that's how people saw Xavier Pascale.

"But I'm not. Papa said my *maman* wanted to call me this. And now that she is not here I do not want to change it. But it is so, so stupid." She rolled over, snuggling into her pillow.

"I think it's pretty. It's like being called Princess."

"And this is not good. The girls at school are mean about it."

I blew out a breath, realizing most platitudes would be a lie. I was also humbled that this little girl had chosen to share her personal pain with me, and I'd only just met her. "I have known girls like that too," I said, instead. "Boys too. It's hurtful. But luckily there are many more people in the world who are nicer, kinder, and better friends. They can be hard to find. Like treasure. But when you find them, keep the friendship safe. It is very, very precious."

I leaned down and kissed her forehead, surprised that this little girl had wormed her way into my heart in a matter of hours. I turned the bedside lamp off. "Sleep well, princess."

"*Bonne nuit*," she said sleepily.

Standing, I moved to the doorway.

"*Peaux-tu laisser la porte ouverte?*" she asked.

I complied, leaving the door open. My brain had obviously tucked away more French than I'd thought. I didn't think I could speak it, but I was happy with how much I seemed to be understanding. I'd go ahead and use the language app on my phone every morning and try to get up to speed.

In my cabin, I brushed my teeth and washed my face in the small bathroom and changed into my favorite soft t-shirt and sleep shorts. It seemed like a lifetime away that I was flinging clothes into a bag and rummaging around for swimsuits. Turning off the light, I slipped between the crisp, soft sheet and the cozy duvet. Lights, chatter, and music filtered through my open window. The hall was dark outside my cabin door, which was open because there was no way I could sleep with it closed.

As tired as I was, mentally and physically, the time change was already playing tricks on me. I looked at my watch, making out the dim glow-in-the-dark hands. It was five in the afternoon at home.

For the first time in two days, I dragged in a deep breath and felt my chest loosen. Even stuffed into a cabin just above the waterline on a boat, I felt a sense of freedom I'd never experienced. I turned the feeling over in my mind, trying to understand it. How long had I felt tense, stressed, and boxed into a package? Great school, serious degree, lucrative job prospects. Always making sure I was doing something my father would have been proud of. Something my mother could brag about. As much as I could get upset with my mother at her decision to marry Nicolas, which had turned into a disaster, she had raised me to be able to take care of myself. I'd been doing just that before I'd fallen off track, in her words, by quitting.

But there was beauty in the fall. I didn't have to be a certain way to please anyone but myself here. No one knew me. No one had any expectations of Josie, the woman. I was not the daughter of a disgraced Charleston socialite, nor the stepdaughter of a dishonest con man. God love Charleston, but the city had a memory like an elephant and a weight of judgment just as heavy. But here, for just a few weeks, I was not an architect desperately trying to carve out my own space in the male-dominated field. And there was a certain freedom in being someone new. Albeit temporarily. A girl with a blemish-free name and no history.

Standing up to Xavier Pascale today, and being true to myself, had been a gamble. But the result was maybe I'd earned a tiny modicum of his respect, and that felt good. I could make the best of the situation here, be the best damned nanny anyone had ever had, and fully embrace the chance I'd been given. That included shutting down my ridiculous attraction to my boss.

I closed my eyes and replayed our evening. Unfortunately, the attraction I'd felt for him was hard to beat back. But he'd made clear in no uncertain terms that it was my problem to deal with. And he seemed like he was the type to respect a power imbalance and never act inappropriately toward someone who worked for him. And I knew there was no way I'd compromise my job of taking care of sweet Dauphine or cast a stain on Tabitha's agency she'd worked so hard to build.

The boat rocked gently, and before long I was dozing. The deep bass of a disco beat in the port thrummed faintly almost in time with my heart. I wondered what the nightlife was like in France and if I'd get a taste of it. Thinking of that made me miss Tabitha and Meredith.

I awoke sometime later, fully alert. The sounds of the port had subsided. Pale waving lines danced like ghosts along the cabin ceiling from the reflection of the water. I strained my ears, hearing a footfall on the steps and then outside my bedroom. I turned my head, seeing a figure in the hall. Mr. Pascale. He fumbled with the latch holding my door open, and it began to close.

"No, please," I said quietly.

He started.

"Sorry." I stifled a chuckle at giving him a fright. "Please leave it open. I can't breathe with it closed."

He was quiet as he processed this. "We leave the port early in the morning. You must close your window."

I sat up.

"*Je le ferai.*" He waved me off and came fully into the room, his silhouette heading to the porthole. He slid it closed and latched it.

I could smell him. His cologne mixed with the sweet scent of scotch. He'd been up late drinking. I wondered if this was a common occurrence. I swallowed, breathed in deeply, the air now filled with him, and rubbed my chest.

"You are okay?" he asked.

"I—I think so."

"Is this why you do not like boats?" his voice rumbled in the darkness.

"Part of it."

"And the other part?"

I only vaguely made out his features in the dark. "The ocean has always scared me a little. It's so dark. Fathomless. Full of things humans don't understand."

"Mystery and miracles too. It all depends on how you choose

to see it. And the Mediterranean ... well, you will see so many parts that are clear and sparkling and seductive. You will forget your fear. You will want to dive down deep to discover her."

"You sound certain."

"I am. Oh. *Merde!*" he cursed. "Can you swim?"

"Of course." I huffed out a laugh. "And I love beaches. It's just the idea of being in the middle of wide open expanses of water that makes me forget how to breathe."

"And that's where the air is the most clean and plentiful. Where you can breathe the easiest."

"I guess so."

"We will cure you, Dauphine and I."

I chuckled. "Perhaps. She is wonderful."

"She is." He stood still for a long moment, then made a slight inhale sound. "Thank you for staying."

It was probably the closest to an apology for our rocky start as I was going to get.

I nodded but wasn't sure he saw me. "Of course," I whispered. "And I'm sorry I reacted so strongly."

He seemed to take my words in, and then without responding headed toward the door and vanished through the opening to his cabin.

I waited for the sound of him closing his door and instead heard his bathroom door close and the distant sound of running water. Then it opened and I listened to the sound of clothing being removed and the soft rustle of sheets. Was he going to sleep with his cabin door open too? I supposed as a concerned parent he would.

I lay awake for what felt like hours, straining to hear his breathing. It struck me how oddly intimate it was for us all to be sleeping separately, but yet all sleeping with no closed doors between us in such close quarters.

CHAPTER TWELVE

XAVIER

I threw my pen down on the report I was trying to annotate in disgust after reading the same paragraph four times and ran my finger around my already loose collar.

I felt the itch of this Josephine Marin under the collar of my shirt like a sunburn. I was used to the *au pairs* from the agency being plain and no nonsense. They were sweet, mostly personality-less, and easily blended into the background. As they should.

It wasn't as though I *needed* a plain nanny. I'd never been the type for that to be a problem, unlike some of the men I knew—my father being one of them, the old dog. I hadn't picked the agency based on the nondescript looks of the childcare professionals. But Tabitha Mackenzie had always sent really fantastic professionals with endless amounts of patience, and who were much more sensible than beautiful. As long as Dauphine was safe and well-cared for, looks had nothing to do with it. Maybe some of them *had* been pretty, but I'd certainly never noticed.

But now ... now it was a different story.

My first meeting with Josephine Marin yesterday had me second-guessing the decision from the instant I saw her. I knew immediately that she'd been the woman who'd stumbled into my video call with Tabitha. Who I was ashamed to admit to myself I may have also thought about again, in graphic detail, that night in the shower. I'd almost put her back on the train right then. I couldn't even remember how to speak English properly. Me. A man who'd gotten his degree from the London School of Economics. My English was usually flawless. Evan was going to have a field day with me, since he'd witnessed the whole thing. As it was, he'd given me massive side-eye the whole drive to the boat. It was like he knew she'd knocked me for six. Her green-gray eyes seemed to shoot straight into my soul.

Something about Josephine Marin messed with the carefully ordered equilibrium I'd honed over the last few years, like a faint earth tremor along a catastrophic fault-line. The kind that made my hair stand on end. And last night when she'd tried to quit ... well, I wasn't going to even admit to myself that her tirade and the way she'd stuck up for herself had been like a blunt force awakening of my libido, so there was no point thinking about it. If it had been anyone else reacting like that I'd have been glad they quit. But for some reason I'd found that unacceptable.

As much as I'd sort of encouraged her to stay, I realized now after a long night of barely any sleep that she was far too dangerous. I should send her home. I had to send her home.

I pressed the intercom button in the master stateroom where I was using the desk while on board. "Evan? See me in my office please?"

Minutes later Evan appeared at the door.

I waved him in from the desk where I'd been trying to concentrate for the last two hours to no avail.

"I have the tender ready to take you ashore as soon as you're ready," he informed me.

"*Bon.*" I raked my hand through my hair.

"Are you ready for the meeting?" he asked.

Meeting?

Oh, yes. Meeting. I absently looked at all the final chemistry reports, the results of which would win our company a billion dollar contract if we could secure the final round of funding for production. I could pay for it myself, but it was always a good idea to spread risk. My company had been working for years on a special film-like paper that could record the technological knowledge and code languages of the world without deteriorating. We'd gotten it to where it could survive extremes of heat and cold for, we believed, two thousand years in the event of cataclysm. Which, let's face it, with the way we were treating the planet, was bound to happen sooner rather than later. Every government needed it. So did every corporation, to protect their knowledge and survive. But the reports on my desk weren't my primary concern right now. "This situation with the new girl is not going to work. She can't stay," I said instead, leaning forward on my desk.

"I'm sorry. Excuse me?"

"The *au pair*," I explained, picking up my pen and waving it dismissively. "Nanny, or whatever."

Evan smirked.

"What is that?" I made a motion at his face.

"That's me smiling at seeing you so ruffled."

"Ruffled." I stabbed the table with my pen and slid my fingers down to the point before flipping it on its end and doing the same again. Slide, flip, stick, slide, flip, stick.

"Wound up," he elaborated.

I blinked at him. Slide. Flip. Stick.

He rolled his eyes. "You finally realized your male equipment might not be dead?"

The pen flew through the air, smacking him in the forehead. "I could fire you for that. Don't think because I've known you practically my whole life that I wouldn't."

"Ow," he grumbled, rubbing his forehead. "Wow. Pulling out the old *firing you* card, X? Things must really be hard." He raised an eyebrow. "Pun intended."

"Fuck you." And he was the only one I let call me X, instead of Xavier or *Monsieur Pascale*. And only when it was the two of us.

"Sorry, that was crass." He didn't look sorry at all. "Anyway, here's her contract and non-disclosure if you want to look at it before she signs. It just came through from the lawyer."

I took the paperwork but stayed quiet since I was incriminating myself. I knew it was unfair to send the girl home just because I couldn't stop the thrum that slid through my deepest core with one look at her. And now I'd admitted my weakness to Evan and confirmed all his assumptions.

Also, beyond the fact that I had no time nor willingness for distractions, it was also reminiscent of my father lusting after my nannies growing up. Except my father *acted* on those impulses. I blew out an annoyed breath to cover my cringe, trying to get my head away from *her* and back into business. It would be fine. She was just an attractive woman. I'd spent time with plenty of those. No big deal. I'd give it a couple of weeks. I focused in front of me. "The reports for the meeting look good. I'm ready." I shuffled the pages needlessly. I knew the results were solid. I didn't need to re-read the reports this morning to know.

"Good. I'd like my goose to keep fattening. I'm not ready for the *foie gras* just yet."

"Such a strange expression." Every year, instead of a bonus, I gifted Evan a small amount of stock in my company. It had been his idea, and he was building up a nice retirement. It was a symbiotic relationship—his skin in the game if you will. He protected me since I was, literally, his investment.

"Sometimes, I like to fantasize you protect me because I'm your friend and not because I'm making you rich," I said.

"That's cute," he deadpanned. "Okay, also on your agenda.

Your father sent another request to meet for this bridge project he wants you to look at."

My stomach tightened. "Invest in, you mean. I was hoping he wasn't pushing that."

"*Pas du tout*. He's anxious to share some numbers with you."

"He's convinced that now we have our hand in some boutique hotel projects I'd like to get into infrastructure too." Newsflash, I didn't. Save the government building contracts for the unscrupulous. There was practically no way to avoid the systemic corruption, and I wanted no part in it.

"He's setting up a lunch," Evan went on while I brooded at how my father couldn't ever take no for an answer. "Next week. Marie-Louise put it on your schedule. She just put a bug in my ear to ask if you'd seen it."

My poor long-suffering assistant who had to contact Evan because I was playing a game of avoidance with my own father.

I flipped open my laptop and after passing the facial recognition software opened my calendar to see how Marie Louise had shaped up my next two weeks. Luckily it was fairly clear, like I'd asked her to keep it, apart from a couple of meetings, a visit with my late wife's estate attorney and the lunch with my father. At least Dauphine would be happy. The lunch was at *Le Club Cinquante-Cinq*, her favorite. I gritted my teeth and hit the confirm button on the invite. "Fine. Done." Sometimes it was easier to keep the peace and invest a bit here and there with him.

"Okay, the other update is that we got some chatter from one of our contacts in the port that there was a guy asking about us, which is why we took precaution yesterday. He surmised it was just a journalist."

"*Mais?*"

"But, what?"

"I'm asking you. You have the look like your spiders are tingling."

Evan rolled his eyes. "Spidey-sense. When will you get that right?"

"Evan."

"Sorry. Yeah. You're right. Something feels shifty. I looked into Michello." Evan paused. "He was released."

"He's *out*? Shit." Arriette's stepbrother. My stepbrother-*in-law*. He'd been arrested for possession outside a nightclub and briefly taken off the streets. But he'd always been a bad seed. Always hitting his sister up for extra cash when he was short. I blamed Ariette's addictions on his enabling. He'd spiraled after her death, presumably thinking he'd be inheriting her estate, racking up IOUs with the type of people who liked to tie up loose ends when they didn't get paid, or even when they did. And sadly, they were also the type who knew I was his relation. Michello was a wild card. I didn't like wild cards.

"Okay. Keep an eye on him."

"Already got someone on it."

I nodded, satisfied, and glanced at my watch, hoping Evan wouldn't wind back around to my comments about the nanny. "I'll be ready to go shortly."

Evan didn't move.

"What?" I asked.

"I was just thinking that it's been a really long time since I heard you laughing like you did last night."

"*Oui*, maybe it was overdue. They say time heals, no?"

Evan cocked his head to the side. "Maybe. Anyway, just give her a chance."

Internally, I knew what I'd asked about having her sent home was ridiculous. And I could have come to this conclusion on my own instead of clueing Evan in on my struggle. I waved my hand with a chuckle as if I'd been joking all along. "Apparently I don't have much choice, do I? It was difficult enough to get a nanny at such short notice anyway. Did the background check come in?" Despite The Tabitha Mackenzie Agency always promising vetted placements, I'd be a fool not to do my own research. Especially when Dauphine was involved.

"Preliminary is clean. Couldn't find a driver's license but she has a birth certificate, social, and passport."

"Maybe she doesn't drive?"

"Maybe. She lives in downtown Charleston. So it won't be hard to figure out a full picture."

"*Bon.*" If I remembered, Charleston was a quaint little city with a young but well-preserved history. It was also a walking city so it wasn't surprising she didn't have a car. I'd really enjoyed my brief trip to meet with a super yacht company who had bid on and won my business for the more eco-friendly yacht I was planning to upgrade to. I loved the ocean, and these gas-guzzling and oil slicking beasts weren't very good for it. "She's an architect," I offered.

"She's what?" His eyebrows hit his hairline.

"An architect. She'd have a degree or something with her name on it. Start there."

"That's impressive. Beautiful *and* smart."

"Apparently." I growled at him.

Evan turned to the door. "Oh, by the way, I told her she wasn't allowed to leave. You're welcome. I felt like you both needed a cool down period."

"You did what?" Fuck. The last thing I needed was her feeling like a prisoner, especially if she had issues with being on a boat. "Evan."

He shrugged with a cryptic look. "New security measure I just implemented. No one on or off the boat twelve hours before we move port."

"Twelve hours?"

"Okay, fine, we can make it three. But with Michello skulking around, it's a good idea anyway. I want to make sure we're safe."

Somehow, I didn't think the new security feature had much to do with my ex-brother-in-law and everything to do with the fact that Josephine had quit and Evan wanted her to stay. What was my old friend up to?

A stray thought popped into my head. My hand clenched.

I scowled at him. "Wait. You're not ... you don't ... you know there's no fraternizing."

"What?" Evan stopped with his hand on the door, and then busted out laughing. "Jealousy is a good look on you, my friend."

"Get out."

He raised a palm. "*Pas de problème.*"

CHAPTER THIRTEEN

JOSIE

First morning jet lag was like a heavy beast in my head hanging on tight to my eyelids. I persuaded Dauphine out of my room where she'd bounded in to wake me up, telling her I needed to shower and change and then I'd meet her upstairs. The boat was moving. I sluggishly showered, rinsing my hair again, since I'd slept on it wet and woken up looking like a cast member from Sesame Street. I tied my hair in a low bun and pulled on a simple sundress I'd found on sale last fall while out shopping on King Street with Meredith. With my best friends on my mind, I checked my phone for a message.

Tabs: *How was your first night?*

I quickly typed back, cognizant of the time. It was late morning here already, and I had a little girl to look after.

Everything is great. Food delicious. Boat on the move. Jet lagged. I hope you're good. Miss you. More later xo

I realized the sound of the engine was so loud because there was a door open in the hallway down to what looked like an engine room. The walls were cream and well lit. I peered down the metal stairs. "Got it?" a man's voice said. I didn't think it was Evan or Paco. "We'll have to replace the ballbearing, over," the British voice said and then the body it belonged to emerged— sandy haired, skinnier than Evan, and wearing a white polo and khaki shorts that now had black grease stains smeared in places. "Oh, hullo," he said with a broad smile, revealing slightly crooked teeth when he saw me. He was young, but sea weathered. Perhaps an ex-surfer. "You must be Miss Marin."

"I am." I held out my hand.

He held up his black grease-covered one apologetically. "I'm Rod. I'm a deck hand. I missed you when you arrived yesterday, I was taking a bit of time off. Sorry about my hand being greased up. Just had a wee problem with one of the systems. No big deal."

"No problem. Nice to meet you. When did you get on board?" I asked conversationally.

"Uh." He scratched his head. "About five this morning, right before we set off."

"Is that right? Well, I'll leave you to it." I waved and stomped up the stairs. Evan was going to get an earful from me. Imagine telling me no one could get on and off the boat for twelve hours before we moved? I growled.

As soon as I got to the main living area, I took a moment to look outside the window. We were cutting through the water, land to our right. The morning sun sparkled off the blue waves. I wanted to appreciate it more, but my need for caffeine outweighed the gorgeous view. I had yet to see where the chef worked, so I looked around for where the kitchen might be. Wait, was it even called a kitchen? A galley?

The sound of masculine laughter came from the bridge.

I headed that way to say good morning and perhaps be pointed in the right direction for caffeine.

Dauphine sat in the captain's chair, her hands on the large wheel, and Captain Paco stood behind her, pointing into the distance. A breeze blew through the open windows and the scent of salted air was a welcome jolt to my tired brain.

"Good morning," I greeted.

"Look! I drive the boat," Dauphine gushed when she saw me.

I chuckled. "I can see that, no wonder it's such a smooth ride. You must be doing a great job."

She flushed with pride.

"I was wondering where I might find some breakfast leftovers and some coffee."

Dauphine abandoned post, sliding off the high wooden chair. "I will bring you." She was in tiny white shorts and a blue t-shirt. Her hair needed a brush.

Paco patted her head.

"Sorry you have to lose your co-captain," I told him, setting my feet farther apart to allow for the motion of the boat.

"Did you sleep well?" he asked, sticking an unlit skinny cigar in his mouth.

"Not enough. I'm still on American time."

He nodded. "It will take a few days."

Dauphine tugged on my hand. "Come."

I raised my other in a goodbye wave and allowed myself to be led back down to the main living area and through a doorway on the opposite side of the stairwell I used to go downstairs to my cabin. The galley was long and narrow with high end appliances. The counters were stainless steel and spotless. It looked as though it could be the kitchen of some sleek, New York City loft. Chef was nowhere to be seen, but next to an expensive looking coffee machine, which still had a glowing red light, there was a plate, a linen napkin-wrapped set of utensils, a bowl of fresh cut fruit, and a basket of bread and pastries including a croissant wrapped in a linen napkin. Croissants. My weakness. Also nestled in the basket was a small ramekin of soft yellow butter and a tiny jar of red preserves with a checkered lid.

First things first, I made myself some steaming fragrant coffee and added cream from a small metal jug left out. Then I plopped a croissant on the plate, as well as butter and preserves, and sat at the small banquette along the wall. Dauphine found another plate and helped herself to some of the fruit and joined me.

"So, what's the plan today?" I asked her, tearing an end off of a croissant and smearing it with butter and strawberry jam. I closed my eyes as I began to chew and let out a moan of appreciation.

"You love food so much." Dauphine observed with a giggle.

"I don't think you understand. In America we *think* we know how to make baguettes and croissants, but I can tell you for sure we do not. I'm planning on putting on some weight while I am here." I patted my belly.

She laughed with delight. "But they make good hamburgers in America, no?"

"Perhaps. I'll let you know after I have one here. So, you never answered. What's the plan today?"

"We go to *Antibes*. We will anchor in the bay. Papa has a meeting." She rolled her eyes. "We will stay on the boat today. Paco said there might be treasure. You'll swim with me?"

I nodded.

"I am only allowed if someone comes in the water with me."

"As long as it's okay with your father and Paco. I'll need to borrow sunscreen, I forgot to bring some."

"We have much. I will show you."

I finished off breakfast, draining my cup of coffee, and located the dishwasher. Like everything else in Chef's kitchen, it was clean and empty, breakfast having already been cleaned up and put away. I loaded our plates and utensils and wiped the crumbs from the counter and the table.

Then Dauphine led me through another short hallway and to a door. She rapped sharply and opened it. "Papa?"

"No, Dauphine," I hissed in a whisper when I realized she planned to go into his quarters. "It's okay. Don't disturb your father."

She waltzed into the sunlight-filled room. "He is upstairs, I was just checking. He told me I must always knock when a door is closed."

"Good advice."

The cabin we entered was clearly the master stateroom—a huge bedroom, spanning the width of the boat. A king bed centered the space. On one side, closest to us, was an office area and desk with papers piled neatly and the other had a large sofa and seating area. There was also a treadmill and some workout equipment in one corner. Her father was nowhere to be seen, and while I knew he was using a cabin downstairs to sleep rather than this one, I still entered cautiously. He obviously worked and got dressed here too, if the men's dress shirt hanging on a valet hook in the corner was any indication. Dauphine danced across the room and disappeared through a door. I followed her into a bathroom and walk-in closet. While not huge, the bathroom was luxurious and certainly bigger than the ones downstairs.

The closet was full of both men's and women's clothes. My stomach shifted uncomfortably as I looked over what had probably been Dauphine's mother's things that had never been cleared away. Two years and they were still here?

Dauphine fingered several of the dresses as she passed, then whipped her hand away as if she'd remembered she wasn't supposed to touch them. She opened a deep wooden drawer on a soft hiss to reveal an array of sunscreens. "*Ici,*" she said. Here.

I selected a thirty sun protection factor. There was a hairbrush on the counter, but there were no toothbrushes or anything that made it seem like the bathroom was currently being used on a daily basis.

I fingered the hairbrush. "Your mother's?" I asked. But surely not after all this time.

Dauphine nodded, and then looked toward the clothes, her face marred with a pained emotion. I doubted a ten-year-old could really define the feelings that must be stirred up by having to see this reminder of their loss every day. For that matter, what about her father? Was that perhaps another reason why he slept downstairs?

"Do you like to braid your hair?" I asked to try and switch her attention.

"*Oui*. Andrea does it for me sometimes, but I do not know how to do it myself."

"May I?"

Dauphine nodded at my reflection. "But my hair is ... I don't know the word. It gets stuck?" She frowned and said something in French that I presumed meant tangled.

"I have something for tangles."

"Tangles?"

I picked up a particularly rats-nesty lock of her hair. "Like this. You have beautiful curls, but you must keep them from being knotty."

"You have curly hair?"

I glanced at my reflection and made a so-so hand gesture. "Wavy. But it's wet right now. Did your *maman* have long hair like you?" I asked, fingering the dark blonde curls.

"Yes, but it was different." Her brow furrowed as if trying to remember. "She liked my hair. She liked to use the comb."

"She brushed your hair for you?"

Dauphine nodded, and her lower lip suddenly began to tremble. "She made some blonde sometimes in her hair. It's ... difficult to remember."

"It makes you sad to think about her?"

She nodded. "But I'm sad also when I forget things about her."

"Do you have a picture?"

"In my room at home. I should have brought one here so you could see." She blinked rapidly, her blue eyes watery. "She was very, very beautiful. But she was very, very sad. *Papa* said being sad can be like getting sick. Some people die when they get too sick."

Jesus. Swallowing a wave of grief at her loss, I squeezed her shoulder. "He's right." I blew out a steadying breath. "Would you like me to brush your hair before you go to sleep tonight? I might not do it the same way, but you have such beautiful curls, we should make them shine like your *maman* liked."

The boat's engines slowed, and the rocking grew a little more pronounced. I hung on to the door frame, my stomach lurching, and reached for Dauphine's hand. I was glad I'd had something solid for breakfast.

Turning, I stopped short at the sight of Xavier Pascale striding across the cabin. "What are you doing in there?" he asked, his voice with an odd quake. "Dauphine, I told you not to come in here."

She inhaled sharply, and I stepped protectively in front of her.

CHAPTER FOURTEEN

With Dauphine protected behind me, I raised my eyebrows in surprise at the tone of her father's voice. My heart thundered like I'd been sent to the principal's office.

The disapproval on his face suddenly evaporated as if he'd caught himself overreacting.

"I didn't have time to buy sunscreen." I held up the bottle by way of explanation of why we were in the master stateroom. "Dauphine said I could borrow some."

"*Oui, Papa.*" Dauphine slipped from behind me and grabbed him in a hug around his middle. Her shoulders shook. The tears that had been so close to the surface, ones I'd managed to keep at bay just moments before, suddenly burst out at the puncture wound her father's anger had inflicted. She babbled words into his body.

His head bowed down as he hugged her back, and dark brown hair flopped silkily over his forehead. Then he gently pried his daughter off his middle. She'd left wet splotches on his pale blue linen shirt. Seeing her tears, I saw his shoulders slump, guilt wracking his features.

He cooed gently to her in French, and then looked up at me, his eyes miserable.

"My apologies," he said. "I'll have Andrea add sunscreen to the purchase list." His eyes tracked to the hem of my sundress and skimmed down my legs. He seemed to realize what he was doing and quickly shook his head. He hugged Dauphine back and then set her away from him. "*Mon chou*," he said, looking down at her, his earlier frosty expression a thing of the past as he looked at his daughter. "You will be a good girl for Miss Marin, *oui*? Evan will take me to shore for my meeting."

Dauphine wrinkled her brow. "Where will you have lunch?"

"In town."

"You promised me we would go to *Le Cinquante-Cinq*. When?" Her voice pitched hysterically.

"Next week, okay?" He switched to French, and she responded.

Dauphine pouted and stomped her foot. Then she looked back at me, her eyes lighting as if she'd had an idea. "Can Miss Marin come? Please, Papa!"

He looked up.

I had no idea what had just been decided, so I shrugged.

"If she would like." He looked at me a beat, but his mouth twisted like he'd swallowed a bug at having to invite me along.

I managed to find my tongue. "If Dauphine would like me to go with you all, it would be a pleasure."

"*D'accord*. It's a plan. Dauphine." He turned to his daughter and kissed her head. "Will you leave me and Miss Marin for a moment. I must speak with her privately."

My stomach tensed with nerves.

Dauphine pouted but pirouetted toward the door. "Paco!" I heard her calling out as she hightailed it to the bridge.

He followed her route and closed the door behind her. "Is this okay?" he asked me, indicating the closed door. The gesture of concern was surprising.

"Um. Sure." I looked toward the long but narrow windows and inhaled. At least the boat had stopped rocking so much.

"You are ..." he paused. "Claustrophobic?" he asked as if he'd had to retrieve the word from the recesses of his mind.

I nodded. "A little. It's not crippling. But it's there." This room with its wider space and more windows felt less confining than my cabin downstairs.

"Sit?" he indicated toward the couch. "I have some employment paperwork for you. A contract and a non-disclosure agreement." He picked a stack of paper off his desk and handed it to me with a pen.

I sank down on one end of the couch and skimmed through each page. It was in English, which I appreciated.

"You can look it over and give it to Andrea when it is signed." He leaned against his built-in desk, crossed his ankles, and folded his arms across his chest. Along with his blue linen shirt that matched the color of his eyes today, he wore distressed jeans and brown boat shoes. He looked like a model in a menswear commercial—brow expertly furrowed, careless masculinity oozing from everywhere.

He's my boss, I reminded myself. I dragged my gaze away. I'd have to pray the contracts were standard because I couldn't focus on a damned word. I signed the employment contract and the non-disclosure agreement. "Here."

He took the papers. "I must apologize," he began. "I am normally more ... smooth. Even."

Inwardly, I chuckled at him calling himself smooth. "Even-tempered?" I supplied.

"Yes. I reacted from concern. Dauphine ... she gets upset sometimes when she comes to see her mother's things. I have been meaning to remove them ..." He lifted his shoulders helplessly. "Her emotions. They are elevated sometimes."

I licked my lips and cocked my head to the side, unsure what to say. I had so many questions about Dauphine's mother, his late wife, and what happened. "If you think it would help in my relationship with Dauphine, perhaps you could explain the circumstances around ... her mother's passing. It's just Dauphine mentioned—"

"What did she say?" His eyebrows snapped together, and he set the signed paperwork on the desk next to him.

"Just that her mother was sad. And maybe she thinks the sadness had something to do with her death," I supplied.

Mr. Pascale's eyes grew unfocused, and tension wound through the seemingly relaxed stance of his body. I could tell by the slight tick under the skin at his temple and the way his folded arms went from something to do with his hands to a tight bind he held against his chest. It was a subtle change, but unmistakable. Like a cage around his heart.

"If you don't want to talk about her, it's okay. I'm sorry I asked." I backed off. "It's not my place. I just thought, for Dauphine—"

"I'm sure you've read internet stories."

"Actually, I haven't."

He snorted, and I tried not to feel offended. But when I held his gaze with sincerity, he seemed to accept it.

The boat's engine cut off and the sound of a heavy chain clanged dully.

"That's the anchor," he said, and it was clear he wasn't going to answer my question. Not today anyway. Then he let out a small sigh and the tension broke. "We have arrived. What will you two do today?" he asked, moving to sit on the end of the perfectly made bed and facing me.

He braced his elbows on his denim-wrapped thighs and looked at me earnestly. A lock of hair fell forward again.

Blinking, I tried to ignore the image of Xavier Pascale and a bed being in the same frame, impressed with his ability to change the subject so easily. "Actually, I was hoping for some direction. How does Dauphine usually spend the day on the boat?"

"She has some school reading to do and some simple exercises to keep her brain—*comment dit-on*—?" He circled his hand in the air as he clearly tried to think of the word.

"Active?" I supplied.

"*Oui*, to keep her brain active before school starts again."

I gave a nod. I remembered going brain dead during long summers between school years in the Charleston heat. "Wow, sounds fun," I said, trying to convey a tone of irony.

"But also, I have asked Paco to take the boat over to the little bay at *Cap d'Antibes* and come back for me later," he went on. "You two can go swimming. I will have Rod put the slide out."

"A slide?" I asked.

Monsieur Pascale broke into a lazy grin. "The best boats have toys."

I rolled my eyes. "The *best* boats, huh? Trying to impress me?"

"Simply trying to change your mind about boats," he corrected with a chuckle.

Damn, his laugh was sexy. Husky and warm.

"Is it working?" he pressed.

You have no idea, I wanted to say. *But it has nothing to do with the boat.* "Not yet," I deadpanned. "What other toys do you have up your sleeve? I distinctly remember seeing a helipad on one of the *other* boats. Are you not rich enough?"

He cracked out a loud laugh, his eyes crinkling almost closed with mirth. He was stunning when he laughed. I'd noticed last night, and it caused even more of a giddy jolt inside my chest today. Shaking his head, he pinned me with his gaze. "I cannot believe you just said that to me."

I swallowed and tried to rein in my smiling lips. "Yeah, me neither."

"No helipad, I'm afraid."

"Then *I'm* afraid I'm not impressed," I joked. This was flirting, I was sure of it. No. No. No. My lower belly was flooding with fizzing warmth, but alarm bells clanged on my brain. Distance, distance, distance.

There was a sharp, sudden knock at the door.

"Ex?" Evan's voice sounded. *Ex? X, for Xavier?*

"Here," Monsieur Pascale responded.

The door opened and Evan poked his head around the opening.

"Ready to go when you are, Mister Pascale," Evan said, his eyes switching from me to his boss, then back to me.

A strange sense of being caught with my hand in the cookie jar dowsed all the tightly wound energy inside me. I smiled uncomfortably.

"I'll be right there," my boss said, making no move to get up.

I stood. "I was just leaving."

Evan paused a moment, then retreated and closed the door behind him.

Tension bloomed as my boss stood too. He scrubbed a hand through his hair, seeming embarrassed. Suddenly his face closed down to all business, and he drew a deep breath. "Dauphine has had a difficult time the last two years," he said, his hands slipping into his pockets. "She needs someone she can trust. *I* need someone she can trust. Unfortunately, I haven't always done the right things and reacted the right ways. I have kept her from her grandmother more than I should, a mistake I hope to rectify this summer. Her grandmother would have her most weekends. Or more if she could. But it's difficult with my schedule, and hers." He stepped around to the other side of his desk then and sat down, steepling his fingers. "Dauphine needs a friend. She needs privacy and space to just be a little girl and not to be scrutinized by the media. I know you are her nanny, but it's clear already from the way she interacts with you that you could be a friend too. It seems the chance I took on hiring you without proper background checks coming through quickly was the right one ... for

Dauphine," he tacked on after a pause. "Please don't disappoint us."

It was a grave and earnest plea. I swallowed, my throat thick.

It didn't escape my notice how he parsed out himself from Dauphine. I was good for *her*. By default that meant not good for him. The distinction caught me off-balance.

"Are you okay?" He stared at me.

"No. Yes," I corrected with a slight voice break. "I, yes. I'm very fond of Dauphine already. I can tell she's had a rough time from the little she has shared. She can trust me. You *both* can," I added.

"*D'accord.* You can go," he said, his voice stiff. His expression had become troubled.

"Of course." I headed for the door but paused with my hand on the latch. "You know," I said, my voice soft. "I've lost a father, so I have some idea of what families go through—what it's like to lose a parent. I'll be here for Dauphine, and I'll keep her safe." I hesitated. On the tip of my tongue was to tell him I could be there for him too, but I bit my lips closed instead. It wasn't wise to get any closer to this man. He was damaged, and I didn't think it was solely to do with the loss of his wife.

I walked out and closed the door behind me, heading into the living area.

"What was that about?" Evan asked, making me jump. He was leaning against the wall just as I emerged from the hall.

I placed a hand on my chest. "What?"

He tilted his head, an odd, contemplative expression on his face.

"He wanted to talk to me about Dauphine," I found myself explaining. "And paperwork. I signed—"

"Relax. I was just curious. I'm glad you signed the paperwork. Good to have you aboard." He smiled and headed out through the main living room onto the back deck, leaving me confused.

Hearing Dauphine's chatter, I followed the sound to the galley.

Only later when Dauphine and I stood on the stern of the boat and watched the small tender with her father and Evan motoring to shore, did I remember I'd meant to have a talk with Evan about him saying I hadn't been allowed to leave the boat when that had clearly been made up on the spot.

I breathed in the sea air, the breeze caressing my skin, the waves below so blue it looked as though a giant had spilled a pot of indigo ink.

I looked down at my young charge, her tangled curls blowing in the breeze and her eyes, just like her father's, matching the swirling blue depths of the sea below us. In just a day, she and her father had wormed their way under my skin and I knew, even when I went home, they might never leave me.

CHAPTER FIFTEEN

After Evan and Mr. Pascale had left, Paco anchored the boat in a little bay nearby he said literally translated to False Silver. Dauphine was sure that meant treasure. We lathered ourselves with sunscreen, and I decided to wear one of my bikinis since it was just she and I. Paco and Rod had disappeared down to the engine room to tinker at whatever had been giving them trouble, and Andrea was last seen with a pile of linens, napkins, and silver polishing cream. Chef was chopping and prepping things for whatever menus he was preparing for lunch and dinner.

I followed Dauphine out onto the back deck and did a double take when I saw a large inflatable slide had been fastened from the deck past the lower platform to the water. "Wow," I said, stopping.

The sun sparkled across the water. The boat rocked gently, and Dauphine clapped her hands in delight when she saw that Rod had unfurled and inflated the long slide off the side of the boat.

I leaned over the railing. "Well, that looks a little daunting."

"We need to be wet first." Dauphine raced down toward the back deck in order to jump in.

"Wait," I called and hurried after her to the edge of the lower platform.

Below us the water was like a jewel. I could tell it was deep, but it was so clear and translucent it was almost like looking through a kaleidoscope made up of turquoise, vibrant greens, and dark blues. "This is amazing," I said.

"We count, yes?"

I laughed. "Sure," I said. "One, two, three!"

We both leapt.

The water exploded upwards, cool and sharp against my skin as we plunged in. It sucked the breath from my chest and loosened my worn bikini top, which I quickly held on to with my free hand.

Dauphine's small hand left mine as the weight of my body drew me deeper, and my feet caressed eddies of even colder water. With my eyes closed, I reveled in the feeling of the quiet. Already I could sense the saline on my lips and teasing at the seam of my eyelids. For a moment I fought the urge to kick straight back up, eking out a few more precious seconds of the novel feeling. Had I ever plunged into an ocean without fear of the unknown, the unseen? I felt a swell of water and knew Dauphine was treading water nearby. With a kick I rose easily and burst through the surface with my face turned to the sky. Salt hit my tongue as I opened my mouth to drag in a breath. I wiped excess water from my eyes and opened them to meet Dauphine's rapturous smile.

"*Fantastique*, non?"

I laughed, unable to contain my joy at this simple pleasure. "Yes. Amazing. It's chilly at first."

"Yes. It is wonderful. Papa says in one more month it will be too warm. Now it is *parfait!*"

"Perfect," I said.

"Perfect," she mimicked. "Now we do the slide. Me first. You will wait for me here?"

"Sure. Go on ahead."

She turned and moved toward the swimming deck and ladder, and I kicked my legs as I tightened the bikini strap around my neck. The navy hull and bright white of the yacht decks made a sleek and majestic picture against the cloudless blue sky and perfectly unmarred horizon. It took up almost all my view. To think, this time last week I'd been sitting at my little cubicle desk at the back of a building in downtown Charleston, my eyes straining over numbers, angles, sketches, and budget spreadsheets in the harsh fluorescent light. For the first time since my world had turned upside down, I felt a sudden rush of relief and escape. I didn't know what that meant practically because I loved architecture and buildings. But I hung on to the lightness in my chest. Somehow in the arduous trek toward trying to get promoted, I'd gotten a little burned out.

I turned, treading water, and looked toward the gray rocky edges of the bay and up at the few mansions from modern to old-worldly stone that clung to its edges. Here and there steep steps were carved in stone among rugged green brush. I imagined the feats of engineering architects of old had to devise in order for these palatial cliff-side dwellings to stand the tests of hundreds of years. I wondered if the more modern ones would have such longevity. If we were still anchored here later, I'd love to sketch the houses. I hadn't quite broken the habit of carrying a sketch-book with me everywhere I went that had been drilled into me by one of my first drafting professors.

I heard Dauphine call out to me.

I turned in time to watch her settle herself at the top of the slide, and then push off. She screeched the whole way down, her small body dumping into the water in a splash of gangly limbs. She came up gasping, making us both laugh.

"Not so graceful," I said. "But it looks fun."

"Your turn."

"Will you wait for me here?"

She shook her head, feigning fear at being left alone in the water.

"I didn't used to like being in the water by myself when I was younger either. Not even in a pool. Come on, I'll race you."

Dauphine giggled and squealed as she half doggy-paddled and half swam breaststroke furiously to the swim deck.

I pretended to try to keep up with slow strokes through the water but let her win.

Paco was watching us from an upper deck, chuckling. He'd finally lit his small cheroot, the smoke a faint apparition circling his head.

For the next couple of hours, we jumped, swam, and raced each other. Dauphine tried to convince me that it was okay to stop messing with my bikini top, as apparently many French women simply went topless. For a hot second, I imagined walking around the boat topless with her father's eyes staring at my breasts. "I'm not French," I explained in a choked voice, trying to shake the image.

"Yet!" She grinned. "I will make you more French, and you will make me American."

I gave her a weak laugh.

We tried the snorkel gear, but Paco asked us not to go too far from the boat since Evan had taken the tender, and if we got into trouble by the rocks, he wouldn't be able to get to us as the main boat was so large. Still, being able to float along the surface of the crystal-clear water at a depth of what I assumed to be about thirty to forty feet was mesmerizing. It was incredible to see the sandy and rocky bottom and the small silver fish with yellow tails that darted about here and there. Sadly, we also saw several pieces of half-buried glass, aluminum, and plastic trash. Dauphine saw it first, and motioned to me, before pointing and then making a crying action at her mask with balled up fists. I loved that this bothered her. It bothered me. I made a heart symbol with my thumbs and forefingers and pointed at her.

Eventually our hungry bellies called us back to the boat, and we lay on the swim deck to dry off in the bright sun.

I hadn't had such carefree fun in quite some time. My skin was dusty and tight with salt, I was thirsty, and my eyes stung slightly, but I felt so at peace. I let out a long sigh and turned my face to Dauphine. "Thank you," I said sincerely.

"*Pourquoi?*"

How to explain in a way she'd understand. "It's been a long time since I enjoyed swimming so much," I told her, but it didn't come close to expressing the joy and relief in my chest.

She grinned, clearly pleased with my gratitude.

"Lunch is ready," Andrea called from above us.

Dauphine leapt up.

Shading my eyes, I sat up and squinted to see Andrea. "Be right there. Are we eating outside or should we change first?"

"Outside. We'll eat on the lower back deck since Mister P is off the boat."

I stood and followed Dauphine, climbing the short built-in step ladder.

Andrea handed us fluffy navy and white towels.

Paco sat at the head of the table on the back deck and Chef at the end. Rod, Andrea, Dauphine, and I filled in. There were a couple of large baguettes, hams, and salami, cheeses, and a large *Salade Niçoise* with green beans, boiled eggs, olives, and tuna over luscious green leaves. Chef pointed at the large bowl. "No anchovies for the little princess."

"*Merci*," Dauphine told him and stood, leaning over and giving him a big smacking kiss on the cheek.

Chef looked so taken aback that we all burst out laughing.

He grinned ruefully.

Andrea poured everybody some sparkling *San Pellegrino* water. "So," she said, tucking a stray hair behind her ear. "We've all been wondering what you said to Mr. P to make him laugh so hard last night."

"Oh," I said, feeling heat rising up my throat. I glanced sideways at Dauphine, and she looked at me with interest. Last night she had thought that we were laughing at her. I looked nervously back at the four sets of curious eyes. "Um," I stammered. "It was just something silly. I hardly remember."

Andrea and Chef looked disappointed and unconvinced at my non answer.

"What happened?" Rod asked.

"Something Ms. Marin said made Mr. P lose it."

"Call me Josie, please," I said.

Rod quirked an eyebrow as he slathered butter on a piece of baguette and laid a circle of salami on it. "It's been a while since he's had something to laugh about."

"Well, whatever it was," said Andrea, "It was lovely to hear him laugh. Right, Dauphine?"

Dauphine nodded with her mouth full.

"So how did each of you end up working for *Monsieur Pascale?*" I asked, desperate to divert their scrutiny.

"*Moi,*" began Paco. "I used to captain for the older *Monsieur et Madame Pascale.* I have known Xavier since he was a boy." He let out a gruff chuckle with a shake of his head. "I could tell some stories, but *non.* All I can say is I'm very grateful to the family. And it has been an honor to work with Xavier." He paused, suddenly looking somber. "There is no finer man," he finished and picked up his glass of sparkling water, staring at it as if he could see distant memories within it.

"Well." Rod cleared his throat. "For me, let's just say I was a rather naughty boy, got myself arrested a couple of times, and Evan who's a mate of my older brother just pulled me aside one day and gave me a bit of a shake. '*What you gon' do with your life, Roddie,*' he says. Or something along those lines. Told me I needed to man up, like. He helped me get back on my feet and gave me a job. I'll always be thankful Mister P trusted Evan enough to give me a fair shake. So, you could say I'm dedicated to never letting either of them down."

I chewed my piece of salami, and then forked some salad as I turned to Chef.

Chef sat back with his arms folded. "Not sure when it became confessional lunch. But you may as well know. I'm an alcoholic. I've been sober for six years and one month. I lost a restaurant, my wife, and custody of my son." He glanced at Dauphine, and words seem to halt in his throat. I surmised he had a lot more to say but felt it was either too difficult or best for Dauphine not to hear. "Anyway, my restaurant was one of Mr. and Mrs. P's favorites. When he heard what happened to me, he offered me a job if I could get myself cleaned up. He said the job was mine as long as I needed, and that anytime I was ready to start again with a new venture he'd ..." Chef cleared his throat as if choking up, "... he said he'd back me. Not sure I'll ever take him up on that. But for now, I'm happy here, talking to you sorry lot." He raised his glass of water. "Cheers."

I reached for my glass, a lump in my throat. "Cheers," I said.

"*Chin chin*," sang Dauphine.

"To Mister P," added Rod and Andrea in sync.

We all took a sip.

Andrea stood. "Anyone need anything? I just have to run to the kitchen, I put another baguette in to warm up. Be right back."

We all helped ourselves to seconds and thirds of the delicious salad and cold meats and cheeses. The baguette was warm, crunchy, and delicious, especially when slathered with a little lightly salted butter. I had far more of it than I should have been comfortable with but couldn't bring myself to care.

A while later, after Paco had regaled us with a story about a run-in with some modern-day pirates early on in his boating career, he sat back with a pat of his belly and a satisfied smile. "Time for a nap."

Dauphine let out a sound of disappointment.

"You want to watch a movie or something?" I asked her. "You don't have to sleep, but maybe we should lie down for a bit until the food settles and the sun is not so strong."

"You can set up a movie on the screen in the main salon," said Andrea. "I'll show you how everything works."

I smiled. "Perfect."

Everyone grabbed their plate and some glasses from the table, and we had everything cleared up in no time. Before long Dauphine and I were on the couch watching a singing Zac Efron, and it was only then I realized that Andrea hadn't shared her story of how she came to work for Xavier Pascale.

If the stories at lunch were to be believed, every one of his employees had needed rescuing, so I had to assume Andrea's story was a similar situation. So my new employer had a white knight complex. I supposed there were worse faults to have, I thought to myself wryly, irritated that I was finding more reasons to like than dislike him. A crush on a handsome man, I could get over quickly. A crush on a handsome and kind man ... well *kind* was my kryptonite.

Dauphine lay on the sectional, her eyes drowsy, but glued to the movie. She'd pulled a cerise cashmere-looking throw over her bare legs.

"Be right back," I whispered. The boat rocked gently beneath my feet as I stood.

The swimming and salt and sea air had tired her out.

I hoped they did the same for me come bedtime.

I caressed her hair and then got up and made my way to the galley to find Andrea and chat. Unfortunately, she was busy going through upcoming menus with Chef.

After making sure it was fine with Andrea that I leave Dauphine relaxing where she was, I retrieved my sketchbook and climbed to the top deck. I spent a blissful hour under the awning, sketching the houses built into the rock. Dauphine found me soon enough and was delighted that I knew how to draw. I tore a sheet out of my book, making a mental note to buy more paper when I could, and gave her a pencil. She drew a seascape, complete with a mermaid.

The sun was low, and the light hitting the villas and rocky outcrops as we gently swayed in the water made my heart twist in contentment. I found myself longing to explore the tiny villages. How close together were all those houses after all? Were all the alleys cobblestoned? Did little French ladies stand in front of their pale blue doors and sweep their stone steps and shoo the stray cats? Did they all walk home with fresh baguettes every day? How strange to have been plucked from my small Southern life I'd thought I'd wanted and plopped into the middle of the Mediterranean. This was the kind of thing I should have been putting on a vision board as a teenager. Not that I'd ever finished one. It had always been Meredith's idea, and my logical left-minded brain didn't put much stock in such a practice. Although Meredith was always trying to convince me that my Pinterest board about France was the same thing. Maybe it was. Maybe fate had indeed brought me here.

Dauphine and I ate with the crew again since Mr. Pascale had not yet returned, and later, I found myself restlessly trying and failing to sleep. My internal clock was still locked into American time. The boat rocked more heavily anchored in the bay than it had in port, and while the motion should lull me, all it did was make me constantly aware I was enclosed deep inside a vessel with no fresh air and surrounded by dark water. I debated getting up to go to outside, but then I heard the sounds of Xavier coming down the stairs and getting ready for bed. So he was home. Something inside me relaxed now that he was back.

CHAPTER SIXTEEN

I peered into the galley, expecting to find at least Chef in there too, but it was only Andrea. I didn't think I'd missed breakfast this time as there were plates and food still on the table. She had her back to me as she fiddled with the coffee machine. "Morning," she greeted as she looked over her shoulder. "Would you like a coffee?"

"Yes, please. Desperately. But just one, thank you. This jet lag might keep me awake again tonight, so I don't think adding too much caffeine into the mix is a good idea. I'm still six hours behind."

"Let's sit and chat before everyone comes in," she said and indicated the banquette seating. "The jet lag will take a few days, I'm sure."

I slid onto the banquette with some fruit and a croissant. "What time do you all usually eat?"

Andrea sat down opposite me, setting two frothy cups of cappuccino in front of us. She glanced at her phone. "Around now, but they're all trying to figure out the Wi-Fi. It's glitching." Her blonde hair was scraped back like she normally wore it, in a low bun behind her head. She wore minimal make-up, and her skin glowed healthy and smooth. "You probably gathered from lunch yesterday, but Monsieur Pascale ... he likes to, uh—"

"Rescue people?"

She trilled tension-filled laughter. "I guess you could say that. I don't even think he realizes it." She waved her hands in the air dismissively. "It's probably best to bring you up to speed. And I didn't want to talk about it in front of everyone. They know of course, but not Dauphine ..." She cleared her throat. "You see," she said. "I was, uh, in an abusive marriage."

My eyes widened. "God, I'm so sorry," I said.

She waved her hand again. "Not looking for sympathy. It's been long enough I can say it for what it was without all the shame I dragged myself out of there with. But it's important you know about it because I have no doubt my husband would come looking if he knew where I was."

"I don't know what to say. God. I'm so sorry you went through that."

"There's nothing to say," Andrea said. "The thing is, I ask myself why hiding out with an employer who's a paparazzi magnet like Xavier Pascale ever seemed to be a good idea. But then I ask myself what else could I do? He's been an amazing person to work for, and all of us who work for him would do anything for him. And so far I've stayed under the radar."

I twisted my fingers together, fidgeting as her words chilled me. "Is there a chance your ex-husband could find you? Like, do you think he's actively looking for you?"

"I don't see how he is after all this time. If I do go for a drink or dinner with the crew, they know we don't take pictures, and we keep a low profile." She blew out a breath. "Unfortunately, he's not my *ex*-husband. I've been too nervous to file for divorce in case he could use that as a way to track me down."

"My God, Andrea. I'm so sorry." Jesus. I couldn't imagine living with that kind of fear.

"Yeah. Well, I'm just telling you this because you need to keep a low profile too. Everyone on this boat is a target in their own way. Either themselves, as in my case, or as a way to get to Mister P or Dauphine."

I pressed the side edge of my thumb nail against the highly varnished wood tabletop. "If you're worried about me betraying your confidence, or attracting attention, please know I'd never willingly do that."

"Thank you."

"Of course."

"Anyway" she said finally, "we all have something to lose. So, I hope you understand how seriously you have to take your job here."

I nodded. "I do. Did I give you a different impression?"

"No, I don't think so. But then again people have misled me before." Her lips flattened.

"I do take my job seriously."

"So far, we've been nothing but impressed with you."

I was thankful to hear it, even though I didn't think I'd done anything special beyond what a normal person would do.

The door to the galley smacked open behind me, and Dauphine flew in. She leaned over and planted a big smack of a kiss on each of my cheeks, then did the same with Andrea, and grabbed a plate, and then sat down.

"Wow," I said. "Somebody's in a good mood this morning."

"*Oui!*" Dauphine clapped then reached for the butter. "Can you guess why?"

I shared a look with Andrea.

Dauphine pointed her knife. "You must not tell her, Andrea!"

Andrea made a zipper movement across her lips.

"I don't know where to even start," I said, amused.

"It is something to do with ..." Dauphine paused, frowning, then said the word, "Shopping," to Andrea.

"It is the same word in English. Shopping," Andrea offered.

"Ah! *Oui*. Shopping."

I raised my eyebrows. "We're ... going ... shopping?"

"Not just shopping ... we are going to the market! Papa said we can go today to the market in Antibes. It is not as good as the one in St. Tropez, *mais* ... that is okay. You will love it! It is my favorite thing!" She was practically bouncing in her seat.

Confused at Dauphine's excitement, I looked at Andrea for help. "A market has her this excited?"

"Well, the markets in France are a pretty big deal in the summer. Antibes is one of the best. Well, the covered market is there all summer, but they have a street market too where they close down the streets and vendors come from all over to set up their stuff."

"Like a farmer's market?"

"Sort of. But better. They sell everything. Even amazing antiques. The one in St. Tropez is famous but pricey. But after you've done this stretch of coast a few years, you realize that a lot of the same vendors travel to each place. You can buy linen dresses from Italy, amazing cheeses, unique jewelry, leather bags, cover-ups, flowers ... you know what? I can't do it justice. You'll understand when you get there."

"You aren't coming?"

"Nah. I've been to lots. I have no room for any more clothes. Besides, I have a ton of stuff to do on the boat. Chef always goes though, to pick up supplies."

Rod and Chef emerged from the crew stairs.

"Where am I going?" asked Chef.

Rod helped himself to a plate and sat down opposite me. "Mornin'."

I nodded at him.

"The market," Dauphine answered Chef through a mouthful of croissant. She swallowed. "You can get a beautiful new bikini, Josie. Then you don't have to worry about your top falling off all the time."

There was a beat of silence where heat traveled up my throat to my face, and eyebrows around me raised.

"Well," Rod said, giving me a wink. "None of us would mind if you wanted to go topless. All the French ladies do. It's one of my favorite things about France."

Chef cuffed him over the head. "That's a stereotype, and you know it." He growled at the same time I felt the breeze of the door to the salon open behind me.

"Rod." Mr. Pascale's voice was an arctic rumble.

In front of me, Rod's face suddenly went purple as he swallowed whatever he'd put in his mouth whole.

"*Viens ici,*" said Mr. Pascale's low voice behind me. I turned to see him holding the door open and gesturing through it with one hand, his eyes like icicles trained on Rod.

Rod nodded with a gulp. "*J'arrive.*" He slid out of the banquette. "Sorry, Josie," he mumbled at me as he passed.

"I—it's fine," I said. "I know you were just joking."

His eyes darted from me to his boss.

Feeling awful for Rod, I chanced a look at Mr. Pascale, completely torn, but not wanting to undermine his authority. He glared at me, and I sank into my seat. Jeez. Was it *my* fault now? Rod went through the opening, followed by Mr. Pascale, and the door swung shut.

Silence ensued.

"*Bien,*" Chef said. "I think I speak for all of us when I apologize for Rod's comment. He just doesn't think sometimes. His emotional intelligence is still a work in progress."

I grimaced. "It's fine. I promise." I knew it was technically sexual harassment, so I didn't say anything else.

Chef shook his head and threw his arms up. "I must go and do my list. We should already be there, all the best things will be gone," he muttered as he exited the galley.

"The Antibes markets are frequented by some of the best chefs," Andrea explained as I frowned at Chef's departure.

Dauphine glanced from one to the other of us. "I do not understand why Rod is in trouble. It is true, *non?* We do not mind if you go with no top."

"It's all right." I patted her hand. "Maybe your dad wanted to talk to him about something else."

"Hmm," she said, then slid out of her seat. "I will go and get ready."

Andrea gave me a tight smile. "Evan said you're an architect, Josie. What on earth made you ditch that to nanny for the summer?" She gestured around us. "Not that it's not a sweet gig."

Dauphine pirouetted out the door.

I grabbed on to the topic change gratefully. "Well, uh, I realized I had no future at the firm. I was passed over for a promotion that should have been mine. Add in the fact one of the partners is a bit of a misogynist. And definitely implied I was easy on the eyes," I lifted a shoulder, "and, well, I quit. It was hasty. I'm just ... I'm not fully to terms with the fact my career I worked so hard for just exploded. And you all needed a nanny. My roommate runs the agency. And Mr. Pascale was convincing."

"Ha. He normally gets what he wants. But yikes, sorry about your promotion. Wow. An architect." She laughed, seemingly with discomfort. "I'm impressed. A bit overqualified for this, no?"

Xavier Pascale had said the same thing. I looked her straight in the eyes. "I'd never treat it as something beneath me."

She nodded. "I never had a chance to go to college."

I didn't know what to say to that. Maybe she thought I'd feel above her or something. I wasn't sure how to fix that. I'd just have to work hard to make sure she knew she called the shots and try not to second guess her like I had at dinner the first night about the wine. "Do you have anything you'd like help with. I'd like to be of use if I can."

She looked around, and I could tell our easy camaraderie might have taken a blow. But I was sure we'd get it back.

"Not really. You guys should go and enjoy the market. She handed me a small flip phone. "Been meaning to set you up with this. Mister P seems to trust you already," she went on, and I inwardly cheered. "Which I have to say I'm relieved about. I don't know what I'd do if we hadn't found someone. I have my own work to do, you know? Although Dauphine seems more laid back this year than she has been before. But anyway, Mr. Pascale needs us to stay put near Antibes a few days. Things have come up." Her mouth turned down.

"Oh?" I asked, not liking the expression on her face. I took the phone and slipped it into the pocket of my shorts.

Her eyes cut nervously sideways and she gave another nervous laugh, her finger running around the lip of her coffee cup. "Antibes is where Mrs. P's family lives. It's, well ... for a while after Mrs. P died, there was a lot of denial and blame by all parties. Things have always been tense. But more so after." She took a sip while I wondered what this had to do with me. "Anyway, when we come to Antibes, it's usually because Mr. Pascale has to go and see things regarding his wife's estate, and in particular regarding her stepbrother, Michello." Andrea shuddered. "I never liked that guy. But he's in prison for drugs right now, so that's a relief at least. I shouldn't be telling you all this, but I guess it's good you have the lay of the land." She shook her head. "Anyway, I wanted to talk to you because you're being thrown in at the deep end, there might not be a day off this week, and I need to make sure you're okay with it."

"I'm not sure I have a choice. I wanted to quit the first day because he accused me of being attracted to him, and I couldn't stand his arrogance. But then I got to know Dauphine, and ..." I lifted a shoulder.

"Are you?"

My eyebrows pinched. "Am I what?"

"Attracted to him?"

My throat immediately clogged. "He's gorgeous," I admitted.

"It was a bit difficult *not* to have a reaction. But also he acted like an ass the first night. Turn *off*."

"I appreciate your honesty." She smirked. "And do you *still* think he's an ass today?" she asked, knowingly.

"No," I admitted. How could I be after learning the things I had at the lunch table yesterday about what a good guy he was. I guessed they could all be making it up, but I doubted it.

"Still turned off?"

I met her gaze, steady. "I'm professional. It won't be a problem. Plus, let's just say I have a trust issue with men in general. It won't be a problem," I repeated.

She held my stare, appraising, but with a small smile playing around her mouth.

"What?" I asked, amused and relieved we were somehow inching back to our initial rapport.

"Nothing."

"Seriously. It won't be a problem."

"I know. I don't think *you're* the one who's having a problem." She took a sip of coffee with a smirk. "Sure you don't want another?"

I shook my head and slipped out of the bench to put my plate in the dishwasher. "Wait. What does that mean? Have I upset someone?"

"God, no. Not at all." She shrugged. "Nothing. Really, I misspoke. Just ... be yourself."

I tilted my head, but when she offered nothing more I sighed. "You're strange."

"Probably," she said. "Have fun with Mr. Pascale and Dauphine at the market."

The three of us were going? I swallowed. That didn't feel intimate and happy-little-family-ish. Not at all.

Maybe I could hang out with Chef.

Dauphine opened the door. "*Dépêche-toi s'il te plaît!*" she whined. "We are leaving soon. Hurry!"

CHAPTER SEVENTEEN

The streets of the village of Antibes were even better than I'd imagined a French town to be. From the boat, I could see the medieval sea wall that surrounded the village, and now that we'd come into port, the streets were close and ancient. The old stone and stucco buildings valiantly supported new and improved shopfronts. In the streets, there were awnings in red, and blue, and every color imaginable, providing shade over the offered wares. Baskets of all shapes and sizes, some lined and filled with varieties of olives, trays of cheese, some tall filled with baguettes, crowded covered tables. There were barrels of fresh garlic, bundles of lavender, cases filled with pungent truffles. I walked with my mouth open, Dauphine dragging me along to look at dresses. It was a good thing I'd just eaten breakfast. Xavier trailed behind us, unwilling to hurry like his daughter, or perhaps not wanting to be grouped with us. He'd waved us ahead as we stepped off the tender and slipped on dark sunglasses and a ball cap pulled low. A disguise of some sort, I imagined.

"This is amazing," I muttered, inhaling the scent of spicy salami, and noted the endless array of different types and lengths.

Back home, salami was just salami. Unless you counted the odd fancy, over-priced charcuterie board that served to educate us that there might be more than one type. But even the most well-trained chef in Charleston would do his nut seeing the array of food in this market.

"*Viens!*" Dauphine whined as a cute guy in a white chef's jacket offered a piece of fresh baked bread with soft cheese and dripping honey on it in my direction.

I reluctantly shook my head, with a mouthed *merci, non.*

But behind me, my boss' voice cut in. "Try it," he commanded, though his tone was soft.

I glanced back at him and wished I could see his expression behind the shield of his sunglasses.

"Go on, it's worth it. Dauphine, *attend*," he said past me.

I flicked my eyes back to the earnest young chef and reached out for the morsel he laid gently in my palm. I heard the chef offer a bite to Xavier, but I blacked out to everything around me the moment the flavors hit my tongue. Letting out an audible groan, I chewed, my mouth flooding with saliva. "Oh my sweet heaven," I managed when I came to.

"Lavender honey." Xavier's voice was gruff. Then he bought three baguettes, two rounds of cheese, and two pots of honey before Dauphine managed to get us moving again.

I seriously hoped he was going to share his bounty with me. That was why he bought it right?

Around us people shouted out greetings and hummed with oohs and aahs, and others called out for separated friends and family members. There were colors everywhere you looked. Smells ran from melting cheese, to fish, to rotisserie chickens and fresh herbs and spices. Under foot, the uneven cobblestone streets were cast in multicolored shade from the sun beating through the awnings.

I'd never been a big social media user, but suddenly I wanted to take pictures and post everything I saw. But none of the pictures would capture the sounds and smells and the utter feast for the senses. I was in awe, and only when I looked over my shoulder and saw Xavier Pascale still following us, keeping pace, his hands stuffed stoically in his pockets, did I become self-conscious enough to realize how like a gawking tourist I must look and snapped my mouth shut.

Dauphine dragged me to several stalls where even I had to admit the dresses were gorgeous. I bought a couple of linen summer dresses at Dauphine's urging, one in white and one in black, as well as a jade green halter neck bikini. "I've never bought a swimsuit without trying it on." I grimaced, wishing at least Meredith were here to give me advice. Even Andrea. The sizes made no sense, so I held a bikini top up and fitted the strap around my chest. Dauphine grabbed the sales lady's hand to get her attention and garbled something to her. The no nonsense sales lady gave me a look up and down, then suddenly grabbed my boobs in her hands, letting go before I could even gasp in shock. Then she grabbed me by the shoulders and whipped me around side to side and back to face her. Heat plumed along my chest and cheeks. She muttered something, sounding irritated or unimpressed, and then grabbed my hips and waist.

Dauphine giggled, her small hand covering her mouth.

"What just happened?" I managed.

"She measured you."

"With her hands?" I whisper-squeaked.

Mr. Pascale stood loitering, dark glasses still on and phone in his free hand. For a moment I thought he hadn't seen until I saw him sucking in his cheeks, trying really hard not to laugh.

Before I could process whether he was actually laughing at me or something on his phone, since I couldn't see his eyes, the woman was back. She twisted me around again and nodded.

"Um," I tried, my eyebrows practically in my hairline.

"*Bon*," she said and ripped the original bikini out of my hands, replacing it with another the same color.

"You needed a bigger size, she said," Dauphine told me.

"Uh, okay."

The woman rattled off something else.

"She says it's eighty euros for the dresses and the bikini, but I think you can offer her fifty."

"Wait. Really?"

Dauphine shrugged. "I think it is okay. Papa always says they charge more to Americans."

I reached into my small cross body purse to get some cash and timidly handed the woman a fifty euro note. She snatched it out of my hand and then said something terse to Dauphine.

"Okay, she said she'd take sixty. Do you have ten more?"

I dug around and found a twenty. "Here," I told the woman, feeling bad. "Make it seventy."

"Bon," she snapped and took it, looking less than impressed with my bargaining, even though it was in her favor. Then she was off helping someone else.

"You're welcome," I whispered under my breath, feeling like I'd just been in some kind of battle where I'd also been violated. "Not sure that was worth the discount," I told Dauphine. "She wasn't very friendly."

"They never are," Mr. Pascale's voice cut in. "They do six market mornings a week, traveling every day. I think they gave up being charming a long time ago."

I looked up at his profile but couldn't get a read on his face with his mouth set so sternly.

"Come," he said with a shrug. "Let us go and find a cafe. I have to make some phone calls, and it is too noisy here."

"Uh, thank you Mr. Pascale, for letting us stop to shop. Sorry it took so long."

He waved me off and took Dauphine's hand. "If it means you

have a proper swimsuit and I don't have to worry about Rod making inappropriate comments, then it is nothing." His neck flushed. "And call me Xavier, please. Mr. Pascale is my father." He strode ahead.

I let out a breath and followed them, feeling again as if I'd just been reprimanded for the Rod thing. I hung back as Dauphine pointed out things here and there, and Xavier pulled out his wallet again and bought her a pink summer dress, a set of sparkling scrunchies, and some beaded bracelets. I admired everything I passed but didn't dare stop to admire too long in case I lost sight of the two of them or got caught up with another scary sales lady. My earlier awe for the market had morphed into a bit of sensory overload.

Finally, they took a right turn out of the market and down a side street. We approached a super cute street cafe with small wooden tables spilling onto the sidewalk. A trellis wound with some kind of flowering plant, and there were bright tangerine-colored umbrellas. There was a single table with two seats available and Xavier pointed Dauphine toward it before speaking briefly with a nearby table and stealing an extra seat. In seconds, we were all closely seated.

"What did you think of the market, Josie?" Dauphine asked.

"It's amazing."

"You see? *Je l'ai dit, non?* I told her, Papa. She did not believe me."

Xavier gave a small smile, and I wished I could see his eyes. "Is that right?"

I lifted a shoulder, then cleared my throat. "I've never experienced anything like it. It was also a little overwhelming."

A waiter appeared. Dauphine ordered an Orangina, and Xavier looked expectantly at me. "Uh ..."

"May I order a drink for you?"

"Okay. Thank you. Nothing alcoholic."

He nodded. *"Un citron pressé,"* he told the waiter. *"Pour nous deux."*

"What am I having?" I asked.

He took his sunglasses off, and I was momentarily frozen in the snare of his blue eyes. "Wait and see?"

Swallowing, I nodded.

"Sorry if the saleswoman embarrassed you. I had a tailor measure my inseam at the market once. I know the feeling." He gave a small grin, and my stomach unclenched slightly, grateful he was trying to make me feel at ease.

"It was certainly unexpected."

He smirked, and I had a feeling he wanted to ask something else, but it never came.

"So, where's Evan today?" I asked. "Isn't he supposed to be your security?"

"He's around here." Xavier's mouth twitched, and his eyes went over my shoulder. "Ah, here he is now." Xavier leaned back and lifted a hand.

I turned to see Evan strolling down the street from the other direction.

"No room for me at the inn?" Evan said as he eyed our table. "Dauphine, there's an acrobat I just passed. Shall I take you to go and see him?"

She jumped up. *"Oui! J'adore!"*

"I just ordered her a drink," Xavier protested.

Evan smiled and looked at both his boss and me. "And it will be here when we get back."

Xavier scowled, and I felt like I was missing something.

Dauphine grabbed Evan's hand, and they disappeared into the throng of pedestrians, leaving Xavier and me alone. At the next table a woman with dark hair kept looking over at us. Xavier noticed and slipped his sunglasses back over his eyes. Silence stretched.

"I'm sorry about the Rod thing," I said.

"What are *you* sorry for? It wasn't your fault."

"I know. I just mean sorry it happened. If it helps, I know he didn't mean anything by it."

"He didn't. He's young and doesn't think sometimes. But still, I can't have him making comments like that. He won't learn if no one corrects him."

"True. So how do you know Evan? I get that he works for you, but you seem to be friends too."

Xavier leaned back, and his fingers drummed on the table. "I've known Evan on and off since we were kids. His father worked with mine. And after Evan joined the British military, I knew one day when he was ready, I'd hire him."

I cocked my head to the side, waiting for him to elaborate.

"Since I was a boy, it was always a bodyguard who usually spent the most time with me." He paused, his jaw setting. "Apart from nannies, of course. I figured out early on that it may as well be someone I respected and consider a friend. Real friends ... are hard to come by the more successful my company becomes. Oh, I *know* a lot of people," he responded to whatever he saw on my face, and I could tell he was uncomfortable talking but he didn't stop, though he kept his voice low. "You don't come from my family or get to where I have in my business life by not knowing a lot of people and cultivating every relationship you can. For the sake of the other staff who work with me, Evan and I are always simply boss and employee in public. But in private we are friends."

"And I'd guess if anyone can understand the things you face, it would be him?"

Xavier shifted and ran a thumb across his bottom lip back and forth. "He's been with me during the best and the worst times of my life. And now you have gotten more from me than most magazine interviewers."

The waiter arrived with Dauphine's drink as well as two tall glasses containing an inch or so of what looked to be pure squeezed fresh lemon juice, a jug of water, and a small carafe of something else clear.

"Sugar water." Xavier motioned toward it. "What do you call it? Simple syrup?"

"Oh. Yes."

"This is very French. It used to be my favorite as a boy." He showed me how to add the sugar and water and make my own lemonade to taste. We clinked glasses and sipped. It was tart and delicious.

"Do you like it?" he asked.

I nodded.

The dark-haired woman laughed loudly, flipping her hair, her eyes raking over my table-mate again.

I leaned forward with my elbows on the table. "Does she know you?" I asked.

"Who?" He sat up.

"The hungry woman at your nine o'clock."

He pressed his sunglasses against the bridge of his nose and pretended to stretch and look down the street both ways. Then he leaned back. "She may know me. But I don't know *her*. But I think you may be aware that I have some following here and there. People like to know what I am doing and make judgments about me."

"You're famous, you mean."

"Well-known, perhaps."

"And will it be strange for you to be seen sitting at a table with me? Will they wonder who I am?" Oh God, what was I implying?

His lips flattened. "Because they might think we're ... together?"

A strangled laugh broke from my throat. "No, no. Just—"

"People will think what they think."

And what will they think? I wanted to ask. *What do you think?* "So it doesn't bother you what people think?" I asked instead.

"It does. And it doesn't. It is beyond my control. And there

are other things that are ... easier to control. Does it bother *you?*"
he asked.

"I don't know. I had a brief brush of notoriety when some stuff
with my stepfather went down." I traced a drop of condensation
down my glass, and then took another small sip and swallowed.
"It turned out he'd been investing huge sums from Charleston
families—our friends and neighbors—in an elaborate Ponzi
scheme. It was hard to escape the press and the shame. Even
though my mom and I had done nothing wrong. I don't think I'd
like to be scrutinized like that again."

He seemed to ponder my answer. "That's ... difficult," he said.

"Papa!" Dauphine appeared, Evan close behind.

My shoulders relaxed. I hadn't realized how on edge I'd been
sitting with Xavier on my own, being pinned by those eyes that
seemed to see right into me. And it occurred to me that even
though we'd left the market so Xavier could make a phone call, he
hadn't touched his phone.

"Josie," Evan said. "I'll accompany you and Dauphine back to
the boat. Xavier has a meeting."

"Oh." I took one more sip of lemonade and then stood. "Of
course."

Dauphine grabbed her Orangina, asking if she could carry it in
the bottle. Then Xavier handed me the package with the
baguettes, cheese, and honey, with his eyebrows rising above his
sunglasses in challenge. "Try not to eat it all at once? At least save
me some."

I thanked him awkwardly because I was so touched and
surprised and frankly shocked he was teasing me and giving me
gifts of food, which was basically the fastest route to my heart,
then the three of us headed back toward the market stalls. I tried
to enjoy the glimpses of the old town that I could see past the
market setup and relished the feeling of being on firm ground.

But soon the port and the water were in sight.

It had been a fun day and I felt as though I'd finally gotten a glimpse of the real Xavier Pascale, and it hadn't done a whole lot to squash my attraction.

That thought sent a ripple of panic through me. This situation was just a tad too seductive to be safe. As soon as I got back to the boat, I would work on my resume. The sooner I had a plan to get out of here on time, the better.

CHAPTER EIGHTEEN

I gasped for air, sitting straight up as the pressure in my chest woke me from a fitful sleep. Moonlight streamed a blue glow across my bedding. The boat rocked gently, and all was quiet. I opened the small window and dragged in a lungful of warm salty air.

And another.

The water lapped and tinkered.

It wasn't enough. I slept with the cabin door open every night, but even that didn't stop me from waking with a gasp every now and again. This week, I'd taken to tiptoeing up the stairs to the top deck and peeking carefully around to make absolutely sure I was alone. Only then could I inhale lungfuls of fresh, cooler, night air to tide me over. I never stayed long. After a trip to the upper deck, I'd often fall into a much deeper and undisturbed sleep until morning.

Exiting my cabin, I quickly glanced in at Dauphine. She lay almost sideways across her bed, covers all kicked off, gangly legs off the edge, and her fingers clutched tight around the trunk of Babar the Elephant. I smiled and shook my head. I'd move her when I came back down.

I slipped silently upstairs, level after level, pulled by the fresh night air I could almost taste. Stepping out onto the top deck, I was met with a night sky that had exploded in black ink and diamonds. I breathed out a soft, "Wow," and filled my lungs again, more consciously this time as I crept forward toward the railing and the velvet darkness where the horizon lay. Xavier was right, out here on the ocean one could really breathe the easiest. The deepest. Especially at night. I concentrated on my breathing, in through my nose, out through my mouth. Trying to get my fill. My hands gripped the railing.

After a few minutes, I tilted my head back and tried to make out familiar constellations, wondering how different they'd be from what I saw back home. France was also in the Northern hemisphere so technically, I should be able to make out familiar patterns.

As my eyes drew more accustomed, I could see the cloudy swath of the milky way start to take on more definition and pick out some individual stars.

A breeze picked up and lifted the small hairs on my arms. The scent of salt spray, teak oil, and eucalyptus danced on the breeze with notes of smokey scotch. Scotch?

My skin prickled. The back of my neck specifically.

I whipped around and gasped.

My eyes, now accustomed to the dark, made out the long form of a man reclining on a lounger.

Xavier cradled a tumbler of amber liquid in one hand on his abdomen, his other behind his head. His eyes watched me, lazily. Like a very, very, attentive jungle cat.

The sight of him made my mouth go instantly dry and shattered the peaceful relief I'd found. "W-what are you doing here?" I asked, lamely. And how long had he been watching me?

There was such a long pause, I became self-conscious. I was wearing sleep shorts and a spaghetti strap tank, more than I'd wear to swim in, but suddenly it didn't feel like enough. "It's your boat, of course, you're here," I babbled. "I just didn't expect you. Andrea said you were gone this afternoon. You didn't eat with us. So ..." My words trailed off. I looked around. Faint lights from some of the high up cliff houses twinkled in the dark and across the water behind him. Whatever peace I'd found up here was gone. I took one long last deep breath of abundant air. "So, I guess, um, I guess I'll just go ..."

"You know the origin of Marin means *sailor* or *seafarer?*" His accented voice was rough and soft, stopping me. His long legs, in shorts, were crossed at the ankle. His feet were bare. And the sight of them more than anything gave me an odd sense of intimacy.

I swallowed.

"And Joséphine ... well, she was a wily and cunning empress."

"Napoleon's wife," I confirmed, licking my lips nervously. The last few days he'd been cordial, if not that chatty, eating meals with Dauphine and me, but things felt different tonight. I also hadn't really been alone with him. Dauphine was always around. Now that it was just us in the dead of night, it was painfully obvious what a good buffer she'd provided.

He raised his glass and took a long sip. There was no clinking of ice. He was drinking neat. "And so ... you have a French name. A French name that would also imply you like the ocean. Yet, you are not French. And you hate boats."

"Actually, I am descended from the French Huguenots," I whispered, my voice seeming to have failed me. "My father spoke of our history all the time when I was a girl."

He offered nothing but a cocked head.

"Trouble sleeping?" I asked, trying to change the subject, then inwardly cursed myself. I shouldn't be trying to talk to him. *Leave, Josie. Go back to bed.* He was clearly in a mood.

"Trouble sleeping?" He echoed my question and gave a soft laugh. "*Toujours,*" he said. *Always.*

When I looked closer, he was far from predatory. He looked ...

beaten. Weighed down by sadness. He hid it well during the day. But here, now, I had an inkling I was seeing him in a way most people normally didn't. His alone time. His solitude that he chose to spend looking at the stars and numbing himself with whiskey.

I stepped back toward the railing again and rested my elbows, leaning my weight back. My heart beat erratically in a way I hoped my relaxed posture hid. "Does the whiskey help?"

Waves lapped softly against the hull, the sound of the water soothing in the quiet night. I had no idea what time it was. Well after midnight, I was sure.

He didn't seem inclined to answer.

I inhaled deeply. "After my father died, my mother ... she would do this. I'd find her some nights when I was sneaking in the back door at three a.m., sitting alone at the window in the dark sunroom. Staring blindly, sipping neat."

"Whiskey?"

I nodded.

"A woman who knows how to get the job done." There was a long silence, then, "So you know what it's like."

"I do." My throat suddenly felt crushed tight with remembered grief. When I could breathe again, I added, "It was a sudden heart attack. One day here. The next gone forever."

"I'm sorry for your loss."

I looked him in the eyes. "I'm sorry for yours."

"How long will Dauphine remember?" he asked.

"Forever."

He winced at my honest answer, so I hurried on. "But the pain gets less. She's a bit younger than I was, so maybe it's better. Less memories. I don't know." I turned my head so I couldn't see the pain in *his* face and blinked. The black water glittered.

Xavier took a long and deep sip of his drink. The dull thud of his swallow seemed loud in our silence. "But you have many memories. I can't tell if that's good or bad."

"It's good, I suppose. Now that time has passed. We would go for walks every Sunday afternoon. The French Huguenot Church was Gothic revival, but then we would walk around and he'd point out the Greek, the West Indian influences, and the colonial British."

I closed my eyes and enjoyed the air moving along my skin and the lap of water. It helped calm the deep buzz low in my belly where the muscles refused to relax. Where they seemed to feel the pull of Xavier the most. Something I couldn't control. And was trying to ignore with my babbling. "I learned to pay attention to the details of a building that speak to the observer without being loud. Like a whisper in their minds. It's what drew me to architecture. It felt like I'd be closer to my father." I trailed off. I'd probably put him to sleep with my boring building talk.

"What were you doing sneaking in at three in the morning?" he asked, breaking the silence.

I frowned. "What?"

"You said you saw your mother when you snuck in at three in the morning."

"Did you never do the same?" I volleyed back. "I liked dancing. Were you a very good boy growing up?" I teased.

His eyes narrowed and became hyperfocused on me.

My throat closed in response.

"I was bad." He took a deep inhale through his nose. "Very, *very* bad." His accompanying chuckle lessened the coiling tension. "My parents fought." He paused then and took a drink of his scotch, almost biting it through his teeth. "My father strayed. My mother was bitter. I stayed out of the way as much as I could. That resulted in lots of unsupervised time and poor decisions. The kind only an angry, horny teenage boy with money to burn can make." He took another sip.

The moment felt like a gift. I doubted he really wanted to share this history with me, and perhaps tomorrow he'd regret it. But for now, I accepted the offering with gratitude.

"I met Arriette then," he said, and I held my breath. "We were the wild ones. After university we got back together. Then, I grew up. It took me a long time to realize she never would. Her demons were too deep. I thought marriage would help tame her. It did not. I thought having a child would help her. Help *us*. But it seemed ... it seemed to make it worse. Or perhaps it was *me* who made her worse. I don't know. The more I tried to save her, the deeper she went—"

His words stopped abruptly. And I felt inexplicably guilty as he seemed to realize how much he was sharing. I closed my eyes and opened my mouth to say something. I didn't know what. Reassurance?

"You must go." Monsieur Pascale's sudden rough bark made me jump, and my eyes snapped open.

His eyes were dark and his glass empty. Deliberately he set it down on the deck to his side.

I gave a small frown. "Why? I'm not—"

"Parce que je veux te baiser. Parce que je veux que tu me fasses oublier."

"What does that mean?"

His face hardened. "It means you need to get the fuck downstairs."

My mouth dropped open, heat flooding my chest and face. I was pretty sure that wasn't what he'd said. But if that was the more palatable version, I felt even more like shit.

"Go," he growled.

"Fine." Pushing off the railing toward the stairs, my heart pounded. "Asshole." I couldn't help hissing the word under my breath as I started down the steps.

He gave a bitter laugh, letting me know he'd heard me. "It's best to remember that."

I hadn't meant him to really hear me. But what had just happened? One minute he was opening up, the next he was snarling. Why had I agreed to this job, again?

Calming my breathing, I counted to ten as I went downstairs. He didn't have to be so damned rude.

Although, I'd blundered in on a really raw and private moment he was having. I supposed he was snapping at me like a wounded dog would. Not meaning to inflict pain, but not being able to see past his own. Perhaps he'd been about to lose it and hadn't wanted me to see. Or was suddenly embarrassed at realizing how much he was sharing—vulnerability making him attack.

I made it the last few steps toward my cabin as I became sure he'd simply been protecting himself.

I was still offended.

But from his point of view ... I sighed, knowing I'd apologize tomorrow. I'd make sure he knew his secrets were safe with me.

Or was it better to pretend it hadn't happened?

Ugh.

My brain was too tired now to think about it. But I knew I wanted to know him more. Even when he was cold and cutting. And that alone was a dangerous thought.

Dauphine was still sprawled sideways across her bed, and the sight of her fizzled my upset like a popped balloon, and I was again reminded that everyone on this boat was hurting in some way. And my job was to take care of her, not get to know her father. Letting out a long deep breath, I gently shifted her and pulled the duvet over her. "*Bonne nuit*, sweet girl."

Then I went to my own cabin and climbed into bed and replayed everything over again. I heard the French words he snapped at me in my head, though I didn't know what they meant.

CHAPTER NINETEEN

The morning sky was cloudless, the breeze still cool, and sun sparkled across the deep blue of the water in a bay off an island called *Île Sainte-Marguerite*. The water was especially clear and magical here, and because it was a nature preserve, the fish were incredibly abundant. I'd downloaded an 'Introduction to Marine Biology' course for Dauphine and me to work through together and planned to bring it up later today.

The last few days had begun to form a sort of routine. While her father worked in the mornings, Dauphine and I would have breakfast, then do her reading for school followed by me teaching her some yoga poses. Then we'd follow her curiosity, which most often led to her asking me about architecture. I was super tickled she had such an interest, and in the course of explaining and sketching elements for her, I found my original passion coming back. It was also fun to realize our time together was also like French lessons for me and English lessons for her as we bumped into concepts we couldn't easily talk about because of the language barrier.

In the afternoons, usually after lunch, Xavier would come and find his daughter. Sometimes we all swam, but more often than not I'd take the opportunity to give them some time alone and retreat with my sketchbook or do a couple of online continuing education courses I'd always meant to do but never seemed to find the time for at home.

When Xavier left the boat for in person meetings, I'd encourage Dauphine to stay out of the sun and we'd watch movies, play board games, or cards before dinner with the crew. In the evenings, we'd compete to see who could wish on the first star. It was blissful in so many ways. But it was also clear that whatever fragile camaraderie Xavier and I had built up after our rocky start, it had shattered the night on the deck. And I wished I knew why. He wasn't rude, but he wasn't exactly friendly either. And he definitely avoided being alone with me.

I missed Charleston, my mom, Meredith, and Tabs, in *theory* —even elements of my job, of course—but I'd grown so attached to the crew, the rhythms of boat life, and obviously, Dauphine. My best friend in the world right now was a ten-year-old girl. And Andrea, of course. She was fun too, and she and I had grown closer over the last week, chatting after Dauphine went to bed.

Finally on French time, I'd actually woken up earlier than usual this morning. So before leaving my cabin, I spent some time emailing my resume to the few architectural firms I knew of in Charleston. And then, biting my tongue, I'd applied to some farther afield. I didn't want to leave Charleston, but I was slowly starting to realize I might not have a choice if I wanted a job in the field I'd spent eight years training for. It would be a step down in prestige, and many of the firms were responsible for some outright monstrosities. But beggars weren't exactly choosers. And as gorgeous as this little sojourn on the Mediterranean was, I was well aware I needed to get back to reality at some point. I quickly read through the requirements and submitted for a senior position at a firm called *Kendrick & Rutledge* in Columbia, saying a quiet prayer of forgiveness for going over to the dark side of office park and strip mall architecture, and then closed out the connection.

After another delicious breakfast, I laid my hands on my belly at the table in the galley, wondering how long until the carb fest would catch up.

Andrea noticed and chuckled. "I was going to offer you this last piece of baguette, but I'm guessing not."

I groaned. "Back home, yoga and spin kept me toned while at my desk job."

"At least you're swimming a lot," she said.

"True. But perhaps Dauphine and I should step up the yoga too." I'd found a YouTube yoga class on Dauphine's iPad that was a perfect mix of beginner and advanced.

Dauphine slathered a huge dollop of strawberry jam on her baguette. Apart from a small tantrum last night when she'd found out her father was going to be off the boat for another business dinner, she was actually such a delightful little girl. We'd spent the evening making up K-Pop dance routines, styling each other's hair, and generally doing everything to get her over her father not coming back for the night. I hadn't slept well. I'd snuck up to the top deck, being sure to check I was alone first, to get some air. The sense of claustrophobia when I woke in the middle of the night was not getting better. Lying back on the lounger Xavier had been on that one night, and watching the stars, I realized I also missed the energy that permeated the boat when Xavier was around. I found it, I found *him*, addictive. The little bit of him I knew, made me want to know much, much more.

"I'm giving a list to Evan later. Is there anything you need?" Andrea asked from across the breakfast table, bringing me out of my reverie.

"Actually," I glanced at Dauphine who wasn't paying attention, but I dropped my voice lower anyway, "I've been meaning to ask how you deal with ... periods?"

Of course Dauphine reacted to my lowered voice and zeroed

her gaze in on us. I had to hope her English hadn't improved that much yet.

"Just tell me what you need, and I'll make sure it's on the boat."

My expression must have remained unconvinced or uncomfortable looking because Andrea laughed.

"I live for asking Evan to pick up the most obscure and/or embarrassing things to see if I can shake that unflappable demeanor. Lay it on me. Special-order-sized tampons?"

"La la la," said Rod, loudly walking into the galley with his fingers stuck in his ears. Over the last few days, I'd pegged the deckhand as the class clown of the group. And he'd been ridiculously courteous to me since his comment about me going topless. He loved to make lame jokes, but even he had his limits apparently. And tampons were his limit.

I chuckled at his expression and turned back to Andrea.

"Having your period on board is a real pain," she said. "I started getting three-month shots last year. Works great for me. Expensive though."

"Okay, I'm out," grumbled Rod and left the room, coffee in hand.

"Isn't all birth control?" I asked

"Luckily in France, despite being a traditionally Catholic country, they'd rather provide contraception than abortions, and they understand gender equality and access to healthcare when it comes to things like that. Actually, in a lot of things."

"God, in America they don't want people having abortions *or* cheap access to birth control. Makes zero sense."

"Ahh, the patriarchy alive and well. You on the pill? Maybe you can go back-to-back on a pack to avoid having your period just this once."

I was on the pill, so I guessed I could consider doing that.

"What's a period?" asked Dauphine.

"*Tes règles*," Andrea explained, translating it to the French.

Dauphine shuddered, her eyes wide. "I do not want to get that. The girls at school say you have blood. Is it true?"

I slipped an arm around her small shoulders. "Every woman gets them. It will be a sign you are growing up."

"Is it with pain?"

"It can be a little, yes."

"Then I do not want to grow up. And I do not want them." She frowned as if remembering something. "Last year one of the girls, Cécile, I think she got them and everybody was laughing at her. She cried."

"It's okay, when it happens for you, you don't have to tell your friends, just tell your—"

Shit.

"Papa," Andrea jumped in. "Or me."

"Or me," I added. "You have my phone number, and you can call me whenever you need to." And I found that I meant every word. I'd only been here a week when Dauphine had cornered me and asked me very seriously if we were real friends, and if I would call her when I was back in America. I'd given her my American number and told her to use it anytime.

I shared a look with Andrea.

Dauphine sat in troubled silence and continued to eat.

"Anyway, put whatever you like on the list for Evan," Andrea said to me. "We'll see how he handles it." She stood and took her coffee cup to the dishwasher. "And put at least one outrageous thing on there. I swear, one of these days I'll find something he can't get me." She gave a smirk. "That man sure is resourceful."

"Anything going on there?" I asked with a sly glance at Dauphine to make sure she didn't get my meaning.

A cloud passed over Andrea's face. "No," she said emphatically, but somehow I didn't quite believe her. "I don't ... date. I can't. You *sure* you don't want this last piece of baguette?"

"Ha. No chance."

"Oh, before I forget, you and Dauphine are accompanying Mr.

P for lunch today. You are all going to *Le Cinquante-Cinq*. It's a famous beach club."

Dauphine clapped with joy. "Today?"

"We are?"

Andrea smiled at Dauphine's excitement.

That didn't leave us a whole lot of time. "Come on, Dauphine. It's time for our morning yoga class."

She hurriedly stuffed her last bite of baguette in her mouth.

"Oh," I said. "Is Evan picking us up to go to the beach club? What time should we be ready?"

Andrea shrugged. "I've given up trying to get Evan to pin down times. Let's say, be ready by noon. He said it's safer to be unpredictable. "

"Which drives me crazy," said Chef, entering the kitchen.

"You and me both," Andrea responded.

I gently guided Dauphine toward the door. "We'll be upstairs if you need us."

In the cool breeze and bright morning sun of the top deck, I cued up the yoga video. I inhaled deeply and exhaled per instructions, trying to expel any negativity inside me. I cracked an eye. Beside me, Dauphine was cross-legged, finger and thumb of each hand touching, and eyes closed. I loved how seriously she was taking our yoga.

Closing my eyes again, I tried to drown out the Jet Ski and a small nearby motor as well as all the feelings of guilt that I hadn't called my mother in days to see how she was. The uncomfortable feeling inside about my work, and how I hadn't heard anything back from sending out my resume yet, pressed against me. I didn't want to face the fact I'd quit when I could have just hung on a bit longer at *Donovan & Tate* while looking for another position. I'd been hasty. And now I was sitting on the other side of the world. It was gorgeous, but it was a fantasyland. In more ways than one.

But ... gratitude, I reminded myself. The female yoga instructor told me to let any thoughts blow away like clouds, and I tried. I really tried. But there was a stubborn ice-eyed one that was hard to dislodge. Then we started into the first set of poses.

We had to pass on some because there was no way to balance while the boat rocked even gently. I mean Warriors One and Two, sure. Tree pose? Forget about it. Eventually we ended back in Downward Dog for a final set of Vinyasas. I tipped my butt up, trying to get as much into the stretch as I could one last time. I opened my eyes and was staring vacantly through my ankles when a set of familiar white-soled boat shoes and strong male ankles stepped into view from the stairwell.

There was a strangled sound from the man in question, and then Dauphine's excited gasp next to me.

"*Papa!*" Dauphine almost tripped in her haste to extricate herself from her pose and get herself into her father's arms as fast as possible.

"Oof," he sounded.

I got to my feet awkwardly, light-headed from being upside down. I'd just displayed my butt in skin-tight leggings straight at my employer. "Hi," I managed, face throbbing.

He nodded, looking everywhere but at me. "*Bonjour.* I'm sorry to have been gone so long."

"It was fine. Dauphine and I are doing a yoga class."

He cleared his throat. "I see. Which I interrupted. Apologies."

Dauphine stripped off her t-shirt down to her bikini and stepped into the plunge pool. "It is so fun, Papa."

"We were almost done," I said. "Uh, I didn't know you'd be back. I thought we were meeting you at lunch."

"Josie, are you coming in the water?" Dauphine asked me, not waiting for her father to answer my question. I'd promised her we'd get in the plunge pool after our class to cool off.

There was no way I was stripping down to my bikini in front of my boss. But I also didn't want to break my promise.

"Papa, you should do yoga with us in the mornings. And you must come in the pool, yes?"

Oh God, no. Get in that tiny plunge pool with my hot boss? I didn't think so.

"Non, *mon chou*. I have to go and discuss plans with Paco. But I will be up again in about twenty minutes. Ok?"

She stuck out her bottom lip but nodded.

A twenty-minute warning to not be in front of him with my butt in his face when he came back up. Embarrassment crawled through me.

After a cool off in the pool, Dauphine flew downstairs to get changed, and I followed at a more leisurely pace. I was passing the open master cabin when I heard Evan and Mr. P talking inside. They were talking in low voices. And I was sure I'd heard my name. I couldn't help slowing my pace. In fact, after a moment, I realized I'd stopped completely and was straining my ears. I thought I heard Monsieur Pascale say something was impossible and a word that sounded like "coo," to which Evan chuckled and said something in a teasing tone. I frowned as I tried to make sense of it with my limited French. I shook it off and reprimanded myself for being nosy. Just in time, I realized, because when I rounded the corner to head down the next set of stairs to deck two, I heard the master cabin door close as if they'd just realized it was left open. Whoever had closed it would have seen me listening.

CHAPTER TWENTY

XAVIER

After interrupting yoga on the top deck, I stumbled back down the stairs, my normally reliant, powerful legs untrustworthy.

"Whoa. You okay?" Evan asked, just leaving the bridge.

"Fine." I ran a hand over my stubbled chin. "I need to talk to Paco about the lunch plans."

"Already taken care of."

"Good," I said distractedly and headed down the next half stairwell toward my office bedroom, this time clutching the handrail. "Hey. Please ask Andrea to move me back in here, I don't think I need to be downstairs anymore." God knew I couldn't sleep one more night across the hall from the hot nanny. If I heard her get up and go to the top deck again, I couldn't promise I wouldn't follow.

"All right," Evan responded as he followed me into the stateroom. "As soon as you tell me what just happened on the top deck. You look a little shaken."

I walked to the windows and stuck my hands in my pockets. "They were doing yoga."

"And?" Evan asked.

I turned and shot him a look, the vision of Josephine Marin's round, delectable ass pressed backward, covered in skintight pink, seared into my brain. "And her ass—" I broke off.

Evan's eyebrows shot up to his hairline. "Do go on."

I scowled.

Evan made an inpatient *continue* gesture with his hand. "And her ass ..."

"It was just there," I snapped. "In my face."

"In your face?"

"My God, you know what I mean." My hand scrubbed over my eyes and shot through my hair. "Are you *sure* we can't get another nanny."

"I'll look into it."

"You will?"

"No. Get a hold of yourself, man." My friend laughed. *Laughed.* He thought this was all some huge joke. It wasn't a joke. She had set my equilibrium completely off balance. I gave him a look. *The* look. The one I gave people in the boardroom who couldn't answer a direct question. The look that told him how very thin the ice was.

Evan raised his hands. "Forgive me. But will you listen to yourself?"

"I am. Now if *you* would too, that would be grand. What do I pay you for, anyway?"

"To keep you safe and entertained."

"Does your protection not extend to my sanity?"

Evan pressed his lips tightly together, expelling a breath through his nose, almost choking in his attempt to curb a fresh bout of chuckling.

I snorted in disgust and stalked over to my desk. "And now I have to put her in front of my father." My father, the philanderer, had boned almost every nanny I had growing up. When I was thirteen and no longer in need of one, my mother finally got sick of pretending she didn't know. So of course, her husband started to venture farther afield. Who knew if he was still into the help these days, and I hated that it was automatically where my mind went. I think he liked the power dynamic, which made it sick as fuck.

"Maybe leave her and Dauphine behind?" Evan suggested.

"I promised Dauphine. Plus, it's her grandfather. I'd rather get a visit between them out of the way. It will also give me a reason to get out of there early. No, they have to come with me today."

I didn't want to put into words what happened to me when I was in Josephine Marin's vicinity. I was acutely aware it was most likely a simple case of abject lust. An extreme one, sure. And I also knew it had a lot to do with not having been with anyone since Arriette died, and even for a while before that. And Ms. Marin was amusing, warm, and smart. And beautiful, of course. But in an utterly natural and down to earth way. A vision of the three of us strolling through the streets of a small village looked too much like a family for my stomach. She was sweet and gentle with Dauphine. Never dismissive. It was her job, of course. But she had a way with—

"Are you even listening to me?" Evan said, exasperated.

"Excuse me?"

"I said, I got the background info on her. She quit her job. After looking at the reputation of one of the partners, I think there was likely some sexual harassment." So she quit instead of sleeping her way up. Good for her. And fuck the guy who put her in that position. And that was why, as her current boss, I needed to keep my head around her.

I gave my head a quick shake to clear it. "Anything about her stepfather?"

"Her mother remarried. Apparently, her stepfather perpetuated a massive fraud and got himself jail time. The guy is from

Charleston. By the sounds of it, a lot of who's who in the city invested with him. Did you ever hear the name when you were there?"

God, poor girl. She'd shared as much with me. I was glad to have it corroborated by Evan. But I knew what it was like to have a father who embarrassed you.

"No, I don't think so." I'd only been there a few days, checking on the more eco-friendly yacht I'd commissioned. I'd be sad to say goodbye to this boat, but honestly I wouldn't be sad to leave the memories of Arriette behind. "But that does remind me, "I added. "I need to respond to the email from the yacht company. I'll reach out to Marie Louise, get her to follow up. Did you get any more background on the bridge project my father wants me to invest in?" I asked.

"Nothing more than what I told you."

I rolled my eyes. "Fine. Should be a quick lunch then. Because obviously the answer is no." Hopefully my assistant at my office in *Sophia Antipolis* had gotten us an out of the way table. I was beginning to hate the *who's who* feel the beach club *Le Cinquante-Cinq* had. People wanting to see and be seen. It was worse at this time of year, right after the Cannes Film Festival, too. It helped that my family had been going there every summer for over fifty years, back when it was the only beach club of its type on *Pampelone Beach*, otherwise getting a reservation would have been a joke. Of course, it had new owners now. They'd tried hard to keep the laid-back atmosphere. I wondered what Josie would think of it. I didn't think money and celebrity turned her on, but of course, I'd gotten that wrong about women before.

"I'll meet you on the back deck," Evan said.

Christ, I couldn't think of anything without my mind wandering to Josephine Marin. I nodded at him absently.

"Papa?" Dauphine darted into the room, brushing past Evan who ruffled her hair.

"Yes, *mon ange?*"

She flung herself on my bed and began to chatter. Of course, it all centered around Josie. Josie was so nice. Josie was so talented. Josie was teaching her English, and Dauphine was teaching Josie French. Josie had been teaching Dauphine to draw. Dauphine might want to be an architect like Josie one day. Josie was running out of blank pages on her sketchbook, and Dauphine wanted paper as fine as Josie's because the paper we used for the printer was not good for drawing. And she wanted watercolor pencils just like Josie's. It went on like a stream of consciousness.

I smiled to myself at her happiness and exuberance as I changed into a pair of turquoise swim shorts and a white linen button down in the closet. Pausing at the door to the dressing room though, I suddenly frowned. I fingered the beaded evening dress, one of so many items of Arriette's things I had never dealt with.

"Papa? What are you doing?" Dauphine appeared at the edge of the door. My hand dropped from her mother's dress. Her eyes tracked to my hand.

"*Mon ange,*" I began and cleared my throat. "I was thinking perhaps I would move *maman's* things. Would that be okay with you?"

She chewed her bottom lip, her blue eyes big. "I don't know," she whispered. "Where will we put them?"

"I don't know yet. But there are many people who don't have such fine things and maybe we could give—"

She shook her head vigorously, her eyes filling. "*Non,*" she whispered.

"Come here," I said gently, and she fell face first into my belly. "Shh. It's okay. Tell me, what are you thinking?"

Sniffing, she pulled away, leaving a trail of tears on yet another of my shirts. "What if *maman* sees us take her things away and thinks we don't love her anymore?"

"Oh, *mon chou.*" My chest grew tight. "No. *Maman* cannot see from where she is."

"In heaven?"

"Of course, in heaven. In heaven she only sees and feels with her heart, and her heart knows you will always, always love her." I had no idea where that pearl of wisdom had dropped from, but it seemed to have a calming effect on Dauphine.

"Truly?"

I swallowed. "Truly."

We hugged again.

"Is there anything you would like me to keep for you?"

Dauphine looked down the row and the shelves, then she walked to a drawer and opened it. "Maybe some of her jewelry?"

"Of course. I will keep it all for you. I have some at home in Valbonne in the safe too. It will all be yours when you are older."

She slid the drawer shut. "Okay." She gave one last sniff, wiped her cheek, and then checked her hair. "Oh, do you like my braid? Josie did it. Do you know in America they call it a French braid?" She giggled, our previous conversation seemingly forgotten. "Isn't that so silly?"

With a bemused shake of my head, I fingered my daughter's silky hair that had been expertly tamed. "It's lovely. You look very pretty. Now go and find Evan, he'll be wanting to leave to see *Grand-père* soon."

She gave a little wave and pirouetted out of the room, her worries about Arriette's things in the past.

Sucking in a deep breath, I gave one last look at the closet and contemplated changing my shirt again, but then sighed and left the bathroom. I stepped out of the stateroom right as Josie came up the stairs.

"Oh, sorry," she said, stepping aside. She'd changed into a pale green swim cover-up over the jade bikini she'd bought at the market, and all I could see was her clothing matched the color of her eyes. Did she seriously get more beautiful every time I saw her? She dropped her gaze immediately, and I realized I must have been glaring at her.

I waved a hand. "After you."

She turned, presenting me with a smooth tanned back and that wavy hair I'd like to wrap my hands in. Maybe while I bent her over and—

She whipped around to me. "Are you ... did I do something wrong?"

"No," I answered quickly, guilt at my dirty thoughts clogging my throat. "Let's just go."

Her eyes, so vibrantly green with the outfit she wore, narrowed. "Are you sure?"

"*Oui.*"

"I don't know why, but I don't believe you."

I raised my eyebrows.

"But whatever," she said with a determined set to her lips. "I'm good at this. I'm good at being with Dauphine. You seem disapproving of me the last week. I haven't done anything wrong, and it bothers me when I think you might think I have."

"*D'accord,*" I said.

"Okay?"

"Yes," I confirmed. "You have done nothing wrong." Except climb under my skin. "Also ... can you try to be more ... invisible ... today at lunch?" My father would be there after all.

Her eyes popped wide. "Excuse me?" Her tone took a sudden turn toward offended.

Fuck. I was an idiot. I waved my hand up and down. "You are ..." I swallowed. I couldn't say beautiful, she'd see straight through me and realize my blundering crush. Or worse, think I was a sleazeball hitting on her. "I don't want ... um." Oh, good God. Was I this rusty?

"Am I not dressed properly?" She suddenly fussed, her cheeks flooding with pink, and her eyes unsure. "I was told I could wear a swimsuit."

Fuck. Remorse filled me.

"No. You look fine." Fine? She was fucking gorgeous. Unthinkingly, my hand went to her bare arm and squeezed gently for a millisecond before dropping it like it burned. "Let's go," I snapped. "We're late." I brushed clumsily past her rather than stay cooped up in that small space, mainlining her coconut scent and accidentally and perpetually insulting her.

But God, I was a beast around her.

Uncouth.

Erratic.

Horny.

Let's just hope she was invisible to my father. And moreover, that he couldn't tell how tightly wound *I* was around her.

After a moment I heard her follow me, and we made our way to the back deck. Dauphine began chattering immediately and held her braid up while Josie rubbed sunscreen on my daughter's neck, back, and shoulders. Then Dauphine returned the favor, and I knew Josie might end up burned later, but there was no way I could offer to put my hands on her skin. I encouraged Dauphine to do a more thorough job, then when it was done we all climbed in the tender for the short ride to the beach.

I'd hardly seen my father over the last couple of years. As a child, he'd been almost mythical in status to me. He'd put in long work hours, and I had assumed our family money was due to his work. It was years before I discovered our wealth had been my mother's, and my father was simply always a "try-hard" with a chip on his shoulder. And his time away from home had rarely been for work.

I'd spent my youth trying and failing to impress him. I'd thought he'd spend more time with me if he could see how smart I was. Consequently, I became the top student. Though that hadn't been much effort as I was naturally analytically minded. I adored science and mathematics. My father called me a nerd.

Then I thought if I played more sports, I'd garner his praise, so I joined the football team. That had come harder. When other boys had perfected fancy footwork in the streets and parks after school, I had been headfirst in a book or being chauffeured to music and chess. But I persevered, and finally made it, becoming center forward and then captain of our local club team. My father never came to a game.

Then when I was an older teen I thought I could garner his praise if I became a ladies' man. A wild child. After all, he seemed to respect men with a roving eye, who weren't chained to their wives and families. And so, I drank. I fucked. I broke hearts. But all it got me was a reputation as a fuck up, tears from my mother, and contempt from my father who came to see me as a wastrel. As did the French press who so closely monitored our family.

It was only after I realized the family money was just something my father had married into and spent frivolously, and that he'd only respect me if he needed something from me, that I finally got my head out of my ass. The scales had fallen from my eyes, and my father had become ... just a man.

A weak man.

A man who made questionable deals, trusted the wrong people, and slept with the help.

Someone I had no intention of emulating.

When we arrived at the beach club, my father was in true form. His eyes missed nothing, not the tension in my shoulders and not the expanse of leg on display by my daughter's minder. Women at the beach club wore less than her, but Josie still tugged on the hem of her cover-up, and she still drew eyes to her like a magnet. My own included.

"*Papa*," I said, forcing a joviality I didn't feel into my tone as he clapped me on the back more heavily than he needed to.

I could tell he was feeling on top of the world. Bold and optimistic that he could get me to invest in his latest venture. "Great to see you," he greeted me. "Just great. And my sweet little Dauphine!" he crowed as she leapt into his arms. "Who is your new friend?"

"*Papie*," Dauphine babbled. "This is Josie. She only speaks

English. She's American. And she draws amazing buildings. And she's teaching me how. And she's really nice. She swims with me any time I want. And I think Papa doesn't like her. But I like her. Please tell him she has to stay."

"Dauphine," I snapped, my voice coming out like a strangled bark. How had my daughter picked up on my discomfort? "Hush."

My father's eyes homed in on Josie as he took her offered hand. "*Enchanté,*" he greeted and brought her hand to his mouth, pressing his lips to the back of it. "I'm Etienne Pascale."

Josie darted a glance at me before smiling wanly at my father and extricating her hand.

"Ahh," another voice boomed. We turned to the large and swarthy Italian heading our way. I recognized the sleazebag friend of my father's. Alfredo Morosto. He'd been involved in so many shady deals, I was sure my company share price would drop ten percent on Monday simply because we were in the same restaurant. Now it seemed he was having lunch with us.

Great.

CHAPTER TWENTY-ONE

JOSIE

The white sand beach and cool, clear, aquamarine water made the bay perfect for a beach club. Evan took Mister P, Dauphine, and me from the boat to a jetty where we made our way onto the beach. My first few steps on solid land made me feel like dancing.

"You okay?" Evan asked.

Xavier whipped around to look in my direction.

I couldn't see his eyes through his sunglasses. "Forgot what firm ground feels like," I said, probably reminding him how I felt about boats in general. "I'm fine."

His mouth tightened and I raised my eyebrows in question, then lowered my sunglasses over my own eyes.

Dauphine took my hand, and I smiled down at her, and we all continued our walk. Attendants in white linen shorts and turquoise shirts ran between groups of loungers, setting up umbrellas and bringing ice buckets of champagne and rosé and bowls of cut fruit on ice. There was a little beach bar made of driftwood and a boardwalk we followed through some low, thick vegetation until it opened up into a large outdoor restaurant hidden behind the dunes, shaded under driftwood and canvas awnings. White painted chairs and tables with blue tablecloths were packed into any available inch with their legs in the sand. Waiters hurried to and fro, squeezing in and around the occupied tables.

The sound of clinking glass, laughter, and popping corks made it seem like one big party. So, this was how the one percent did the beach? I chuckled to myself, remembering the way Tabs, Mer, and I always had to take turns lugging the cooler and our plastic chairs from where we could find parking, sweat dripping into our eyes, all the way to the boardwalk beach access on Sullivan's Island or Folly Beach. Which reminded me, I needed to call them soon.

Dauphine and I followed her father as he made his way to the front of the restaurant and greeted a tall *maitre d'* who kissed Mr. Pascale on both cheeks and ruffled his hair. I gathered he'd known him for a long time, and it made me smile to see my boss treated like a little boy.

I felt eyes on us, in a sort of who's who way. It gave me a weird, uncomfortable feeling, reminiscent of the days following my stepfather's arrest. Glancing around in my sunglasses, I almost did a double take as I recognized a famous model who'd been big in the nineties and at a separate table the ex-governor of California who had also been a movie star at one point. My heart rate sped up. Meredith and Tabs would freak out. God, I missed them. Meredith, especially, would get off on star spotting.

Not that anyone cared who *I* was, but I suddenly felt extremely exposed being in such a high-profile place. My cheeks burned and I felt vaguely nauseous. Nothing like being given the once over and summarily discarded to remind one of how insignificant one's life could be perceived. Even though it brought a feeling of relief. The eyes definitely followed Xavier Pascale though.

The *maitre d'* made a quick fuss over Dauphine, and then pointed us to a table in a corner of the restaurant under the twisty branch of a tamarisk tree.

Before we could sit, we were joined by an older man I knew instantly must be Xavier's father.

He had the same thick cowlick at his forehead, though his was dark gray, and his hair was cut almost identically, short but curling around his ears and collar. The man and his son were roughly the same height. Interesting that they didn't hug upon greeting each other.

When it was time for my introduction, I inhaled, overcome by nerves. Pushing my sunglasses up to my head, I stepped forward and stuck out my hand. "Dauphine's nanny. Josie. Nice to meet you."

The older Monsieur Pascale took my hand in greeting and then pressed damp lips to my skin. "Enchanté. I'm Etienne Pascale." I gave a fake smile, pulled my hand away, feeling slightly soiled.

Another man approached us, and Xavier's tension seemed to ratchet up seventeen notches. "My friend here is Alfredo Morosto," Etienne told me. Then he chuckled and said something in French under his breath that made our new arrival laugh too, but caused Xavier to wince.

"Come." Xavier pulled the chair out at the closest end of the table, gesturing for me to sit, and I sat down opposite Dauphine. I expected him to sit next to her, but he came around and took the seat on the other side of me, protecting me from having to sit next to either of the two older men. My shoulders relaxed slightly, relieved to have him between me and our lunch companions. Glancing briefly at the menu in French, I told Dauphine to order me whatever she was having to make it easier.

We both ended up with Shirley Temples, which earned me another eyebrow raise from Xavier.

The three men were talking earnestly, though they kept their

voices low. Alfredo Morosto was a beefy man with a massive gold
Rolex on his wrist. His shirt was unbuttoned to halfway down his
torso, and a heavy gold chain lay against his gray chest hairs and
years of over-tanned flesh. He glanced around the restaurant at
least every five minutes. I couldn't tell if he was looking for something or making sure no one was listening to them. I gave up
trying to follow the language because it suddenly seemed like
they'd switched to Italian, and while Dauphine and I played a
game of hangman on the paper table setting, I watched their body
language instead. It took a while, but suddenly I realized why
Alfredo Morosto kept looking around. I thought maybe he
wanted someone to see him, or more specifically to see who he
was having lunch with. That was confirmed when he finally saw
someone he knew and stood and clapped a young man in a pink
polo on the back as they shook hands. Brief introductions were
made to Xavier and his father. Dauphine and I kept playing,
ignoring the visitors. The first greeting seemed to open the flood
gates of people stopping by the table. There were a few curious
gazes my way, but when I didn't smile or catch anyone's eye and
directed all my attention to Dauphine, they lumped me in as the
help soon enough.

Next to me, Mr. Pascale outwardly portrayed a calm exterior,
but under the table, his one leg bounced incessantly in tiny movements. Stress seemed to pour off him in waves, though I had a
feeling I was the only one who noticed.

Under the table, his fingers were making quiet, destructive
work of a small paper placard that had stated the table was
reserved when we first arrived. He'd already destroyed his paper
coaster. Then he moved to picking at the hem of his shorts
against his thigh, surreptitiously checking his watch.

The urge to still his hand with mine beneath the table, or
press my foot against his in the sand, to offer him some kind of
comfort, was overwhelming.

I picked up my glass and took a long sip of ice-cold Shirley

Temple. As I did so, I stealthily slid my paper coaster toward his place setting, earning a small surprised puff of air and acceptance as he casually picked it up and got to work.

Xavier drank sparkling water and didn't touch a drop of the wine his father poured for him.

His father was watchful. Whenever I caught his gaze, I'd paste a quick placid smile and look away. Thank God for my sunglasses.

The whole lunch was awkward and seemed interminable. At least the spaghetti with clams Dauphine had ordered us was mind-numbingly delicious.

"*Alors*, where are you from, Jenny?" the elder Pascale suddenly asked me when Alfredo Morosto excused himself to go to the bathroom.

All eyes turned to me. I was down to the last few sips of my drink, and I'd reached the cherry. "Uh. I'm from America." I didn't bother to correct my name as I fished the cherry out of my glass. Actually, I was rather relieved he'd forgotten it.

"Yes, but where?" he pressed.

"Charleston. It's on the east coast, in South Carolina."

"Ahh, yes. I know of it." His gaze shifted to his son, his eyes narrowing slightly. "You spent some time there recently, didn't you?"

I glanced at my boss, surprised, as I bit down on the sweet and chewy cherry, rolling it around my tongue. He'd been in my city?

Xavier hadn't taken his sunglasses off, but I felt the shadow of his gaze on my mouth as I chewed. Then he shook his head and took a sip of water. His breath hitched and made him cough. His father must really make him uncomfortable. "I was there briefly, yes," he responded. "Visiting a yacht company."

"Oh? Which one?" I asked.

He mentioned a name, and I wondered if it was the one on King Street where the French lady, Sylvie, worked. She and I often ended up getting coffee at about the same time at Armand's Coffee Shop. We didn't know each other well, but over time, we'd started to greet each other and make small talk, which was how I knew where she worked. "I think I know it." It felt odd to know he'd been in my hometown, walking *my* streets. So close. No, not odd. Destined. My insides squeezed tight at the thought he'd been there before I'd known him. As if there was a break in the timeline of my life somehow. Like I *should* have known. How could I have had this strong a reaction to him from the very second of meeting him and not known when he'd been near me before? Which was all ridiculous really. I shook my head, grabbed my water glass, and took a long sip, turning my attention to Dauphine's drawing of a mermaid. "She's beautiful," I said.

Etienne Pascale shook his head with a light snort as if what I was saying was somehow amusing.

I frowned, lost and uncomfortable, this time by the odd tension that thrummed between father and son.

"Papa, can Josie take me down to the beach now?"

"Of course, *mon chou.*" Xavier sounded relieved.

Etienne Pascale leaned sideways and hauled out a fat brown wallet from his shorts. "*Tenez,*" he said to me and Dauphine and held out a large denomination of euro bill. "For ice-cream." He switched to English.

Dauphine snatched it.

"It's a bit much, don't you think?" Xavier grumbled.

His father chuckled. "Let an old man spoil his only grand-daughter."

"*Merci, Papie!* Come," she said to me, and I was all too eager to leave.

"Bathroom first," I said, and I grabbed our shared beach bag. "Nice to meet you," I said to her grandfather.

He stood as I did, and when I offered him my hand, he took it and brought his mouth down to meet my skin again. "Pleasure is all mine. And I apologize for messing up your name ... Josie."

At my side, Xavier was rigid. His leg that I could still see under the table froze as he reached calmly for his water. I glanced at his face and saw nothing but sunglasses and a placid smile before he stood too. Ever the gentleman. "Text me and let me know where you set up on the beach," he said to us. "I'll join you when I am done here."

I nodded.

"Will you swim with me, *papa*? Please?" Dauphine came around me and gave her dad a quick squeeze and kisses on both cheeks.

"*Bien sûr*," he murmured. Of course.

My charge then gave her grandfather a kiss on each cheek, and we made our way into the low slung white-washed clay building. It was dark inside with a large empty room and a cold fireplace. I took a huge inhale, thankful to be free of the tension at the table. There were single unisex restrooms off a small hallway and one was free. I made sure it didn't have a hinky lock and then told Dauphine I'd wait for her.

As soon as she'd closed the door behind her, another restroom door opened and Alfredo Morosto stepped out.

I smiled politely.

"Ahh, *bella*. I was hoping I would get a chance to talk with you."

"I'm just waiting for Dauphine."

"Of course, of course you are. You are even more beautiful up close."

I cleared my throat as I backed to the wall and folded my arms across my chest. "Thank you. They're waiting for you at the table."

"Let them wait." He stepped a tad closer and a hand reached out and I flinched, but he merely picked up a piece of my hair that had fallen from my bun and studied it. "Fascinating color," he said as he immediately dropped it. "Real?"

My heart thudded, and I smoothed my hair and tucked the piece behind my ear as he lifted his hand in an innocent gesture. *Hurry up, Dauphine,* I willed her.

"So how long have you known Xavier? He's a smart one, that. Passing you off as the nanny."

"I *am* the nanny."

"Of course, of course. But a man like him, so much judgment. I bet people are wondering. *I'm* wondering. Listen, uh, here's my number. I always like to chat. I love to know what work the young Pascale is up to in business these days. I'm a fan, you know."

I frowned. "Are you asking me to *spy* on him?"

"No, no, just ... for us to be friends. Good friends. Friends who might do ... favors for each other. Chat. There's a lot in it for you. Information you might have access to. Think about it. Rumor has it he's working on something big. Something I might be able to help with."

I scoffed and glanced at the door to the bathroom. "Why don't *you* call him then." My God. How long did a pee pee from a tiny bladder take?

"You know," he stepped a tad closer, and I had to resist a shudder, "I have an opening for a nanny at *my* home." His fingers hovered over my shoulder, skimming my swimsuit halter string. "Just in case you were looking for something more ... interesting. My kids are grown of course. But I'm generous. We don't have to call it nanny. We can call it whatever you like."

I looked him right in the eyes and held his stare in a defiant challenge and utter disgust. I mean, seriously, what the fuck was happening right now? All I knew was I shouldn't show fear. That suddenly became imperative. I thought I might wait for Dauphine in the main room by the fireplace and not this small private hallway.

I moved.

His hand darted out, stopping me by my shoulder. "You weren't going to say goodbye?"

I fixed him with a blank stare. "I didn't realize there was anything good about it."

Surprise flashed in his eyes, and his face transformed from

congenial to mean in milliseconds. "Quite a little icy bitch, aren't you?" he hissed. "Do you warm up for the little nerd out there?"

The bathroom door unlocked, and he dropped his hand, his face and demeanor melting into a harmless smile.

Dauphine stepped out, pressing immediately to my side. Kids picked up on way more than adults ever did. And this guy was a threat. And not just to me. Protectiveness surged through me. For Dauphine. For her father.

Putting my arm around Dauphine's shoulder, I pulled her with me as I pushed past him.

He stopped me again, this time slapping a card to my chest. The shock of his hand there caused me to stop, and I fumbled and grabbed it.

"My number. I'll be waiting for your call." He winked and strode away, beating us to the door

"Ugh," I said.

"I don't like him," said Dauphine.

"Me neither."

CHAPTER TWENTY-TWO

Dauphine spent almost an hour swimming and making sandcastles before she jumped up and ran to her father strolling barefoot along the small waves lapping at the water's edge. I'd texted the number he gave me, telling him to turn left and walk about fifty yards. He wore his dark sunglasses and held his shoes with one hand. He kissed his daughter's head then stepped closer and looked down at our creation.

I shaded my eyes to look up at him.

The edges of his mouth tipped up into a smile.

"You don't look like you're leaving soon," he said.

I followed his gaze to where I was buried to my waist. Dauphine had begun by making me an armchair dug into the sand. Then it had become a "mermaid throne." And now I had a whole mer-village with mounds and walls built around me and over my legs. I had a stinky piece of seaweed draped across my head. My crown.

"It appears so." I raised my eyebrows. I didn't add that I also had sand in unmentionable places.

Xavier's lips seemed to struggle before he let them go into a full-blown grin, revealing his gorgeous straight teeth and a devil's dimple. I couldn't help smiling back. I knew I looked utterly ridiculous.

"She is the mermaid goddess," Dauphine said with a happy sigh, drawing our attention. "She rules over this whole kingdom."

"Does she now?" he humored his daughter. He looked back at me. "You should have rented some beach chairs and an umbrella to get out of the sun," he said, then frowned. "I apologize. I didn't think of that. Also that my meeting ran long." He pulled his wallet out and flagged down a beach attendant who was jogging past with an ice bucket. "Where's your stuff?"

I pointed over my shoulder behind us and he went to pick my beach bag up.

"It's fine—"

"Dauphine." He spoke over my head. "Swim with me and let the mermaid goddess rest in the shade?"

She dropped the handful of wet sand and went shrieking into the water.

"Hey," I called. "A little help here?" I struggled to get loose in the sand, and when it was clear Dauphine hadn't heard or simply ignored my plea, her father was suddenly crouching next to me and digging the sand from around my legs. God. He was far too close. His hand brushed sand and then skin as he dug me out. He froze for a moment, then took a breath and continued.

I quickly took over and brushed enough off that I could finally wiggle free.

He stood and gave me his hand. And in moments Dauphine's kingdom was destroyed as I was pulled upright.

"Here." He dropped my hand and went around and brushed sand from my back before abruptly stopping and stepping back, thinking better of it.

"Thank you," I said and hurried past him into the water. "I need to wash off."

. . .

As soon as we had a place to sit, he gave me his wallet to put in the beach bag and draped his linen shirt over the chair next to me. I traded his wallet for a towel I handed him for the second chair. He laid it out and then perched on the edge and applied the sunscreen I handed him to his face and shoulders.

From behind my sunglasses I feasted on watching him. His hair was unruly where he'd obviously dragged a hand through several times over. Maybe when he'd run out of coasters. Somehow, I'd never taken him for a nervous person. It didn't jive with his business reputation. And I found seeing the vulnerable side of him did strange things in my belly. I sighed softly.

It didn't escape me that the three of us on the beach looked a lot like a family. And how much I liked it. Really, *really*, liked it.

"Thank you for lunch," I managed in a strangled voice to fill the silence. I looked around, desperate to look at anything rather than at him, and noticed the beach had emptied out somewhat. Dauphine tried to do a handstand in the water and tumbled sideways.

He cleared his throat, and I braced myself for him to ask me to put sunscreen on his back. My hands itched. I might die or accidentally moan out loud if I got to run my hands over that body. He didn't ask, just tossed the cream back in the bag.

"You're welcome. I hope it wasn't too tedious."

I lifted a shoulder. There were so many things I wanted to ask him. Like why he seemed so strained around his father. And about that Morosto character. "Tedious? No. Tense? Perhaps. Forgive me saying, but you ... weren't yourself."

He tilted his head slightly.

"I'm sorry. Perhaps I was wrong," I backpedaled. "I don't know you. I don't know how you normally act—"

"No, you're right." He let out a sigh and looked toward Dauphine who was now trying and failing to do cartwheels in the shallow waves. "I don't see much of my father. And he wants me to invest in something. And of course, he chose the most high profile place to meet."

"Yeah. It's a nice beach club. Seems like it's been there a while."

"Since the fifties. Before that the only exciting thing to happen were the allies landing right here.

"Wow, really? We only hear about the beaches at Normandy, but I guess they came from all sides."

He grinned. "There wasn't much here. A local family built some small bungalows. Then they added a community table in the sand and invited passersby to join them. Brigitte Bardot ... you know her?"

I nodded. The sexy French actress of many a black and white movie.

"She was filming here. The movie *Et Dieu ...Créa La Femme*. And God Created Woman." He chuckled huskily. "My grandfather used to tell me the story. The whole crew ate here every day. And after that, in 1955, the family got a business license and it's been *Le Club Cinquante-Cinq* and full of," he gestured with his hand, "*the rich and famous* ever since."

"Including you."

He shrugged with a smile tugging his lips.

"So, it's the oldest of all these places I see up and down this stretch?"

He chuckled. "Oh no. The Tahiti is the oldest by just a few years. And at the Tahiti, like many beaches in Europe ... clothing is optional."

Heat crawled up my neck.

He smirked, and if I wasn't mistaken his angled face was currently looking at my body. Really looking.

I felt the gaze, even though I couldn't see his eyes. Or did I? Was this the worst kind of wishful thinking? I cleared my throat. "Cool story. Well, lunch was great."

"The food was. It always is. Our company though ..." he shook his head and looked toward his daughter.

"You don't trust that Morosto guy?" I took a chance, though I was pretty sure I was right. I also wanted to make sure he also got the same bad vibes as I had. Especially if he had to do business with the guy.

Xavier turned back to me. Then took his sunglasses off, his blue eyes landing on me with startling intensity.

It was like suddenly being under an alien refractor beam. I didn't know whether he was going to beam me up or fry me on the spot. *Breathe, Josie.*

"I didn't know he was coming. It's bad for my business image to be seen talking with him. He's ... he doesn't have the best reputation. I saw you exit the building right after him, you looked disturbed," he said in a low voice. "Did he say something to you inside?"

I hesitated, wondering whether to tell him, or if it would cause more drama. Drama he obviously wanted to avoid. Who wouldn't? "Nothing I couldn't handle."

Xavier's jaw tightened. "What did he say?"

"It doesn't matter. It was stupid. I almost laughed at him."

"But you didn't."

"No. I could handle it. I got the impression he wanted me to tell him things about you, yet I know nothing. But for what it's worth I hope you don't have to do business with him." I lifted my chin. "In fact ... please don't."

Xavier regarded me steadily. "I don't intend to."

My chest warmed. "What about your father?"

"What about him?"

"I don't know," I said, my answer lame because I didn't want to verbalize my true theories.

He raised an eyebrow. "Yes, you do. *You* could tell when I was tense at lunch. *I* can tell that you have far too many opinions floating around in that head of yours."

"Too many opinions?" I responded archly. "What? For a *woman?*"

He let out a short and amused growl that had the effect of flipping my stomach upside down. God, imagine that sound in a different context.

"You know what I mean," he said.

"Fine. You want my opinion? I think the only way your father knows how to have a relationship with you, now that you are an adult, is through business. Apart from that, I don't think you have anything in common. Maybe not even then." I bit my teeth together hard. *Shut up, Josie.* "Like most parents, they can make you feel twelve years old again, no matter how much better and stronger of a person you've become."

Xavier's eyes narrowed, and he puffed a short breath of surprise through his nose. After a moment, he spoke. "All he wants is a way to make more money, no matter how unethical. He wants people to think he has my ear. Which is why he chose this very public place. He thinks I'm an easy mark."

"Are you?" I asked, my voice soft.

He stood and tossed his sunglasses on the chair. "Not even close," he said and turned to walk down to the water.

"Wait," I burst out.

He turned, his eyes narrowed.

I sat up.

"Yes?"

"Did you need sunscreen on your back?" I asked. Ohhhh, I did not just ask that. I did not. Fuck.

His head cocked to the side, his eyes giving away nothing.

"Never mind." I waved him away. *Go*, I willed him. *Just pretend that never happened.*

He narrowed his eyes, like he knew every thought in my brain, and turned away, and my entire body almost collapsed in relief as I watched him walk to the water. His muscled back tapered into those turquoise swim shorts that made his bronze skin glow even darker. I closed my eyes, even though they were hidden behind my sunglasses, in a massive dose of willpower as if that would help inoculate me against being attracted to him or something.

For another half hour, father and daughter played in the waves while I watched from the shaded comfort of the beach chair. I couldn't believe how I'd just spoken to him about his father. But to be fair he'd asked for my thoughts. If he didn't like them, that was on him. Still, my insides were all sorts of messed up. Every time we actually had a conversation, the line between boss and employee blurred, and he was always cutting it off before it went further. It was as if he forgot sometimes. Which made me think despite Evan being his friend and being surrounded by people, Xavier Pascale was ... lonely. Perhaps it was by his own design. I wasn't a psychologist, but I had a feeling that deep down where he refused to acknowledge, he was yearning for a connection. I wondered what his late wife had done to him to cause him to bury his heart so deep.

Dauphine suddenly came running up toward me. "Come. I need you to play *Jeu de Loup*. It's not fun with just me and Papa."

"I don't know the game."

"One person is the, um ... *le loup* ..." She twisted her lips sideways as her brow furrowed.

"The wolf?" I offered, the word popping up from the depths of my brain.

"Yes! One person is the wolf and the others must try to get away. And when the wolf bites them, they must become the wolf." She clapped and shivered as she explained.

"Come here," I said and dried off her face and shoulders and reapplied some sunscreen.

"Good. You will play?"

I glanced out to the water. Her father was swimming freestyle in large powerful strokes parallel to the beach as he waited for her to come back.

"Please. Papa said yes. And he said I can be the wolf first."

But what happened when her dad became the wolf? I shivered. "It sounds like the game of tag, but with biting." An image of Xavier catching me and biting me flew into my brain, and I kicked it out so fast I had to shake my head. I didn't need an X-rated film reel in my head while there were children present, thank you very much. Things were already bad enough.

"You don't bite, silly." She looked sympathetically at the alarm that must have crossed my face. "You just take, like so." She grabbed my wrist. "Say yes. Please. It's not scary, I promise."

That was debatable. I chuckled. "I don't know how anyone says no to you. I honestly don't."

"Me neither." She shrugged like it was the most confounding thing.

My chuckle turned into a full laugh. "All right. Here, put some more sunscreen on me."

After a rudimentary swipe, Dauphine took my hand and dragged me to the water.

"Now, it's perfect," Dauphine said, her eyes bright. "He is swimming and he does not know I am coming to catch him. I will make him the wolf!" She slowly made her way forward, hoping to intersect him. I saw the moment his head turned sideways for a breath, and his eyes found me and then immediately darted to Dauphine. She must have seen him spot her because she let out an excited squeal and went rushing forward. There was a flurry of splashes and then a triumphant Dauphine squealed again and yelled something that probably meant, I got you. And then she was swimming madly toward me.

"Oh, no, you don't," I said as she tried to use me as a human shield, the form of her father fast approaching under the water like a shark. But she grabbed me like an octopus and then thrust me forward with her feet.

"Ow!" I half yelled and laughed, adrenaline spiking as I tried to swerve out of the way of the oncoming predator, but she practically pushed me on top of him. I screeched as a hand shot forward and grabbed my waist, our bodies sliding together.

Holy fuck.

The entire universe exploded then contracted in an instant to that single sensation.

He let go immediately, but I'd already gone down sideways. I came up spluttering at the same time he surfaced and stood in the waist-deep water. He gave a head flick to shake the water from his hair, his eyes dark and guarded.

My eyes strayed downward as I hauled in short choppy breaths. Water ran in rivulets down his body, his chest speckled with dark chest hair. I swallowed against the remnants of the flash fire that had left me aching. I'd never experienced chemistry like that. Ever. I wondered how my body hadn't instantly vaporized into steam. With sheer force of will, I made my brain and my mouth work. "Dauphine, you are a traitor!" I called, my voice rough and transparent, and tore my eyes off him. I looked around for her but she was already paddling away as fast as she could. I glanced back at her father, and he too was backing away from me fast. He better make sure I didn't catch him, I thought hysterically.

I couldn't be held liable for my actions.

I might actually bite him.

CHAPTER TWENTY-THREE

By the time we got back into the small tender at the beach club jetty, it was late afternoon. I hadn't all out burned, but my skin felt tight and uncomfortable and I was headachy, thirsty, and exhausted. Dauphine had wiped sunscreen over my back and shoulders, but I could tell I probably had streaks of angry skin.

The three of us were quiet as we rode with Evan back to the looming yacht anchored a short distance away. I imagined I could feel Xavier Pascale's eyes on me, and his broodiness made my stomach feel tense.

"You all have fun?" Evan asked. He couldn't be that clueless to the tension, could he? The smirk playing around his mouth said otherwise.

"Yes." Dauphine nodded, followed by a large yawn. I followed suit.

Xavier smiled fondly at his daughter and squeezed her shoulders.

The water became a little choppy, and my knee swayed sideways and bumped up against my boss' leg. I tried to shift, but it was no use if I needed to feel anchored in my spot. I tried to ignore the sensation as it happened again. I stared at the horizon and the approaching yacht. Our tender slowed. But all my attention was drilled down to the one spot where my skin brushed against his. I must have sunstroke. There was no other explanation for why I couldn't shut my stupid brain off from overthinking and my body from over feeling everything.

And then we were at the yacht, and Xavier moved forward to help Evan, and then helped his daughter out.

Below deck, a quick look over my shoulder in my bathroom mirror confirmed the streaks of sunburn. I showered, moisturized, sprayed some aloe awkwardly over my shoulders, hoping I got it in the right place. Then I put on a loose-fitting t-shirt, drank a whole bottle of water, and lay down for a few minutes.

When I awoke, it was dark. Moonlight streaked in, creating a faint colorless glow. My cabin door was closed. I sat bolt upright, utterly disoriented. I fumbled for my phone and saw the time was just after midnight. I'd missed dinner.

I padded to the bathroom, holding on as the boat rocked gently. Then I went to my open door, debating if I was going to go take a breather up on the top deck. I hadn't woken with a racing heart I suddenly realized. And I didn't feel hungry, so I wondered what else had woken me. Just then I heard a whimper. Then Dauphine talking. I poked my head out of the cabin. I waited in the silence to hear her again. There was another louder cry and then something unintelligible. She was having a nightmare.

Across the hall Xavier Pascale's room sat dark and silent, like he wasn't there. Then I remembered he'd moved back upstairs.

Dauphine's scream pierced the silence, making me jump.

I hurried into her room. "Shhh," I crooned, seeing her whip her head from side to side. I climbed on to the bed, and she sat up with another cry. My arms went around her and she tried to struggle.

"Dauphine, shhh. It's me. It's Josie. You're okay. You're safe. Shhh."

"Josie?"

"Yes, my love."

She collapsed back on the bed.

"What were you dreaming about?"

"*Maman*," she whispered. Her shoulders shook, and she curled onto her side.

I brushed her hair from her temple. It was damp.

"*Mon chou.*" Xavier was a dark figure in the doorway.

"*Papa.*"

He came around the other side and climbed onto the bed. He was shirtless with just a pair of athletic shorts.

I should leave them together, but I was struck motionless at the sight of him. Jerking out of the stupor, I shifted to move.

"*Non.*" Dauphine reached out and grabbed my hand. "*Reste ave moi,*" she murmured.

"Your father's here now—"

"*S'il te plaît.* Please." She took a wobbling breath. "Please, you both stay?"

Over her head, Xavier Pascale watched me, his eyes almost black in the darkness. I couldn't tell if he was appalled by his daughter's plea. But if she needed me, just for a bit, I didn't want to make a scene simply because being near her father sent my body chemistry into chaos.

I nodded and shifted down so I could lie down and face Dauphine. I smelled her coconut shampoo and beyond that the faded smell of Xavier's woodsy cologne, musky male, and warm, sleepy skin. I mashed my lips between my teeth.

Dauphine grabbed her father's arm and wrapped it around her middle and then turned toward me, curling into a ball and nestling her chin under mine.

Stiff and tense with the stark, familial intimacy of the moment, I screwed my eyes shut so I didn't have to face her father less than a foot away from me on the pillows. Her movement had pulled him closer. His hand and wrist were millimeters from my belly. I struggled to think what I could do with my arms. Naturally, one would drape one over her small body, but *his* arm was there. I settled for resting mine awkwardly along my side.

Xavier's fingers must be stroking her arm or something because I could sense the small and gentle rhythmic movements.

Dauphine's shuddering breaths calmed and deepened, and her body relaxed.

I opened my eyes slowly, looking at the top of her head and wondering how long it would take for her to get into a deep sleep so I could slip out.

I couldn't help my gaze moving up to where I knew Xavier lay.

Dark eyes studied me. I saw gratitude warring with conflict.

Keeping my breathing as steady as I could, I held his gaze. Long moments passed. The longest I'd allowed myself to really look at him, I realized. Certainly the longest we'd locked gazes. I surrendered to the experience, as if he was a decadent chocolate mousse after I'd been on a years-long diet. It felt rich, intoxicating, and really, really bad for me. The tension grew, but underneath was an intimacy that felt deeper somehow, perhaps due to the sleeping child resting between us, but also underscoring the fact that Dauphine was the most important element here. And somehow it also came with the message that anything or anyone that might threaten her, Xavier Pascale wouldn't hesitate to cut out, cleanly and without hesitation.

His eyes began a slow roam over my face.

He didn't have to say anything for me to understand just a fraction of how weird this situation must be.

It was too intimate.

It was too much like a family.

It was so intensely personal.

Strange things were happening inside my chest, and making me want to reach out and brush his dark hair from his temples.

Things that made me want to place a kiss in his daughter's hair as if she was mine.

Ours.

For an inkling I understood the pure connectedness, fierce protectiveness, and familial love a mother must feel when she shelters her child with her mate.

His gaze returned to mine. And then suddenly the heat of his fingers pressed against the fabric of my shirt.

My breath stuttered to a halt, my lungs seizing, as a current swept over my skin. Was this really happening?

Fingers trailed down and then they were on my skin, on my belly where my tank must have ridden up.

My mouth parted on a puff of air.

And then there was nothing. His fingers were gone.

He closed his eyes, leaving me alone in the dark, wondering if it had been an accident. Wondering if I'd imagined it.

I let out a long breath, not realizing until I released it how tightly wound my entire body had been in the last few minutes.

Dauphine's inhalations were deep and relaxed, indicating the state of her slumber.

Gently, I rolled away and climbed out of bed. Without looking back, I crept to my room, and leaving the door open, climbed into my own bed.

I blinked in the morning light and found my mental bearings. Images of last night flooded my mind. Dauphine's nightmare. Her damp hair. Her small body. Her father's eyes in the dark.

His fingers on my skin.

My breath caught.

A knock at my door sounded again. "Josie?" Andrea's voice called.

The skin on my shoulders scratched like burning sandpaper as I shifted to my elbow. Sunburn. Ouch. "Come in," I croaked.

Andrea poked her head around the shiny mahogany. Someone must have closed my door. "Hey there, are you sick?"

"No. At least I don't think so. Oh my God, I'm so sorry," I added when I saw the time. "I think the sun wiped me out yesterday." I scrambled to get up.

She waved her hand. "It's fine. I was just checking on you. See you up top."

Sitting up, I clutched my head as it pounded. It was worse than a hangover.

I showered and went to find Dauphine and get some water, some painkillers, and something to eat. I found my charge vegging out in front of a *High School Musical* marathon.

"No swimming today," she groaned. "And no reading. I'm too tired for anything."

"Not too tired for Zac Efron though," I said with a smirk.

"Never." She grinned.

I looked out the window. "Where are we today?" I asked, remembering I'd vaguely been aware of the boat engine running very early this morning as I must have slipped toward waking at some point before zonking out again.

Dauphine shrugged, her eyes never leaving Zac's chiseled cheekbones. *I feel ya, girl.*

"Okey, dokey," I said. Truly, I was relieved to have a calm day. I hadn't taken a day off since I arrived. After checking with Andrea that it was all right to do so, I went out on the shaded stern deck to sketch. I was down to my last page.

The next day the boat would be moving out to sea, and we'd be heading back along the coast toward Nice and Monaco. I glanced longingly over my shoulder toward shore. I'd been doing some online research about all the architectural influences up and down the coast. The fact that the area had remnants dating back thousands of years made me desperate to experience some more of these little places. And Corsica, an island that had some of the most wide-ranging architectural influences, from pre-Roman to

Pisan to Genoese still standing, was only four hours away by boat.

By boat!

And I was *on* a damn boat. I wanted to weep. Then I wanted to laugh at how much I was beginning to appreciate boats.

"What is so amusing?"

I jerked in surprise and turned to see Xavier had come out the sliding doors. He reached up and held the outdoor stair railing, spreading his feet to find balance as the boat sliced through the waves. The wind whipped his black hair over his forehead.

"Sorry. What?"

"It looked as though you laughed out loud to yourself."

"I did?" I ducked my chin, embarrassed that he'd caught me changing my mind about boats. "I was just thinking I might be learning to appreciate boats."

He raised an eyebrow. "Indeed?"

"Don't get too ahead of yourself," I sassed. "It's a long way from appreciating to loving them."

"Did you have a bad experience with a boat?"

"Not every feeling has to be rooted in the past." I lifted a shoulder.

He cocked his head. "But they normally are."

Interesting. "Well, not that I remember," I said. "I've never really spent any time on a boat before this one."

"Even living in Charleston? That's an accomplishment," he said. Good lord, Xavier Pascale was ... joking with me.

I let out an awkward laugh. "True."

I noticed then that he held a white canvas tote bag in his other hand. Seeing my gaze made him look down. "Oh. I came to give you this." He cleared his throat. "I'm not sure if they are the right things."

I stood and took the bag he offered. Inside were two large blank sketchbooks, a set of really expensive drafting pencils, watercolor pencils, and a hardback book. "Wow." I smiled.

"Dauphine said you were running out of paper." He waved a hand, dismissively, suddenly gruff and looking extremely uncomfortable. "It's nothing. I'm simply replacing since Dauphine has been using up your supplies."

"Thank you, really." I looked back down at them, and then to the book. It was a hardcover, small coffee table type book, and the picture on the front was of a castle. I turned it over. "And this?"

"It's, uh, about the architectural influences in the area around where I live, in Valbonne. I thought you'd be—I thought it would be good for Dauphine. My mother, she, uh, helped raise the funds to produce the book for the historical society she is part of. I had a copy. I thought you would appreciate it more. And perhaps show Dauphine. It's in French, of course."

"Of course. Thank you. This was extremely thoughtful."

"As I said. It's nothing." Then he added, "I was only thinking of Dauphine."

I looked up at him and gave him a grateful smile. "All the same, I really appreciate it."

He nodded.

The boat suddenly slowed its motion, and I lurched forward. My hands were full, and unable to catch myself, I was suddenly face first in Xavier Pascale's hard chest.

"Oof," he huffed out a puff of air, his arms catching me.

The smell and heat of him rushed in, and before I could even get my scattered wits together to peel myself off him, his strong hands gripped my upper arms and roughly set me away from him.

"Watch yourself," he snarled.

I almost stumbled backward from the force of action and his words. I blinked in shock. My cheeks burned with heat. "I didn't —I'm sorry, I—"

"Careful down there," called Paco from behind Xavier. And I realized he could see us from up on the bridge. "I should have warned you. I thought I saw a piece of wood in the water. Must have been a trick of the light."

Anger fought with my embarrassment. Had Xavier honestly just thought I'd purposefully fallen into him? *God.* I yanked the canvas tote open and stowed my other sketchbook in with the new stuff. "Thank you for the supplies," I said stiffly, unable to look at him. Then I brushed past him.

His hand reached out and took my arm, stopping me.

I swung around. "What?" I snapped, though my voice felt choked up, and I prayed to God I didn't burst into tears.

He let go but said nothing.

I stared at him, both of us locked in a battle of God knew what. Was he so emotionally constipated he couldn't fucking apologize for acting like an arrogant tyrant?

"I'll be downstairs if Dauphine needs me," I gritted out, hoping I didn't sound like a woman unhinged.

He gave a small nod, his face devoid of any recognizable emotion, and I raced down to my room.

Alone in my cabin, I angrily refreshed my email. God, maybe I'd just get an amazing job offer to, I dunno, redesign the façade of Charleston's ugliest building, the Holiday Inn in West Ashley. Though honestly, that building should just have some carefully laid charges and be put out of its misery. I dialed my mom's number, unsure if she'd answer. It had been weeks since we'd spoken. Meredith had set her up with an app so I could call over Wi-Fi.

"Hello?" Her voice sounded small and vast at once. She sounded like home.

My ears and nose stung with instant homesickness. "Ma?"

"Josie. Sweetheart. Is that you? Hello? Hello?"

"Yes, Ma. I'm here." I smiled, my eyes flooding. "I'm here. How are you?"

"Gosh, darling. I almost didn't hear this blasted thing bleating at me. I thought it was another weather report. How do you all live with these constant beeps and buzzes going on telling me about everything. I've got no interest in whether Wappoo Cut is going to flood its banks in high tide. Wait, I'm so sorry, this is probably costing you a fortune and I'm prattling on. How are you, love?"

My face hurt from smiling so wide from the joy of hearing her voice. I grabbed a tissue and wiped my eyes and nose. "It's good to hear your voice, Ma. I'm good. It's beautiful here. And I'm calling over the internet so it's free, okay? Don't worry. Though, there might be a bad signal sometimes because we're on a yacht."

"You hate boats!"

"I do. But this one ... well, it's as big as a house. Let me tell you about Dauphine, the little girl I look after." I picked at the cuticles on my toes as I told her all about Dauphine and the water in the Mediterranean, the food and the crew.

"Sounds like a fun little diversion," my mother said when I was done, and I smarted a bit at her dismissal. "Have you been working on your resume? I spoke with a lady in my bridge club. And she thinks her husband might know of a position at the Historic Charleston Foundation. I know it's not an architectural firm. But it's respectable and it fits well in your resume ... unlike this, this, what do you call yourself? An Au Pair? A nanny?"

"Either."

"Yes, well, we'll pretend you took a long vacation or something, and then after a while maybe no one will notice the gap on your resume."

"Ma. I appreciate you trying to help. But I'm concerned enough for the both of us. You trying to get me a job is just stressing me out more. I've actually applied for several positions at real architectural firms. And it's *my* career, okay?"

"I'm just trying to help."

"Don't, okay?" It came out harsher than I'd meant it. "I'm sorry, I—"

"It's embarrassing," she hissed. "I don't know what to say to people when they ask."

I blinked, my voice hardening. "Well, you tell them Ravenel Tate is a misogynistic asshole, and your darling daughter couldn't work there anymore."

My mother gasped. "Josie—"

"I'm kidding," I said, annoyance in my tone. "Not about what he is, but that you should say that." My throat closed up on the last few words. It wasn't that I was homesick necessarily.

"That's not funny, young lady."

I blew out a breath and squeezed my eyes closed against the slight pricking. It was not homesickness, it was simply that I suddenly felt very far from home. Xavier Pascale's coldness had me feeling adrift. And like I'd mentioned to Xavier about his father, there was something about talking to my mom that made me feel twelve years old again. We reverted to old patterns. It was partly comforting. It also drove me nuts.

I rolled my eyes. "No. You're right. It's not. Because it's true. Anyway, why do you have to discuss *me?*"

"Because you're my daughter, and I'm proud of all you've accomplished." Her tone suggested an unfinished thought.

"But?"

"But I don't understand why you had to run away. That's not what we do, Josephine. You didn't see me running away from Charleston when your father died. Nor when all that unpleasantness with Nicolas happened."

I snorted at her word choice. *Unpleasantness?*

"No," she went on. "We stay. We look people in the eye, and we hold our heads up high."

I tore at tiny piece of dry skin next to my nail. Was that what I'd done? Run away when things got tough?

"And don't think I didn't notice that you haven't even mentioned your boss."

I licked my lips. "What about him?"

"Josephine."

"Mother," I shot back.

She let out a sigh. "I've seen pictures of him, you know?"

"I'm—it's going to be okay." I dismissed her mention of him. "It's fine to think of this as an extended vacation, all right? That's what it is. I'm not throwing in my degree to become a professional nanny."

"Okay. I just miss you." Her voice wobbled.

I squeezed my eyes closed. "I miss you, too. Hey. Can you wrap your arms around yourself and squeeze? That's me hugging you. Everything's going to be all right. Listen, I have to go. I love you."

We said goodbye and hung up. I stared at the phone. I didn't need to go anywhere, but talking to my mom hadn't made me feel better at all.

An hour later, Andrea texted me that I would eat early with the crew and Dauphine would eat alone with Monsieur Pascale. I couldn't help the horrid feeling in my belly that I'd done something terribly wrong. But what?

The next day, it happened again for both lunch and dinner. Feeling mildly betrayed, I was torn between relief and disappointment. They played board games on the upper deck and went swimming, and he barely glanced in my direction. When I woke in the night and crept up to the top deck, I was equal parts relieved and disappointed not to find him there. Every morning, I felt crabbier and more tired.

Xavier had business on shore and he was back and forth. On one of the days, it was my day off, so I hitched a ride with him and Evan to shore while Dauphine stayed with Andrea. We were in a small town near Marseille, and as much as I'd looked forward to moments like this, I felt overwhelmed wandering around all day by myself in a strange town. The museum I'd read about online was closed and nowhere had good Wi-Fi, so I couldn't even check in with home or check my email to see if I'd heard back from any of the jobs I'd applied for. I sat awkwardly by myself at a little café and ordered a *citron pressé,* which wasn't as good as the one Xavier had ordered me because it came with packets of sugar that didn't dissolve instead of the simple syrup. The baguette sandwich came with anchovies on it, which permeated the entire experience even though I picked them off. And weirdly, I missed Dauphine and wondered why I hadn't just invited her along even though it was my day off. Security, I reminded myself. That was why.

I met up with Xavier and Evan at the quay. Xavier was on the phone, the other hand shoved into the pocket of his tan pants and his linen shirt tails carelessly rumpled. Against the backdrop of the Mediterranean, he still looked like a million dollars. He nodded in my direction.

"Have a good time?" Evan asked, and I tore my gaze away. Luckily, I was wearing sunglasses.

I shrugged and followed him toward the tender. "It was all right. There's not much to do here. But it was nice to stretch my legs and walk more than fifty feet in one direction."

He grinned and stepped into the shallow boat, turning to help me in. "I'll bet."

"I was disappointed not to see the museum though. It was closed. I read they have an exhibit of the Huguenot expulsion since Marseille was one of the ports many fled from."

"Do you know where your father's ancestors left from?" Xavier suddenly asked from behind me, clearly having caught up with us and our conversation.

"Um." I shifted over on the bench to give him room. "The south, probably Marseille. But I'm not sure."

"I apologize. I should have told you there is a Huguenot Memorial on Ile Saint Marguerite."

"Where we just were a few days ago?" I asked, dismay lacing

my tone. I quickly schooled my features and hoped I hadn't come off as annoyed. This was not my vacation after all. But I *was* annoyed. I couldn't help it. Suddenly I asked myself why I was still working for a man who didn't even like me half the time. But then I thought of Dauphine. She'd told me she loved me when I was putting her to bed the other night. And I surprised myself my returning the sentiment.

"What was all that Huguenot stuff about anyway?" asked Evan. "Wasn't much for history in school."

"People being persecuted for being protestant, so hundreds of thousands fled the country," I supplied as he steered the vessel past the quay and toward our huge floating home.

"So you're technically protestant," Evan mused, eyeing me. "And Xavier here is Catholic. Interesting. Destined to be at odds."

I kicked Evan's shin, acting like I was being playful, while inside I was asking what the hell? "And what are you?" I asked Evan, trying to brush over the weird vibe.

"Thirsty. Hey, the crew is all going out when we get to St Tropez. You should come with us."

I glanced at my employer, who was staring very hard at his phone. "Sure," I said. "That'd be fun. As long as Dauphine doesn't need me."

"She'll be seeing her grandmother for a bit," Xavier responded, letting us know he had, indeed, been listening.

"Oh," I responded. Surprised. "How long for?" What was I supposed to do when I wasn't watching Dauphine?

"I'm not sure yet. Evan?" He turned his head toward his body-guard. "When are we due in St. Tropez?"

"Day after next. Why?"

He switched to French, and they spoke so rapidly that between that and the sound of the tender motor, I let their conversation go and drifted into feeling the sun and wind on my face. Turning toward the elements, I breathed in deeply.

I didn't understand why my mere presence had suddenly made

Xavier act so damn uptight. He'd so very thoughtfully bought me sketchbooks and even gave me a book he thought I'd be interested in. But then in the same breath, he'd acted like I was to be avoided at all costs. Days ago at the beach, we'd talked, and I felt as though we were actually starting to become friends, but today he'd leave the room if I walked into it rather than be alone with me. Up on the deck in the middle of the night he'd shared intimate parts of his past. I had too. Then suddenly he'd barked at me to get lost. A pervasive feeling of discomfort plagued me as if I'd misstepped, but not sure how to fix it. And I couldn't forget the touch that night in Dauphine's room. Maybe it had been by accident, and now he felt awkward about it. Though I was now beginning to think I'd imagined it.

Having a few hours to myself when we got back, I decided to head down to my cabin.

I dialed Meredith's number. I had to talk to someone about what was going on. I felt like I was going crazy.

CHAPTER TWENTY-FOUR

Meredith answered on the third ring. "Is everything all right?" Her voice was sleep-infused.

"Yes, yeah," I responded to Meredith's sleepy greeting. "Wait, Why? What time is it there?"

"Let me peel an eyelid open and I'll tell you." There was a snuffle. "Ugh. It's ten."

"Can't believe you're still sleeping, but sorry I woke you. It's five in the afternoon here."

"It's Saturday," she grumbled. "And I got trampled by Moscow Mules last night."

"Nothing that a bit of Polish water and tomato juice won't cure." I grinned, thinking of Meredith's drive for the perfect Bloody Mary. "Hope you picked up some more Tabasco. You were out last time I checked."

"Yes, goober. Life doesn't just stop when you're not here."

I laughed. "Oh, I thought I was indispensable. Hey, on the subject, I saw an Instagram post from Skull Creek boathouse in Hilton Head that had a whole spicy deep-fried soft-shell crab perched on a Bloody Mary. You need a road trip. It's only two hours away."

"I'm not driving two hours for a Bloody Mary," she griped.

I lay back on the bed and swiveled so I could have my feet up the cabin wall. "*I'd* drive you two hours for a perfect Bloody Mary. I love you that much."

"You would. If you had a driver's license. Gah. I miss your face."

"Me too."

"So ... how's it going?" she asked.

My bottom lip was getting bruised by the amount of time I spent gnawing on it. "It's fine. Xav—Mister P is on and off the boat, so often it's just me and Dauphine. And the crew, of course." I paused with everything I wanted to say weighing down my tongue to silence. "But it's fine. Good."

"What's the kid like?"

"She's ... she's great."

"A hellion?"

"No, actually. Not at all. No more than a normal kid who's lost a parent and desperately needs attention from her remaining one."

"Ah. So, a pretty good fit for you then, huh?"

I quickly got up and closed my cabin door for the sake of privacy, and then opened the small porthole window in order to be able to breathe. "You could say that." I wanted to add a caveat that it would be far better if I wasn't cripplingly attracted to her father.

"Just keep your head down. And your pants up," she added as if she'd just heard my thoughts aloud.

"Hey!" I lay back down on the bed, a smile on my face at being able to catch up with one of my best friends, bantering as if we weren't thousands of miles away from each other. I wanted to talk to Tabitha too but worried she'd notice the elephant-sized crush in the room.

"I know, I know. Just, oh my God," she whined. "I've been Googling the shit out of him. Hoping I'll catch a glimpse of you.

Oh, and I think I did. Did you all go to a beach restaurant a few days ago?"

A shiver of dread snaked through me. "Um, yes. How——"

"You were snapped in a paparazzi pic. I have no idea what they were saying, and before you freak, they had no idea who you were because your name was nowhere."

"Oh my God. Was it just one picture?" I thought about our afternoon swimming.

"Yeah. I'll send it to you. Damn that man is a smokestack. How do you not drool all day long?"

I giggled in spite of myself. "I do. It's a real problem," I admitted, then cringed. "Like, Mer, a seriously, serious problem. And I think he pretty much knows it too."

"Shit. Really?" She laughed. "You always had a bad poker face."

I covered my eyes with my free hand and lowered my voice. "I know. But it's not just his looks, I am so drawn to him, and he does these nice things for people," I added lamely when I couldn't think how to describe the things I knew. "It's hard to describe." And he also just acted like an asshole to you, I reminded myself. "But he's also complicated," I added.

There was a short pause. "Tabs is so relieved this worked out," Meredith said in a tone pregnant with unsaid warnings.

My belly felt sludgy with guilt, even though I'd done nothing wrong. "Anyway, apart from at the beach club, he's avoiding me. I think. Or I'm avoiding him. I don't know. Maybe both. But it's a feat when you're on a boat, I'll tell you." But then that strange touch in Dauphine's room. What if it really was accidental? It probably was.

"I do give you credit, you know I do. But if he's avoiding you too, then have you entertained the fact the feeling might be mutual? Maybe it's making him uncomfortable."

Despite the fact I was lying down, my insides seemed to drop away. "Ugh," I moaned and covered my eyes again. "Don't say that. I've never been so ... *aware* of someone in my life. I don't know how to explain it. And I can't even *think* it might be mutual —my insides might implode." They felt as though they were imploding right now. "If that's the case, he'd never do anything about it. Which is ... good. But, honestly, Mer. I think Evan, that's his security guy, and Mr. P were talking about me. Maybe that's why he's been so distant and hot and cold. He doesn't trust me or something."

"He wouldn't have you watching his daughter if that was the case."

My teeth continued working on my lip. "True."

"What did he say exactly?"

I thought back to the morning before the beach club after yoga when I'd passed the stateroom and heard him and Evan talking in French, convinced I'd heard my name. "I don't know. I was sure he said my name. It was in French and I was eavesdropping. He said something about *impossible*. Something, something *coo*."

"Coo?"

"Yeah. I know. I told you, I couldn't really tell, but I definitely heard my name." I thought about that night on the top deck. "And I don't know a lot of French, but I felt like the gist was he didn't want me around. He also says stuff in French on purpose, like he knows I won't understand him."

Meredith hummed. "Like what?"

"If I knew—"

"You'd know. I get it. Jeez, that's uncomfortable. But are *you* okay?" she asked. "Like you're having a nice time apart from him, right?"

"I've been applying for jobs and haven't heard back, which is making me panic a bit. I'm missing working. Designing. Using my brain. I know that's odd to say. I think Dauphine is awesome, but I feel like my brain might turn to mush. How do people lie around in the lap of luxury all day and not get bored and crazy? I've started doing online courses. By choice!"

"Jeez, Josie. First world problems. Haven't you ever taken a vacation? Pretend it's a vacation."

"I get bored on vacation, you know that. That's why I'm always wanting to do stuff, go for a hike, go sightsee or whatever."

"Grr. I know. And *I* can think of nothing better than lying around with a good book and nothing else to do. So why don't you do stuff, then?"

"I'm stuck on a boat. If I didn't have cabin fever before, I sure as heck do now." But an idea began to form in my head. "Actually, maybe that's the problem. I'm antsy. You're right though. I think I need to tell him I need to do some field trips with Dauphine." And ask him what I was doing wrong.

"Perfect. And I'm always right."

I rolled my eyes as if she could see me. "Whatever." I smiled.

"And I'll bet I'm right that the attraction is probably mutual. But relationships between rich privileged billionaires and the girls who work for them ... I don't think they normally end well. *Pretty Woman* not included. The power dynamic is whack. Plus his history, you know? It screams baggage. And there's Tabitha. So be very, very careful, okay?"

My throat felt tight. "I know. I am." I forced out a slow breath. "I will. I promise."

I didn't want to hang up, but after a long goodbye, I groaned in frustration and mashed the end button before I rolled my face into my pillow and screamed.

Xavier sat in a lounge chair with a laptop, two phones, and a tray that held a large glass of iced water. Or vodka. Who knew?

"Oh." I stopped. "Hi."

He watched me from over the top of a sheaf of papers.

I guess now was as good a time as any to have that talk with him I'd said I was going to have.

"Um, do you have a few minutes?" I asked before digging my teeth into my lower lip.

He set down the papers and removed his sunglasses, and for a second I saw his gaze slide down to my attire. Or lack thereof. Dammit. I felt exposed in my swimsuit and not full of the confidence and bravado I'd armed myself with leaving my cabin. What did I want to discuss exactly?

"Well?" he asked when my silence grew awkward. His tone had gentled, as if he knew I was struggling.

"Dauphine," I said, latching onto a safe topic. "I was thinking she and I should do more field trips. When you go to shore, perhaps she and I can do something in town sometimes."

He cocked his head to the side. "We can ask Evan, of course. He would have to accompany you."

"C-could you accompany us sometimes? I mean, I think Dauphine would like to do more things with you. But only if it's safe obviously."

"What did you have in mind?"

I wracked my brain that seemed to have lost most of the information I'd been feeding it over the last few weeks. "If we go back to Ile Saint Marguerite, she and I could go and see the Huguenot Memorial you mentioned. And then also, I was reading about this amazing turquoise river. It's like a gorge or something, the color of the water is milky blue, and you can kayak—"

"*Les Gorges du Verdon?*"

"Yes! The Verdon Gorge. Is it far?" I leaned against the stair railing behind me.

He pursed his lips. "If we drove when we were back in Nice, perhaps it would take two and a half hours."

"Oh." My shoulders slumped. "It was just an idea."

"It was a good idea. Dauphine has always been interested in going there, actually. Her class went on a school camping trip a while ago, but she couldn't go. She was afraid she would wake up with a nightmare and be teased by the other girls."

My chest constricted. "Poor Dauphine. Wait, do you have to camp there or can you do it in a day?"

He snorted a laugh at whatever he must have seen on my face. "I see you are not a fan of camping?"

"Are *you*?" I defended.

"Not particularly. But somehow I don't think I have quite the same reaction to the idea as you do."

"And what reaction was that?"

"Like someone just asked you to try a chocolate-covered locust. Or a mussel."

I cracked up. "Yeah. That sounds about right. All power to the campers, it's just never been my thing."

"No boats, no camping," he mused. "So, is that all you wanted to talk about?"

I opened my mouth then closed it again.

His eyes were steady on mine. Intense. It was now or never.

"It's just. This ... this chatting with you is nice. Then sometimes, you just snap like I've done something wrong, and you're cold again. I mean, I'm not saying I'm the best person in the world, but I think I'm a nice enough person. Dauphine seems to think so. As well as practically every other person I've ever met. I have to be honest, I've never come across someone who simply tolerates me one minute and seems repelled by me the very next."

He stilled, his eyes narrowing. His arms folded across his chest.

Shit, I'd really just put it out there, hadn't I? My heart thudded heavily all the way up my throat. "I mean ... I, it's fine if you don't like me. But," I swallowed. My mouth had gone dry as paper. Earth, or ocean, swallow me up. Please.

"You're nice one minute and snappy the next."

He sat forward, legs astride the lounger. "Snappy?" His work was cast aside.

"Snappy," I reiterated. "The way you look at me feels like ..." I trailed off, then cleared my throat. "Never mind. Anyway, it feels as though you have been avoiding me. Have you?" I asked before my brain caught up with my mouth. Might as well ask him straight out.

His expression remained unchanged, though there was a long pause before he answered slowly. "Why would I do that?"

"It seems like you have been." I lifted a shoulder as if it had been just a casual observation.

"I think I have too much work going on and too many important things on my mind than worrying about where you are at all times. I ... like you just fine. I'm sorry if I've made you feel otherwise," he said flatly. "That was not my intention. As long as my daughter is safe, that's all I should care about."

"Of course." I bit down hard. "Okay. As long as there is not something I can do differently."

"I don't think that's possible," he said cryptically after a long pause. "Now if you'll excuse me, I have a few more reports to read."

CHAPTER TWENTY-FIVE

My American phone beeped with an incoming text as I pulled on a fresh t-shirt from my laundry pile. After Dauphine and I swam while Xavier was on a conference call, I'd had a quick shower to get the salt off. This morning we'd stopped off at a small bay, and this afternoon we'd be docking back in St. Tropez. I was looking forward to getting off the boat again and having a night off.

I hurriedly swished some mouthwash to freshen up and wound my wet hair into a top knot, then grabbed my phone. There were two text messages from Meredith.

Mer: *Update! I think I know what he said in French. Lol. Call me later.*

Mer: *Oh crap. Tabitha just said she got an email from him and asked if I'd heard from you. Call me!*

. . .

My heart thudded, and I frowned and perched on the edge of my bed while I dialed Meredith's number. It went to voicemail. "Shit," I murmured and gritted my teeth as I dialed Tabs.

"Hey, Josie," she answered on the first ring.

"Tabs! How are you? Isn't it the wedding this weekend? You must be so busy."

She gave a short laugh. "My sister has the world's most intense wedding planner. Everything is ready, but I'm so busy because the damn planner and my sister have micro-managed everyone's time down to the minute. We're on a packed schedule. I have hair and make up for the rehearsal dinner in, I kid you not, seventeen minutes. Not fifteen. Not twenty. Seventeen."

"Yikes. That does sound intense. But you're having fun though, right?"

"I am."

"And what about the hometown guy you were worried about seeing? He there?"

"He's here," she said. "But I don't want to talk about him. How's it going there?"

"Fine. I mean, I think. Dauphine is amazing. And we've totally bonded."

"But?"

"How do you know there's a but?"

She let out a short breath. "Listen, you'd tell me the truth if anything had gone on between you and Mr. Pascale, right?"

My belly flipped over. "Um," I managed through a throat now filled with rocks. "What do you mean?"

"Josie, don't make me say it."

"But that's the thing. I mean, I think you're asking if anything sexual has happened, to which I can categorically tell you no. No way."

She let out an exhale. "Thank God."

Her reaction of relief should have made me feel better, but somehow, I felt worse. And what had happened to even have her ask that question. She seemed to be waiting for more from me, so I decided to share my thoughts. "But I think he has a problem with me for some reason. He's nice and chatty one minute, and then snapping at me the next. Basically, I love Dauphine, but I'm not having the best time with him, if that makes sense. But I mean, he's not my job. She is."

"Right."

I licked my lips. "Why did you ask that?"

"I haven't checked my email in a few days, and I dunno, maybe I missed it when I did check, but he sent me an email."

My forehead creased up, and I tried to ignore the uncomfortable feeling brewing inside me. "And," I pressed when she paused.

"And he asked me if I could find a replacement for you."

My stomach plummeted, and ice swept over my skin. "Are you serious?"

"Yeah. Like I said, it was a while ago, and I overlooked it. I just thought I had everything with the business squared away and put an out of office note on my email, and we've been nonstop here, and I feel awful that I didn't see it and respond to it. I should have seen it and called him. But of course, I wanted to check in with you first and hear your side."

My heart was drumming in my throat, the sick feeling now spreading through me. "My side? There's no side. I feel like—"

I felt betrayed by him, is what I felt. "How long ago was the email?" I asked instead and waited as she looked it up.

She named a date. Almost two weeks ago. I guessed that should make me feel a little better.

"And he hasn't sent you another one, calling off that request?" I clarified. "Even though you didn't respond?"

"Maybe he thought I was still working on it. What happened two weeks ago?"

"I don't know," I said truthfully. "I mean, the night I arrived he was so rude to me that I kind of quit. It was clear he wanted me to stay. And I didn't want to let you down. So I stayed. And since then ..." Since then he'd been hot and cold. Kind, then mean. Friendly, then icy.

"Since then, what?"

"Nothing. Honestly. I've been busy with Dauphine. She's happy. I just ... I don't know, Tabs." I picked at a tiny piece of peeling skin leftover from a sunburn on my knee. "Can—can I ask? What did his email say exactly?"

"Josie, I know we're friends, but I can't divulge that." Her voice sounded pained.

"Shoot. I know. I'm sorry."

"Maybe one day when you're home. I—I guess I'd better give him a call."

"Okay," I said, deflated. Almost two weeks ago was the incident on the top deck in the middle of the night. But I had no idea if that was the inciting incident for him emailing Tabitha. But maybe it was. Nausea rolled through me. What exactly had I done that was so bad? And what exactly had he said to me that night?

We said our goodbyes, and I mashed the end button. Inexplicably, tears burned at the back of my eyes. I knew I'd done nothing wrong, but the sense of betrayal and rejection was so strong, I felt helpless. And he was a goddamn successful billionaire for God's sake. If he had a problem with me why couldn't he just damn well tell me to my face?

Around the table with the crew in the galley a few hours later, I tried to follow the animated banter, but my stomach had been churning for hours. My bludgeoned pride was allowing all manner of thoughts to join the pity party parade. Now I began wondering if Dauphine had been sweet to my face and then complained bitterly about me to her father at all the meals they'd shared without me. Because how else could I explain him taking the drastic step of asking for a replacement?

I'd found Andrea right before dinner and told her what had happened. She'd been as surprised as me, and completely clueless. "I'll try and ask Evan later," she said before giving me a hug. "He may know."

I thought I'd been doing an all right job. It wasn't exactly hard. And I thought, despite the concern I'd voiced to him earlier, he at least liked me. But who had I been kidding? From the moment I'd arrived, Xavier Pascale and I had been at odds. The friendly boss-employee relationship I'd caught glimpses of were clearly an illusion. I thought of the hard look he'd given me after I fell against him when the boat slowed so abruptly. I'd never known it was possible to repulse someone you had a crush on so utterly.

"What do *you* think, Josie?" Rod asked me.

I blinked, a forkful of forgotten ravioli halfway to my mouth, and realized everyone was staring at me. Everyone but Captain Paco. He was having dinner with Monsieur Pascale and Dauphine this evening on the upper deck.

"Um, I'm sorry, what do I think about what?" I managed, my voice dredged from somewhere far away.

Rod smirked. "About whether Chef should wax his back?"

My eyebrows shot up.

"Fuck off," growled Chef, and there was a screech as he pushed his chair back and leaned over the table, grabbing Rod by the collar and knuckling his head. "That's not what I said and I don't have a hairy back."

"Oi, get off," yelped Rod. "Joking, mate. Joking."

"Say sorry, you—"

"Children, children," said Evan calmly as he deftly moved his glass of water from under Chef's elbow where it was in danger of being batted off the table.

I held my breath as Rod tried to jerk himself free from the merciless ribbing. And I cringed as I waited for something to actually be knocked over.

Finally, Chef let go, straightened his shirt and sat. "Hmmph," he sounded grouchily.

"Bloody hell." Rod rubbed his head. "Sore spot was it?" he baited.

Chef feinted another move, chuckling as Rod jerked back on instinct.

"The ravioli is delicious," I told Chef, even though until now I'd barely tasted a thing. But I was eager to help move the group along. I focused on my plate and took another bite. It was homemade as always, filled to bursting with a soft buttery cheese, herbs, and a hint of truffle. God, I'd miss his cooking.

Chef shrugged. "Simple food. I don't get inspired cooking for this lot." Even though this ravioli was far from simple to my palate, and he was clearly being humble and also throwing in a dig at Rod.

"No complaints on preferring simplicity here," said Rod, deliberately pushing the scrumptious and far from simple pasta around his plate, his tone sarcastic. "I'd rather eat baked beans on toast than this swill, anyway."

Chef growled.

Everyone else laughed.

Clearly this was a long running play-feud because no one seemed to take it seriously. And being here with them every day had slowly started feeling like a family. I blinked as tears threatened again. It reminded me of when my dad was alive and both my mother's and aunt's families and extended families would have Sunday lunch every week that lasted past dinner time. All that had changed when Mom married Nicolas, of course.

I'd miss these new friends. So, so, much. It was clear, I was going to have to resign. I couldn't stay in a situation where I wasn't wanted. I certainly didn't want to be fired, if that's what he was getting ready to do. Besides, I needed to be available if any of the firms I'd contacted wanted me to come in and interview. I couldn't really ask them to wait while I hopped off a boat in the South of France. Jesus, my mom was right. I should have stayed. It was too late for that, but I needed to go home now. Dauphine was going to her grandmother's anyway. It was perfect timing.

"All right," said Andrea with an eye roll. "Enough, Rod. Josie, we were discussing getting off the boat later. What do you think, do you want to join us? We might take a wander along the port and wind up in the town. It's gorgeous. Maybe you and I can pop into a few boutiques since they stay open so late. We can meet the guys for a coffee later."

We'd docked in *St. Tropez* just before dinner. It should have excited me, as I'd finally have a chance to get off the boat onto solid ground and explore the town I'd heard so much about. But now it was probably the place I'd be leaving from.

"All right, so no answer from Josie then," Rod said.

I took a breath. "God, sorry. I-I think I'll stay on board. I'm not feeling that great." I couldn't face going out with everyone and having to pretend I was happy and not about to leave. Plus, I needed to write a resignation letter, pack, and make arrangements to leave.

My breath hitched as I fought back an almost hysterical laugh mixed with wanting to wail.

Andrea reached across the table and squeezed my wrist. "It's going to be okay."

Blood rushed to my cheeks that she'd draw attention to me in front of everyone when I was feeling so raw.

"What is it?" asked Chef.

"Yeah, what's wrong, sweetheart?" Rod said simultaneously.

Andrea gave me a quick look and then turned to the others. "Does anyone here have a complaint about Josie they'd like to share with the group? All of you have told me to my face you think she's great. So can someone," she looked pointedly at Evan, "tell me why Mr. P said he's looking for another nanny?"

"What?" Rod exploded. "That's ridiculous."

"Ahh, fuck," growled Evan and stood. He flung his napkin down on his unfinished food, making Chef flinch. "Bloody fool."

Evan and Chef then shared a look.

"What?" I asked. "What's going on?"

Chef chuckled and shook his head.

"For the love of God," Andrea complained. "Evan?"

"It's nothing," he said. "Relax, Josie. I'll get it sorted out."

"There's nothing to sort out," I said. "I'm definitely not staying where I'm not wanted or needed. This is probably my last night."

CHAPTER TWENTY-SIX

Evan didn't return before dinner was cleared. Back in my cabin, it took less than twenty-five minutes to pack my belongings. Glancing at my watch, I saw it was almost Dauphine's bedtime. I nibbled the corner of my thumbnail as I debated what to do. Should I go and find her? It was my night off, but if I left tomorrow, I wouldn't see her. I checked my emails on my phone for something new from Tabitha. Or a response to any of my job applications. There was nothing. I opened the text from Meredith that I hadn't had a chance to look at yet.

Mer: *I found out what coo means. I think he said "cul." It's pronounced a similar way, and I bumped into that French lady at Armand's so I asked her too.*

And? What does it mean?

. . .

Mer: *it means 'ass.'*

Ass? As in butt?

Mer: *Yep. He was talking about your ass. I'm sure of it.*

About getting rid of it? Like fire her ass.

Mer: *Maybe.* *Cringe emoji* *Sorry. Did he do it? Did he ask you to leave? Tabs said he might but not why.*

Andrea appeared at my open door. She'd put on some make up and wore a soft blue sundress and sparkly flip-flops. Out of her starched, white yacht uniform, she looked so much prettier. Beautiful, even.

"Hey," she said softly. "You okay?"

"Not really. But there's not much I can do about it. Not sure what Evan was on about, but trust me—I don't want to hang around to be fired. I'll draft my resignation letter in the morning. You look stunning, by the way."

"Thank you." She looked around. "You packed."

"I'm leaving first thing tomorrow," I answered by way of explanation. "This is where I came on the boat, this can be where I leave it."

"I can't believe he didn't discuss it with me. Or Evan. Though he may have sent an email, but I didn't get it. The Wi-Fi has been on the fritz. We haven't been able to send or receive email for the last several hours."

I breathed out a sigh. "Oh. I was waiting to hear from Tabitha —she owns the agency. She was going to call him."

"Why don't you come out with us? There's no point staying on board."

"I'm not really in the best mental place."

"Come on. Your mental state the best reason to come out. You haven't even had a night out since you started. You must be stir crazy."

"You have no idea."

"You need one. Besides, it could be your last night."

"It *is* my last night." I felt my resolve caving.

"Well then."

Looking around, I realized I would have to stay holed up in here all evening and probably wouldn't sleep a wink come bedtime. And I certainly wouldn't be visiting the top deck. God knew, I didn't want to be anywhere else on the boat and bump into Xavier Pascale when he couldn't stand the sight of me and I made him so uncomfortable. "If I come with you, any chance you won't judge me if I decide to have a few or hundred drinks." Even as I said it though, I knew I didn't want to be hungover while making the ride of shame to the airport tomorrow.

She laughed. "No judgment from me, I promise. I may even join you in a few. Come on."

I rummaged through my bag and pulled out the only thing I could find. It was the plain black linen t-shirt dress I'd bought at the market in Antibes, but it was short and nicely cut. With the right accessories it could double as a little black dress. I also pulled out my makeup bag. "Give me five minutes?"

Andrea broke out in a wide smile. "You betcha. See you on the back deck. We won't leave without you. Don't wear heels, the cobblestones are a nightmare."

"Don't have any." I shrugged. "See you in a few."

My hair had dried into waves I was getting used to since I

hadn't seen a hairdryer since I'd arrived. It helped that I'd wound my locks into a low bun while it dried. Being in the sun every day, the copper tones had really lightened and caught the light as I separated the waves. I applied some light make up, focusing mostly on my eyes. The tan I'd built up over the last few weeks negated the need for much else. I slipped the dress over a black bra and panties, put on some dangly earrings that sparkled, and my black flip flops. It would have to do. I grabbed my small cross body purse, lip gloss, phone, and some money and left my cabin to go say goodnight to Dauphine before I left, only to bump right into her and Xavier coming down the stairs.

My cheeks throbbed as I was once again swamped with embarrassed heat. I couldn't look at him, so I dropped my gaze to Dauphine, and then bent to her level. "*Bonne nuit*, my little mermaid," I said and kissed her cheek as I felt the weight of her father's gaze on me. "Sweet dreams."

"I am going to see *mémé* tomorrow!" she crowed. "I must pack my clothes. And then you can read to me too later, after Papa?"

My heart squeezed. God, I'd miss her! I shook my head. "I'm going out with Andrea."

"Where are you going?" Xavier's harsh tone jerked my face up to meet his gaze.

"I have no idea." I telegraphed don't-fuck-with-me vibes as hard as I could.

His jaw flexed. "Be safe."

I narrowed my eyes. Like he cared. "I think I'd like to have a few drinks and ... dance," I goaded. "Is that safe?"

His nostrils flared briefly. But he tamped down whatever he'd been about to say. He gave a curt nod that seemed like he'd rather do anything but agree with me.

"You look so beautiful," said Dauphine. "Doesn't she look pretty, Papa?"

I smiled down at her. "Thank you."

"*Oui*," came her father's gruff voice.

I glanced back to him, my smile fading as his eyes seared into mine briefly.

I blinked.

"Excuse us," he ground out and urged Dauphine forward. I flattened myself to the wall as he passed me, my eyes closed, and allowed myself a last surreptitious inhale. Wood. Man. Amazing that this condescending, control freak of a man could still make my lady parts do a tap dance. Even with my eyes closed, my body could feel the moment he was safely past me. I wondered how cell-deep awareness this strong could be one-sided. And I wondered if I'd ever experience it again in the rest of my life. My analytical brain couldn't make sense of it.

I turned and hurried up the stairs without a look back.

On the back deck, the sounds of the port restaurants and the balmy evening breeze soothed my frayed senses. Paco sat on a deck chair holding a skinny brown cigar. A gun and a copy of *For Whom the Bell Tolls* rested on the table next to him.

Wait.

I spun back around so quickly, I hurt my neck. "Is that ...?"

He casually glanced down. "A gun? Yes."

I swallowed. "Okay."

Right. Of course, someone would need to stay and guard the Pascale family. "Didn't know that was a thing in France to just be casually packing. And Hemingway?" I arched my brows, playing off my shock.

"Sorry to be so cliché." He chuckled.

"That's not what I'd call it," I said and caught Andrea's amused expression.

Evan had finally ditched his starched uniform and was dressed in a t-shirt that hugged his impressive physique and a pair of worn chino pants. His hands slipped into his pockets and he shrugged. "I need to do a couple of things in town for an hour or so, so Paco will be guarding the fort." I was relieved he was coming with us as I was hoping to find out what he'd discussed with Monsieur Pascale.

Chef and Rod were already off the gangplank and ambling down the pier toward the security gate that would let us out of the marina and into the throngs of the port nightlife. Apparently, they were getting along now.

I teetered down the gangplank, hitting *terra firma* for only the second time in a week, and grabbed Andrea's arm. "Good lord. I have sea legs," I moaned. "I feel like I weigh ten tons. Please tell me this is a known phenomenon and not that I ate that much pasta and baguette."

Evan steadied me from the other side, looking concerned. "I hope you don't have *mal de débarquement.*"

"Mally what?"

"It's like reverse sea legs. People can get dizzy, their center of equilibrium is off from being on a boat for a long period. Hopefully it's just an episode and will wear off soon. You didn't have it at the beach club, right?"

I thought back. "I felt heavy and tired when we first arrived, but not dizzy. And it didn't last."

"Just hang on to one of us as we walk."

"Wow, you're serious. This is a thing?" I concentrated on putting one foot in front of the other. "I feel drunk without the fun."

Evan left us then and hurried ahead to catch up with Chef and Rod. By the end of the pier, I felt marginally better but realized I'd missed my chance to talk to Evan.

"How's your head feel?" Andrea asked.

"Good. Fine. So, is it just me, or did you notice Evan made himself scarce before I could ask him about going to speak to Monsieur Pascale on my behalf?"

"Yeah. I did. Coward." She rolled her eyes. "It can only mean he doesn't have an answer yet. I'm sorry."

My stomach sank. "It's fine. It's not like it would have changed my mind about leaving."

"But maybe you can corner Evan later and get the details?"

I nodded.

"Great," she said, her uncomfortable smile morphing into a joyous one. "Now let me take you to my favorite little boutique off the square and then we'll go get some drinks. And then I'll persuade you to stay."

The cobblestones were tightly packed and so were the throngs of people. I clung tightly to Andrea's arm. There were singles, couples, families, and groups of fiery young men and tittering young girls. The outfits ranged from a day out on the water to fancy reservations for dinner.

Music and the clink of glass and hum of chatter emanating from the street cafés and restaurants lent a festive mood to the atmosphere. The evening felt full. Vibrant. Unmarred by the silly stresses of family worries or low paying jobs. Or the humiliation of failing at being a nanny. Real life didn't seem to exist here.

A family with two little toddler darlings dressed in matching Vilbrequin and Gucci gesticulated wildly as they talked and walked and browsed the shop windows. After several little shops, I'd put a marginal dent in my credit card with some cute items for Meredith and Tabs, a gorgeous linen scarf and a necklace with peacock feathers for my mother.

"Come on," Andrea said and squeezed my arm. "There's another little boutique I want to pop into up ahead. But first, I'm buying you a real French crepe."

The smell of warm batter and caramelized sugar had already grabbed my attention and made my stomach growl. She dragged me to an open window across the street and ordered two lemon and sugar crepes that were served to us in sticky goodness, dripping out of wax paper. The tart and sweet flavors exploded across my tongue and I devoured the delicious treat.

"Ohmygooooood," I mumbled with my mouth full. "Shmazing."

Andrea laughed. "Right?"

When we were both done, Andrea pulled out a couple of wet wipes from her purse, and we cleaned off our fingers and lips. Then we made our way farther up the road.

Tucked into an alley no more than five feet wide was a little store. There was a planter full of colorful flowers below the picture window. The antique wooden front door, with peeling light blue paint, was propped open. Several pretty summer dresses hung from it and swayed in the breeze. The smell of baked waffle cones and coffee drifted from the busy ice cream shop on the corner.

Andrea greeted the saleslady who seemed to remember her from previous trips, and they chatted in French. Andrea pointed at me, and they both looked me up and down. "She has a new shipment of gorgeous dresses that haven't been seen by anyone," Andrea addressed me. "What size are you? Actually, don't tell me American sizes, they're nauseatingly small. I'll always remember Julia Roberts in *Pretty Woman* telling the personal shopper that she was a size six, and everyone watching in the common room at uni let out an audible groan." She laughed. "Oops. I'm dating myself, aren't I?"

I smiled. "I know the scene you're talking about. If only we had Richard Gere and his unlimited credit card. That would make this trip even more fun. Or better yet, our own unlimited credit cards, no men required."

The sales lady disappeared into the back and came back out with her arms full, and Andrea and I spent a fun half an hour trying on little flirty dresses.

The last one I tried on was a simple but stunning short dress in a golden silky material that seemed to float around my body like a "wisp of sexiness," to use Andrea's expression. It was so thin, it ought to be see through but wasn't quite.

"It'll be a crime if you don't buy that," she said persuasively.

"You know," I said wryly. "I think you'd get on with my friend

Meredith. I can almost hear her telling me to buy the dress even though I have absolutely no idea when I'd ever wear such a thing. Are you sure you're not channeling her right now?"

"Ha. Clearly a sensible girl."

"But not a very sensible dress."

"Wear it now." She shrugged, her eyes gleaming. "Nothing is sensible in St. Tropez."

"What? No."

"Yes!" She clapped her hands excitedly. "There's no better time. You're all tan and gorgeous. It's your last night." Her smile dimmed a little. "We should make it count. I don't normally party, but I think we should at least go hit up *Les Caves*. It's famous. All the celebrities have visited over the years. You can't be young and beautiful in St. Tropez and not go to a nightclub. Now *that's* a crime."

"Um. What happened to sensible, chief steward, Andrea?" I asked, an eyebrow raised.

"She hasn't had a night out in a long time. And in case you haven't noticed, hasn't had much female companionship lately either. And I'm seething that this could be your last night. So I say we make it one to remember."

"I don't have the right bra for this. The material, while not see through, felt thin as gossamer. The delicate spaghetti straps were marred by the black bra straps underneath.

"So take the bra off."

"Andrea. Wait. *Are* you Andrea? Meredith, is that you?" I stepped forward and rapped lightly on her head with my knuckles. "You are insane."

"You're young, you're perky, and you know no one here. Not that anyone would judge you. People sunbathe topless here, for God's sake. Come on. I'll get this emerald green one." She held up the first dress she'd tried on that I'd tried to persuade her to buy.

"You hustler," I griped. "You were going to get that all along."

"Nope."

"Yep."

"Okay, I was debating. But now I will if you will. Come on. We'll tell Evan we're going to the club so no one worries about us. But let's go have a dance for a few hours. Let's feel like the awesome powerful gorgeous women we are. Maybe we'll even be hit on."

"You ever thought about starting a motivational podcast?" I deadpanned.

"Is that a yes?"

"Fine. Yes. But I don't care if I'm hit on. I'm over men right now."

Andrea clapped again.

"I can't believe I'm doing this." I reached under the dress and tried to unsnap my bra. "And I'm still not convinced you are actually Andrea."

"I'm going to get offended if you say that anymore. Am I really such a stick in the mud?"

"No. Sorry. Just ... sensible?"

"This is the most sensible idea I've had in ages."

I rolled my eyes with a laugh and slipped my bra out from the dress under one arm. I winced when I saw myself in the mirror. "Are you sure about this?" I asked.

"You are stunning," Andrea responded from behind a curtain where she'd disappeared to put her dress choice on. "You need a stunning dress and a stunning last night. I can't bear to think you'll go home with such a bad taste in your mouth from one of the most divine places in the world and one of the loveliest families I've ever worked for."

I snorted at the last one.

"No, seriously," she said as she whipped the curtain aside. "I don't know what's gotten under Mister P's skin lately. But he's a good man. One of the best. Now, let's call Evan and let him know the plan. I'm sure he's back on the boat by now. His primary protection duty is to Mr. P and Dauphine after all. And then you and I can go get us a glass of champagne."

We paid the sales lady, and she fussed around us a couple more times, clipping out a label and folding up our own dresses into shopping bags. Then I linked arms with Andrea and let her drag me out on the town.

CHAPTER TWENTY-SEVEN

It was either the dresses or the intention to have fun, but from the moment we left the store, eyes followed us appreciatively wherever we passed. I collected the looks like gold shillings and felt like a million dollars by the time we made it back to the bars and restaurants along the quayside. We headed for where Rod and Chef were sitting at a café, so we could ask them to take our shopping bags back to the boat.

A loud wolf whistle pierced the air, making both Andrea and me jump and drawing even more eyes. In the same instant I realized it came from Rod.

"Gorgeous, ladies!"

"God, Rod. You are such a builder," complained Andrea. "Can't a girl walk down the street without being harassed?"

"You love it. Now come here and sit with us two geezers and make us look good."

Chef chuckled at Rod's antics, and I was glad to see they actually did seem to get along.

"Sorry, lads. We can't. Josie and I are off to the nightclub. *Les Caves.*"

"Did you get enough to eat?" intervened Chef, like a gruff dad.

"We had crepes," Andrea assured him. "Anyway, take our shopping, would you? I've texted Evan, but let him know you saw us and we're fine, and if we're not home by one a.m., would one of you come looking for us?"

"After midnight?" sputtered Rod. "What about my beauty sleep?"

"God knows, he needs it," Chef muttered.

"Oi."

"Boys, boys. Rod, you're always up late. Yes or no?"

"Yes. Fine. Why can't we come with you?"

Andrea laid a hand on Rod's sandy hair. "Next time, yeah?" Then she grabbed my arm and we waved goodbye as we left them.

Tucked into a corner behind a row of restaurants off the main port was a small dark doorway flanked by two palms and a red rope with brass fittings. There was a line that snaked around the corner into the alley. A wide man with square shoulders, shaved head, and a non-existent neck stepped out of the darkness. His face was set in a hard scowl.

"Umberto!" Andrea greeted, and he burst into a grin that transformed him from scary mother fucker to ball of sugar.

They fired a string of greetings at each other in ... "You speak Italian?" I asked Andrea. "That's Italian, right?"

Andrea shrugged bashfully. "I know a few words. This is Umberto. Umberto, this is Josie. Dauphine's nanny."

"Of course." He smiled and shook my hand. "And you, my dear. You are also *bellissima, like my Andrea*! Come in, come in!" He unhooked the heavy rope and ushered us past him, and we stepped into a dim and quiet vestibule where a heavy base beat was barely audible.

"How do you know the bouncer? I thought you didn't party much," I asked.

"Oh, we dock here off season too, and we let his kid come and hang out and play on the boat. Umberto and Paco know each other from way back. I think they crewed on the same boat back in the day. It's a small world in the hospitality industry, especially in the mega-yacht world."

"You call yourselves *yachties*, right?"

"Sadly, yes." She pushed open an interior door. "Anyway, you ready?"

I nodded.

Music and laughter blared out. The music was something from the nineties but over a dance beat. Inside, the club was dimly lit. There was a central oval area surrounded by red velvet covered benches and round tables occupied by small groups of people. A long bar backed with smoky antique glass covered one end of the room and at the other was a white light-tiled dance floor and a DJ booth. It didn't feel overly busy, but we still had to edge in at the bar. Andrea flagged down the bartender and in seconds I had a *coupe* of champagne, eighties style.

"This place is so old school, I love it!" Andrea yelled. She held out her glass to clink and we both toasted and then drank. The DJ began a dance mix of "Gangsta's Paradise" and we hit the dance floor.

"You were right," I told Andrea after an hour where we'd danced, had water, more champagne, and danced some more.

"What?" she yelled.

"This is so fun!" And I'd needed it so much.

She nodded with a grin.

Since it was early and most of the groups there were part of couples, no one had really approached us to dance with them. But men sure watched us. Some girls too. We may not have been the most gorgeous or glamorous in the place, but even I knew there was something mesmerizing and attractive about a person full of joy and happiness. And for a few hours, that was exactly how I felt. The room filled. I was gently but firmly pulled into the embrace of a guy with swept back blond hair and ripped jeans and a Dolce and Gabbana t-shirt who barely looked like he was out of high school. He was absolutely beautiful but far too young for me.

I laughed at his overblown confidence and enjoyed two songs with him. At least he was respectful about where his hands went. Andrea danced with his friend. When they tried to urge us off the dance floor, indicating a dark corner of benches, we declined and my guy held a hand to his chest, feigning a mortal wound. But it didn't take long for them to find new conquests.

My hair clung to my neck, and it got smokier and warmer as more people showed up. I made a drink motion to Andrea and we forced our way through to the now crowded bar. After a glass of water, I motioned to the ladies room.

Down the hall, the air was cooler on my damp skin, and my ears rang with muffled throbs. It was comparably quiet. I held onto Andrea's arm, still feeling slightly off-balance.

"Whew! That was fun," she enthused as we pushed open the door. There was a small sitting area before the bathrooms.

A girl was fixing her hose and gave us a once over.

"Haven't had a good old dance like that in ages," Andrea said as the other girl left.

"Those two young guys were fun." I peered into the mirror and wiped at the mascara shadow under my eye.

"Ahh, he was whispering and begging me to "bring him to heaven." She laughed, raising her fingers in quotes. "If I were ten years younger," she crooned. "Your guy was stunning."

I chuckled. "And also twelve."

"Yeah. Makes an old maid like me feel like she still might have it though." She made her way to the mirrors to join me and grabbed a tissue to blot her glowing face.

"You aren't an old maid!"

"Josie. I haven't had sex in over ten years," she said at my reflection. "I'm as old maid as it gets. And the last time I did it was ... well, I left him, didn't I? So that's that."

The mood plummeted.

I squeezed her arm, and she sniffed, turning around. "Argh. Look at me—a sorry-for-myself wreck after champagne. It's always made me gooey. I just miss it, you know? The intimacy. The tenderness even, not that I got much of that."

"You're fine. You can feel sad about that if you need to. I mean, ten years?" I exclaimed in a teasing tone.

She leaned away and punched my arm good-naturedly. "Hey."

"I'm kidding."

"I'm not. I'm ... lonely. The boat and all the people on it are lovely, family, almost, and I feel safe, I love my work. I feel valued but ... I also feel invisible. Like there's this whole other life out there I'm supposed to be living and that bastard stole it from me." She sighed as she turned back to the mirror. "I'm a hologram in this life."

I wanted to say that I didn't think she was invisible to Evan, or that he saw her as a hologram. But it also was a heck of a long time for Evan not to make his move if he wanted to. "I don't feel like I'm wise enough to give you advice," I said softly. "I mean, look at me, I'm supposed to be an architect, but I've ended up a nanny. Not that there's anything wrong with that, but I've studied and invested huge amounts of money and *years* into getting a job my dead father would have approved of, and the man my mom married after him threw it all into jeopardy. The last guy to ask me out ghosted me after one date. And before that someone dumped me because of who my stepfather was. Utterly humiliating. And worse, I'm really damn attracted to my boss. I mean, God, could you get any sadder than that? I'm crazy about *my boss*." I shook my head with a cringe. "I'm setting feminism back a hundred years."

The sooner I got that resignation letter written, the better.

I could tell Andrea wanted to say something but didn't know what.

"Hey, I'm sorry," I said. "I wasn't trying to make it about me. Can I say one thing though?"

"Hit me."

"I don't think you're invisible to Evan." There, I'd said it.

Andrea went pink, and then pale.

"Shit, sorry. Are you going to pass out?" I asked.

"No. No, I'm fine. But since we're being honest, I don't think you're invisible to Mr. Pascale either." She took my arm. "I could tell from the beginning that there's something between you. And maybe it's just a physical attraction. Maybe it's more. But it's there. And that man deserves some happiness. Some joy. And if you leave tomorrow, he's going to be a grouchy mother fucker. And you are so fantastic with Dauphine. Not that you should throw your own life plans away for a widower and his daughter. But I've never seen him even have the twinkle in his eyes he's had the last few weeks. Even when he's not in a good mood he has ... spark. He hasn't had that in a while. And never mind the laughing. My God. The man hasn't found anything funny in years. *Years*. Long before *she* died." She let go and stepped back.

The silence that followed felt like the heavy, deafening aftermath of a resounding explosion.

I realized I was stunned still, my pulse pounding. I closed my mouth, my jaw snapped shut.

"Yeah," she said. "I can't believe I dropped that bomb on you. I blame the champagne."

We both turned by unspoken agreement and went to the bathroom stalls to do our business.

Nerves climbed from their dance party in my belly up to my throat as I washed my hands at the sink. The bathroom and retiring area were a lot more crowded now. We needed to get back out there and have fun, dammit. "I don't know what to do with the information you gave me. I'm too champagne-headed for this," I said. And I wasn't sure I believed her. But I *wanted* to, and that was pretty terrifying.

"I don't know what to do with what you told me either," she said with a wistful grin. "So I'm going to pretend you didn't."

We agreed to one more drink and a few more dances, and then we'd call it a night. I was hoping to be too tired to even think let alone wake up breathless as I still did most nights. Outside the quiet chatter of the retiring room, the deep throb of the club resumed. The music had changed from 90's classics to sexier, deeper beats. My thoughts were whirling. Back at the bar we ordered two more glasses of champagne. The place seemed even more electrified than it had been before we went to the restroom. The bartender looked up and past us into the distance for a moment, and then turned to grab an open bottle from a silver ice bucket.

I turned to look behind me to see what had caught his attention and only saw the dark, smoky club—laughing faces, and dancing bodies on the dance floor. Then something made me look up. Maybe it was because there was an energy drawing attention upward.

My throat closed.

He was there, on an upper level, his white shirt turned up to his elbows that leaned on the railing, looking down over the crowded club.

Xavier Pascale. Scowling like he'd kill anyone who came near him. The energy of the entire room seemed swept into his orbit even though he stood alone, telegraphing don't-fuck-with-me vibes.

In slow motion his gaze found us then found *me*, and my mouth went dry.

Andrea must have seen me staring, or she felt the shift along with everyone else. "Holy shit," she said. "I think I need a cold shower."

"Huh?" I forced my eyes from him and turned to her.

"Never mind. I guess you're going up there."

"What?" My heart pounded in my chest and ears. "No. I'm staying with you."

"No. You need to go talk. I don't mind. Trust me."

"*I* do. I mind. We came to dance. We came to have fun. Let's do that." I tilted the champagne and gulped it down, the tiny bubbles almost threatening to explode out my nose, I drank so fast. My eyes watered.

"I'll go back to the boat and check on Dauphine and make myself scarce." She put her mouth close to my ear, so I could hear her properly. "You go up and talk to him."

"I can't," I said, turning my head slightly in case he could read my lips. My nerves made my legs feel like jelly, and I gripped the bar top tightly. "No. Come on. Let's pay for our drinks and get back out there."

"He already bought them for us."

I let out a long breath. "Of course he did."

"Go talk to him."

"Ahh, *les filles élégantes!*" We turned to find our two young admirers looking a little sweatier and just as enthusiastic as before. "*Voulez-vous danser encore un fois?*"

"Yeah, I don't think so." Evan appeared on the other side of us. His gaze burrowed into Andrea's. "Having fun?" he growled.

Whatever was on Evan's face had the two boys disappearing into the crowd as quickly as they'd shown up.

"Hey," yelled Andrea over the noise. "What was that?"

Evan said nothing, though I could tell he was biting his tongue, and Andrea looked ready to spit fire. Whoo boy. If anyone had chemistry around here it was these two. It was pretty funny that she couldn't see it.

My eyes left them and found *him* again. He hadn't moved. He watched us still. He watched me. Like a leopard from a tree.

"I'll make sure Andrea gets back safely." Evan's voice was loud in my ear, presumably so I could hear him over the noise. "He wants you upstairs."

I flinched. "He does?"

And then, in the time it took for me to process Evan's words, he and Andrea were gone.

Xavier Pascale took a drink from a heavy looking tumbler, then he set it down somewhere next to him I couldn't see.

My legs shook, and my heart pounded in my throat. I knew if I went up there, it was going to forever change me.

A spark of anticipation and nerves, hot and searing, scorched through me from my neck to my navel. And then I was halfway across the room, pressing through the people, my pulse racing at Mach speed and my breathing not much better. Apparently, I'd started toward him before my mind could give me permission.

There was a bouncer at the bottom of the stairs. A rope. But somehow I was past them. The bouncer hadn't stopped me. The stairs were glass as I found my footing. The railing was cool wood and steel under my palm.

By the time I'd reached the top, I'd run a marathon. Adrenaline pumped. My lungs bellowed.

He waited for me, retreating from the railing and inclining his head slightly toward a small couch and table in the dim corner. I felt curious eyes on me from the darkness and dismissed them.

"Is it true?" I stalked up to him.

He dragged his eyes from my face to my feet and back again. "Is what true?"

"You want to send me home," I snapped. "You emailed Tabitha. Don't be dense."

He hissed and his eyes flashed in warning. He circled me, and I turned with him. "Evan?" he asked.

"It wasn't Evan." Shit, I didn't want Tabitha getting in trouble either. "I overheard you."

"No, you didn't." He stepped toward me, and I retreated to the darkness of the wall next to the couch. There was no way I would sit down and share a nice congenial moment with him. I needed to clear the air, and then I was getting out of here. There was a danger to this man tonight. Who was I kidding? There was a danger to him every night.

Why did everyone else see a kind, handsome, and broken pussycat?

All I saw was a lethal predator who I felt sure had the means to snatch my heart from my chest with a single swipe.

He loomed.

"What are you doing?" I gasped as my back hit the wall and he kept coming. "Y-you're scaring me."

"Good." His palm smacked the wall by my head, and the smell of stale, smoky and alcohol fueled club air sifted slowly into linen and rough pine wood. "Because you scare the shit out of *me*," he said. "*Tu me détruis.*"

I swallowed but my throat was stuck. "Wh-what does that mean?"

He leaned in, nose skimming up my cheek, inhaling me. We'd never been this close. My body lit up like a glowing tinder.

My breathing grew shallow.

Fingers lightly pressed into the hollow of my throat, resting. His skin to mine. "You don't seem like a girl who scares easily." The words, delivered so softly right into my ear, made every molecule of my skin vibrate.

"I'm not," I managed, though I knew that wasn't what he'd said in French. My hands, pressed to the wall on either side of my hips, dropped and I fisted them to keep from reaching for his waist. To stop my fingers curling into the belt loops of his jeans and tugging him closer. I was enclosed in the energy of his body, aching. But resisting. This was my boss. And he'd taken leave of his senses. One of us had to keep our head.

"What about me scares you?" he asked.

I squeezed my eyes closed, like I could gather my courage. I dragged in air laden with his woody scent. The same air that was weighed down with the heady and heavy atmosphere of the club. We were suspended in time. His face hovered next to mine, his mouth by my ear. My nerve endings screamed for contact as his every exhale stirred across my skin.

"The way you make me feel," I uttered finally. Oh, Josie. You *did not*.

His body stilled. His breathing faltered. "Again."

"What?"

"Tell me again," he growled in my ear.

"I'm scared of the way you make me feel," I said louder. "It's not ... it's—"

"*Oui*," was all he muttered. Yes. The fingers at my throat, flattened into a hot palm against my chest. "*Oui*," he said again.

I blinked as my breath stuttered. Okay, this was happening.

CHAPTER TWENTY-EIGHT

My fingers found Xavier's waist, the soft nub of his linen shirt, and then curling into the tense muscle beneath, hard lines that trembled at the contact.

He trembled as I touched him. What sorcery was this?

The darkness of the club and the loud beat of the music seemed to channel all my senses to feel the scent of him. Telling him I was scared of the way he made me feel might have been the most reckless thing I'd ever done. Until I'd started touching him. But I couldn't make my hands stop.

Against my ear, I heard his breathing falter as my fingers moved. Then my name tore through his lips in his French accent. "*Joséphine*," and my insides spontaneously melted.

I turned my face, my mouth finding the rough skin of his jaw. I wanted, no *needed*, him to kiss me.

A tremor snaked through him under my palms.

And slowly, deliberately, our bodies moved and pressed closer.

I breathed calmly, consciously, trying to slow this heady rush that felt like I was plummeting downward. I had to keep my head, but it was almost impossible. I was giddy, flying, and pinned to the ground with lust and panic all at the same time.

His palm slipped up my throat and around to cup my nape. My skin burned.

A rough, denim-covered knee touched mine and pressed slowly, insistently, parting my legs. A hard thigh slipped between mine.

Oh my God.

My body arched, my mouth opened, and a whimper escaped. His mouth was so close, a slight turn of my face pressed against the sublime roughness of his jaw, and I could have it. But his mouth remained stubbornly out of reach. He was going to kiss me, right?

What was this torture? And when had I lost all control of this situation?

The hand against the wall by my head was suddenly an arm, hard as steel around my waist, locking me against him as heat blazed through me.

He growled in what I thought was a French curse, and his hand drew my hair into a tight fist, tilting my face up.

I was trapped. Unable to move.

His eyes in the dark seemed fevered and low-lidded. And then our mouths were there, millimeters apart. We breathed together. My heart hurled itself against my ribcage. My body throbbed and ached. And my hips made a small movement against him beyond my control.

"What about this?" he muttered into my breath, and his hips responded to mine and ground up in a slow roll. God. He was huge. And hard. "Does this scare you even more? We should both be fucking terrified."

Holy shit. I was going to die. Arousal was going to cause an arrhythmia and my heart would stop. It burned through me. And I was literally going to die from lust. How could people experience this and not want it all the time? It was like a hit of the most potent drug there was. There was no way this was normal. Allowed, even. He hadn't even kissed me. I wasn't even naked with him yet, and I'd never been so turned on in my life. It made me want to cry. My eyes burned.

His hips moved again, but they were already meeting mine as I pressed forward.

I bit my lip in an effort not to gasp at the contact. My dress was too thin. His thigh too hard.

His face moved back slightly, his eyes finding mine, burning with intensity, watching me.

He moved again, harder, grinding up. Testing me.

My dress was nothing. The sensations too acute. "Oh, God." The friction was perfect. It was too much. It was too fast. Lightning began flashing white hot as I pressed myself back at him. On him. Small movements, but they were enough. I couldn't stop.

The hand in my hair gripped tighter, he stared at my mouth, and I licked my lips. I wanted his mouth. I'd never needed a kiss as badly as I needed his. I thirsted for it. I tried to reach him but he held me back just out of reach.

"No," he whispered. "Not yet."

"But—" His thigh pressed. My hips rocked. Perhaps people would think we were dancing. "But, it's okay to make ... make me come like this," I choked out. I couldn't breathe. God, I was almost there.

"*Merde*! No." He released me so abruptly, I swayed back against the wall, my legs almost giving out.

But it was too late. The sensations had gathered and built, and the pressure had mounted so high, my brain no longer controlled my body, if it ever had around him. I shattered past the point of no return. It was exquisite. It was maddening. It was shocking. And so very, very ... empty of him.

His mouth dropped open and his hands caught me around the waist as my entire body quaked, and I slipped down the wall.

He cursed again and hauled me against him.

"Oh my God," I whispered, my breath choking out of me. I managed to get my palms between us on his hard chest and pushed away. *Jesus*. Had anyone seen? Shame swamped me, erasing all the incredible sensations that were ebbing away too fast. My face burned. My head whipped left and right. The groups of people in the dark shadows of the upstairs area seemed to be absorbed in their own business. They either hadn't seen us, or people up here were used to giving and demanding discretion. We hadn't kissed, maybe they really did think we were dancing. Jesus. *We hadn't even kissed.*

An aftershock wracked me. I was dizzy. I suddenly wanted to laugh hysterically.

"No one saw," he answered my unspoken question. "But we need to go. Now. That cannot happen again." His tone sounded shocked. Awestruck. Horrified.

No kidding. "I didn't start it," I said, sounding like a petulant child. I was shaken to my core. In literally every way.

He grabbed my elbow and we started toward the stairs. "The fuck you didn't with that dress.

"Are you kidding me, right now?" I wrenched my arm free.

He turned to me, scrubbing a hand down his face. "Please," he said. "Not here. I'm sorry. That was ... inappropriate. I can't think. I was wrong. Can we go?"

We glared at each other.

I folded my arms. "I swear to God, Pascale."

"*Xavier.*"

I ignored him correcting me. "We better be having a normal conversation when we get back to the boat. And no telling me to fuck off again in French."

His brows knitted in confusion. "I didn't tell you to fuck off. When—?"

"You did! That night on the top deck. We were talking, and then you told me something in French that meant—"

He stepped right up into my space, his voice dropping. "I said I wanted to fuck you." He cocked his head. "Not that I wanted you to fuck off. A very important difference."

What was left of my breath was sucked right out of my chest.

He inclined his head at whatever he saw on my face. A lock of dark hair fell across his forehead. "And, yes, I was mad about it. At myself. Not you. And yes, it's crude. But it's true. I can't work. I can't sleep. I can't fucking *think* straight with you around. You are destroying me. And I cannot let that happen. Not for me. Not for Dauphine. That's why I sent that email. Now, unless you want a picture of us arguing in a nightclub splashed over *Voici or Stars* tomorrow morning, I suggest we get out of here."

The mention of the tabloids was like a bucket of ice water. There was no way I wanted to invite that kind of media scrutiny into their lives. Or mine. I snapped my jaw tight, the words he'd said bulleting around my brain, causing maximum damage.

"You leave first," he went on. "I will be a few minutes behind you. Head straight for the quay. Don't stop to talk to anyone."

I nodded. I could do that.

"I'll have Evan meet you at the gate. It has a code." He leaned forward and whispered the number in my ear.

There was no way to remember a gate code for fuck's sake. I hardly knew my own name. I brushed past him. This was all too much. And his words were too much.

"*Joséphine*," he said.

I turned back.

"You look beautiful," he said. His eyes swept over my dress and back to my face. "You are beautiful. I didn't mean to imply otherwise. I'll see you in a few minutes."

The night outside felt different. I felt eyes crawling over me, the breeze like pin pricks on my skin, the sounds jarring. My flip flops smacked on the cobblestones, and I almost fell. I moved to the flatter concrete sidewalks where available, dodging people, and then crossed to the quayside. I followed what Andrea and the guys had done when we passed the security gate and waved like I knew where I was going. They weren't concerned about pedestrians since all the jetties where the mega yachts were had coded gates. Oh shit. I couldn't remember which one it was. The third or fourth jetty? Or was it the fifth one?

Now, if only I could go back and erase the last twenty minutes. I'd known my life would change before I'd gone up the stairs to him at the nightclub, but I hadn't been prepared for this. For him. To discover that he was struggling with his attraction to me as much as I was to him. My brain could barely compute. And I hadn't been prepared for the way I'd fallen apart for him, leaving me feeling like roadkill. I said a prayer that it had been far too dark for anyone to have gotten a clear photo or video. My heart climbed up my throat with nerves and shame.

"Josie." Evan's voice, amplified by the concrete and water reached me right as I was starting to sweat with panic. "You okay?" he asked as I reached the gate where he stood. He opened it before I had to try and remember the code.

"Fine," I said.

"I thought you guys would stay out for a while, have a chance to—"

"I don't want to talk about it."

"He's a good guy—"

"I said I don't want to talk about it. And I don't feel good. Dizzy or something. Maybe I still have that *mally*-thing."

"*Mal de démbarquement?*"

"That. Tell him I've gone to bed. Tell him ... goodbye. How early can we leave in the morning?"

"What? What are you talking about?"

"I know about him asking Tabitha about canceling my contract, okay? I have to resign. I can't work for him." I couldn't work for him when I felt the way I did. Especially not now. Not after what happened. "I can't."

"Josie. Don't do this to him."

"To him? What about me? I don't know what to do here. I

didn't sign up for this." My hysteria grew. "I can't have an affair with my boss," I hissed with a squeak.

"Okay. So you resign. But you don't leave."

"Evan. God. Listen to what you're saying. This ... this is too much for me. Is that why he kept me around and didn't fire me because he was hoping he and I could have a thing?" I cringed as the words came out.

"Fuck, no. Xavier would rather die. Jesus. You have to talk to him. It's not my place. Just please don't leave before you've talked to him."

I knew I'd told him I wanted to talk to him, but my mind was a mess, and I felt crushingly embarrassed by what had just happened. Weak. In danger. Like I'd throw away everything I was if I stayed. I'd become his concubine. His concubine that looked after his daughter. An unpaid escort as well as a child minder. And I'd do it willingly just to feel that all again, this time with him inside me.

No. No. No. And no.

Evan cleared his throat, the look on my face clearly unsettling him.

"Please, Evan. Just promise me that if I do decide to leave, you'll drive me."

He let out a long breath. "Okay."

I nodded and turned to the gangplank.

"Josie?"

"Yeah."

"You've been a wonderful addition to Dauphine's life. And a pleasure to have on the boat. I'm sorry it didn't work out."

I blinked and blew out a wobbly breath, suddenly swamped with emotion. "Me too."

"But I'm not saying goodbye to him for you. You need to do that yourself."

. . .

Downstairs I checked on a sleeping Dauphine, taking a moment to press my lips to her hair. Then I went to my cabin and flung my tiny cross body purse that held my phone and money on the bed. Our shopping bags from earlier were placed neatly by the door. I emptied them and carefully packed the little trinkets among my clothes in my suitcase. I had a quick shower, threw on a long t-shirt, and packed the gold dress. Then I unpacked it again and hung it in the closet. It would always remind me of him, and I couldn't fathom ever wearing it back home. Some things just didn't travel well. Summer flings and little gold clubbing dresses among them. Maybe Andrea would wear it.

I stood still, shifting from foot to foot. Was he back on the boat? He'd moved back up to the master stateroom, so I didn't have to worry about him sleeping in the cabin opposite me. I checked my email, but there was nothing from Tabitha. And no more texts from Meredith. I debated calling her. Especially if I was going to start traveling back tomorrow, but I couldn't face talking about it. I didn't know how to articulate everything that had happened and the things I was feeling. The sound of my name, the way he'd whispered it, was on a loop in my brain, making me feel weak. "*Joséphine.*"

I brushed my teeth, washed my face, and climbed under the duvet, and flicked off the light. Light streamed in from the busy port, and the boat was mostly still.

Closing my eyes, I was immediately back in the darkness of the club and the intensity of his gaze, watching me as I fell apart. The memory of the feeling as I couldn't catch myself falling over the edge had me losing my breath again. Arousal swam through me, squeezing my insides. I cringed. The memory was almost as intense as the reality. I curled to my side and bit my fist.

"*Joséphine.*"

He hadn't meant for us to go that far, I knew. Not in public. Maybe not ever. I couldn't be angry. He was right that we should have both been terrified of our physical attraction. It was the kind of connection that could burn the world down around us. And he couldn't afford for that to happen. Not with a daughter to take care of.

I couldn't either.

I heard when he got back. The low voices of him and Evan. I imagined Evan relaying my message, and I wondered about Xavier's reaction. Would he be disappointed? Angry?

Without thinking I slipped silently from my bed to the door. And for the first night since I'd arrived, I released the catch that held it open and quietly swung it closed.

The latch clicked loudly in the silence, and I laid my palms and forehead on the back of the door, breathing slowly, and counted to ten.

CHAPTER TWENTY-NINE

XAVIER

I stood outside the closed cabin door belonging to my daughter's nanny, staring at the wood and gripping the door frame. It didn't escape my notice that she'd closed it for the first time since she'd arrived. She couldn't have sent a louder message. A message my libido wasn't hearing. My heart was in my throat as I rested my forehead gently against the varnished wood and began to count in an effort to chill the fuck out. "*Un, deux, trois ...*"

She was giving me an out—maybe even forgiving me for crossing the line.

And I was going to respect her closed door.

I *was*.

And yet ... and yet.

I'd revealed my attraction.

And she shared it.

I hadn't experienced this kind of intensity in so long. Had I ever? Perhaps it was so strong because it had been so long since I'd felt *anything*.

Now I knew the feel of her under my hands. Her curves under that ludicrous scrap of material. The quake in her body. Those tiny sounds she made in my ear like the whimpers of a small trapped animal. The heat between her legs. The smell of her. *Christ.* The way she'd fallen apart just from our connection.

I'd just had the most erotic experience of my life, and no one had been naked. I felt like a sixteen-year-old again. As desperate and as clueless as one anyway.

What sounds would she make when I stripped her naked? When I flipped her onto her belly, wrapped my hands in her hair, and drove myself into her body? *Fuck.* My stomach clenched and my head grew light. I shook it to clear the image.

But the image remained. It got dirtier. Sweatier. Would she scream? I wanted to know. I *needed* to know.

I was drowning.

I felt out of control and I didn't like it.

Walk away from the door, I told myself. *Walk the hell away. Nothing good can come from this.*

An uncomfortable thought suddenly slid under my skin, making me want to peel it off. I shuddered. Was this how it started for my father? Wanting to fuck the nannies and unable to leave them alone until he had them? No. This was different. Wasn't it? I wasn't my father. He had nothing to do with this. I was basely and purely attracted to her, dammit. I would have been even if I'd just met her in the street. Or seen her over a video conference, a little voice reminded me.

What if I fired her? Then she wouldn't be working for me. That would solve that at least. Then I could—

You asshole, I raged at myself. What kind of man fires someone so he can sleep with them? My clenched my fingers on the door frame.

"Papa?" Dauphine's voice came from behind me and I jerked upright. "What are you doing, Papa?"

I sucked in a breath and scrubbed my hands down my face. "Um, ah. I was thinking." Shit.

She cocked her head sideways as she let out a yawn.

"I was resting," I amended. "I had a headache. Come on, let's get you back in bed. What are you doing awake?" I gently steered her back to bed. Straightening her duvet, I pulled it open and she crawled in. My throat felt thick, like I'd been caught stealing. At least Dauphine's appearance had doused my raging lust.

"I had a nightmare," she said.

"I'm sorry, sweetheart." I leaned down and kissed her damp forehead. "It was just a dream."

"I dreamed you were sending Josie away. I love her so much, Papa. Do you think she can come with me to *Grand-mère's*? I really want *Mémé* to meet her. I think she will love her like I love her."

Guilt flooded me, and I tried to swallow it down my already closed throat. I tucked in the duvet around my daughter's small body to stall. "Shh. It's time to sleep, okay? We'll talk in the morning." I kissed her head again. "Goodnight, *mon chou*."

"Good night, Papa."

My shoulders slumped as she let me off the hook. I left Dauphine's room and walked straight to the stairwell and went to my stateroom, ripping off my clothes. There was no fucking way I was going to have a tawdry affair with the nanny and sneak around on my own damn boat and try to hide it from my own damn daughter and everyone who worked for me.

I was not my father.

I didn't screw the help.

I flicked off my light and lay under the sheet. Immediately sensations and images assaulted me. I was harder and longer than a circus tentpole. Sleep was impossible.

I finished my morning workout, feeling tired, troubled, and out of sorts. The boat felt ... empty. Or maybe that was me. A ping on my phone told me Evan had taken the Mercedes out of our parking bay in St. Tropez. He would be running some errands and picking up some stuff for me at my office in Sofia Antipolis and meeting us at my mother's later. But Evan often left the boat, and it didn't leave the place feeling like something was missing. My gut felt troubled.

Andrea sat at the table in the galley with a cup and saucer and didn't say anything when I walked in. It was her day off, so I could hardly complain. But it was totally out of character.

"Good morning," I tried, anyway.

She stood and took her coffee to the sink and poured it away. "Is it?" she asked cryptically, and then disappeared down the staff stairwell, passing Chef who was on his way up.

I frowned and made myself an espresso and asked Chef to make me an egg white omelet.

He grunted. "No problem, *Monsieur*," he said in a tone that made me wonder if he would spit in it.

"Great. I'll take it on the top deck in fifteen minutes. Everyone all right this morning?" I asked.

"*Oui*," Chef responded in a decidedly "no," tone.

"Okay, then," I muttered sarcastically. "I'll just go get cleaned up."

I'd just gotten out of the shower when Dauphine came slamming into the room.

"Excuse me," I grumbled. "I'm getting dressed."

Her face was thunderous, and she stamped her foot. "I don't care!" she screamed. "Why did you let her leave?" Her face collapsed into a loud sob and she ran forward to bury her face against my stomach.

"What are you talking about?" I hugged her to me with one hand as I held up my towel with the other.

"It's all your fault!" She pushed off me and began pummeling my stomach. "Ow," she complained. "Your stomach is too hard."

I laughed. "I'm tensing so you don't hurt me."

"Stop laughing. It's not funny. I knew you didn't like her. I knew it. Why, Papa? Why?"

"Christ." I let out a long exhale and tightened my towel firmly around my waist and then padded into the bedroom. I pointed at the couch. "Sit."

My daughter stomped over and sat.

"What are you talking about?"

"Josie has gone away."

My stomach dropped to my toes, and my heart felt like ten tons of concrete. "She ... left?"

That's when I noticed a folded letter crumpled in Dauphine's small fist. She smacked it on my leg. "It's in English. Read it to me."

"Dauphine! Do not speak to me like that," I warned and took the letter.

Instead of her normal chagrin when she knew she'd pushed me too far, I got a look of pure sparks. I sighed and looked at it. *Monsieur Pascale* was written in delicate cursive. She even had beautiful handwriting. "This is to me. So I think I should read it."

"Andrea and Evan both already read it so it's not private."

My eyebrows shot up. "Oh, they did, did they?" I was going to have words with both of them. "Well, you are not reading it. It is addressed to me. Not you. Did she not say goodbye to you?"

"She did." Dauphine nodded dumbly, her tears still streaking hot and fast down her cheeks, her small chin wobbling.

I hugged her closer with one arm.

"I knew you did not like her," Dauphine warbled. "You were mean to her sometimes. You are not mean, Papa. Why were you mean to Josie?"

"I liked her just fine. And I wasn't—" I broke off. "Maybe I was gruff sometimes."

Dauphine dissolved into tears again.

Fuck me. My heart was twisting in my chest at the thought of Josie leaving and at seeing my daughter so distraught.

"I did like her." I winced. "I like her a lot." God, if I could only explain the half of it.

"She's so nice."

"She is." I nodded.

"And kind."

"*Oui.*"

"And smart."

I pinched the bridge of my nose. "*Oui.*"

"And she makes me laugh."

Me too.

"And she teaches me things. And I can tell her my secrets and she doesn't laugh. And she makes me feel safe in the night. And she knows how much I miss *Maman*, and she doesn't say the stupid stuff."

"What stupid stuff?"

"Like everyone says. My teachers, you, the doctor you made me talk to. They all say, it will get better. They say they're sorry. Why are they sorry? Sorry doesn't bring *Maman* back."

"No. It doesn't."

"And ... she's my friend. My *best* friend. If you don't bring her back, I will never speak to you again. Never."

I sucked in my lips. "Okay. Well. Now we're going to sail around to *Cap Ferrat* and you can tell *Mémé* all about it."

"I'll tell *Mémé* you made Josie leave. I heard Evan and Andrea talking. You fired her!"

I squeezed my eyes closed, then let out a long breath. I wanted to deny it, but I'd as good as done it. Firstly, with sending the email a few weeks ago to Tabitha Mackenzie and never retracting it. And secondly by acting like a fucking beast last night. But in the end, her leaving was the best thing for everyone. Maybe not Dauphine, but ... "You'll get over it," I said gently to Dauphine. "You will make new frie—"

"I hate you!" She ran to the door and slammed it behind her.

"I guess I have a tweenager," I muttered, and then stared hard at the letter, my guts twisting.

Three hours later, as the yacht made its way around the headland and into the small bay where my mother's villa was, Dauphine hadn't spoken a single word to me. She'd packed almost all her animals, which told me she was making a statement that she wouldn't be coming back on the boat any time soon. My chest was aching with guilt. Despite the businesslike and light tone of Josie's resignation letter, letting me know what a wonderful time she'd had with Dauphine and that a job opportunity awaited her back home, I couldn't help feeling like I was doing the wrong thing by letting her go and also that she was probably really upset. Did I believe she had a job offer? Certainly, it was possible. Anyone would be a fool not to hire her. But somehow, I knew that wasn't the reason. The reason was all me. And I couldn't help the grudging respect I had for her drawing a line in the sand and leaving in the wake of what had happened between us.

Evan had apparently taken Josie to the train station on the way to Sofia Antipolis, and they'd left early to beat the traffic.

My mother was expecting us for lunch on her terrace, so as soon as Paco dropped anchor, Dauphine and I, and her bags, took the tender to the small concrete jetty where one of my mother's house managers who doubled as security, stood waiting with Jorge, her private secretary. Jorge, skinny and always impeccably dressed, had an effeminate air and was, as far as I could tell, utterly ageless. He'd looked and dressed exactly the same since he'd started in this post over twenty years ago. Arriette used to joke that he was a vampire. My mother's house manager, Albert, was part of a husband and wife team that did everything from groceries to maintenance and lived on the property. Albert *had* aged. But he still looked fit and strong.

I threw the line up to Albert and he tied us up to the heavy iron mooring cleat before giving us a hand up.

"Right on schedule," Jorge praised after we'd all said our greetings. Albert and I grabbed Dauphine's bags and headed up the stone steps cut into the cliff.

My mother waited at the top by the wrought iron gate to her villa. She wore white palazzo pants, a brightly colored tunic top, and pearls at her throat. Her hair, still expensively blonde and shot through with silver, was perfectly wound up in her signature chignon. She threw out her hands in welcome. "Ma petite!" she exclaimed, grabbing my daughter into a tight embrace and then kissing her on each cheek. She set her back and looked her up and down. "You are a treat for these eyes. I've missed you!"

After Dauphine had returned the sentiments, my mother turned to me and kissed me on both cheeks. "Come. Lunch is served."

We wound up to the terrace with a stone balustrade that overlooked the rocky bay below and my yacht anchored a short distance away. Her housekeeper, and Albert's wife, Astrid greeted us and poured us some wine and water.

Dauphine and my mother chattered away as they found their seats. Lunch was smoked salmon, salad, and baguette.

"Please pass your father the breadbasket, dear," my mother addressed Dauphine.

"I'm not speaking to him. He'll have to get it himself."

My mother's eyebrows gently raised. "And what did he do to deserve this?" she asked, giving me the eye.

I should have known we'd have to talk about the nanny again.

"He fired Josie and sent her away. And she did nothing wrong, *Mémé*!"

"And who is Josie?" my mother asked.

"She was the American nanny I hired. She had no experience." I bit into a piece of bread. "It all happened so last minute. And I didn't fire her, she resigned. Unfortunately, Dauphine grew rather fond of her. I'm afraid I didn't realize how much."

"Oh." My mother patted Dauphine's hand sympathetically. "There'll be others."

My daughter sniffed. "She was my *best* friend."

"Did something happen?" my mother asked me.

I took a gulp of rosé wine—larger than I'd intended. It almost went down the wrong way and I coughed. I shook my head. Now she was going to draw conclusions.

"Ah," my mother said, her head cocking to the side as she studied me. I couldn't tell if she was amused, disgusted, or simply empathetic. "That's unfortunate," she said, her mouth curling. Perhaps she thought Josephine had come on to me or something. "Evan should have said something."

"It wasn't *her*. I—" my gaze flicked to Dauphine, then back to my mother. "She just wasn't suited. Wait, what do you mean about Evan?"

"As I said. Unfortunate. Because she's on her way."

This time I did cough. "What?" The little minx had been playing dumb. I scowled at my mother.

"Truly?" Dauphine asked, then looked over my shoulder toward the house. "Josie!" She jumped up and ran past me.

I whipped round, and there were Josephine and Evan being shown out the patio doors by Jorge. Josephine's face was all smiles to see Dauphine, but by the way her skin beat bright red all the way to her ears, I could tell she was embarrassed at being here.

I was fucking embarrassed. I glared at Evan.

"Been trying to call you, Boss. Gave up and called Madame Pascale. The train workers strike has shut down all the lines. She won't get to Paris in time for the flight tonight. I've called Marie Louise to try and get her on tomorrow's flight. The strike should end in a few days, so we'll have better luck later this week."

I'd forgotten about the planned strikes and immediately felt like shit for putting Josephine in this position. Well, even shittier than I'd felt not two minutes ago. And then suspiciously annoyed because he could have easily gotten her on a flight to Paris.

"Come, you must meet Josie," Dauphine said to her grandmother. Then to Josie, "*Mémé* speaks English."

My mother stepped forward and smiled in welcome. "I'm Madame Pascale."

"Josephine Marin," my daughter's ex-nanny responded. "Lovely to meet you. I'm so sorry for the unexpected intrusion."

"Nonsense. You'll join us for lunch. We have plenty. You too, Evan."

"Thank you, Madame. But I will grab a bite with Jorge inside, we need to discuss some security details."

Then he gave me a stony look before turning to go inside. Great. Did everyone who worked for me plan on taking Josie's side over mine?

"As you wish." My mother headed back to the table and motioned to Astrid who was already hurrying out with another set of silverware and glasses for the round table. Astrid moved Dauphine and me apart and put Josephine's place setting right between us. Of course.

"These ridiculous strikes," my mother snapped in French. "It's irresponsible."

"Well," I said as I pulled out my mother's chair to avoid having to do Josie's. "They have a point, if they need more pay."

"I didn't take you for a unionist," she said, placing her napkin back on her lap.

"Well, as a product of a privileged upbringing," I waved my hand at our surrounding, "and knowing how good we have it, I can say that they are right to feel pissed off when the world around them gets more expensive and they never get a salary increase."

"*Bof.*" My mother flicked her wrist and switched to English. "Josie. Are there lots of strikes in America?"

"Um. Not really. I mean there are labor unions for manufacturers but not so much for infrastructure." Her eyes flicked back down to where she was helping herself to salmon and salad. She hadn't looked at me once. And I realized we hadn't even greeted each other either. God, I was a prick. How must she be feeling right now?

"It's an inconvenience here. A strike every time I turn around it seems these days."

"There've always been strikes. It's part of French life," I said, amused at my mother's new sense of principle.

"And you don't mind?" my mother challenged.

"Of course I do." I shrugged. "But I work around the obstacle." I offered the bread basket to Josie and then poured her some wine. I managed it all while still staying focused on addressing my mother so I didn't have to cross gazes with her.

"*Oui*," Dauphine piped up. "Mountains are made to find a way over, not to stop your journey," she parroted my favorite phrase I deployed on her every time she told me she couldn't do something hard, like homework. She turned, her eyes sparkling proudly at me.

"Quite right. You're talking to me again?" I asked her in French

She stuck her tongue out. "Josie is back. I'll stop again if she leaves again."

If she leaves?

I finally chanced a glance at the woman in question, but she was focused on her plate, her cheeks still blazing and had probably just heard her name in our French interaction. I suddenly realized how uncomfortable she must feel being forced to eat a meal with me after the way things were left between us. And it wasn't like *I'd* made her feel welcome and invited her to stay and eat. My mother had done that. Tack on the fact that the last time we'd seen each other, she was orgasming in my arms, and ... shit. I shut the image of that down and grabbed a sip of water.

She had to be feeling humiliated and vulnerable and, if I knew anything about her thus far, angry as shit. Had I taken advantage of her?

My stomach tightened. Even the idea of her angry was turning me on. I was a train wreck.

I glanced back at Dauphine and my mom, only to see my mother's eyes narrowed on me.

I gave her a thin smile. "So, Mother. Tell us about your latest charity project."

The rest of lunch proceeded quickly. I tried to pay attention to my mother's news, and soon lunch was cleared and Dauphine was dragging Josie into the house to give her a tour.

"*Alors*," my mother said as soon as we were alone. "How long were you sleeping with the poor girl before she grew a backbone and left you?"

CHAPTER THIRTY

My mother's eyes pinned me with her signature mix of disapproval and pity.

The very worst look.

I remembered a similar look one night eons ago when I'd slunk back home, easing my father's Porsche back into the garage at three in the morning after stealing it to go on a little joy ride. I'd done it in a bid to impress my friends, and a girl of course, though it had backfired royally when the girl's father had found us, her passenger seat reclined, my hand up his daughter's nightie, and my tongue down her throat. I guess I should have felt lucky we didn't live in the land of guns. But back then, the hot humiliation of being caught was like being held up against a wall by my throat. I drove home, carefully mind you—my earlier bravado and machismo gone, and praying like a dying man that a phone call about my behavior didn't beat me home. Alas, my mother waited in the dark of the garage until I'd thought I was almost home free, the idle engine silenced, the dust cover eased back over the sweaty beast, before she'd flicked on the fluorescent garage light and scared the shit out of me. "You will *not* become your father," she'd growled.

"Don't look at me like that," I said to her now across the lunch table. "I'm not sixteen. And I'm not sleeping with her."

"Xavier. I'm not blind. And I'm not being judgmental. At least not about what you think. There's no wife to cheat on," she bulldozed over the scoffing sound I made.

Ouch.

"But *mon dieu,* Xavier. Did you learn nothing from your father's behavior? You don't sleep with the help. How extremely uncouth. Certainly, not in your position. If a lawsuit were to happen now with everything you've built, or the media got wind of it—well, and not to mention how very awful it would be for Dauphine. So confusing."

"Again. I'm not sleeping with her," I snapped. "That's—that's why I didn't stop her when she resigned." I felt the wince at my admission, even as I tried to remain stoic.

"Ah, but you *wanted* to sleep with her." Trust my mother to just put out there what I was dancing around.

I blew out a breath. For all that I'd been an impossible teenager and was mostly responsible for the silver streaks she paid a fortune to have blended into her salon blonde, we'd also become close after my parents' divorce. Grabbing my glass of rosé, I downed the last sip and filled it back up with water. God knew I needed my wits about me. "Whether I want to or not, it's irrelevant. She's leaving."

"Not until at least tomorrow."

"So what? It's one night. I'm not that weak or desperate. Anyway, let's talk about something else. How long are you here? Without some help for Dauphine, I could really use you this week. It's busy for work, and I hate to always leave her on the boat with the crew."

"I'm here for five days. She can stay for all of them. Then I'm due for a board meeting in Monaco for the Roman Heritage Society. Oh, that reminds me, I must tell Dauphine. They've discovered a shipwreck, almost two thousand years old, right here in town down by the old Roman port. They were digging to put in a car park of all things." Her face twisted in disgust. "Honestly, nothing is sacred with these people. Thank goodness we had the sense to insist on the archeological team being involved in the site preparation. You know they would have just bulldozed right through it, none the wiser. Anyway, I've put it on the agenda. We need to raise funds to preserve the thing and then put it on display. I don't suppose you feel like being a patron again this year?"

"As always simply let me know how big of a check to write and where to send it."

"You're a good son to your *maman*," she said affectionately.

"Yes, and I'm sure it makes you the favorite board member."

She lifted a shoulder in tandem with her eyebrow. "It's not the only reason. But it sure does help. On that note, I'm on the host committee again for the gala. If you could buy a table, I'll find the other nine people."

"Sure. Of course. But no matchmaking."

"Xavier, how am I supposed to invite a spare lady to make up numbers and not hope that you might hit it off? But lucky for you, I have no one in mind right now."

"Good. Don't think too hard on it. I'm not ready."

She gave me a steely look. She'd never gotten on well with Arriette, and I suppose she thought I should be over her faster. "It's been two years—"

"I'm not ready," I reiterated. "Besides, I thought *you* were my date."

She glanced off toward the ocean, the breeze blowing a strand of her perfect chignon free. "I—I may have met someone," she said, her voice getting quiet, unsure.

"Really?"

She smoothed the errant strand back behind her ear, her fingertips pressing it back into her do. "I haven't wanted to say anything. Not until I was sure. Of *my* feelings. But, yes. I think so."

"Anyone I know?"

"I hope not. No offense. But he's ... Italian. I met him through some acquaintances in Monaco. He lives in Sanremo." Sanremo was just a bit farther along the coast across the Italian border. "He's nice. Uncomplicated. *Kind*. He hasn't been here yet."

"Does he know who you are?"

"He knows I have a son."

"Are you hiding your money?" I asked, my disbelief obvious even to my own ears. My mother loved to live a level above everyone else. At least, I thought she did. "And hiding me?"

"Well, look at you." She gestured her hand up and down. "You're a behemoth in business. God knows you didn't get that from your father. I'm happy to take credit. But I think you could perhaps ... intimidate an ordinary man. Not that I'm saying Giuseppe is ordinary. Not in that way. He's remarkable in so many ways ..."

My mother trailed off under my scrutiny.

I pulled down my sunglasses to really study her. "Are you blushing?" I asked.

"Nonsense!" She tossed her napkin at me. "I don't blush."

"You are." I laughed.

"You're laughing. That's good, no? I expected you to be more protective."

"I *am* protective. I'm still going to have him investigated." I tossed a remaining piece of cucumber that was on the edge of my plate into my mouth.

"Okay."

"I was joking. I trust your judgment."

"I don't. Not in matters of the heart. Not after your father." She looked back out to sea.

I inhaled deeply through my nose. That was the thing, wasn't it? One could have all the good judgment and intuition in the world, and be successful in business, but those you chose to give your heart to, who had power to hurt you the most, that was where the Pascale family seemed to have a blind spot.

I was aware of all the dark spaces in my heart. Never more than right now. They'd grown comfortable, those dark spaces. But I suddenly realized, over the last couple of weeks, they'd become like grit in the cracks, broken and irritating. And I definitely wanted to brush them out of the way and let the light in. Looking at my mother, noticing the glow I'd missed when I arrived today, it looked as though she was living again.

I wondered how that felt.

I wondered if I'd ever feel brave enough to try it.

Dauphine came running across the grass to the stone patio, Josie trailing behind her. She'd been smiling at something Dauphine said, but it slipped a bit on seeing me. She refocused on my mother instead. God, why did I feel so shitty about her?

"You have a beautiful home," Josephine addressed my mother. "Belle Epoque Architecture?"

"That's right. Built in the 1880s. You like history?"

"I do. And architecture, of course."

"Josie is an architect!" Dauphine said with pride.

My mother looked at me, her eyebrows raised again before turning back to our visitor. "My goodness! My son didn't tell me."

"No," Josephine said, her eyes trained solely on my mother. "I don't suppose he did. I've been qualified for several years now. Some of my favorite courses in college were the architectural influences in this part of France. I also have some French heritage. It's always been on my list to come here in person."

"Well, I know you're headed home but hopefully you were able to see some of the architecture along the coast. It spans from before Roman times."

"Um, no. I wasn't able to see that much actually. Not up close anyway." Her eyes flicked to mine briefly. "I'll have to plan a trip here some other time."

"What? Have you been a prisoner on that boat?" my mother admonished.

She's the fucking nanny, I wanted to protest. *That's where her job is. Was.* Whatever.

Josephine gave a small, tight laugh. And while I knew I wasn't required to provide day trips and excursions for people I hired to look after my daughter, I was suddenly filled with guilt and remorse. Which felt like just about the stupidest thing ever. My mother was leading Josie to the table to sit and motioning for Astrid to bring us coffee after she'd cleared the table. "So," she was saying, "how does an architect find herself working as a nanny for my grumpy son?"

"Excuse me," I said. "I have to check in with Evan and make a few calls." I leaned down and kissed my mother on the cheek and turned my back, striding toward the patio doors that led inside. I didn't need to sit there while I was needled passive aggressively by my own mother. "Do you have to leave right away?" I heard her ask Josie. "Perhaps you could stay in the area a few more days. You know I'm on several preservation committees, and I can point you toward some wonderful areas to visit."

A few days? She was here for one more night. That was it. The sooner she left, the sooner I could forget the feel of her under my hands and get her out of my head.

"Fuck," I muttered as I entered the cool interior of the house, my shoes squeaking slightly on the marble floor.

"Was just coming to find you," said Evan, rounding the corner. "Should have just followed the cursing. What's up your bum?"

"I hate that expression."

"I know. That's why I use it."

"Are you seriously telling me you couldn't figure out a way to get her to Paris for her flight? We have a helicopter for fuck's sake."

"I'm going to pretend you didn't ask me that. You insult me."

I blew out a breath and scrubbed my face. "Sorry. But she must have felt like shit having to come here and face me after ... after ..."

Evan cocked his head sideways. "After she found out you wanted to have her replaced, against my advice by the way? Or after what happened last night at the club?"

My head whipped up and I narrowed my eyes. "What about last night? What did she tell you?"

He raised his palm and smirked. "Jeez. Calm down. I was guessing. She didn't tell me anything. But you just did."

"Nothing happened."

"Right."

"It didn't," I insisted. Not really. Except it did, didn't it? She fell apart under my hands, and the memory of it even now made my legs weak. "Anyway, it's none of your business."

"But you wanted something more to happen?"

"Evan. I know you're my friend and I tell you a lot of shit. But if you don't stop talking right now, we're going to have to explain to my mother why your teeth are on the floor."

He reached out and placed a hand on my shoulder. "I'll take my chances. You have a few days. Even if I can get her to Paris, I can't get her on a flight until Thursday at least. Maybe you'll change your mind by then."

"Thursday?" My stomach flipped. That was four nights of having her close without Dauphine as a buffer. "She can stay here. Or on the boat and *I* can stay here, or a hotel in Nice, or—"

"That bad, huh?"

I was being ridiculous. Seriously, what was I going to do? Barge into her cabin like a caveman and ravish her because I couldn't control myself? No. I wasn't a beast. At least, not normally. But also, she closed that door on me last night before we had a chance to talk about what happened. That told me there was little chance she'd give me another chance. Yes, she was beautiful and sweet with my daughter, and smart, and fun. So were a lot of people. I could handle a few days, just she and I if she stayed on the boat. I'd probably hardly ever see her either. I had work to do, same as always. She could eat with the crew. I'd have meals on shore. In fact, she could go and do her architectural sightseeing or whatever during the day. "Whatever," I said and shrugged. "It's no big deal. So she stays until Thursday. And maybe we should get her to Paris by Wednesday so there's no problem getting her to her flight."

One less night with her on the boat.

"How very thoughtful of you," Evan deadpanned.

I lifted my shoulders again with casual nonchalance, though the tightening of my insides told me I was trying to fool myself as well as Evan. "All right then," I said. "Let's go say goodbye to Dauphine and pick up the stowaway."

I turned toward the exit, and Evan stopped me, a hand on my arm. "X, wait. You deserve some happiness. Or at least some good sex. Not one of us will judge you for it."

"I don't need your permission," I snapped and shrugged him off. He put his palms up and continued walking.

But there was no way to lie to myself. The idea of being alone with Josephine Marin on a boat, with the tension between us, was making me feel all sorts of things again. Physical things. Things I'd long denied myself. Now that it was decided she was staying an extra few days, a thrill pricked at me—that little tingle I got when I could tell I was on to something at work that was going to be a game-changer. A challenge that would be worth it. Maybe Evan was right. Maybe I did just need to get laid. Josie was no longer working for me, so I could mentally cross that off my list of reservations. If, *if*, we had a fling it would have a built-in expiration date, which was about the only way I could contemplate it.

And the chemistry between us told me it was going to be good.

Oh so, so good.

I stepped back as Evan opened the patio door and discreetly adjusted myself. Okay. I took a breath. I was going to do this. If she still wanted me, that was. My heart thundered with terror.

We walked outside, and I shaded my eyes in the afternoon sun.

"Great news," my mother called. "Since you no longer need her on the boat, Josephine is going to stay *here* with me for a few weeks and help me with my foundation work. Isn't that wonderful? You don't mind, do you?"

CHAPTER THIRTY-ONE

JOSIE

Xavier Pascale had mastered the art of keeping his face expressionless, so I had no idea what effect his mother's pronouncement had on him. If any.

Dauphine came back to the table from throwing some leftover bread to the seagulls over the balustrade just in time to hear Madame Pascale's pronouncement. "You will stay with me here?" she asked me, her eyes big and round. "But why you will not come back on the boat? Now you will stay here in France and not be with me?" Her tone told me she found this incomprehensible. Her eyes grew watery, her chin wobbling. "Papa told me he likes you very much. So now you do not have to go."

"Um, I ..." I looked helplessly toward Xavier.

Say something, I wanted to yell at him.

"Perhaps we'll share Josephine," Madame Pascale soothed her granddaughter. "She can help me *and* help your papa? Besides, I will be in and out of town." She looked at her son, and I glanced between them. Evan, of course, was biting back a grin. It was as if he found Xavier's predicament funny.

God, this was torture. I'd started the day off feeling like I wasn't wanted at all. It wasn't like he'd come and knocked on my door last night. Nor even called when he'd found out I left with Evan. Talk about a knock to my ego. And now I had the distinct feeling they were fighting over me, and Xavier Pascale had suddenly been outmaneuvered by his mother, which didn't make any sense.

He didn't want me to stay.

Did he?

The idea of being able to stay a few weeks in this gorgeous home and explore and learn about the local architecture of the region was sorely tempting and a lovely consolation prize. Added to which it would mean I still got to see Dauphine a while longer before heading home. Madame and I had had a wonderful discussion, and she was full of information I wanted to mine. She seemed to find me equally enchanting.

Also a sad truth? If Xavier wanted me back on his boat, and in his proximity, there was about a zero percent chance I'd say no. Which made me rather pathetic.

Xavier Pascale cleared his throat and seemed to come to his senses. He turned and had a quiet conference with Evan, which left Evan looking bemused.

"Dauphine, you enjoy a few days with your *grand-mère*," Xavier said, turning back to us. "I have business to attend to in Corsica tomorrow. I was going to suggest that Josephine may want to come along to view the architecture since she has a few days free, and then I'd bring her back the day after tomorrow."

I opened my mouth then closed it.

Evan had his head cocked to the side, looking at his boss but quickly shook it off. "Yes," he suddenly said and turned to me. "Andrea told me you had read up on Corsican architecture, and I was just coming out to tell you we can't get you on a flight until Thursday. It seems like a good idea."

"Well, you can rebook that flight for a few weeks' time," Madame Pascale said. "Better yet, just leave it open." Then she turned to me. "I wish I could accompany you and be a tour guide. But please feel free to return here after your trip and be my guest, unless you'll be staying on with Xavier and Dauphine." She smiled. But it was the kind of gleeful smile that had me digging my teeth into my lip with suspicion. Go to Corsica with Xavier on the boat? Without Dauphine as a buffer? Or as a reason to even be there?

"*Pouah!*" said Dauphine with her nose turned up. "It takes so long to get there. I'm glad I get to stay here with *Mémé*." She wrapped her arms around my neck. "I will miss you!"

Xavier sat next to his mother and leaned in to tell her something.

I ran my hand up Dauphine's back and returned her embrace. "Me too, sweetheart." When Dauphine pulled away, I looked up at Evan. "Sure. Tagging along to see Corsica sounds great. And thoughtful. I appreciate you including me."

Evan looked awkwardly at Xavier, then smiled thinly. "No problem. Well, you should get going if you're going to get there by dinner. Paco is all fueled and ready to go. I'm sure he wants to get ahead of the fog that's predicted here for tomorrow."

"We're heading there now?"

"Xavier has an appointment in *Calvi* tomorrow."

"Oh, ah, of course." I turned to Dauphine. "You have fun, little mermaid. I'll see you when I get back."

"When will that be?" Madame Pascale shaded her eyes as she asked her son.

"We'll probably spend tomorrow night there and head back the day after, and then I have business in *Cannes*." I knew Cannes, where the famous film festival happened every year, was between where we were now and St Tropez. I was dying to see it.

Madame proceeded to give me a list of places to see both in *Calvi* and in *Cannes*, including the infamous Carlton Hotel. "You know it is rumored that was where Grace Kelly met Prince Rainier of Monaco? Such a romantic and tragic tale." She placed a hand on her chest.

"Okay, Mother," said Pascale after a bit. "Let's get this show on the road."

I bit my lip. "Um. Madame, would you mind terribly if we swapped contact information in case I have questions and need more advice about where to go and what to see?"

Madame Pascale beamed. *"Bien sûr!* Of course."

A few minutes later after saying our goodbyes to Xavier's mother and daughter, Evan and Xavier helped carry my bags down the cliff stairs to the tender. I wasn't sure how I felt about being on that tiny boat with my suitcases. It seemed a bit precarious.

"Your mother is absolutely charming, I love her," I told my ex-boss in an attempt to make conversation and keep my mind off the idea of potentially capsizing. My anxiety had spiked, and it probably wasn't a hundred percent due to worrying about falling overboard, and instead to do with this strange turn of events.

"You sound surprised," he said as he handed my bags down into the boat.

"Have you met you?" It was out before I could check myself.

Evan barked a laugh at his boss' expense that echoed across the rocky cliff and bounced back at us off the water. "Sorry," he apologized quickly.

Xavier gave Evan a glare and said something rapidly in French, to which Evan smirked and shrugged, then stepped carefully into the tender. Evan handed me down, and Xavier held out his hand for my other. I grasped it—warm and firm—then stepped gingerly into the shallow vessel.

"I'll see you in a couple of days." Evan gave a salute, then set off up the stairs, grinning.

"Wait. You're not coming?" I called after him.

"He has business to attend for me," Xavier said, his mouth straightened with concentration as he pulled the choke on the tender.

"Oh. Okay. So, you don't need a bodyguard in Corsica?" I asked skeptically.

He raised an eyebrow and gunned the engine. "It's an unplanned visit."

"But didn't you say you had a lunch meeting? How is that unplanned?" I raised my voice to be heard.

"You ask a lot of questions."

I texted Andrea. *Don't be surprised. I'm headed back to the boat.*

The afternoon sun was warm on my bare arms and simple white t-shirt. Though the water was slightly rough. A wind had picked up. I slipped my sunglasses over my eyes and focused on our traverse across the water, holding tight to the plastic handles on the tender sides.

Another yacht was in the small bay. A hulking gray monolith that could be military looking if not for the spacecraft-style design elements of curves and reflective glass and the two bikini-clad girls dancing to unheard music on the sun deck. A Russian flag flew from the aft deck. I glanced toward Xavier to see if he'd noticed, but he looked directly ahead to our destination.

"I'm confused," I blurted, trying to be heard over the wind.

"What about?" He steered toward the stern of our anchored boat.

"Your change of heart. I'd have thought you'd have been glad to be rid of me. You almost were. What changed?"

He slowed the engine and pointed at the rope coiled by my feet. I'd seen him and Evan do this enough times that I knew he needed me to grab the cleat of the swim deck and tie us on when we neared.

I grabbed the rope and focused on getting us secured. "I

mean, I know Evan thought it would be nice for me to see Corsica, but you didn't need to go along with it."

"It was *my* idea. Not his."

My head snapped up to his, but I could read nothing behind his sunglasses.

"Josie! You're back." Paco came down the steps, effectively ending the chance of getting any kind of elaboration to that odd statement.

I returned the captain's grin because it was impossible not to. "Captain Paco. The fates didn't want me to leave today. There was a strike and I couldn't get the train."

"I heard." Paco took my baggage up to the steps, and Rod grabbed it and took it inside. I stood in the breeze on the main deck as Paco and Xavier stowed the tender. Above us, on the cliff, I searched out the balustrade of Madame Pascale's home and saw her and Dauphine standing at the railing, looking tiny from this distance. I waved. They waved back.

Xavier soon joined me, and we stood silently next to each other as the engine turned over and Paco pulled the anchor, then maneuvered us out of the bay. A cool wind had picked up, and goosebumps erupted over my bare arms. Or perhaps it was standing next to this man.

He made a soft throat clearing as if he was about to speak. When nothing came, I turned to him, waiting, as he looked out over the water.

"I don't know what I am to you right now," I began. "I mean, are you still my boss? Am I your guest?"

His face swung to mine, blue eyes as complex as the ocean beneath us, fixing on me "What do you want to be?"

My heart bobbed into my throat, shutting off air.

He shook his head suddenly. "I'm sorry, I—" cutting himself off. He winced his eyes shut. "I know you must be angry—"

My head bobbed back in surprise. "Angry? Why would I be angry?" That was the last emotion I was feeling.

"After last night. After what I did. And then you left. I didn't stop you. I let you leave, thinking ..." he trailed off.

"Thinking?" I prompted.

"I'm sorry. I don't think I can do this. I thought I could. I ..."

Panic flared. But for exactly what I couldn't tell. I simply acknowledged the feeling, knowing I'd have to examine it later. "Can't do what?" I asked.

"I don't know." He swallowed and looked away.

Clarity hit me. He'd asked me back on the boat. Without Dauphine. My stomach flipped. And I knew.

He looked vulnerable all of a sudden. As rich and powerful as he was, he was also just a man. He was attracted to me. He'd admitted it. *Shown* me, actually, in no uncertain terms. To be fair, he probably just wanted to get laid. But my relationship with his daughter had complicated things.

And now, for whatever reason, he didn't know whether or how to proceed. That was what he meant by not being able to do this.

My heart seemed to swell into a heavy beating beast as I contemplated whether to help him bridge the gap between us. I'd be risking my heart, I knew it. It might be just lust for him, but I was attached. To both him and his daughter. Shit. It would hurt when I left. It had fucking killed me this morning, saying goodbye to Dauphine and leaving without seeing Xavier one last time. Maybe it was better to leave us uncomplicated.

"You asked what I wanted to be to you," I said quietly. I watched his hands on the railing clench tight. "How about ..." God. This was it. Make the first move, or not. After the way I'd felt leaving this morning, after what we'd shared last night. No. I couldn't do it again. "How about ... just ... friends."

He inhaled through his nose and closed his eyes.

"Of course." Then he pushed away from the railing. His hand went up to his hair, and he turned away, then back. Then he turned away a final time and went inside.

His departure was like a flame being snuffed out. I was a chicken shit.

I stood there, breathing in the wind, and wondering if I'd made a mistake. I examined my hesitancy. And his. Yes, Dauphine complicated things. I wasn't a stranger. I had attachments to his family. But I also wasn't living here. I was going home, if not on Thursday, then in a few weeks. No one was asking for a commitment. I wasn't. I couldn't. I had a life to head back to. A career to rebuild. This wasn't some fairytale. Who said we couldn't just enjoy each other for a couple of days? Get it out of our systems and move on? For a second I let my tightly-reined in mind go and conjured the image of him and me together.

The chemistry of last night.

No clothes between us.

My belly went into free-fall, and I struggled to catch myself and turn off the images.

I drew a shaky breath and replayed our conversation. I'd offered simple friendship. *Of course,* he'd said. Had his reaction been relief or disappointment? This was Xavier Pascale we were talking about. He was the kind of man who went after what he wanted. He hadn't gotten to where he was in life by not going for it. He didn't wait for permission. He created opportunity. So what was different about this situation? Didn't he trust me to not make it emotional?

Was I capable, at this stage, of not making it emotional?

I shook my head at myself. Of course. I wore my emotions out there for everyone to see. And he could see mine. He saw my love for Dauphine. I wasn't "no-strings-attached" material. That was definitely dangerous territory for a single dad. Certainly one in his position. I sighed. This was probably for the best. I tried to hang onto the sense I'd talked into myself last night when I'd gone back to my room and made the decision to leave. The attraction between us was dangerous. It felt reckless. And if it felt like that to me, it must feel worse to him. He had so much to lose. A little girl's heart to break for one.

We rounded the headland, and the low afternoon sun washed gold across the deck and over the water. The yacht cut through the waves, undulating gently. I cast my mind to what I'd read about Corsica to distract myself.

Behind me the door opened again. Andrea probably. I turned around.

It was Xavier. He stopped and we stared at each other.

The sun was blazing fire around his dark hair, and his eyes glowed, spitting gold in the afternoon light. He was so beautiful, it actually hurt my chest.

Then he came toward me and kept coming until he was inches away.

My breath froze.

His arms caging me against the railing. "Friends," he said gruffly.

Prickles swept up my arms.

God, he was so close. "If ... if that's what you want," I managed. He smelled so good—cedar wood and ocean salt melted into my senses. "I mean, you could always use another. Friend, I mean." I was trying to tease, but coming off all wrong.

He shook his head. And then he swayed forward and his forehead came down on mine. "But that's not what I want. *Je veux* ... I want your mouth." He paused and I inhaled his breath. "This delicious but annoying mouth. I want to devour it. I want to invade it. That might be a little bit more than friends, *non?*"

I had no legs. I was just fizzy air and lust melting against him.

His hand threaded into my hair, loosening the messy bun, and then twisting the locks around his hand. He mumbled some things in French, then English. Things about my hair. And if Meredith's translating skills were to be believed, something about my ass. I was delirious.

He could be telling me he was about to dangle me over the side, and I wouldn't bat an eye.

He tilted my face up.

My mouth watered.

His eyes burned. "And what do *you* want?" he rasped.

I didn't hesitate. I couldn't. Not now. "You," I managed soundlessly. "Please. Please kiss me."

And then sweet merciful angels, his lips closed the distance and slanted across mine.

I grabbed onto his shoulders and the lapels of his cotton shirt. Was this really happening?

He was kissing me. Finally.

God, was he kissing me.

His lips were heavenly—soft in touch, hard with intent—the stubble of his chin sending shots of flames cascading over my skin and into my belly—burning me from the inside out. His lips nipped and tasted. They pulled, and then opened. His tongue slipped against mine.

Oh God.

A moan filled my ears. Mine. Then his.

I opened to him. Tasting him. My body flooded with heat. My tongue pressed forward, needing more, and he took. Deeply. His hands held my head, they tipped my jaw, his thumb opened my mouth farther like he couldn't get enough, and his tongue delved in. Caressing. Drinking. I was being devoured and I loved it.

This was what kissing was supposed to be. I'd never be able to kiss ever again and not compare. I felt it throughout every cell of my body as it burned its way through, leaving ashes in its wake.

Jesus. It was heady. Addictive. I was ravenous. I didn't think I could get enough of this. Of him. Of his mouth. I never wanted to stop. My breathing was so erratic I was getting lightheaded. But I didn't care if I passed out kissing him.

I shouldn't be doing this, I thought from the dark recesses of my mind. We shouldn't. But I could only press forward, wanting more.

My fingertips slipped up his neck and into his hair. My nails raked across his scalp and a tremor rolled down through his entire body. The body that was now against mine, hard for me, pressing against my belly.

Please never let it stop.

His mouth slowed, and I whimpered my disappointment. His lips slid to my jaw, the heavy sound of his breathing brushing the lobe of my ear and down my neck, reminding me I actually had skin, and a body, and I was standing on something solid and not floating like a mess of inflamed and combustible atoms somewhere.

"*Mon dieu,*" he said, then went on in French.

I wanted to know the meaning of his words, but just the music of them, breathy and desperate, sliding over my skin was enough.

He inhaled, sliding his nose up the side of my neck, making my entire body shudder.

And suddenly a throat cleared next to us. We both leapt apart, Xavier turning to face the railing and me to face the visitor, my breath laboring in my lungs.

Andrea stood there, her eyes wide, cheeks bright pink and trying to bite down on a gleeful smile.

CHAPTER THIRTY-TWO

I covered my mouth with my fingertips. With Xavier turned away and facing out to sea, Andrea and I shared a moment. Her mouth dropped open in exaggerated surprise. Then mouthed, "Oh my God!"

My expression, I hope, communicated, "*I know! Crazy right?*"

She cleared her throat again, trying to school her expression. "So sorry to interrupt, Monsieur Pascale, "she said, her voice a little squeaky. "But Captain said we might hit some rough water soon and wanted to make sure everyone was, ahem, not about to go overboard."

My cheeks burned and I pressed my cool fingertips against them to calm down. I had a leprechaun in my belly leaping up and down, flinging rainbow confetti all over the place.

Xavier turned, his expression nonchalant. Bored even. God, I really needed to know how he did that thing where he wiped his expression clear as a poker player. "Thank you, Andrea. Please tell Chef we'll need only aperitifs this evening before docking in *Calvi*. Mademoiselle Marin and I will be having dinner in the port."

"We will?" I whipped to face him.

His eyes locked with mine, and I saw only a flicker of warmth and familiarity I'd seen moments before our kiss. But it was enough to know the man I'd kissed was still in there and apparently not regretting it.

I turned to Andrea, lifting a shoulder and fighting a grin. "We will."

I had a feeling he'd presented it as a *fait accompli* to reduce the chance of my refusal. As if I would. But it made my heart swell to think that was something he was worried about. I vowed to peel back that gruff exterior in the next couple of days and understand the man underneath.

"Very well." Andrea returned my grin and spun on her heel, leaving a scowly Xavier on the deck.

"You don't like them knowing, do you?" I asked, still unable to scour the giddy grin from my face.

"There's not much the crew of this boat doesn't know, but *oui*, I have never forced them to witness my social life."

My grin finally eased. "I'm assuming by social life you mean the women you date?"

Xavier's hand came up and a thumb pressed a smoothing caress between my eyebrows. "Interesting," he mused with a slight chuckle. *"Un peu jalouse?"*

Jealous? I wasn't answering that.

His grin spread wide.

I blinked. "When you smile at me like that, my heart skips a beat," I told him.

He stared at me, his expression growing serious again. I began to second guess my honesty. God, this was definitely supposed to be just a fling, and here I was having conversations with myself about finding the man inside and talking out loud to him about my heart. "I'm sorry," I mumbled. "It was just a turn of phrase." I shook my head, my cheeks warming again, but this time with embarrassment.

"Protect it."

"What?"

"Your heart. Please. I cannot be responsible for it."

My throat clogged. "Of course, I—"

"I cannot ... I am not able to give more. You must forgive me." He shook his head, his French accent stronger with his distress. "We have two nights and two days. Just two. Just us. Give them to me?" he asked.

My breathing stuttered, and heat in my belly grew. "Is that a request or a demand?"

"You can say no."

"God, no."

His expression dropped. "No?"

"No! I mean yes. Yes. *Oui*. Two days." My face blazed. "Two nights." I blew out a breath and a self-conscious chuckle. "Good to see how disappointed you were though." I sucked my lips between my teeth.

He growled. God. That sound. Then he brushed a finger across my bottom lip and down my throat to hook into my t-shirt. He tugged me close and pressed his lips to mine. It wasn't enough and he'd already pulled back. "We don't have to do anything you don't want to," he murmured. "You can change your mind at any time. You don't owe me anything."

God, I appreciated him saying that so much. I smiled. "You can change your mind too, but I'd really hate it if you did."

He gazed down at me, his blue eyes honing in on my mouth again. "I have to try to get some work done now," he said. "*Mon dieu, aide-moi*. But meet me for champagne on the top deck at seven?"

I licked my lips and nodded, my hand reaching for the railing as the boat dipped into another wave. "What did you just say in French?"

"*Mon dieu, aide-moi*. It means, God, help me. Because I don't know how I'm going to concentrate on work. It's been impossible for weeks already."

"Huh." I grinned, pleased. "Oh, by the way. How do you say ass in French?"

"Ass?"

"Yeah, like 'he's got a fine ass.'"

"I do?"

"Shut up. You know you do. Soo, what is it? What's the word in French?"

"*Cul.*"

I laughed. "Meredith was right."

"Meredith?"

"My best friend back home. I heard you talking to Evan, and she said you were talking about my ass."

He chuckled out a breath and scrubbed a hand down his face. "Nobody can keep a secret on a boat."

"So you were?"

"Talking about your ass?" He winked, and his hand slipped down behind me and grabbed a handful, bringing me hard against his body.

I squeaked.

"Yes. Do you have a problem with that?"

Oh yes. This playful Xavier was a really nice surprise. "I'd rather not have my anatomy discussed by the boys in the locker room." I feigned annoyance, even while the heat of his hand burned through me.

He laughed, teeth gleaming and eyes crinkling, making my heart rate triple.

"*D'accord.* I'll only discuss your ass with you." He leaned forward and pressed a lingering kiss on my lips.

My hand left the railing, and I clutched the lapels of his shirt. The boat dipped again, and my stomach whooshed. It broke the kiss.

He scowled, looking out to sea. "It's getting rough. Do you get seasick?"

"I haven't before today. But then again, I don't really like boats, so I have little experience to know if I will." I shrugged and brushed a strand of hair that suddenly blew across my face. The wind had picked up.

"You like *my* boat."

I lifted a shoulder. "It's okay."

His eyes narrowed.

"But I like *you*," I added. "And Dauphine. And everyone who works for you. Well, I guess you're right. I like *your* boat. Anyway, you better go and get that work done before I climb you like the jungle gym at my favorite playground." I reluctantly let go of his shirt and smoothed it out.

He frowned, a smirk playing around his mouth. "Jungle gym? Is that some American thing? It sounds kinky."

I laughed, loving that he could actually joke with me after the rather gruff demeanor he'd worn since I arrived.

"All right." He stepped away, his palms up. "I'm going. I have to rearrange all the meetings I blew off to stay in Corsica for two nights. The water is getting *very* rough. If you feel sick, ask Chef for ginger tea. Look out at the horizon. Or come find me."

"I will." I nodded, processing what he'd just said. He may have needed to go to Corsica tomorrow, but his decision to stay an extra night was made with me in mind.

I dug my teeth into my bottom lip to fight the grin.

As soon as he ducked inside I turned and dragged in a lungful of sea air. I replayed the last hour, and with it giddy anticipation swirled. Two nights. My skin prickled with lust. I pressed my thighs together to quench the deep ache that had settled between them. I knew what this was. A two-day affair. That was it. I had no doubt it would be highly sexed and searingly hot. I just hoped my heart could handle it when he turned it off after time was up. Would I be able to do the same? And then what? Should I go home? Or did I take up his mother's offer to stay on a few weeks with her? That seemed far more of an intimate prospect now than it had before everything had changed between me and her son. I chewed my lip. I should call Meredith for advice. But somehow I didn't want to. Telling someone, even Meredith, that I was planning to have a two-day affair with my ex-boss on his yacht made it feel ... sordid somehow. And of course, there was Tabitha. I didn't know what this situation fell into. Technically, I was no longer his employee. But it was still Tabitha's reputation that could be affected if people knew about us. They wouldn't care about the technicalities. They would still only see that Xavier Pascale boned his daughter's nanny.

Land was a distant blur and around us was nothing but wide-open ocean. A shiver rippled through me. Now that Xavier wasn't out here distracting me, and we were farthest from land than we'd ever been, the reasons for my dislike of boats came back strong. My stomach lurched queasily.

I left the railing and made my way inside to find some ginger tea.

In the galley, Chef was wedged into the banquette reading a newspaper spread across the table.

"I think I'm getting seasick. I held the edge of the table. Do you have some ginger tea I can make?"

"We have sachets, but best bet is I make you some fresh. Also, we have anti-nausea meds if it gets bad, and," he pulled himself out of the booth and grabbed a basket from a small bottom shelf, "we also have these. Acupressure cuffs. They actually work great." He held up a package of rubber bracelets in light blue.

"Really?" I asked skeptically.

"Really." He tossed them to me. "They press on the *Nei Kuan* acupressure point on the inner wrist. My ex-wife swears by them. And she's right about most things."

I felt an odd smile cross my face.

He waved a hand. "Yep. I'm the sad sack who's still in love with his ex-wife. Sue me. Anyway, I'd go for ginger tea and a bracelet over the anti-nausea meds because the meds will knock you right out. And from what I understand you have ... a date, tonight?" He gave me a look with an eyebrow raised.

"Can't keep a secret on a boat," I mumbled. Clearly word had spread fast. Thanks, Andrea. "Is it weird? I mean is everyone okay with this ... development?" What did I call it? A two-day booty call with their boss?

"It shouldn't matter to you what we think." He rummaged around in the vegetable basket, pulling out some ginger.

I lifted a shoulder. "But—"

"We're happy for him. Trust me. Just ... be careful."

"Careful?" It was sweet of Chef to worry about me getting hurt. The boat leaned and my stomach complained. I pulled a bracelet off the card display backing and put it on. Better than nothing.

"He's been hurt," Chef went on. "He's closed off. I know it because I ... well, I recognize it. If he opens up to you, please take it for the gift it is and don't take advantage."

My eyebrows pressed together. "Of course." I swallowed, feeling silly now I'd thought his concern was for me. And almost guilty, even though I'd done nothing wrong.

Chef sliced the ginger root. "You know that song 'Graceland?' By Paul Simon?"

"Vaguely."

He turned on the fancy coffee maker and set out a mug to fill with hot water.

He held up a bottle and inspected the label. "Honey?"

"Uh. Sure. Thank you."

"Lavender honey."

"Oh, I love that. I thought we were out."

"I hid some. It's from the farm next to Pascale's estate. The place is famous for lavender. You should see it all in bloom. Bloody gorgeous. Anyway, you ever listened to the lyrics?" He dumped the chopped ginger and a generous spoonful of honey into a mug.

"To 'Graceland'?"

"Yeah. It's about this dad, a single dad, and his kid. On a road trip. And he says ..." He looked up in thought. "Hmm. I'll butcher it. Hot water's ready." He put the mug under the hot water spout and filled it. Then he gave it a stir, took out the spoon and put a saucer over the top. "Needs to steep. It says something like when you've lost love, it's like everyone can see inside your heart and see that you're blown apart."

I swallowed, my throat thick.

"Anyway, it's true," Chef went on. "It feels like everyone can see your damage, so you brick that hole closed in whatever way you can, with whatever you can. And it's not always a sound structure, if you know what I mean."

"I—"

"Hey you," Andrea said, hurrying up the stairs. "Just got the downstairs bedding out of the dryer and remade the beds." Then she looked at me and back at Chef and back at me.

"He knows about Xavier," I said. "You told him?"

"I had to, remember? You have a dinner date in *Calvi* tonight."

"Oh yeah." I grinned. "Sorry, my mind is a bit ..."

"Mushy? I bet. That was some kiss."

"It was, wasn't it?" I tried to rein in my smile by biting down on my bottom lip. But there was a bubble of giddiness inside that wouldn't be kept down.

Chef whistled and waved a hand as he tidied up his small work station.

"I have a few minutes," Andrea said. "You want to go sit in the living room? Or we can go down to your old cabin. It's actually better to be lower in the boat on days like this, the rocking isn't so bad."

Chef took the saucer off the top of the mug. Steam rose. "Have at it."

'Thank you so much," I told him, accepting the mug gratefully.

"Just remember what I said, yeah? Be careful."

"I will."

I followed Andrea downstairs. My bags were back in my room. "You said my *old* cabin, and it gave me an odd feeling like it was assumed I'd be in Mr. Pascale's room tonight."

"Okay, two things," Andrea said, flopping down on the edge of my bed. "One, yes, you probably will, oh my God. But I thought you might need your own space if you want it."

"You're a good friend."

"I know we're new friends, but yeah, I feel the same way."

"I miss Tabitha and Meredith. But having you here totally makes up for it. Except that you are bearing witness to my ex-boss' booty call. Which is not ideal."

"Nah. I already chatted with the crew. Paco will stay on, but the rest of us, if it's okay with Mr. P, are going to take two nights off in *Calvi*."

My belly flipped, and I was filled with gratitude. "That's nice of everyone."

"It's gorgeous there. And a bit different from the usual hoity-toity Riviera scene. And a break is welcome, trust me."

"You said two things when we got down here? One I should have my own cabin. And two?" I took a careful sip of the hot ginger tea I was carrying and set it down on the dresser on a leather mat designed to stop things sliding off the varnished surface.

"Ah right. Two, you're not going to call him Mister Pascale now that, you know, you're ...?" She waggled an eyebrow.

I chuckled. "Right. I guess I'm supposed to call him Xavier. I mean he's asked me to before. It feels weird."

"Not weirder than," she lowered her voice to a sultry moan, "'oh, yes, Mister Pascale—'"

"Stop!" I hissed and snorted a shocked laugh. "Shhh, oh my God." I gave Andrea a playful slap on her arm, my cheeks burning. "Gross. Makes it sound like he's my teacher or something." I shuddered, still laughing but also feeling more than seasick. An image of Tabitha's disapproving expression floated through my brain.

"Sorry." She bit her lip in an exaggerated grimace. "Out of line."

"A bit. I know, it's weird. Look." I sobered and took another careful sip of tea. "This feels ... scary. And real. Nothing has even happened yet. Nothing irreversible, anyway. Apart from that kiss, which was, phew. But the chances of someone being hurt are high. *Me.* I'll just say it. The chances of *me* being hurt are high." I blew out a measured breath. "I'm in over my head. So I'm probably going to play things close to my chest. I feel as if sharing it will make it more real, you know? Please don't ... please don't be offended."

She reached out and squeezed my hand. "I understand. You can trust me. I'm fond of you both. And to be honest, I've wondered how I'd feel if this happened. My allegiance is to him because of history and circumstance. But I'm rooting for you. I'm rooting for you both."

"It's only two days."

"It's more."

"Please." My stomach clenched. Seasickness or panic? "Please don't say that. I can't ... I can't afford to think that." Xavier's warning to protect my heart came back to me. "I'll be disappointed. And I shouldn't be. I have a life to go back to. This can't be more."

She reached out and took my hand again. "Keep an open mind, yeah? And maybe an open heart?"

"It's too open already. This relationship feels like juggling with newly sharpened knives."

"And I take it you're not a good juggler."

"No shit." I took another larger drink of ginger tea. My stomach was feeling better already.

"All right. Well, I'll leave you to relax. I'm going to pack a few things up and call ahead to get a hotel room. A whole day off tomorrow where I know no one and have nothing to do? I'm salivating."

"Do you all go and stay in the same hotel when you have time off the boat?"

"Not if I can help it. Besides, Rod and Chef both know people in *Calvi* I think, so I'm sure they'll get themselves sorted. We should be there in a couple of hours."

We stood and I gave her a hug. "Thank you," I said. "Enjoy your time off. And be safe."

"Always."

After Andrea left, I partially unpacked and finished my cup. I didn't want to assume I'd be spending the whole night with Xavier. And even if I did, I wasn't planning on hanging out amongst his dead wife's things. Just the thought that her memories surrounded him up there was enough to make me wonder for the millionth time what the hell I was doing. Despite the rocking, I decided to take a quick a shower, shaved everywhere that needed it, debated my bikini area and decided the risk of messing up, cutting myself, or ingrown hairs in the wrong place was guidance enough to simply neaten things up.

The boat lurched suddenly, then fell, my stomach hollowing to zero gravity. I crashed against the shower wall and slipped across the fiber glass. I caught myself on the sink, but not before I left a razor cut on my thigh. The plastic razor clattered to the floor, along with everything on the counter. I belatedly registered the sound of things in the room falling, my suitcase I'd left on the edge of the bed. Probably the tea cup. Just how big of a wave had we encountered and would there be another? My stomach tightened in fear and then rebelled. Shit.

I heaved, just making it to the toilet bowl before retching up my insides.

Naked, wet, and shivering, my stomach emptied, my eyes watering and throat burning. Reaching up, I grabbed a white fluffy towel, pulling it down to cover myself as I sat back, trying to catch my breath. My heart pounded. My toiletries bag had fallen beside me. I weakly squirted some toothpaste on my brush and reached behind me for water from the still running shower. I cleaned my mouth as best I could to get rid of the taste and spat in the toilet again and flushed it.

Ah shit. This was no good. I'd taken the nausea bracelet off to shower, and it now lay beside me on the floor. I pathetically worked it back on. I'd vomited up my strength it seemed. I leaned my head back on the shower stall and closed my eyes, my body feeling weak. The boat rocked again and my equilibrium went with it. I groaned, willing myself not to vomit again. There was nothing left.

"Josephine?"

I cracked an eye just as Xavier came barreling around the corner of the bathroom. "*Merde!*" he yelled. Then he was on me, trying to pick me up.

"I'm okay," I protested weakly.

He babbled in French, turning the shower off, and in a display of super human strength managed to pick me up off the bathroom floor, slippery and wet and tangled in a towel. And underneath naked. Very naked.

"I'm okay. I'm okay." Embarrassment crawled over my skin as he lay me down against the pillows on the bed with jerky panicked movements.

His hands raced over me. Then indicated the blood on the towel. "You're bleeding. Where are you hurt?"

I grabbed at the towel and tried to keep myself covered. The cut was high on my thigh. It was a graze really, now that the blood had been wiped clean.

"I'm fine. It's nothing. The razor slipped." I gestured to the area of the cut.

His hand shoved the towel aside and revealed the tiny wound for a second, before he then covered his face with his other hand. "*Pardon.* I'm sorry. I panicked. I thought you were hurt."

"I slipped. Then I got sick. But I'm okay."

"You are seasick?"

I nodded and took a moment to take stock of my body. "I think so. But I feel better now." Nothing like being rescued by a hunky Frenchman to sort your body's priorities out. Seasick? What? Short memory.

"You feel better?" he asked.

I nodded.

He squeezed his eyes shut, his shoulders slumping. "I thought—"

My fingers reached out and curved around his upper arm and squeezed. I wanted to sit up and hold him to me—to offer him comfort from whatever nightmare had just surfaced in his memories.

I became aware of his hand on my thigh and of my towel, which was in danger of baring all. I couldn't see how much of me below the waist was revealed. My attention fell to the air cooling the damp skin between my legs and realized it was probably a lot. He was being a gentleman not to look, and I forced myself not to try and cover up lest I draw more attention. Nonetheless, heat pooled, my skin prickling.

Then his eyes trailed downward. A dark lock of hair fell across is forehead. His lips parted as a soft puff of air escaped, then closed as he gave a heavy swallow.

He looked up at me and caught my gaze, his denim eyes burning, pupils large, worry ebbing. His expression—so desperate, so vulnerable, so hungry—made my breath falter. Then he glanced at the open door.

He got up, his hand sliding off my skin, and went to the door. He closed it.

It shut with a soft snick. And he slowly turned the catch, locking us in.

"Is this okay?" he rasped.

I didn't think he was asking about the closed door this time.

CHAPTER THIRTY-THREE

XAVIER

I turned the latch, heart pounding. My skin was too tight for the energy and want pounding through my body. I counted to five, waiting for the sensation to pass, with no luck. I'd been on a call when the boat tipped forty-five degrees with no warning and plummeted into the space left by a fast rolling wave. There were crashes and thumps as everything that wasn't secured went flying in every room of the boat, including my laptop. Then I'd heard Rod shouting and cold fear clutched me. I'd left Josie at the railing.

Laptop forgotten and phone abandoned, I'd bolted to the deck. No Josie. Rod was clipped on, trying to rescue a chair that had flipped from the upper deck and caught by a leg on the lower railing. I should help, but— "Josie?" I yelled. Rod's eyes widened and he shook his head. Logical thought reasoned with panic as I went through the galley and was directed by Chef who was on hands and knees in a mess of plates down to Josie's cabin. Thank fuck.

But then I swear, my fucking heart stopped. Reason was over-taken, and all I saw was Arriette in a crumpled heap, unconscious. Bleeding where she'd hit her head. Evening dress covered in vomit.

I screamed a curse, my throat tight with remembered fear.

No. This was Josie. *Mon dieu*. She was hurt but she blinked up at me. And God, I hoped I hadn't scared her.

But now, minutes later, my heart was still thumping and adrenaline was ebbing, being replaced by something else. I was at the door, locking us in. I squeezed my fists tight. I wanted her so bad. I turned from the door just as she whispered my name. "Xavier."

It was foreign from her lips.

She reached a hand up. "Come here."

I stalked to the end of the bed. She was as I'd left her, towel barely covering anything. Smooth, long legs, the skin like silk where I'd touched her inner thigh. Her hair was a damp mess, cascading over the pillow.

She shifted her legs apart a fraction and the towel rose. A noise broke free from my throat.

"Did you just growl at me?" she asked, her voice breathy. "You sound like a wolf."

I pressed a knee on the bed. "I was going to take you to dinner first," I said.

"Except it looks like I'll be your dinner." The corner of her luscious mouth tilted up as I chuckled in response, grateful for the tension valve release. Her expression grew serious again. "This is just sex, right? Two days. So let's throw the rules out the window."

Swallowing down an unexpected denial in my throat and leaving her just sex question unanswered, my fingers began unbut-toning the cuffs of my linen shirt. One wrist, then the other. She was right. Just sex. Two days. It was what I wanted. What I needed. After that things could return to the way they were before. The buttons worked loose down my front, and then I peeled the shirt off.

Josie licked her lips, her cheeks flushing pink as her gaze trailed downward.

Guided by the want in her eyes, I flicked the buttons on my shorts open and peeled them down my legs.

There was no hiding what I wanted from her now. I was hard and aching, my briefs no match against the strain.

She sat up and the towel fell to her waist, revealing her milky white tan-lined breasts tipped with mouthwatering tan nipples that puckered and hardened under my gaze. *Jesus.*

"I have to warn you," I choked out as burning need dragged down my spine, and then held me in its steel grip. I was light-headed. "It's been a while. And I've been fantasizing about those." Among other things.

Grinning and leaning forward, she tucked her legs behind her and took a hands-and-knees move toward me.

My gaze raced down her pale lower back to the curve of her ass where the suntan line ended in lily white soft globes. "*Ton cul* ..." I breathed.

"My ass?" she asked, amused, reaching for my cock. Her eyes glowed luminous in the soft glow of afternoon light that flooded through the tiny window. God, she was beautiful.

I nodded just as she palmed me through the fabric, and my head fell back on a groan of unsatisfying relief. Grabbing her hand as she dipped inside the band of my underwear, I stopped her. "I wasn't joking. It's been a while." As much as I wanted that mouth of hers on me, my hands sifted into her hair and I leaned down to kiss her. She tasted like mint toothpaste and need. Her hands clasped my wrists where I held her head. She rose up, still kissing me and wrapped her arms around me, holding me close. Her tits mashed up against my bare chest, the sensation of being skin to skin setting off goosebumps.

"You feel so good," she whispered against my mouth.

"*Oui*," I agreed.

Wrapping my hand around her waist, I picked her up and moved her back up the bed. Then I stood and took off my last remaining piece of clothing. My eyes feasted on her naked form. Her breasts glowed soft and pale against the rest of her tanned skin. "I don't know where to begin." I crawled over her, dipping down to lick around the stiff peak of her nipple before drawing it into my mouth.

She arched and whimpered, fingers scraping through my hair to hold me to her breast. "There's good."

I sucked and licked and an urgency grew as her body responded. I switched sides, giving the same attention, loving how she arched and writhed, her leg hooking onto mine. I sucked harder, teeth nipping, hands kneading, testing how much she wanted. She cried out, a guttural sound, and her lower body surged toward me, seeking relief. Her hands gripped my hair in a tight fist that bordered on painful. Good. She was no fragile flower. Because my need was so brutal right now I was likely to break her. I should take my time, I knew I should. But she'd been invading my mind and body for weeks, and my greed for her knew no bounds now that it was unleashed.

I left her breasts, sucking and biting and devouring her skin as I moved down. It would leave marks, and somehow, I wanted to. I shoved her legs apart, and she spread them wide. I boldly lifted one, pressing it back, opening her fully. My dick strained against the bedding and towel beneath me, urging me to rut with the bed just to get some relief. Especially as I inhaled the scent of her, lightly soapy from her shower laced with the faint musk of her arousal that glistened in her pink folds and on her tight little entrance.

My mouth watered, and lightening zipped down to my balls. I was in danger of coming too soon. I tried to slow myself down. I breathed her in and snuck my tongue out for a quick taste, licking up the seam of her.

She gasped and thrust her hips up. I did it again. Softly. Torturing us both, trying to slow my heart down that pounded so heavily she could probably feel the vibration through the bed. I began whispering things between each little taste. French things. Things I knew she couldn't understand, and it made me feel free. Things about her body only, to remind myself this was just sex. I told her how gorgeous her pussy was. How pink. How perfect. How sweet. How wet. How she'd bewitched me. With my fingers, I spread her open, tasting deeper. Telling her how I couldn't wait to be inside her. I tested her with my fingers, the burning heat closing over my skin. The sounds she made like last night in the club, sang through my senses. I closed my whole mouth over her, tongue probing, and ending with a deep suck on her clit.

She thrashed and her legs tensed. "Xavier," she whimpered. "Please."

I did it again, and again, honed in on that sweet spot with rhythmic persistence. Inside her, my finger pressed upward.

"God. Yes." Her hands held my head, her body hardly moving it was coiled so tightly. "Right there. Please don't stop." She didn't even breathe. It was like every single part of her stopped and coiled as I worked her.

She waited.

She strained.

And then she snapped. Her back arched, her hips bucked. I felt the shudder as it rolled down her body, and a cry tore through her and reverberated around the room. The sound slammed into my gut, imprinting itself on my memory. I took one last taste, her body quaking in an aftershock, then gave a small kiss to the little cut that had left a blood smear on her thigh. My hips were grinding into the bed. God. I needed her so bad.

Fuck. "I have no protection," I gritted out. And it wouldn't take long. There was no chance I'd be able to withdraw.

She pulled me up to her, hands running over my face, caressing me, running through my air. "I'm on the pill. I'm religious about it. I'm clean. I—are you?" Her eyes were warm, luminous, watery, questioning.

"It's been more than two years—" the confession was out before I stopped myself. *Fuck*. I squeezed my eyes closed against the fleeting look that crossed her Josie's flushed face. I didn't need her pity. "Yes, I'm clean." I gave the answer I should have before.

"Then come inside me," she whispered, her thumb pad running over my closed eyelids. "No rules, remember?"

Jesus. I never did that. Never. But ...

I couldn't look at her. I didn't want to. Didn't want her to see something I didn't want to show. Eyes still closed, I sought her lips, kissing her languidly, letting her taste herself on my tongue. Then I pushed upward on my arms, and slipping a hand under her back, roughly flipped her over to her belly.

She squeaked.

Now my eyes opened and I feasted on her. Her ass. I grabbed the soft skin. Pushed, kneaded. I dug my fingers into the skin and ran my hand up her spine and fisted it in her hair. "No rules. Two days. Just sex," I said.

Her neck arched and she gasped.

I let her hair go and pulled her hips up. My cock was ready to yell at me. I closed my hand around the hard length and found her wetness, running my tip up and down. Readying it. "That's all it can be."

"I-I know."

I notched my cock at her entrance and warred with my patience. My stomach clenched as I willed the wave of lust to recede just a bit. The boat rocked, and I slipped farther inside. I groaned and tried to stop myself. I wasn't ready for it to be over, but she rocked back, taking more and letting out a soft cry.

I gritted my teeth, stopping myself from pressing in farther, hands digging into her hips. She was so tight. So hot. "God, I love your body," I breathed, my eyes greedily taking in the view. As my gaze slipped up her back past her shoulder, it snagged on hers. Her face lay sideways, pressed to the pillow, cheek flushed, mouth slightly parted, eyes soft—watching me. Her fingers clutched the bedding, knuckles white.

"No rules," she whispered. "Just let go. I've got you."

"Ah, fuck," I breathed. "I know." I slipped forward. "I know you do." And she did. That was the most terrifying thing. I switched to French. "I'm worried I won't be able to stop wanting you," I admitted, knowing she couldn't understand, and hissed as the feel of her enclosing the length of me swept up my body and down my legs. Pressure grew in the base of my spine. I gritted my teeth and withdrew, letting myself slam forward. Knowing, *trusting*, that she could take it. Again. Again. Words fell from my lips, but I wasn't cognizant of them. It took all my effort to try and stave off the explosion that was building. She'd started by meeting my thrusts, and now she braced herself, back arched, offering what I was taking. Sweat beaded and pooled, rolling down my temple and splashing on her skin. She still watched me. I could feel it. I didn't want to look. I didn't want to. I thrust harder, punishing myself for my weakness. Punishing her for it. Making myself wait. Finding the last of my control from the very depths of me. Admitting to myself I was taking advantage of her attraction to me. Of her love for my daughter. And hating myself for it. Because I knew if I opened my eyes, hers would be telling me it wasn't just sex, and it wasn't just two days, and there *were* rules. And we were going to smash everything down. Including ourselves.

My eyes snapped open. She was there to meet me with everything I already knew. In that moment, something inside me snapped free. I wished we were face to face, my body cradled in hers as she took me in. I sank down, my chest to her back, hands slipping down her arms and entwining with her fingers, the need for connection overriding every argument I had. I rocked my hips, rolling out and thrusting back in. The angle had changed and she cried out and pressed back, seeking more. I buried my face in her hair and let her surround me. I was giving in to it. Giving in to her. Letting go like she asked.

I couldn't.

I shouldn't.

This way lay utter destruction. I'd been down this road before, and I wouldn't go again.

But my body wouldn't listen.

Josie's soft cries and needy whimpers held me captive. Her fingers gripped mine as if I could be her salvation. Or she could be mine.

I had to pull back. I had to. Too late, the sensations boiled over, catapulting through me, dragging destruction and absolution in their wake. "*Joséphine*." Her name tore through my lips as I let go, pouring myself out and leaving myself like a broken dam and utterly exposed.

CHAPTER THIRTY-FOUR

JOSIE

The weight of Xavier—hot, hard, and sweaty—pressed me into the bed, teasing out the last of my orgasm. It was soft and rolling on the heels of his. Not near the explosiveness of the first one he'd given me with his mouth and hands, but no less intense. Deeper even. The feel of his breath in my hair and on the back of my neck underscored the utter rawness of the moment.

I squeezed my eyes shut, feeling the moisture that had gathered and the rise of emotion that had just choked my throat closed. Shit. Crying after sex? This was new. I tried to even my breath before I sobbed and utterly embarrassed myself.

Something had just happened. I'd felt it, experienced it as it happened to him, and whatever it was had tried to grab at my heart, trying to take me with it. What I'd just experienced had felt a lot less like fucking and a lot more like making love. Maybe it was a French thing. Perhaps this was what lovers were like in France. Soul sex, with lots of emotion, but able to simply switch it off. If this was his idea of just sex, two days, no rules, I was in so much trouble.

His hand brushed my hair off my damp shoulder and his lips, soft and prickly with his stubble, pressed against my skin.

I cringed into the pillow, fighting off the way his tenderness was confusing me, the way it made my eyes leak. He'd been rough in the beginning. Rougher than I was used to. Rough in a way I didn't know I liked, apparently. The memory of it prickled over my skin. The roughness kept things simple.

He needed to get up right now and clean up and leave me here. I was inside out.

He eased off me. Out of me. I was bereft. "*Dis moi* ..." he whispered.

I wondered if he knew how often he'd slipped into French with me in the last little while. I wondered what it meant that he wasn't mentally checking himself. Listening to him mumbling in French, saying God knew what, as he did those wicked things to my body, was just about the most erotic thing I'd experienced. I groaned and squeezed my thighs together. I wanted him again. This was bad.

His fingers caressed my hair again. I turned my face away so he was on my other side. I wasn't ready to look at him yet.

"Josie," he murmured. "Are you okay? Tell me ... did I hurt you? I'm sorry." His lips found my shoulder, my spine. Warmth moved through me.

I answered him in my head. *Not yet. But you will. Of that I'm sure.*

Counting silently to three, I turned my face to the side he was on, trusting that the pillow had wiped away all traces of my strange emotional reaction. He lay, temple propped up on one hand, looking down at me. His blue eyes were soft and dark. Intense.

The boat's rocking had calmed, though the engine still chugged, propelling us on our journey. "That was an interesting way of taking my mind off feeling seasick," I mumbled and watched as his mouth spread into an open smile.

I closed my eyes. "Don't do that," I grumbled.

"What? Smile at you?"

"Mmm."

"Are you so grumpy?" He trailed fingers down my spine to the curve of my ass. He was obsessed. My flesh rose with sparks in his wake. "I would have thought you'd be relaxed now."

"Like you are?" I mused. "You're like a tamed panther."

"But still hungry. Hungry animals are never tame." His palm circled over one mound, then the other before his fingers trailed up the crease.

I was awash with aching heat again. I couldn't believe I could be turned on again so quickly. Nor that *he'd* gone so long without sex. With the stamina and skill he had, it was a crime to deny the world so long. Ugh. Jealousy thumped me in the gut quick and hard.

His hand left my back and his finger pressed between my eyebrows. "What happens in your mind when you get this line?" he asked.

"I don't want to talk about it."

"Tell me."

"It's stupid."

He waited, gaze on mine.

"I was jealous of all the other women. Past and future."

Seconds passed and then he flopped onto his back, both arms coming up to cradle his head, and he stared at the ceiling, letting out a long breath.

A chill swept over me at the loss of his heat.

Me and my big mouth. I shifted, wincing at the feel of him, sticky and slick between my legs. I'd never let anyone do that. It was so intimate. And dangerous, to be honest. But this man could get anything from me. I should clean up. Finding the towel from my earlier shower bunched up beneath me, I made a move to get up and cover myself.

His hand shot out to my arm. "*Reste un moment.*" He shook his head. "Stay? *S'il te plaît.*"

I grabbed the edge of the duvet and pulled it over me and rolled toward him.

"Don't hide."

"I'm not. I'm cold."

Looking down his body, I saw he was hard again.

He followed my gaze and chuckled. "Lots of time to make up for," he joked.

"Surely ... surely there have been others. Other chances?"

His smile faded. "My life has been all about Dauphine and work. I know it seems easy from the outside. Other single parents have it harder. After all, I have a mother and plenty of staff who want to look after her. But," he paused, brow furrowing as if thinking how to express himself, "I was scared. Scared I would not be a good father, and Dauphine would grow up being like her mother. I ... keep looking for the signs. I don't ... it doesn't seem like much else is important. I have my work. Many new challenges. Inventions. And I have my daughter." He seemed to be dancing around something else. "I don't like the way people—women—look at me. Like I'm broken. Tragic. A man to be pitied. Or saved. I *am* broken. I'm very aware of it. But it's *my* business. And I don't like to see it in people's faces. In women's eyes who think they can fix me. I don't want to be fixed. I don't trust easily. Not after Arriette. And I want to keep it that way. It's safer. It works. But that hasn't left me many opportunities. Women always want more."

Wow. *Offense taken.* I was equally awash with pity for him and sadness for us. And hurt. As if he was rejecting me personally. "Everyone should want more. Everyone should expect more."

He didn't offer a response.

It was one thing knowing the man you were with had walls.

Quite another being personally told about their height, their breadth, and their utter impenetrability. And being warned not to try and scale them lest I be just another one of *those* women. Was I supposed to feel lucky he picked me? I was on the verge of feeling used. Irritation bubbled. No. I knew what the parameters were. What he wanted them to be anyway. I swallowed the bitter sting of rejection and hopelessness that rose up in me and tried to lighten the mood. "And now I get to be the lucky girl who enjoys this for a few days?" I reached out and closed my hand around his girth. Internally, I winced at the superficiality of my response. It sounded hollow to my own ears. But what other response could I have?

He took my hand off him and brought it to his mouth and kissed the back. Then he sat up. "I should let you get ready. We'll be docking soon."

Whatever connection we'd found during our lovemaking, because I was sure that's what it had turned into, had waned in the aftermath. "Sure," I said. "Are we still going to dinner?" I asked because, frankly, after what he'd just said, it would be anyone's guess. I mean, wasn't taking a woman you were sleeping with out for dinner kind of romantic? A way to get closer? Talk more? Have her ending up wanting more?

"Yes, of course," he said.

Right. "What should I wear?"

"Not that gold thing, or we won't leave the boat," he said with a laugh as he pulled his shirt from the floor and punched his arms through.

"I don't have a lot to choose from, but I'll figure something out."

He stood and pulled on his underwear and shorts, fastening the button. He raked his one hand through his dark hair, then leaned forward and gave me a quick kiss. "You always look beautiful. Wear whatever you like." Then he winked and unlocked the door and left.

I flopped back on the bed.

Good God, I was confused.

We docked in a small port near *Calvi* that sat nestled beneath plunging cliffs and a huge, ancient wall. "Whoa," I breathed out the word, shading my eyes as we approached. The sun was setting across the ocean behind me, to the west, and the light danced up the limestone cliffs, making the rocks look like pure gold.

Andrea joined me on the bow. "You look lovely," she said.

I'd embellished my simple black linen dress with a gorgeous jade green and turquoise necklace I'd bought with Andrea in St. Tropez. It brought out my eyes, if I did say so myself. I'd borne witness to that in the bathroom mirror after my second shower of the afternoon. "Thank you."

"You doing all right?" she asked.

"Stratospheric," I replied.

She gave a grim smile. "That's a long way to fall."

"No kidding." I squeezed her hand. "Enjoy your time off."

"You too." She winked and left me.

I was due to join Xavier on the top deck, but I needed a second to myself in the fresh air. We were the only boat on the one long pier, side-to, probably due to the depth of the water available and the size of the boat.

Rod was moving around, tying things up and righting things that had fallen. He and Chef would probably take a while to get off the boat. Andrea must have pulled the long straw because I watched her stride down the concrete jetty away from us to the gate at the end.

After my shower, I'd checked my email again for any responses to my applications. There was an email from my mom. She'd sent me her contact's name at the Charleston Historic Foundation. I was pretty sure I might even enjoy working there for a while. Certainly, the contacts in the city would be invaluable. People who valued what I did and weren't out to make the fastest buck. Then after that, who knew? I hadn't heard from anyone else, but for some reason, I still resisted applying.

I'd keep in touch with Madame too, regardless of what happened here with Xavier. There was a lot I could learn from her that could be useful in my work back in Charleston. Besides, I genuinely liked her. So to that end, I'd messaged her and formally asked her if I could stay and shadow her for a week before returning home while I figured out my next steps. I'd give myself one more week in France, not the weeks she'd suggested, so I could minimize my run-ins with Xavier after this two-day affair was over. She responded immediately with the word: *Absolument*! Which I took to mean absolutely in French.

Then she sent a cute selfie of her and Dauphine holding up some freshly painted nails. Dauphine's were tangerine with little mermaid stickers, and Madame's were a classy French manicure. I'd meant to ask Andrea what the French called a French manicure. Was it even French? French fries weren't French, so what did I know?

A whistle drew my attention.

I looked up.

Xavier was casually leaning over the top deck rail, looking like an Instagram model. "Will you be joining me?" he asked and let out his megawatt smile that was like a shock starter to my chest.

Everything inside me was a complicated mess of emotion. I was upset at the things he'd said as we lay on my bed after the most incredible sexual experience of my life. Annoyed and hurt. And I had no right to be.

Why couldn't I shut off my stupid brain and heart and just enjoy this for what it was? He'd made no promises. I didn't want promises anyway. And just because it had been earth shattering for me, didn't mean his sexual experiences weren't always like that for him.

But, shit.

I was crazy about him. Beyond attracted to him. Addicted to getting him to laugh or smile. And the way he'd cried out my name as he climaxed? Well, that would haunt me soul deep for pretty much ever. And his daughter. God, I loved her. And I was enamored with the way *he* loved her. I had to make sure I didn't confuse my love for his family with being in love with *him*. But I feared the waters were already too muddy.

My stomach, utterly empty, growled.

"Well?" he asked

"On my way."

CHAPTER THIRTY-FIVE

Xavier Pascale and I walked side by side from the concrete jetty down to the small fishermen's huts that clustered in a semi-circle around the port. The heat of the day hadn't ebbed fully yet, but a breeze had picked up.

"So, this is *Calvi*?" I asked.

"Yes. The quieter part of the port. More fishing boats, less tourists. And I know it better here."

"And is this where your meeting is tomorrow?"

He stopped at the entrance of a narrow cobblestone alley we were about to head down and pointed up past the hulking citadel wall that overlooked the rocky bay and to the top of the cliff. "Up there."

I raised my eyebrows. "Okay."

He gave me a side grin. "Long story. Maybe I'll tell you over dinner." His hand brushed against mine and then he clasped it, his fingers sliding between mine.

My belly gave a flutter of pleasure. The handholding came just in time as my flip flop caught on a cobblestone and I tripped. Or maybe it was the distraction of the action. "Whoa!"

His arm wrapped around my back as he caught me. "*Attention.* I'm sorry. Be careful. Are you okay?"

I winced and wiggled my foot. "Tripping in flip flops is painful."

"Will you be all right?" he asked, his brow furrowed in concern. He dropped to his haunches and inspected my foot before his fingers trailed up the back of my calf. "The restaurant is not far. Perhaps a foot massage when we get back tonight?"

I knocked on his forehead. "Are you real?"

"Ah." He rubbed his head, a funny smile on his face.

"Sorry. It wasn't too hard, was it?" Who was this sweet, smiley, playful man?

"For this head? No."

"Ha." I wiggled my toes. "I think I'm fine, let's go. Did I mention how hungry I am?"

He stood and leaned forward. What was he—? Oh. His lips pressed against mine. Soft, persuasive, and over too quickly. He stepped back.

My eyes fluttered open. "What was that for?"

He suddenly looked unsure.

"I'm sorry. That was just unexpected." I glanced around. "And the handholding too. I thought you were worried about people seeing you. Recognizing you?" Pedestrians went on their way around us. Shopkeepers were hanging out on their front steps smoking and chatting to each other, paying us no attention. It reminded me of St. Tropez, but less flashy, and less groups of perfectly dressed catalog families.

"No one knows I'm here. And people here don't care who I am. Mostly. It's not like on the mainland."

"Wait, we're not technically in France? I feel so stupid. I mean, I thought we were. I just didn't think. No one wanted to see my passport."

He chuckled and brought my hand up to his mouth for a

quick kiss before tugging us on our way. "Actually, this *is* France. Though, it wasn't always. And Paco sent our passports ahead to the port master."

"Oh?"

"You never used to have to do that. But we have so many refugees in Mediterranean waters from the genocide in Syria. Every country is feeling the strain, so officials are checking credentials of boats. And I have a good relationship with people here."

"You do? How come?"

"Another long story."

"Hmm. What language do locals speak here? French?"

He guided me up a hill and into a small stair-filled alley that was only a person wide, and guided me ahead of him. "Yes. But many consider themselves Corsican, not French. They have their own customs." His voiced floated up from behind me as I climbed. "Their own dialect in many areas. Lots of Italian influence. It's actually closer to Italy. France stole it from the Genoese in the 1700s. And *putain*, it's really hard to be going up the stairs with your ass in front of me."

I whipped around, catching him staring at the area in question. He raised his eyes to mine guiltily, his palms up and a smirk playing around his sexy mouth.

"Well, now I can't walk ahead of you."

"Yes, you can."

"No. I can't." I folded my arms.

He bit back a smile. "That's a pity. I'll just enjoy it later." He took my hand. "Besides, we're here. Though a bit early." We'd stopped outside a green door. It was set into a chipped stucco wall, the paint of the door peeling to reveal ancient wood. All of a sudden it swung open and a small man came out and propped it open and laid a blackboard against the wall. Then he looked up, and his graying face morphed into a wide tobacco-stained grin. "*Pasqual-ey!*" he erupted.

The tiny man rushed forward, grabbing Xavier by the hand and slapping his back in a half embrace. It was returned with big smiles. "Cristo." Xavier greeted the small man who came up to his elbow, if that.

"*Venga! Venga!*" the man named Cristo commanded excitedly. Xavier and I were ushered inside. Before my eyes had adjusted there was a fuss of greetings from staff in the kitchen and a few introductions made to waiters Xavier didn't know. It was clear they were being told royalty had arrived. I hung back, letting Xavier catch up. He was responding in what sounded like rough Italian, definitely not French. And then slowly everyone kind of remembered I was there. I swallowed as one by one curious eyes turned to me. Xavier stepped back and took my hand. He held it up and said something, something, *Joséphine*.

There were some collective sighs and sounds of surprise. "Josephine," a few people whispered reverently. Okay. Weird. And then my other hand was grasped and kissed and shaken and we were ushered to a couple of stools by an upturned wine barrel. "Um?" I asked. "What just happened? Are you like a secret soccer star or something?"

He chuckled, then scratched his nose. "Something like that. Not the soccer thing. I wish. Not that I was half bad in school."

"And? Get there faster," I encouraged.

He looked around. "They are getting us a table ready upstairs," he evaded.

"And this is another long story?"

"*Oui.*"

"We might need more than one dinner together," I quipped.

"We might," he said, his voice dropping to a low octave and his eyes finding mine in the dim interior light.

Suddenly we were presented with a basket of bread, olives, and an earthen-ware jar of red wine with two short stubby glasses. For some reason I'd pegged Xavier Pascale as someone who frequented extremely fancy places. This was as basic and as charming and as real as they came. "You are full of surprises," I told him and bit into a tart and firm green olive, the smooth bitter flavor zinging across my tongue. Heaven. I moaned. "We don't get olives like this back home. Wow."

He smiled enigmatically and took a sip of red wine.

Cristo arrived back at the table saying something to Xavier that sounded like the words *ten minutes* in my European Romance language basic understanding. Then he poured some dark green yellow oil onto a saucer and kissed the tips of his fingers. He was so sweet.

"Our table upstairs will be ready in ten minutes," Xavier told me. "He said he wants it to be perfect."

"Mind if I gorge myself on bread and olive oil in the meantime?"

He tilted the basket toward me in offering. I took a piece of bread, tore a chunk off, and set it to absorb the oil Cristo had just poured. "Thank you."

"I love watching you eat. I have from the very first night. It became impossible. I had to avoid it whenever I was able. I had to tell Andrea you needed to eat with the crew."

I paused mid-chew, staring at him. "Uh." Oops. Mouthful. I hastily chewed and swallowed. Too big. I took a swig of wine and almost choked. Nice. Someone tells you he likes watching you eat, and you decide at that moment to choke on your food. Great.

"But save some room. Cristo's food is the best. Simple. But the best. And there's a *lot* of it."

I had one more bite of bread, and then reluctantly put it aside and took a sip from my glass. "The wine is amazing," I said. "What type is it?"

"Just a local blend that's left over from the vineyards, probably. They sell it as a house wine. It can vary slightly from year to year, depending on what's exported."

We locked eyes.

I set my glass down. "What do you do exactly?"

His gaze flicked to his glass where he trailed a finger down the side of it, then back to me.

"Long story," we both said at the same time. Mine a question, his a statement.

He smiled, and I laughed into my wine.

"I love that you don't know."

I frowned. "And you want to keep it that way?"

He blew out a breath, his eyes growing serious. "I find myself wanting to tell you everything. You are so easy to be with." He picked up his glass and took a healthy sip. Now that he was letting himself be with me was the unspoken follow up.

"I wish I could say the same."

His head cocked to the side, wordlessly asking me to explain. A faint look of hurt rippled behind his poker mask.

"I mean *this*, here, *you*, right now. It's ... great. But on the same day you tell me women want too much of you. I can imagine, I *know*," I corrected, "how they could fall into that trap of wanting more of you than you're willing to give them. To give me. This version of you is ..." I took a small sip of wine, wondering how honest to be and deciding I'd said enough. What I wanted to say was "this version of you is easy to fall in love with." But the truth was every version of him was.

I couldn't look at him. I picked at a small piece of my bread. Then Cristo was there, gesticulating and pointing to a small rickety wooden stairwell.

We got up and followed him. At the bottom of the stairs, Xavier waved me after Cristo and ahead of him. After what happened outside, this should have been funny. But I'd ruined the vibe. I moved ahead of him. But the moment my foot touched the first stair, he took my arm stilling me, and stepped up behind me, his mouth at my ear. "I was talking about *other* women," he whispered.

"What am *I*?" I turned my face to his.

His dropped his forehead to my shoulder for a second, then he looked up at me, his expression helpless. "You're ... you."

I nodded at his non answer, knowing it was probably all I'd get, then I continued following Cristo upstairs.

CHAPTER THIRTY-SIX

After following Cristo up four flights of ancient wooden stairs, that got narrower, and more rickety, I was seriously ready to question the safety of this adventure. "How old do you think this building is?" I asked Xavier over my shoulder.

At each turn, we passed closed wooden doors set into whitewashed stucco and kept climbing.

"Five hundred years, give or take. Maybe more."

"Wow. Do they not have termites in this part of the world?"

"Normally, I'd say 'what are you talking about?' But I just read a frightening article. They are going to become more prevalent in Europe with the average temperature rising every year. We'll lose so much history."

"That's so sad, I—" My words died on my lips as we reached the top and climbed through a trap door where I'm sure I flashed Xavier my black thong, and then we were on a roof terrace. It was strung with twinkling lights and potted plants. Full grown orange and lemon trees in halved wine barrels created a sanctuary but left the view open down to the harbor and the ocean. There was even a grape vine over our heads. The last of the day's light had spilled mercury across the blue ocean. On the terrace in front of us was a single linen covered table for two with a candle in a glass jar in the middle. Soft classical music played from somewhere unknown.

Cristo fussed and moved us toward the table. My mouth was open and I closed it. "It's beautiful," I told him sincerely.

Apparently he knew what that meant. "Beautiful, beautiful, *si*, *si*," he said, delighted. He turned to Xavier, gesturing to the wall in the corner, explaining some kind of dumb waiter contraption and a bell before turning back to us and filling our wine glasses with the last of the carafe. Apparently, the upstairs table got the fancy cut crystal. It was old and heavy. Beautiful. After seating us, Cristo disappeared back down the stairs.

I looked around, still in awe. "This is ... stunning." The breeze was cooler up here and caressed my bare arms.

"It is. I had no idea."

"Wait. This isn't your special romance table?"

"I think I covered how much romance I've had recently," he said tightly.

My gut thumped. "I'm sorry. They seem to have known you a long time. I—didn't you bring your wife here?"

"I take it back about you being easy to be around. You're challenging me tonight." He chuckled and picked up his crystal glass. "*Chin chin.*"

"Cheers," I returned carefully.

We both set our glasses down.

"The truth is I did bring her here. Not up here. This was never offered to me before. I didn't know it existed. Arriette, she didn't enjoy when I came to visit Corsica. Perhaps Cristo could tell." His voice was low, and his eyes strayed to the left as if lost in memories.

"What really happened to her?" I whispered. "How did she die?"

His shoulders moved, and he slowly unfolded his arms, setting his palms on the table edge as if steadying himself. He looked down at his fingers. "The sordid stories say she partied too hard and overdosed." His voice carried shame.

"And you?" I managed. "What do you believe?"

He looked at me with hesitation, with so much pain that my chest cinched tight. "I ... I believe she took her own life," he said. "I believe it was ... deliberate."

Shit. I let his truth hang out in the air between us, fighting the urge to refute it, to reassure him, to crawl across the table and hold him so fucking tight. "Today, when you saw me in the bathroom, you thought of her, didn't you?" I asked quietly when I could breathe again.

He nodded then lifted his palms from the table with an inhale and reached for his wine. "So. Now you know. And I would like for you not to discuss it with anyone."

"Of course," I croaked and cleared my throat. "I would never. I'm so sorry."

"Not your fault." He grimaced. "If Dauphine had to think about the fact her mother didn't love her daughter enough to stay alive, well, you can understand why we do not talk much about it."

I picked at the hem of my dress as I quaked inside at his painful truth delivered so bluntly. And I'd bet he felt the same way—that she hadn't loved *him* enough to stay alive either. No wonder he had trust issues. This was more than someone lying to you. This was trusting someone with your heart. With your life. With your daughter's life. And it not being enough. My eyes stung and filled. I shook my head, blinking and looking out at the dark night view. I swiped a quick hand to my eyes before he could see. "Dauphine said you told her that sadness was a disease that people could die from. I think you have handled it well with her. It's not that people who suffer don't love their family enough," I said slowly. "It's that the disease is stronger."

He gazed at me for a beat, and an understanding seemed to pass between us. "Are you real?" he asked softly, tossing my words from earlier tonight back at me far more poignantly.

There was a clang at the wall where the dumb waiter was. Cristo materialized out of the small roof door as if summoned, bearing a tray of goodies and breaking the morose atmosphere.

He set the food down on a cart that he wheeled over and began laying some of the dishes out on the table. Heavenly scents rose up, making my mouth water. Herbs, garlic, something lightly fried. By the time he'd also retrieved what was in the dumb waiter, my stomach gave a loud growl. Cristo's eyes darted to me, startled.

"Excuse me," I said, my cheeks blazing, sucking my lips between my teeth. I glanced up to see Xavier, head down, shoulders shaking as he tried to hold in a laugh.

He caught my eye, and we both cracked up.

Cristo was smiling his stained and gap-toothed grin and started talking to me.

"He's saying he's flattered that the food they've prepared will be so enjoyed."

"Tell him you've been starving me in preparation to experience his cooking."

"*Je*—no. *Mon dieu.*" Xavier flashed a semi amused and semi shocked glance at me before relaying some sort of message to Cristo. Cristo seemed gratified, and then began pointing and explaining.

Some didn't need too much explanation. There was a charcuterie board with a selection of meats and cheeses, some more olives, small fried squid, large glistening pink prawns lightly dusted with something and surrounded by big, fat, juicy lemons. There was some type of lighter colored meat, surrounded by round balls and carrots. "Wild boar and roasted chestnuts," Xavier explained when I stared at it too long.

All the dishes looked sumptuous but small so we could taste everything.

Cristo opened a dusty bottle of red wine and set it to the side for now, and then shuffled away and disappeared.

"My mouth is watering." I pointed at a bowl. "To be honest this looks like southern grits."

"Grits?"

"Made of coarse cornmeal."

"Ah, like polenta. Yes, this is Corsican though. So it will be made of chestnut flour. It's to be served with the lamb or with anything you like."

"Served the same as grits too, then. Breakfast, lunch, or dinner. Certainly in South Carolina. And people either love them or hate them. There's no in between."

"How are they prepared?"

"Simple butter and salt, sometimes with cheese, sometimes with sausage gravy," I listed. "Definitely with shrimp and bourbon gravy. You name it. Some people even have it sweetened with syrup." I made a face. "Though that's a sin in my household."

Xavier served my plate with a little bit of everything, and I began eating. The flavors were incredible. No herb was overpowering, but everything tasted fresh and bursting with flavor. I identified fennel, garlic, rosemary and, of course, chestnut.

"Tell me about growing up," Xavier asked after we'd all but decimated the initial offerings, neither of us able to talk for too long before putting something else in our mouths. It was hard not to moan aloud.

Cristo had just been up and ladled out some kind of seafood bisque that was making me delirious. I was getting so full, and the now finished carafe of wine had made us both languid, relaxed, and laughing freely.

I answered Xavier, telling him about growing up in downtown Charleston and going to private school. We shared similar stories of what that was like and the kind of friends who lasted from that time.

He told me about the nuns at his Catholic private school and how he credited them with keeping him on the straight and narrow.

I talked about losing my dad. And I told him about the morning I woke up at boarding school and was summoned to the principal's office. I was told my stepfather had been arrested, and I was being asked to leave due to the fact my fees hadn't been paid since the beginning of the school year. "I wasn't even allowed to go back to my room and pack my own things. Or even say goodbye. Everyone was in assembly." I swallowed the ball of shame and humiliation that always lodged in my throat when I thought back. "My mother was there to pick me up, and she was so shocked and humiliated by everything she couldn't even talk to me. We said nothing the whole drive home. When we got there, there were press at the gates. We could hardly get through. The police arrived so we could get through the gate but had to endure walking to the front door with that audience. I left all my stuff in the car rather than unpack in front of them."

Xavier reached for my hand. "I know what wolves they can be."

Blinking away some moisture in my eyes, I continued. "I remember asking as we closed the front door behind us, 'Is this house even ours, or will we be kicked out of here too?' The answer was, of course, yes, we would be kicked out. The mortgage had not been paid in six months. It was that question that broke my mother. She loved that house. She and my father had bought it together, well before my stepfather had entered the picture." My wine glass empty, I picked up my water glass and took a long sip, remembering how she'd all but collapsed and I'd had to try and get her to the sofa. "Not many friends reached out to me. Even friends I'd been in school with for *years*. Meredith did though." I smiled. "I've known Meredith since elementary school. Tabs only since college, though it feels like so much longer. I miss them. They're also my family really."

Xavier reached for the dusty bottle of red wine Cristo had opened earlier and poured us both new glasses.

"I'm sorry that happened to you," he said. "I can't imagine how that must have felt. Like an earthquake under your feet."

"Something like that. If the earthquake destroys the whole world around you and leaves you standing and wondering where it all went. It still haunts us. Charleston has a long memory. The day I accepted the job to come here, I'd just been passed over for a promotion at work, and the senior partner made some mention of my stepfather. After all these years, we are still paying for his sins. I was told that I'd never get a promotion."

Xavier scowled. "Fool," he said acidly.

I chuckled. "I appreciate your blind allegiance, but you have no idea if I'm good at my job."

"You're extraordinary. I'd stake my life on it. You are passionate about everything you do. Interested. Curious. Talented, if the sketches Dauphine has shown me are anything to go by. You can draw out the exact detail in a façade that makes it what it is. And top of the class student."

I raised my eyebrows, flushed with pleasure. "A top student? And how would you know that."

He took a breath, and then looked me in the eyes. "I have your college transcripts. I make a habit of thoroughly investigating everyone who comes near my family."

"That sounds lonely," I fired defensively, not sure how I felt about him looking into me. It made sense given his position. It's still didn't feel right.

"It *is* lonely."

Somehow that deflated me. "So, you knew everything about me. Why bother asking?" I asked tightly.

"Because those were facts. But there was no story. You're the story, *Joséphine*."

He picked up his glass and sniffed the new wine. In Charleston, I used to find that pretentious. But Xavier swirling and inhaling wine was sexy as all hell. Maybe it was just the confident way he sat, leaned back, legs slightly splayed. Candlelight and the glow from the overhead twinkle lights played across his features. Maybe it was the way he held his glass. And the fact that we were sitting on a rooftop on an island in the middle of the Mediterranean. But more than that, it was his presence. His intellect. And the way he was clearly a successful and important businessman, and yet he was looking at me like I was the most fascinating creature he'd ever encountered. It could go to a girl's head.

After he took his first sip of the new bottle and didn't spit it out or wince in horror, I assumed it was probably excellent. Not that I'd expected otherwise.

I took a mouthful and slow swallow. Wow. It was. "Mmmmm."

Xavier cleared his throat. "Um, what was that?" he asked, his voice rough.

"What?"

"That face you just made. That small sound especially."

"I made a sound? The wine's so good, I guess. It conjures up images of lying in a dark field, staring up at a starlit sky surrounded by the scent of blackberries."

"You have a way with words."

"Ha. Not usually." I gave him a small smile.

He set his glass down. "I don't suppose while you are lying there inhaling the blackberries and staring at the stars I am between your legs, pushing up your dress and tasting you?"

I choked. "What? Oh my God." My voice came out in a breathy squeak. The faint buzz and warmth of the simmering chemistry between us flared like a struck match and spread throughout my lower belly.

He gazed at me. "I love that sound you just made. I'm addicted to that sound. And that look you get on your face. You are intoxicating, *Joséphine*."

My hand shook slightly as I took another small sip of wine in an attempt to not look as though I'd just been blown sideways.

"You should give a girl warning before you make love to her from three feet away."

He inhaled through his nose. "Is that what I'm doing?"

I set my wine down, licking my lips. Uncrossing and crossing my legs, I shifted in my seat. A move that didn't go unnoticed by Xavier. "It's definitely what it feels like," I admitted. Just the way he said my name sometimes made my stomach free fall.

Cristo took that moment to materialize, and quietly, as if he could sense the change in atmosphere, cleared up our dishes. He whispered to Xavier.

"Dessert?" Xavier asked me.

I shook my head. I was full and was sure it would be delicious, but I just wanted to be alone with Xavier.

As soon as Cristo left and the dumbwaiter rattled its way down below, we were left in candlelit silence. The strains of soft classical guitar had faded between pieces and now slowly came back to life.

"There's so much I still want to know about you," I said. "Two days doesn't feel like enough."

"Maybe it will be. We are still at the beginning."

I didn't bother to disagree. Instead I nodded, shoving down the odd feeling of sadness that bubbled through my happiness.

"We won't be disturbed again." He slid his chair back and lifted a beckoning hand. "*Viens ici?*"

Come here?

As if I could resist.

CHAPTER THIRTY-SEVEN

Back at the boat, all was dark. Only Paco was apparently on board, and even he had retired for the night.

After Xavier had beckoned me over to his side of the table, I'd ended up on his lap, our arms wrapped around each other, talking for ages and making out like teenagers. We'd stopped short of getting to any indecent behavior out of respect for Cristo and his establishment, but before long it was clear that not even our surroundings might stop us if we didn't get out of there. We stumbled giddily down the stairs, saying swift and jovial goodbyes. In the cobbled streets, Xavier held me close, tucked under his arm, pausing occasionally in darkened doorways to kiss my neck and whisper French things in my ear. My skin was a conduit for his desire, every cell lit up with electrical fire.

I was giddy, breathless, and utterly seduced.

I guided Xavier down to my cabin where we barely made it through the door before our clothing was discarded. Only the mooring lights from the boat and dock filtered through my tiny window as I cradled his body between my open thighs and he slid into me, filling the seemingly endless ache I had for him. His face and eyes were barely visible in the shadows.

Our lovemaking started off slow and deliberate.

He lifted my leg, finding his way deeper, and I cried out at the new angle. "There's no one to hear you," he whispered, moving in and out of me languidly, making me feel every slow inch as he dragged out and pushed back in. "Tell me what you want. Let me hear you."

"This," I'd gasped. "You. You feel so good inside me."

He grunted and mumbled something back to me in French. Then switched to English. "Faster?" he asked as he thrust in hard and fast.

I cried out again.

"*Oui*, like this," he answered for me. "You make me crazy. Hungry. I will finish and need more. How is it possible?"

Then his whispers quieted and it was just the sound of our labored breaths and my cries as he brought me closer and closer to the edge. The sudden silence from him was disconcerting, but, oh God, he was just in the right spot.

"Xavier. Yes." I wrapped my other leg around his firm butt, urging him faster, deeper. Lightning shot up and down my skin.

His body grew tense and strained and we both struggled against and toward the rush to the edge. I got there first, my eyes squeezing closed and my head going back as I gave myself up to the fall.

Then I held his head in my hands, watching his shadowed features as he came apart, wishing I could see what was going on behind his tightly closed eyelids.

He collapsed on me, his heart pounding against mine, and then slid off to the side. Cool air whispered over my sweat-slicked skin as I caught my breath.

I disentangled myself without resistance and crept out of bed to clean up. When I re-emerged, I found Xavier already sleeping, hand thrown up over his head, the other on his belly. The light from the bathroom showed his features were smooth and relaxed at rest, his thick eyelashes resting on his cheeks. I made myself stop staring and clicked the bathroom light off, crawling in to join him.

I lay in the dark next to his warm body, feeling strange and discomfited. There was a struggle going on within Xavier. He was open and teasing one moment and quiet and broody the next. Despite our romantic evening and the foreplay, verbal and otherwise, that had preceded our lovemaking, he'd seemed distant at the end, as though he suddenly found himself being vulnerable and had scrambled to close himself back up.

I awoke with a start, gasping a deep breath. It was dark and hot, and I was suffocating. The memory of the evening we'd spent together slid through me. The heaviness of Xavier's arm draped across my middle and the heat of him curled around my back brought me back to my surroundings.

His breathing changed, then his arm moved, squeezing gently before lifting so his palm ran down my torso. His hand flattened on my belly and ignited the banked heat that hadn't waned since the night in the club.

"*Ça va?*" he whispered.

I dragged in a breath, filling my lungs with much needed oxygen.

He shifted away, rolling me onto my back. "This is why you visit the deck at night? You wake up like this?"

I nodded, then realized he probably couldn't see me. "Yes. It's okay. I'm fine. I just need a second to breathe."

"Do you have a bad experience where this comes from?"

I chuckled. "No. Not that I remember. Not everything has to be rooted in past trauma." I rolled to face him and slipped my hand into the hair at his nape, scraping my nails along his scalp.

He groaned.

Our lips met. Soft, seductive, demanding.

"You just have to distract me," I whispered as his lips slid down my neck and I arched my body.

Suddenly his hands slipped under me. "Come." He made to lift me.

"Whoa. Where?"

"My bed. It's bigger. More windows. More space. More air."

I stayed him with a hand on his shoulder, thinking of all of Dauphine's mother's things in there.

"What?" he asked.

"What about the top deck?"

"Outside?"

"Under the stars," I said, wondering if he'd remember what he'd said at dinner. Not that I needed that. I mean, I wouldn't complain.

"Mmm." He hummed, his fingers pushing the sheet off me and trailing down my belly.

I grabbed his fingers and kissed them. "Insatiable."

"Addicted. Come. The stars it is."

He pulled on his shorts and handed me his shirt lying on the floor. Then he gathered up two pillows and my duvet and we trotted up the levels of the ship until we broke through into the muggy, starlit night. The lights from the port twinkled, and pale yellow light washed up the walls of the citadel high on the cliffs. Out to sea, all was inky black.

Xavier pulled two chaises together and pulled the cushions out of a storage box. We tied the cushions to each other rather than the chair to stop them slipping apart. He lay down the pillows and duvet and then climbed on, holding out an arm for me to slip under and rest my head on his shoulder.

The railing height hid our bodies, but above us the stars blazed. Our only witness.

"Is this better?" he asked.

I smiled, snuggling in next to him. "Yes." The mooring lights cast a faint glow around us, and as my eyes adjusted I could see as well as if there was a small lamp on.

"We will wake up wet and covered in ... what's the word when everything is wet from the air in the morning? I forget it in English. In French it's *la rosée*."

"Dew?" I suggested.

"Yes, dew."

"God, that sounds better in French. Everything does." Especially whatever the hell it was that poured out of his mouth while he was making love to me.

He kissed the top of my head.

"Now, tell me why you are so famous to Cristo. And why does he call you Pasqualey?"

Xavier chuckled. It was a dark rumble under my cheek. "One line of my mother's family is originally from Corsica. There was a famous hero named Pasquale Paoli who at various times tried to help keep Corsica independent, working with the Corsican resistance against the French in the 1700s. Cristo is convinced I'm descended from him somehow."

"Are you?"

"I have no idea. But likely not. Pascale is my father's name, and as far as I know he has nothing to do with Corsica."

I frowned. "Something doesn't add up about tonight. That's a lovely story, but I'm not buying it." I poked him between the ribs and he jerked with a hiss. "Oh em gee, are you ... ticklish?" I laughed.

He grabbed my hand just as I was gearing up to really go for his ribs. "I would be careful if I were you."

We gazed at each other a beat, my face turned up to his.

Then he kissed me on the nose. "I ... maybe .... did something to help clean the area up of crime and corruption by helping the local municipality with donations and contributing to the election of a more upstanding councilman." He paused. "Who also happens to be Cristo's nephew."

"Ahhh."

"They are good, honest, hard-working people. They deserve to run their own city and not give in to the organized crime that is never too far away. It also has a lot of history, which can be easily lost to too much progress. And I mean of the greedy, commercial kind."

I turned my face up to him in surprise. "Really? I would have thought a businessman like yourself would be into applauding business opportunities wherever he could find them."

"You make me sound mercenary."

"Aren't you? I'd heard you were."

He hummed. "Maybe only about things that fascinate me. Technology, innovation. Commercial building development is not one of them."

I chuckled, warmth zinging through my veins. "That's the sexiest thing you've ever said to me."

"How so?" I felt his gaze on me again, curious.

"That idea is kind of close to my heart living in Charleston, South Carolina. I struggle against the commercial developers all the time who want to come in to our city and make a quick buck with no regard for the history of what came before. I love that our city has progressed in so many ways. It's considered a foodie capital now—fantastic restaurants, vibrant with students and a mix of old and new. Of course, there's still lots of social progress to be made, and in my field it's a fine balancing act between progress and preserving history and not only preserving the 'right kind of history.'"

"Explain."

"Well, there are parts of my city that have been underfunded for generations. Forgotten and ignored and systematically repressed. Of course, then crime flourishes. Now people want to come in and 'clean it up,' but that means moving people who've lived there for decades or longer. What needs to happen is those areas should get funding for parks and restoration and better schools and education, not moving people away, just so some developer can get rich." I finished in a huff, not realizing how my blood pressure had spiked up. "We have a shameful history of owning slaves. But the descendants of those slaves have just as much right for their history to be saved as the white slave owner who built a mansion. Perhaps more so, in my opinion."

"You're passionate about this topic."

I blew out a breath. "Yeah, I guess I am. And I'm not saying all development is evil. Capitalism can be good. I just ... there needs to be balance."

"And were you working toward that in your last job?"

I frowned. "No. I mean, I was trying. I got to work on some projects hand-in-hand with the various preservation societies. But my last project kind of broke my faith." I told him about the hotel and the history of the land it was on and how the stupid nepotism and greed of my ex-boss and his nephew had thrown all my hard work and potentially that history out the window. "Not to mention," I added with a grim edge, "that my boss implied he was only keeping me on because I was easy on the eyes. So what could I do but quit?"

Xavier hissed. "What is his name?" he growled the question, his body tense.

I glanced up at his troubled gaze. His eyes glittered darkly. "Are you going to avenge my honor?" I asked, amusement lacing my tone.

He grunted. "Maybe."

I shifted, turning farther into him and walking my fingers across his taut belly. "Why such honor?"

His muscles tightened under my touch. "My father. I don't want to be like him. I already feel like him in some moments when I look at you and my body rages to have you. It feels depraved. Like I'm possessed. And I wonder, was that what it was like for my father? Was that how it began? But then I know, it was about power with him. It was about getting away with it. It wasn't about how mad he was about the girls. Not like the way you drive me so mad with wanting."

"How mad?" I asked.

"Out of my mind," he admitted. "I was torn between being addicted to seeing you every day, knowing I would not, *could not,* touch you and sending you away so you didn't torture me anymore. But then, of course, it would hurt Dauphine."

"Yet, you let me resign and walk away."

"I'm sorry. You became too much. And after the club," his finger traced the shell of my ear, "*J'ai paniqué.*"

Giddiness fizzed in my belly. "I'm assuming that means you panicked. Why?"

"My daughter is everything to me."

I nodded, understanding. "I know."

"And I have not allowed myself to get distracted. Or to be apart from her."

"And now?" I asked as I licked my lips. "What changed?"

"I don't know." His gaze caught on my mouth and his finger moved from my ear to my cheek and over my bottom lip. "I'm still trying to figure it out. After you left, I was telling myself it was for the best. But I felt … I felt like I had made a terrible mistake."

"I bet Dauphine made you feel bad," I teased.

He chuckled. "Everyone did. Even Chef could hardly look at me. And Evan? *Mon dieu.* He's lucky we have a long history."

I smiled. It was nice to know I had allies beyond Andrea, that people were rooting for us. I wondered what they'd say if they knew he'd already put an expiration date on us of two days.

"I thought I'd been given a second chance when you returned today, but my own mother was going to keep you away from me," he said with a chuckle and a shake of his head. "And then I knew my need for you was too strong to resist. I wasn't sure you would agree after the way I'd behaved. Or if everyone would see through me and know what I wanted and laugh. But I took a chance. And now you are here. I can barely believe it."

"Me neither," I whispered. "I'm glad I'm here. I want to be here," I affirmed in case there was any doubt. "I'm glad I had an asshole boss back home, or I wouldn't have been here. I wouldn't have met you. Or Dauphine."

We gazed at each other, understanding the gravity of our admissions. Then his mouth descended and covered mine. His lips were soft and demanding.

My hand on his belly gripped tight as if I could tangle myself into his skin.

His tongue dipped into my mouth and I groaned, arching into him. The low banked fire that endlessly burned for him, blazed up.

"I had dreams of you," he whispered between kisses. "Like that night you came up here in your *miniscule* pajamas." *Kiss*. "I sat in this chair." *Kiss*. "And I fantasized that you came over and took your clothes off and crawled on top of me." *Kiss*. "And made me forget the pain in my heart."

I shifted toward him, and then slipping my leg over his, I sat up and straddled him. "And in French you told me you wanted to fuck me. But I didn't understand." My bare thighs squeezed his waist, and the bed covers slipped down my back. I still wore his linen shirt, and now I unbuttoned the two places holding it together. "But I would have. I've wanted you since the moment I saw you with your daughter in the train station. Every cell of my body wants yours. And I cursed the fact that we were meeting under the circumstances of me working for you."

His eyes were heavy-lidded, his mouth slightly parted as his hands joined mine and he spread the material and bared me to his gaze. Beneath me, his hips bucked up and pressed against my naked center, drawing a moan of aching need from my throat. He whispered something in French.

"Why do you switch to French when I can't understand?"

He gazed up at me, his voice thickening. "I said, you are an angel under the moonlight."

My shaking hands made quick work of his shorts, flicking open the button and zipper and drawing him out, hot, hard, and heavy in my hand. "I need you." I gasped, lifting up enough to slick him through my wetness once, twice, and then sinking down slowly, taking him into my body.

His fingers dug into my hips, pulling me down and driving himself up until I was full to the hilt and utterly breathless.

His gaze pinned me, the look feral, hungry, haunted and pleading. Pleading for something he said he didn't want me to offer. My heart.

Two days was just not fucking enough with this man. It was going to kill me when it was over. I squeezed my eyes closed. It was killing me now, my heart willingly running to its own doom in my chest.

CHAPTER THIRTY-EIGHT

I awoke to the sound of seagulls screeching and cartwheeling overhead. I realized I was alone, wrapped up on the chaises where we'd fallen asleep in the wee hours.

The sky glowed blue with low morning sun even though the bay was shadowed by the massive peninsula. My body was hot and clammy, sticky under the duvet. My face felt damp and cool in the morning air.

"Ah, you're awake." Xavier's voice had me turning to see him stepping up the last step onto the deck, two cups on saucers in his hands.

"I really hope that's coffee." I blinked groggily. "That was too much wine and not enough sleep." And maybe too much sex? Was there such a thing? I ached. But in a good, delicious, satisfied way. "Oh my goodness, did you shower already?"

Xavier was wearing navy shorts and a fresh light pink linen shirt that made his skin glow. He looked utterly masculine and delicious against its soft hue. His hair was wet and shiny in the daylight, and he smelled of cool verdant forests as he leaned toward me delivering a kiss to my forehead and a cup and saucer to my hand.

"*Oui*," he answered and perched next to me. "I had an early call with Tokyo, and then I had to do some exercise before I gave into the urge to come up here and drag you to my bed again."

I smoothed my hair with my free hand, realizing it must look absolutely wild from our outdoor sleeping arrangements.

"You look beautiful."

"Shush, you charmer." I grinned and took a sip of coffee, creamy, bitter, and smooth all at once. I raised an eyebrow. "How did you know how I take my coffee?"

"I called Dauphine."

"You're joking?"

He grinned into his coffee, looking slightly embarrassed. "*Non*." He chuckled.

"Hmm. How is she?"

"Wonderful. This afternoon they are going to visit the newly discovered Roman ship. It's not open to the public yet, but my mother has her ways."

"And Dauphine loves the idea of shipwrecks and treasure."

"She does."

We shared a smile over his daughter.

"She's wonderful," I told him since I'd never outright said it. "And it's a testament to you. You should be very proud. I was scared about taking this position. I've never thought I'd be good with children. But she makes it easy."

"You're natural."

I lifted a shoulder. "I just hope my own children are as charming one day. Maybe I'm only good with *her*." I laughed, but it slipped a little as I realized Xavier had glanced away uncomfortably.

"Why architecture? After everything you told me last night?"

I frowned, slightly taken aback. "What do you mean?"

"I mean, you are passionate about history. It's obvious you like keeping old things, not building new things."

"Well, I—" I let out a surprised huff of air. "You're right, I suppose. I never looked at it quite so black and white. Maybe ..." I knew what he was saying was right, but I'd been working toward being a successful partner at an architectural firm since I'd started college. My father had always known I'd be good at it, ever since I'd known what I wanted to be. He'd encouraged me. He'd fostered my love for the details no one else saw. He'd—

"What?"

Huh. "Um. I think I'm having an existential crisis." Should I even be an architect?

Xavier's concerned face grew more serious. "I'm sorry. I only meant—"

"No. It's fine." I cleared my throat. Of course I should be an architect. My degree was the only one I'd have ever wanted, but ... "Maybe I've been focusing on working at the wrong places. Looking at it wrong. God, to think, I even applied for a job at a firm that builds office parks." I shuddered. "How did you get so smart?"

He chuckled and kissed my hair. "Well, I must do a few more things before my meeting." He stood.

I cleared my throat. "Okay. Thank you for the coffee." I glanced down at my attire of his lone wrinkled shirt. "Is it safe to go downstairs dressed like this?"

"Of course. I was thinking perhaps you would like to stay in my cabin tonight. If you need your own space I understand. But perhaps you would sleep better?"

"It's not that I need my own space, but ..." How did I tell him his dead wife was everywhere in that room? And knowing now what he'd shared with me about her, it felt even more heartrending. As if by keeping all her things for two years untouched that he wasn't ready to give her memory up. Maybe he wasn't. And where did that leave me? I already knew I was temporary for him, but I didn't need the reminder while we made love. Not to mention that was a sure-fire way to say bye-bye to my big O. And I was quite attached to the ones he coaxed out of my body.

I took a breath. "It feels as if your room is yours and Arriette's room. I don't want to interfere with your memory of her. And it's all right," I rushed on. "I'm okay. Not, like, jealous, or anything." I grimaced. Jealous? Of a dead woman? *Fuuuucck*. I needed more sleep, clearly. "Sorry, that was not what I meant." I flailed. "I actually don't know what I'm trying to say. I'm trying to be sensitive to your feelings, and mine, and her memory, and I'm not doing a very good job. I'm sorry."

"*Tu as fini?*" He sat back down, eyebrow raised.

Was I finished? I nodded and studied his face for a clue into how much I'd just offended or upset him.

He looked thoughtful. "I have made a mistake in not taking Arriette's things from the boat. Last summer, it was ... it was the first time Dauphine and I had come to the boat without her *maman*. We did not stay too long. It was difficult. I should have done it before now. But I got busy. And then I worried perhaps I should wait until Dauphine wants to look and see what she wants to keep. But she seems so young for such a difficult task. And so, I waited. Or perhaps I avoided it. I did not expect to have someone ... to bring ... a lover here." He swallowed heavily, his tone had grown thick.

"Then you should wait."

"I've waited long enough. I spoke to Dauphine last week about it. I'll be moving Arriette's things—"

"I'm sorry." I laid a hand on his forearm and squeezed gently. "You don't need to share this. Or explain anything. You don't owe me that."

He took a long breath. "Perhaps we can talk about it later?"

"If you want."

"Thank you." He gazed at me then leaned forward, pressing his lips to mine in a brief, soft kiss. "Perhaps you should come with me today."

I bit my lip. "To your meeting?"

"Why not?"

"I—I don't know."

"Come. You will like where I'm going. It was rebuilt in the eighteen hundreds on a fifteenth century foundation. And it's not open to the general public."

"Mmmm," I moaned in pleasure. "You really know a lot about seduction, don't you?"

He burst into a warm laugh. "Is that why I finally have you? Because I promised you history and architecture?" he teased. "I should have figured that out sooner. Come. Let's get you downstairs so you can get ready."

"A church?" I exclaimed. "You never did tell me exactly what it is you do. Who are you meeting with? Do you have business with God himself?" We'd wound up the mountain in a taxi, past the ancient citadel walls we saw from the boat, and through some rocky scrubland until we came to a chapel perched on a hill. A small sign told me it was called *Notre Dame de la Serra*. It was cream stucco and framed on a rocky hilltop with more stunning mountains around it.

He smiled, amused.

We climbed out of the taxi and walked through a small gate in a stone wall.

"Here she is now," he said, looking past me across the small limestone cloistered courtyard. "*Soeur Maria*," he greeted a tiny nun hurrying toward us.

Her lined face lit up with an excited smile. She was adorable.

"She doesn't speak English, I apologize," he said quietly to me.

"Oh. That's okay. You're meeting with a nun?"

"She worked at the boarding school I went to as a young boy."

"And you're still in touch? And you have a business meeting with her?"

"Another long story," he said just as the small woman reached us, and tucking a folder under her arm, grabbed Xavier's hands in hers. They spoke softly and affectionately, and I figured he'd introduced me when I heard my name and received her attention.

Her cool and papery hands took mine, and her rheumy blue eyes roamed me from top to bottom. I smiled a greeting, unsure what to say since she wouldn't understand anyway.

Seemingly satisfied, she turned back to Xavier and motioned to a pathway that led through an opening in the cloister wall.

"She suggests we walk to take in the view," he told me.

"You both go ahead," I told him. "I'll follow."

He acquiesced with a grateful smile and offered Sister Maria his arm, and they began a slow stroll.

As soon as they turned away, I took a moment to gather myself. His meeting was with a nun? Honestly, I did not understand this man. But everyone we'd interacted with, apart from that creepy Morosto character and his father, seemed to put Xavier on a pedestal. If I wasn't half gone over this man, discovering he was secretly funding some foundling orphanage run by nuns would seriously put me over the edge. Who was I kidding? I was already hanging over the damn edge. I was in so much trouble. My chest swelled watching his tall muscular frame, and let's not lie, incredible rear-view, as he leaned down and attended to a tiny old woman. Who was this guy?

I followed them around the more recently built, cream stuccoed side of the chapel and up a set of rocky stairs toward a statue of the Madonna that rose high and white against a blue sky. They didn't seem in a hurry. They chatted and laughed. I occasionally got the feeling I was mentioned. Especially when Sister Maria asked him something, and he grew very quiet and pensive.

Then suddenly, I wasn't thinking of them.

I gasped.

We'd reached the top of a stone path and Notre Dame de La Serra revealed its biggest secret. It had been built overlooking the entire citadel and miles-long bay of Calvi. My breath caught as I took in the overwhelming view that ranged from the rocky outcrops plunging into the bright blue ocean, over the incredible ancient citadel walls of the city, and over a rolling valley. A turn to my left showed one could also see the towering boulder-strewn mountains behind us. It was spectacular.

I dragged my eyes away to look at Xavier a few feet to my right, only to find him looking at me over the top of the small nun's head, watching my reaction.

I dropped my mouth wider than it already was in a non-verbal expression of wonder.

He grinned.

Sister Maria said something to Xavier and shuffled a bit farther down the path, leaving us together.

"Amazing," I said.

"I knew you would love it."

He gestured down the hillside. "That's the *Vallé Réginu*."

"I have no idea what that is, or why it's important, but this is amazing." I looked back over the bay and pointed. "The water is so light blue there."

He leaned close, pressing his arm to mine. "It's shallow in the bay." He pointed to the left of us where a jagged peninsula thrust out into the dark blue ocean. "That is called *La Revellata*. Parts along the edge are extremely deep. There are caves and grottos and tiny beaches too. I've heard it's good scuba diving."

"It's breathtaking."

My hands were laid flat on the stone wall barrier in front of us, and Xavier's warm hand covered one of mine before plucking it up and bringing it to his lips. He stared at me.

As beautiful as the view was, I found it hard to let go of his look until the polite cough of a small nun reminded both of us of her presence.

She turned toward the sea, but not before I saw her knowing smile. She said something to Xavier, and he turned back to me. "Sister Maria said that you are welcome to go into the main chapel and look around. We will return in a few minutes after we conclude our meeting."

"Oh, of course. Thank you for showing me this." I took a few steps back and reluctantly let go of his hand. My chest was full, my heart-racing. I rounded the corner down the first few stone steps and stopped to take a breath.

Love filled me like a sudden hurricane, as if I'd opened the final window in my soul, swirling through my insides and robbing my breath.

I think I just fell the last step to in love on top of this mountain.

I was in love with Xavier Pascale.

Along with the realization came panic. My hands grew sweaty. I pressed one against my chest.

Breathe, Josie. He hasn't broken your heart yet.

But he will.

Right?

CHAPTER THIRTY-NINE

XAVIER

It didn't take long for Sister Maria to give me her most recent financial update on our joint project. She was a wizard with numbers and also the most kind and generous soul I knew. When I'd first had the idea to help process refugee kids who arrived on island with no parents and provide them with food, safe housing, and education, Sister Maria had been a natural choice. She'd already retired from teaching and transferred her orders to a convent in her native Corsica, and we'd kept in touch over the years. Mainly our interactions had been postcards from her asking me to donate to various charities and reminding me God had seen fit to bless me for a reason. There was nothing like Catholic guilt dispensed by a kindly nun. But now that we'd started this joint venture almost five years ago, I'd found myself coming over to visit her and talk in person at least once a year. And since Arriette had died, many times more.

At the conclusion of our business talk, she made no move for us to leave to join Josephine. "I can see now why you wanted to meet me here, rather than in the citadel like we'd previously arranged."

"What do you mean?" I asked, playing dumb. "Josephine is an architect and loves history. I thought she'd like to see it."

Sister Maria laughed huskily. "You can't swing a cat without hitting an ancient structure down there." She pointed down the hill. "Far more history than up here."

"But no view."

She made a noncommittal grunt of affirmation then eyed the stairs leading down. "I'm assuming you know the legend of this place?"

I let out a controlled breath and nodded. "I do," I admitted.

She took my hand in both of hers. "Does *she* know?"

I shook my head.

"Oh, Xavier. I do not want to see you hurt again."

"Do you think I will be?" I asked carefully.

"It's not for me to say. She seems lovely. Grounded. And in love with you."

My intake of breath was short and sharp. "Do you think so?" I waited for the stab of panic I was expecting, but it didn't come. It would later, I was sure.

"You do not need me to tell you."

"I don't know anything anymore. I can't trust my own thoughts." I tried to swallow. "The guilt I feel about Arriette—"

"Xavier. You know God doesn't hold you responsible for Arriette."

My throat closed so tight I could barely breathe. "Doesn't He? How can you be so sure?"

"I have a close relationship with Him." She winked, trying to lighten my mood, but it was no use.

"I couldn't love her enough to save her, Sister. I think maybe I'm not capable." I pressed my hands on the stone, pushing back and doubling over to hang my head like it could open my lungs so I could breathe, so it could soothe the pain that rushed into my chest at admitting my truth. I squeezed my eyes closed and counted through it. "I don't ... know where my heart is," I said when I could speak again. "I love my daughter, but beyond that I fear it is dead inside for anything else or so deep I can't find it. If I cannot find it, how can I give it to someone again?" I pried my hands from the stone wall, but they shook. My words seemed nonsensical to my ears. And I hated this feeling of vulnerability.

Sister Maria laid a warm hand on my spine, offering quiet comfort. "Your heart is not lost. You wouldn't have brought Josephine here if it was. If anything, it's the opposite. It is found. You just need time."

Time.

I'd given Josephine two days, only one was left, and then she was going away. It was better this way. Wasn't it? Safer for me. Safer for Dauphine. And I didn't know if I wanted more. Not with this person I'd only just met a few weeks ago. It was too soon. Surely it was too soon. Wasn't it? "I brought her here to test the legend, I think. To have God make the choice for me. To unearth my heart ... or not."

"Xavier, you deserve happiness. But counting on a legend that says a couple who come to this place together will be united forever is folly. God can only do so much. He gave you a heart and the ability to love. And I believe He also places people we need in our path. It is *your* choice to take Him up on it."

"What if I'm too afraid?" I asked.

She let out a long, sad sigh. "Then you are too afraid." She looked out to sea and then back at me. "A life lived in fear is no life at all. Look at the families you are saving, people who lived in fear but are willing to face death and hunger and drowning to get themselves and their children to a better life. A life without fear." She took my hand and squeezed.

"Well, that certainly puts my drama in perspective," I said grudgingly.

Sister Maria smiled. "I will say the fact you came here today to find guidance tells me that even though you are afraid, a small voice is telling you that loving Josephine might be worth the risk."

"I think that small voice might be my libido, not my heart," I said drily.

Sister Maria crossed herself and slapped the back of my hand.

I smirked, relieved at the break in tension.

"Here." She tutted and handed me the manila folder she'd tucked under arm. "Let us rejoin Josephine."

Josephine was quiet in the back of the taxi.

I was too. I was raw after my impromptu confessional with Sister Maria. As the car made its way down the winding road, I instructed the driver to take us on a short tour through the old city and to point landmarks out before returning us to the port.

I looked at my traveling companion and was overcome by the urge to touch her—to close the strange gap that seemed to have sprung up between us. I reached out and took Josephine's hand, warm and soft, and held it gently on the seat between us atop the manila folder Sister Maria had given me.

Josie looked down at our hands, then up at me. She smiled tentatively. "What's in the folder?" she asked.

"My project with Sister Maria."

"Can I see?"

I pursed my lips, unwilling to let go of her hand, but then shrugged and did so. "Of course."

She took the folder and opened it.

"I haven't looked yet, myself," I said as we both looked at the front page, which was a list of names and ages.

Josie frowned and turned the page to the first kid. A picture of a young boy with dark hair and eyes, about twelve was stapled to the top corner. "Is this ... a report card?" she asked and turned the page to another kid. This time a bit older. Then another and another.

"Yes. They are not orphans exactly, but they have been separated from their parents. Most of them are from North Africa and Syria. They are targeted to be recruited into a life of crime or worse. So Sister Maria and I work with the local governments and the NGOs to locate them and give them a chance for schooling and a future of some kind, and we also try to locate their families through the refugee camp network." I swallowed, embarrassed suddenly. I didn't know why. Maybe I just felt exposed. Like I was trying too hard. Or boasting about my charity.

Josephine's eyes were on mine, fixed and unreadable.

"I like to see their grades. Maybe give them a further opportunity in time. It's ... it's not an investment in any way," I went on as if she'd accused me of something. "It's just something I do. I think it's important. I was given so much. And I—"

"Stop," Josie said. Then she looked away and out the window, hiding her face. She closed the folder and set it back between us.

My heart pounded. What the fuck was that? I didn't expect her to worship me or anything, but you'd think I'd just shown her the plans for a nuclear power plant that was going to displace a colony of baby sea turtles. A little acknowledgment that I was at least a decent human being would have been nice. "Are you okay?" I asked.

"No."

"What did I do?"

She turned to face me. Tears on her cheeks, gutting me, her eyes translucent green. "Nothing. I'm sorry," she said. "It's absolutely wonderful. I didn't mean to make you think otherwise. I'm just tired. I get emotional when I'm tired."

I lifted my hand and touched the water on her cheek. She closed her eyes.

Debating for a split second, I gave into an instinct and chanced a rejection. "Come here," I said, and meeting no resistance, hauled her across the back seat onto my lap where she burrowed against my chest. I let my face fall into her thick, luscious hair and held her close, breathing her in deeply. My heart raced as I realized how nervous that small simple move to reach out to her had made me. And how relieved I was that she hadn't resisted.

After a whirlwind taxi tour of the major sights inside the Calvi city walls, I had the driver drop us at a small restaurant in the port that employed its own fishermen who went out every morning. It was early afternoon, and Josie and I shared a bottle of rosé and I ordered a late lunch of bouillabaisse and Josie had fresh fish, rice, and seasonal vegetables.

Her fingers were halfway across the table, fidgeting with the stem of her wine glass. Without thinking I reached out and took her fingers in mine and found myself holding hands across the table, something I hadn't done in years. Not since Arriette and I had first met.

It was so natural to want to touch Josie, to be with her. To laugh and to talk. She asked me all kinds of questions about my business, and I shared my work with the alternative energy project power plant that was currently being built near where I lived. I told her about the invention of microfilm that could withstand a cataclysm and last for two thousand years and how everyone wanted to record their technology or their industrial secrets and hide it on the microfilm in a bunker in Iceland in case the world ended. I wasn't bragging. She was fascinated and I let myself talk.

I told her about my successes and also my failures. I told her about Arriette's brother and how he'd felt like he deserved Dauphine's inheritance from her mother. About how I always felt like he was a threat out there and that was why my security around Dauphine was always so high.

"Wow, would he hurt her?"

"I ... I don't know."

Josie's face grew troubled. "Has Dauphine met her uncle?"

"When she was small. I doubt she remembers him."

"It might be worth showing her a recent picture, so she knows to sound the alarm if he approaches her."

"I don't want to scare her. But it's probably a good idea." I shook off a shiver. "Let's talk about something else. What about you?"

"What about me?" She smiled, her eyes dancing. "I've already told you everything."

"I doubt that," I said. "What are your plans when you go back?" I asked.

The question hit the atmosphere between us like a meteor hitting Paris. *Fuck.*

Josie jerked like she'd been slapped, her eyes closing tight. Her fingers in mine moved to untangle, and I grabbed hold of them tighter. "Wait," I said.

I needed to say something. To take it back. But ... I wasn't asking her to stay. She didn't plan to stay.

Words and needs and demands and denials rose up and crashed silently around in my throat.

Her fingers went limp in mine, which was somehow worse. "It's fine, Xavier. We're both aware of what this is. Let's ..." Her voice wobbled. "Let's just enjoy one more day and not think about after tomorrow." She pulled her hand away slowly and I let her.

I still couldn't speak, paralyzed as I was. Inside me, the words rose. *I want more.* But I left them unsaid, not believing them, and unable to drag them through the turmoil even if I did.

Josie pasted a smile on her face, her eyes bright with determination. "You mentioned caves and grottos. And private beaches tucked away in the cliffs?"

"*La Revellata.*"

"Perhaps we could take the boat there this afternoon?" She stood and came around to me. "I need to run to the restroom, but," she leaned down, her lips close to my ear, "I have a fantasy of you fucking me in the ocean that I'd like to take home with me. Let's do that instead of talk." Her mouth slipped down to the side of my neck and her lips pressed against my skin, lighting it on fire. Then she stood and hurried inside, her summer dress floating around her curves, her hair cascading down her back.

I grabbed my wine glass and downed the contents, signaling for the check.

CHAPTER FORTY

JOSIE

I'd thought the water was beautiful off the coast of Southern France, but here, off the coast of a rocky island in the middle of the Mediterranean Sea, it was almost fake. I leaned over the prow of the boat as the anchor plunged down through the water, searching for a bottom that looked closer than it apparently was. When it finally hit the depths and stopped, I couldn't see the bottom. Yet I could see the mottled blues of rocks and sand through crystal clear water.

Xavier had put some music on, and the smooth and clubby beat bounced through the speakers suddenly making me feel as if I was in a music video. Or a dream. The singer sang sexily in a reggae sounding beat. Something about needing to let go, but also about never going back. I inhaled and closed my eyes, a smile on my face even while my heart thumped heavily. I never thought I'd ever have an experience as all sensually encompassing as this—the place, the situation, the man, the emotions. No matter that our time together would end tomorrow and my heart would splinter to leave Xavier and Dauphine and the crew, I was still suffused with the joy of the experience.

"What are you thinking about?" came Xavier's rough voice behind me.

I inhaled through my nose. "I was wondering who this artist was singing?" I lied.

"Dennis Lloyd. He's from Israel. Tel-Aviv."

Strong arms came around either side of me, and Xavier's warm body pressed against my back. "Mmm. I like it," I said, only half talking about the music. "So was Paco mad that you wanted to take the boat around here?"

"*Non*." His lips settled against my bare shoulder, nudging the strap of my summer dress off. Prickles of lust raced over my skin.

I tilted my head back and my gaze dragged up the cliffs to the sea birds wheeling. The boat hardly swayed, the waves were so gentle lapping at the rocks it was hard to believe they could be so scored and sheared. One would expect violent, crashing white sprays battering them up endlessly. There were no other boats around to indicate any other swimmers or divers. A glimpse of white sand between a gash in two towering cliffs could be seen every few minutes over the gentle swells of water.

"Are we swimming to that beach?" I asked, pointing and then letting my other hand scrape through his thick soft hair next to my cheek.

"We can take the tender."

I pressed back, giving myself space from the railing, and he stepped back. Grasping the bottom of my sundress, I pulled it up over my head and off and dropped it on the deck until I stood in my bikini. Then I climbed over the silver rail. "I'll race you," I said to him with a glance over my shoulder.

He was watching, eyes dark, a thumb running over his bottom lip.

I grinned, and then lifted my arms either side of me and dove.

It was graceful, a talent developed in the summers during high school. The water rushed toward me and then my hands and my head and my whole body streaked into the cool.

I was arching back up to the surface when I heard the plunge into the water next to me. My eyes opened into the sting for a brief second to see the white streak of bubbles as Xavier shot downward past me.

Surfacing, I began a fast freestyle toward the beach.

In a moment, he was alongside me and then pulling ahead, his mouth split into a wide grin. It was no use, his strength and speed were no match. I did my best, but soon I lapsed to breaststroke as I approached where he stood waist deep, water running down his finely cut upper body. He flicked his hair and then combed his fingers through it.

We stared at each other stupidly. My cheeks hurt from grinning. When I was close enough, his hand reached out. I took it and he hauled me to my feet. My toe scraped on something hard and I hissed. It was still about thirty feet to the small beach. I let my feet touch down onto the submerged rock he was standing on.

"You okay?" he asked, an arm closing around my waist and locking me against his body.

"Fine," I said, watching a bead of salt water trickle to the edge of his top lip.

"It looked like you got hurt."

"My foot. But your body is a good painkiller." I licked my lips and winked.

He chuckled. Water swelled around us, and he adjusted our stance to keep our balance on the rock.

His erection pressed against my bare belly, and my stomach melted.

Then his lips, salty and cool, were on mine and his tongue, hot and sweet, licked into me.

I groaned, and letting his arm lift me, wrapped my legs around his waist so I was a barnacle on his body. I held his head in my hands so I could get enough of his damn mouth.

"*Ta bouche*," he said on a groan and I giggled, pulling back for a moment, trying to remember the word. Mouth.

"I love yours too," I said. "I was thinking that exact thing." And I gave him another deep kiss, my tongue tasting his.

He growled and his hand slipped behind my neck.

My bikini straps slithered down my chest, and his erection pressed hard between my legs.

He licked his lips. "How much of what I say in French do you understand?" His fingers played over my nipple, pinching gently and making me arch into him with a sharp inhale.

"I mean ..." I gasped as his mouth followed his fingers, and then chuckled. "I get some contextual clues. But not a whole lot."

His other hand slipped down my waist to my butt and he squeezed a handful, pressing me into him. "*Ton cul,*" he began, and then let out a stream of words.

"Tell me in English," I managed as we rocked together. "Or is it too dirty?"

"It's too much of everything. You're too much of everything. It's the first thing I noticed about you. I stood there in the train station and thought ... I can't have you here distracting me away from trying to be a good father. Trying to be a good man." His joking tone had slipped, and his hands gripped, and his mouth took mine savagely.

He swayed in the water and I gripped his body tighter.

"God, I want you inside of me," I said breathlessly as he gave up my mouth for a second. I gazed into his unblinking eyes, his lashes sparkling with sea water. "But I don't want this to be over," I said. "This. Right here. This ache and need I have for you is the most delicious and painful thing I've ever experienced," I admitted. It was excruciating and overwhelming and almost otherworldly. In that moment, I understood how desire could make people do stupid, thoughtless, insane things. Murder, break up families, or take countries to war.

He brought a hand up to my face, cradling it, everything

slowing and gentling. His thumb ran over my lips and then dipped inside. I sucked the tip of his thumb into my mouth, watching as his nostrils flared and his pupils dilated. He swallowed heavily.

"Let's go to the beach," I whispered.

We found a tiny strip of sand hidden from the boat by a boulder. Above us was nothing but cliffs and blue sky. Even the sun was blocked here. With a hand to his chest, I pressed Xavier down to the sand and worked his turquoise swim shorts down. And there he was. Huge, and hard.

"*Joséphine*," he started to say and then the rest of his words disappeared into a groaning, breathless, flurry of French as I took his length into my mouth.

I wondered if he knew all the different ways he said my name. Like it was not just my name, but a prayer. "*Joséphine*."

Every lick and suck pulled more words from him.

His hand tangled in my hair, firm and pleading. His hips strained up.

My hand gripped him hard, mimicking my mouth, touching where my mouth couldn't reach, and the sounds he made sang in my blood, spurring me on, flooding me with hot and wet heat. I couldn't help that my other hand slipped between my own legs, edging my bikini bottoms aside and slipping against my swollen, slick skin.

I sucked him deeper, harder, faster, moaning with the sheer thrill of feeling his pleasure, his vulnerability, and his loss of control. For a few moments, he tried to stop me—muttered things in French I could barely understand like *he couldn't*, or *I couldn't*, or God knew what.

Then suddenly his fingers squeezed to a fist against my scalp, his breathing stopped, and his entire body tensed for two seconds before his breath stuttered and he started to pull my mouth away. I fought him, determined to have him.

I wanted everything.

He let out a strangled sound, and he jerked and erupted down my throat, shuddering violently through his orgasm.

Time slowed and then came back.

The waves lapped gently up the sand in whispering rushes. Birds cried.

"*Merde, Joséphine*. You will kill me," he added after a few moments, his voice cracked.

"I wanted it. I wanted you." *Every single piece of you I can get,* I added silently. *Because I love you.* I sat back, and his eyes opened and swept down my body.

Suddenly his eyes narrowed at the hand that was still between my legs, and he grabbed it.

Xavier's flushed face turned agonized as he sucked my fingers into his mouth. "*Pour moi,*" he said. "I should punish you for trying to take your pleasure away from me when you just stole mine. You cannot have it all."

Jesus. His erotic words sent me even closer to the edge without laying a finger on me.

Then his fingers replaced mine, then his mouth, and as I gazed up at the cliffs a few moments after that, I realized how fleeting my control was.

We pulled ourselves up the ladder onto the swim deck, laughing and out of breath from racing each other. The music on the boat was still playing. It was slow and powerful, and the woman's voice sang familiar lyrics in an echo of the feeling I'd just had on the beach with Xavier about it being strange what desire could make foolish people do. I inhaled, feeling the words hit my chest as she cried out desperately that she didn't want to fall in love. "Is this 'Wicked Game'? I only know the Chris Isaac version," I added, my voice nonchalant in a bid to draw attention from the fact that the words were the theme to our entire relationship. And that I was going to fucking cry if I stopped to listen to them.

"The artist's name is Ursine Vulpine," Xavier said, handing me a towel from the stack Paco must have left out for us.

"It's beautiful," I said as my hair stood on end, and goosebumps raced over my skin. "Haunting. But you need to turn it off."

Xavier stopped and swallowed. He seemed about to say something and stopped himself. Around us the female singer's voice grew and enveloped us in her desperate plea to not fall in love.

I watched as Xavier understood what I meant, the words registering, and surprise and regret rippled across his face.

Turning my back on him, I bit down hard, and pretending I needed further drying, concentrated on my legs and arms.

Then his arms were around me. "I'm sorry," he whispered into my hair. "You are amazing." He swallowed loudly. "But—"

"I know," I said quickly, desperate for him not to finish that sentence. I squeezed his forearm. "It's okay. I meant what I said at lunch. I know what this is. It's just ... this thing between us ... it's more than I planned ... it's difficult."

He inhaled deeply. "It is," he admitted. "It is for me too."

I turned in his arms, and for a moment I could believe he might give us a chance for something beyond two days if he only knew how I felt. It was a scary leap for him. What if I made it first? "I ... I've never felt like this before." My voice broke on the admission.

"I'm sorry, Josephine," he murmured, instead. "I don't know if I can ever ... you deserve so much. You deserve a whole heart."

His eyes were fixed on mine, begging me to understand.

I laid my hand on his chest. "I'd be content with your broken one," I whispered.

His throat bobbed thickly, and his eyes closed.

Water filled my vision, spilled down my cheeks, and dripped to the deck.

"*Monsieur Pascale!*" Paco's voice suddenly broke the silence.

"You are back. Thank God. I was about to sound the emergency horn."

We both swung around to Paco. He'd aged fifty years since we'd seen him two hours ago.

"There has been an urgent call from the mainland." He stopped, his face crumbling. "It's Dauphine," he said.

CHAPTER FORTY-ONE

I wasn't a mother, but even I knew as the shaft of terror cut through me that there was nothing worse than this.

As the anchor clanged back up into place, Paco haltingly repeated what he knew. Madame had taken Dauphine to see the Roman ship exhibit. Arriette's brother had approached Madame while she waited for Dauphine to return from the restroom. While they talked, someone else must have somehow managed to get to Dauphine. She'd disappeared into thin air. Dauphine was missing.

Xavier's knees buckled. Both Paco and I lurched forward to grab him. Immediately he shook us off, but his eyes went to another place. His mind had disconnected from his body. We were strangers to him. I followed as he scrambled to find his phone, cursing and yelling as he threw things across his desk to look for it. I saw it peeking out from his pink shirt lying across the bed. Grabbing it, I held it out. He snatched it from me and seconds later was barking down the phone at Evan.

I didn't know whether to stay or go. I was invisible right now, and I was okay with that. I just wasn't sure what to do. How I could help. God, I hoped Dauphine was okay. Surely, her uncle wouldn't hurt her. Especially if money was what he wanted. I yearned to say this to Xavier, but it seemed inadequate comfort for the terror rolling off him in waves. I could tell he was contemplating how to get back to his mother's house faster.

Why hadn't people invented teleportation yet?

The boat was moving at a fast clip. The afternoon waves were rough, and my stomach lurched. Wondering how best to help, I reluctantly left Xavier on the phone and went to the bridge, clinging tight to every handrail.

According to Paco, the boat needed to refuel before heading back on the hours long trip to the mainland.

"I should have done it this morning," he cursed, his face scrunched in agony, and I could see he was on the verge of tears. "Why did I not do it this morning?"

I squeezed his wrinkled hand where it gripped the wheel.

Paco had already called Andrea, Rod, and Chef, and we would pick them up at the dock in Calvi as soon as we could get around the headland.

Every moment counted.

Feeling helpless, I went downstairs and slipped the rubber seasick bracelet back on my wrist. I quickly stripped off my wet bikini and holding onto the towel rail for balance against the rocking motion, rinsed the salt off my body. I pulled on shorts, a t-shirt and running shoes, and threw my wet hair up into a bun. Then, trying to keep my hands busy and my mind distracted, I packed all my belongings, unsure where I'd be sleeping tonight or *if* I'd be sleeping.

Poor little Dauphine.

God, I hoped she wasn't scared. What kind of monster might this uncle of hers be? Xavier had mentioned he'd had problems.

My stomach twisted in fear, I felt ill. What must Xavier be going through?

I wanted to be with him and comfort him through this. Trying to think how I could be most helpful, I thought through what we might need when we found her, or what the night might bring. She'd probably have to talk to the police. There'd probably be a lot of waiting. I went to her room. It was freshly made up. A few of the animals she'd left behind were sitting on the bed. I could pack a bag with a change of clothes for her. I went and grabbed the beach bag she and I had been using and took a set of clothes and pajamas from her drawer. Then I selected a small, soft, clingy monkey from her animal collection. In the bathroom, I went through her drawer to see if she'd left an old toothbrush. I found a new unopened one and threw that in the bag too. Going back to my room, I dug out my sketchbook and rolled up a few blank pages with two pencils and used one of my hair-ties to secure it and laid that in the bag too.

I could feel the weight of Xavier's desperation and fear emanating through the entire boat. Taking the bag I'd packed for Dauphine, I headed up to the galley and threw in a bottled water and a granola bar. What if it wasn't her uncle? What if his appearance was coincidence? What if some sick fucker had taken her? Not for ransom, but for terrible, unthinkable, unfathomable reasons. My stomach heaved, and my heart pounded. It had to be a thousand times worse for Xavier. And what about *Madame Pascale*, his mother? She'd lost Dauphine on her watch. God, this was agony. Outside the window was open ocean. I couldn't tell how close we were to picking up the crew and refueling.

This second night in Corsica had been for me. If I hadn't been here, Xavier would already be heading home. He might even be there already. My skin grew clammy with the thought. Was it my fault?

I slung the bag on my shoulder and left the galley to the sitting room, so I could see if we were almost back to Calvi. We were. This was taking too long. I went to Xavier's room.

It was quiet and his door was open. Poking my head around the door, I scanned the stateroom, expecting to see him on the phone.

"Xavier?" I called softly.

There was no answer, but I heard a muffled sound. I entered and rounded the bed, rushing to Xavier's aid.

He was hunched over, rocking, his head hitting the ground. He jerked when my hand touched his bare spine, sucking in a hitched breath.

"Shh," I soothed, falling to my knees next to him, and rubbed his back, my own eyes filling with stinging tears. "Shhh. We are going to find her," I whispered. "She's all right. She's going to be all right."

He leaned sideways, his head finding my lap and his arms coming around my waist. He was shaking—a full body tremble. He was in shock, I realized, and probably also having a panic attack and some form of PTSD episode. I bit my lip as I gave in and cried with him, holding him as tight as I could.

I didn't know how long we sat like that, but the phone he was clutching in his hand behind my back suddenly rang, loud and shrill.

Xavier jerked away from me.

I barely got a look at his face before he scrubbed it with his arm and got up.

"*Oui*," he barked, stalking away. He was still in his swimsuit. "*Bon. Immédiatement*," he said and hung up.

Getting up off the floor, I realized he needed some things too. I picked up the pink linen shirt on the bed. "You need to get dressed. Can I help you with anything?"

"*Non*," he said. He turned toward me but walked straight by me to the bathroom. He closed the door.

I sank down to the end of the bed, holding his shirt. There was nothing worse than this feeling of impotence to help. I got my phone out of my shorts pocket and thought about texting or calling Madame. My fingers ran over the texture of Xavier's shirt, and I brought it to my nose and inhaled the comforting scent of this man I loved—the father of the little girl I adored.

Then I started praying.

Please, God. Please let Dauphine be safe. Please touch the heart of the person who has her and ask them to return her to her father, safe and unhurt. He needs her. They only have each other. Losing her will kill him, she's all he has left. Please, please. Please. Please.

I swiped the tears that had rolled down my cheeks.

The bathroom door snapped open and Xavier came out.

"You're still here," he said in a flat voice.

"Have you heard anything more?"

"No."

I swallowed. "Is there anything I can do?" I asked helplessly.

He gave a bitter laugh as he buttoned his cuff and headed to his desk. Papers were all around it from his earlier frantic search for his phone. "You've done enough."

"Wha-what do you mean?"

He blew out a breath as he leaned down and began gathering paper.

I stood and bent to help him.

"Leave it," he barked.

I raised my hands. "S-sorry."

He pinched the bridge of his nose. "I shouldn't have even been here."

My fear exactly. Guilt tore through my stomach. All of our beautiful and sensual moments turned sordid and dirty. Like we were being punished for stealing these selfish moments of pleasure. "I-I'm sorry," I said. And I was.

I wished I could rewind time and plan to stay with Dauphine and Madame Pascale until my flight.

I would have been with her. I would have been an extra set of eyes. Extra protection. She would be safe right now.

My hand settled on my belly, feeling the pain and guilt settle deep in my gut. *Oh, Dauphine, I'm so sorry.* I sniffed and wiped my eyes. "How soon can the boat make it back tonight?" I asked.

How many more hours of agony will we endure waiting and unable to do anything to help find her?

"I'm having my helicopter pick me up from Calvi. The boat will follow."

"Oh. That make sense." Gesturing to the beach bag I'd packed, I stood. "You should take that. I packed some things for Dauphine for ... when you find her. In case it's late and you have to speak to the police or something. There's a change of clothes and things."

"Thank you," he said and then looked down at his phone, scrolling, his brow furrowed.

The engine of the boat changed, and I knew we were approaching the port. He pulled out a small brown leather bag of his own and threw in some clothes, then took the beach bag I'd packed and reached in to add the contents to his bag. He transferred the monkey and the clothes and the toothbrush.

"And water and a snack," I prompted. "It could be late. She could be hungry."

He nodded.

"Wait, there's also some sketch paper in there. If there's any waiting around. She might be bored."

He reached back in and drew out the paper and an old receipt or something that he stared hard at.

"Okay, well." I wrung my hands. This was agony. I wanted to go with him and be there when he got her back. And he would. He had to. I wanted to hug Dauphine so tight against my heart when he did. But I had to step back and let him do this himself. It was the only way he knew. "Please tell her I love her when you get her back."

He looked up at me, the small square of paper still in his hand. "Were you part of it?"

I looked at him, confused. "What?"

"I asked, were you a part of it?"

"Of what?"

"Taking her."

The words detonated between us.

My skin grew cold as the blood in my body seemed to drain away. I was paralyzed in shock, unable to even form a reply. He thought *I* had something to do with this? Why?

"Are you asking me what I think you are?"

"Yes."

I opened my mouth, then closed it. *Jesus.* "I—I can't—"

"It's an easy question." He cocked his head, his mouth twisting in disgust. "A question I think you are having trouble answering."

"What are you talking about? What's the question exactly? Are you kidding me?"

He held up what was in his hands.

I narrowed my eyes on it. It was the business card that the creep Alfred Morosto had given me as Dauphine and I left the bathroom at *Le Club Cinquante Cinq.*

"Evan believes that Michello, Arriette's brother, is working with Alfred Morosto. That somehow Morosto tipped Arriette's brother off about our plans."

Oh. *Oh.*

"I need you to tell me every single thing he said to you that day on the beach, and what you told him, and I want to know what he promised you."

CHAPTER FORTY-TWO

The approaching helicopter was sleek, black, and shiny with minimal markings. There was just a tail number that began with XP, and I guessed it was the helicopter version of a vanity plate. It drew a crowd in the port as it touched down at the end of a long seawall.

I had no idea what kind of string-pulling had happened to allow Xavier to use the port as his own personal airport.

Xavier barked at me to follow as he ducked low. I hadn't thought I was going with him, but everything suddenly changed. I'd gone from his lover to a traitor in the blink of an eye.

He was reacting out of fear and panic, and I was trying really hard to keep that in mind.

But internally I was seething and hurting, my fists clenching, and my head aching from grinding my teeth.

The wind in my ears and thump of the blades was deafening. I held my hair out of my eyes as best I could as I followed him, running low to the loud beast. If it wasn't for Dauphine, I would have told him to fuck off when he suddenly demanded I leave all my things and accompany him. But with a chance to get to her sooner, help find her, or at least be there when they did, I was biting back my anger.

He twisted the handle of the door and wrenched it open, gesturing me inside.

I climbed up into the cool dark interior, dipping my chin at a single pilot in a black helmet and headset with reflective glasses who nodded back. There were four black leather passenger seats, two pairs facing each other. I sat on the farthest one, facing toward the cockpit. I didn't know much about being in one of these things, but if it was anything like a train, I wanted to be facing in the direction I was heading. Nerves slipped through me, upending my stomach.

Xavier secured the door before taking the seat just inside, catty corner to me, his back to the cockpit, his long legs folding next to me. The closing of the door didn't diminish the sound, just muffled the sharpness.

I found a seatbelt and secured it and tried my best to smooth and retie my hair. Then I looked over at Xavier.

His eyes were bloodshot, his hair wild from the wind, and I suddenly noticed he'd misbuttoned his shirt getting dressed earlier. I hung on to that small detail to remind myself he was a human and terrified father and not a megalomaniac billionaire who thought I'd wronged him. Not deep down. At least I hoped so.

He turned his head to nod at the pilot over his shoulder and unhooked a set of earphones from his headrest, putting them on. He tapped them and pointed to beside my head.

I turned my face, seeing the headset right next to me by the window.

My stomach lurched as the machine rose, and the pier rushed away beneath us. Fumbling with the earphones and the mouth-piece, I managed to get them on.

Silence.

My ears rang in the void of sound as I adjusted. Then Xavier spoke, something in French. The pilot responded. They conversed back and forth a few times.

Outside the window, the low sun cascaded over the peninsula of *La Revellata* and over the azure bays. It was hard to believe what had happened down there just a couple of hours ago. I should have been building emotional armor instead of falling all the way in love. Because damn it, my heart was splintering, and I wanted to double over with the pain of it.

Fear for Dauphine was the only thing keeping me functioning.

Then the helicopter banked, causing me to grab onto my seat with both hands, and turned out to sea.

"Josephine," Xavier said in my ears.

I looked up at his flat mouth and his blank eyes.

"I have told the pilot to put us on a separate channel. Can you hear me?"

I nodded, my belly nauseous.

"Start talking."

I took a calming breath and counted to three. "About what?"

"Don't be diff—"

"Difficult? I'm trying really hard right now to give you the benefit of the doubt," I snapped. "I didn't resist when you basically frog-marched me onto this death-trap of a machine only because I'm also terrified for Dauphine. And every second you think I had something to do with her being taken is wasting precious time figuring out who actually has her."

His eyes narrowed. "What did he say to you?"

"Morosto? You already asked me that on the beach that afternoon."

"And you didn't tell me."

"Because there was hardly anything to say," I said and leaned toward him. "He made a pass at me. He told me I could come and be a nanny in his house."

Xavier's jaw tightened and he bared his teeth. I was guessing he knew Morosto didn't have young children.

"Or," I lifted a shoulder, "spy on you for him."

His head cocked. "And did you?"

I gave a humorless laugh as I shook my head in disbelief, sitting back. "Fuck you."

Xavier made a strangled sound in his throat, and his fist pounded the seat in front of him.

I gasped, my jaw dropping. "You asshole," I hissed, my heart leaping into my throat with fright. It was in no way aimed at me or even close, but the violence of it left me shaking. "Calm down or I'm not speaking to you ever again. I had nothing to do with this, and you damn well know it," I barreled on, shaken. "Alfred Morosto is a creep. He asked me if I was interested in an 'arrangement.' I said, no. He called me an icy bitch and asked me if I warmed up more for *you*. He assumed we were fucking." I dragged in a breath. "Like father like son, right?"

Xavier flinched.

Fuck. I looked away, squeezing my eyes shut, so I didn't have to look down and see how high we were over nothing but water. "And he called you a nerd." I remembered the final detail. "Are you happy now?"

Xavier was quiet and when I glanced back, he was leaning down, cradling his head in his hands.

Silence crackled between us over the airwaves.

His muscular shoulders outlined against his shirt heaved as he breathed deeply, and I itched to reach out and soothe him. To comfort him about Dauphine, to take back my biting words. Even after his actions.

But I turned my head to the window, hanging onto my anger.

"Where was Dauphine?" he asked after a few moments.

"In the bathroom. I was waiting for her outside it. He cornered me in the hallway."

"Why did you take his card?"

"Because it was either that or he was going to slip it between my breasts himself." I glared at Xavier, and he stared right back.

He was a master of non-expression, and I knew I wasn't. I only hoped he could see in my face how utterly outrageous his accusation was and how much he'd hurt me with it. To think how differently we'd gazed at each other not so long ago, our bodies slick with sea water and desire.

I'd known our relationship was temporary, but there was no way I could have predicted the hammer that would come down on us. I swallowed and set my chin. "I think you're forgetting who I am. I have a life waiting for me back home. A career." If I could build it back up. "I am an architect. Something I worked hard for. I didn't ask to be here. And I don't even work for you anymore." My chest heaved. "I was going to leave, *Xavier,* remember? This trip to Corsica, that I'm now regretting with every fiber of my being, was *your* idea because you were horny and lonely. And don't you forget it."

Without his brief display of rage a few moments ago, and his general dishevelment, you wouldn't even know what he was thinking. His gaze on mine flickered, the only clue that he heard what I was saying.

I tore my eyes away and stared out at the graduated blue canvas of the horizon. Then I closed my eyes and conjured Dauphine's sweet, joyful, laughing smile. She was going to be okay. That certainty struck me deep. "Stop pointing fingers at me, and let's start thinking about how to find her," I added tiredly.

"You are correct."

"Excuse me?" I opened my eyes.

He looked back at the phone in his hand and read a text and then began texting someone back. "I should be focusing on Dauphine, not you," he said after a few moments not looking up.

I blinked at his coldness. My eyes flooded, and my breath left me like I'd been winded. A little girl was missing. This wasn't the time to indulge the tsunami of rejection and pain engulfing me. But my heart was breaking, tearing off in great jagged chunks. And I simply couldn't hold it together anymore.

My chest constricted, unable to hold back the choking sob. Yanking my mouthpiece down so he didn't have to hear it, I stuffed my fist in my mouth and curled over as if I could keep my heart from falling out of my chest.

The rest of the helicopter ride was silent for me. Xavier had gone onto a channel with the pilot, and I was left hanging in the muffled silence as we sliced through the air to mainland France. I could see the coastline, littered with the towns and cities of the Riviera.

I'd barely registered we were coming down on the roof of his mother's house and then we were touching down. Clearly, I'd missed the flat roof and helipad on my tour. I glimpsed Madame out the window. She clutched the sleeve of her secretary, Jorge—both shielding their eyes from the sun and the wind of the blades.

My legs were jelly as we disembarked.

The elegant *grand-mère* I'd met had been replaced by an old lady with shaking hands who grabbed Xavier into a close hug, tears streaming down her face. Then she turned to me, and it was the most natural thing in the world for us to reach for each other, and in a moment I was wrapped in a hug full of warmth and sorrow and shared fear.

The engine turned off and the blades slowed, the roar slowly dying. My ears rang.

"Come, we will speak to the police, they have arrived downstairs," Madame all but shouted.

Xavier nodded and stalked ahead. He looked broken, and terrified, and so utterly alone, and I wanted to support him.

Instead, I held out my arm for Madame, and she clasped it tightly while we followed.

Jorge held open a door to a stairwell with stucco walls and tile steps. The metal clanged closed behind us.

The sound of Xavier's phone bleated loudly in the echo

chamber of the stairwell. Ahead of us, he brought it to his ear, mid jog down the steps. *"Allo."* He stopped dead, his hand reaching for the railing. His legs collapsed as he sat.

My stomach bottomed out. *Oh fuck.*

Beside me, Madame's bony hand squeezed my arm like a vice. *"Ô, mon Dieu, ô mon Dieu,"* she wailed.

"Shhh," I soothed. There was no way Xavier could hear anything if she cried any louder. "Shhh. Let him listen."

We hurried down, stepping around him so we could see his face and try to get any kind of indication of what news he'd just received. Inside, I found myself chanting *please be okay, please be okay.*

His eyes squeezed closed as he listened to whoever was on the other end.

Madame laid a hand on his shoulder, and he grabbed it and held tight, taking the comfort. But by the rigidity in his body, I could tell that he wanted to kill whoever was on the other end of the line.

"Oui," he said, the word wrenched from him like it cost him everything he had. Then he took the phone from his ear.

CHAPTER FORTY-THREE

"*S'il te plaît*," Madame begged as the phone slipped from Xavier's ear.

I watched as his entire body and spirit seem to collapse in on itself with ... wait. Relief?

"*Elle va bien,*" he whispered. "She is okay. For now. Michello has her. He wants money. But he'll be lucky if he sees blue skies ever again. Evan knows where he is. God willing, Dauphine will be home by bedtime."

"Oh my God." I breathed the words, my voice failing me. It wasn't over yet, who knew how crazy this Michello person was, but knowing who had her was hopefully more than half the battle.

Madame and I embraced with relief, and then as Xavier stood, she grabbed him and wrapped her arms around his back.

I stepped back, hugging my arms around myself.

Xavier released his mother. For a moment he stared at me.

Desperate to reach for him, I clenched my fists at my sides.

Our eyes locked for milliseconds that felt like long minutes.

I licked my lips. "I hope you get her back soon. W-what can I do to help?"

He blinked, his eyes cutting away. "I'm going down to speak to the police, so they can coordinate with Evan. Then I will take the helicopter. Accompany my mother by car to my villa in Valbonne." His jaw flexed. "Please."

I swiped at my leaking eyes. "Of course."

He and his mother had another quick emotional exchange.

His eyes cut to me again briefly, and then we were on the move again.

Downstairs, two plainclothes men who were identified as policemen, took my name but didn't ask any questions. Madame and I left Xavier with them and followed Jorge and Madame's housekeeper Astrid to a waiting black Mercedes in the circular driveway. Everything was happening in a blur. I clutched Madame's hand.

"It feels wrong to leave Xavier to find her alone," Madame said as we got in the car.

I squeezed her hand. "I know. I feel the same. Will he be okay?"

"The police will accompany him. I ... yes, I hope so." Her voice shook, betraying her terror.

"They didn't ask me any questions," I said, just now realizing how odd that was.

"Xavier told them you had nothing to do with it and that you were with him in Calvi."

My eyes filled again. So he could tell *them*, but not me? I clenched my jaw and willed myself to understand that he was a man in panic. An apology might come later. Right now, he just needed to get to Dauphine. "He'll bring her home, and she'll need you there waiting for her," I told Madame reassuringly.

I, on the other hand, felt like a burden in a family crisis. My passport and belongings were stranded on a boat in the ocean. I couldn't leave. Although at this stage, I'd happily leave everything I owned behind not to have to face Xavier's coldness ever again. A sigh wrenched from my emotionally tired body. I was terrified for Dauphine and desperate to see her safe. And fear and heart-break had depleted me.

I just wanted to go home. I wanted to wake up in my shoebox room in my aging apartment I shared with my two best friends. I wanted to look out the kitchen window and see a brick wall that I knew. I never wanted to see another yacht. I wanted to walk to my favorite little coffee shop and hope that the French lady, Sylvie, didn't remind me of Xavier. Or a little girl I'd lost my heart to. Then, for a living, I wanted to draw, create, imagine, and protect history all day.

And I wanted to go back in time—back to before—to my safe life in my small city. A place where I didn't know how many shades of blue an ocean, or a broken man's eyes, could be.

Madame smiled a watery smile, unaware of the turmoil and sadness that had suddenly overcome me. "Dauphine will need you too."

"Maybe. *I* need to see her safe." And then I needed to see myself safe. There was no ignoring my throbbing heart that still gasped like a gutted fish in my chest. After I held Dauphine close, I'd need time to heal away from all this. *Breathe, Josie.*

"She loves you. So much."

"I love her too." I was going to crush her tiny body in the biggest hug when we had her safe. God, I hoped she was all right and not scared. The poor girl already had nightmares. My stomach swirled with rage at thinking of the asshole who had her, of how terrified she must be. I understood an inkling of how Xavier must be feeling. He must want to tear Michello limb from limb. It was a pity he was a legitimate businessman and not a gangster because I'm sure with his resources he could make some-body disappear. I took a deep breath. God, I wanted to hold him. Comfort him. Even after his brutal accusations today. The image of him curled up, his head in my lap, in a rare moment of vulnera-bility flashed through my mind, and I blinked back the burn of more tears.

"And my son? Do you love *him?*"

I jerked, my deep inhale interrupted.

"I'm sorry. I did not mean ... to shock you."

My head shook with a will of its own, but I couldn't answer.

Her hand squeezed mine.

I blew out the long, slow, steadying breath. "It doesn't matter."

"He deserves to find love again."

I closed my eyes against the burn of tears and nodded. "He does."

"You must forgive him. He is not easy. He was always a wary child. His father ... and myself, if I am honest ... we did not show him the best example of love. It was ... how do you say?" She pursed her lips. "It was ... currency? We used love, and Xavier's love, against each other."

I winced internally and nodded in understanding at the way she gave her explanation as a question, due to the language insecurity. But I turned her explanation over in my mind.

If Xavier didn't feel worth loving ... if he didn't think he had emotional value, or wasn't worth investing in, or being a risk worth taking ... or worse, if he didn't feel he was worth *living* for, then yes, perhaps that was how he saw it. Maybe even the way he gave it. "I agree he thinks he doesn't deserve love."

"He blames himself for Arriette." Madame's patrician profile was silhouetted as we sped along the highway, streetlights glowing amber, casting her in sharp relief.

"Yes," I agreed, and after a brief hesitation, added, "I got the impression from him you did not approve of her."

"I should have been better about accepting Arriette when she was alive. I always thought he was too good for her. Perhaps a mother's pride. But in the end I was right. He had to fight that battle alone. He didn't feel he had my support when things got bad. And of course when she died he probably thought I was saying ... I told you so ..." She shook her head.

"Have—have you told him your regrets?"

"Not in so many words. Besides, their union produced Dauphine."

"I think he probably needs to hear it. Maybe not the part about where you think you were right. I think he already knows that."

She gave a humorless laugh, then sighed. "I have not been the best mother. And with the terrible example his own parents set, it's no wonder he chose poorly."

My chest squeezed. "He loves you. And no one is perfect. We all do the best we can," I soothed. And suddenly I ached for my own mom. She'd said similar things to me growing up when she and I had crossed wires, about how she was just doing the best she could. And she did. I never doubted her devotion. Even when she chose Nicholas De La Costa as my stepfather.

Madame patted my knee. "Yes. I hope you will remember your own words of wisdom when you and Xavier are working out your differences. When this is all over and my granddaughter is safe. We all do the best we can."

I narrowed my eyes at her emotional outmaneuvering, but she pretended not to notice. "He accused me of being involved in what happened today," I said instead.

Her inhale was sharp. "*Non.*"

"*Oui,*" I responded.

She flicked her hand through the air. "Ridiculous!"

"*Oui,*" I repeated, waiting for the inevitable question of why he might have thought that with a hint of suspicion. None came. Instead she said, "He is looking for an excuse to set you away from his heart. And that tells me all I need to know."

She picked up my hand in hers again. "After we have Dauphine back in our arms, please ... please give him a chance. Love is ... true and real. And deep love is ... so rare. I am only just discovering it myself. I saw the way my son looked at you yesterday when he thought none of us would notice and," she caught my eyes and held them, "and the way you looked at him. You have been ... healing for him. For Dauphine. Real love from the right person will do that."

Thinking of all that had passed between Xavier and me, and how little time we'd really had to cement who we were to each other before a crisis showed me just how ill-built our connection had been, I steadied my voice. "Sometimes love doesn't come fast enough. And sometimes it's not enough."

"And sometimes love is all it takes." She winked cheekily, even while her shoulders were still tense with fear. Neither of us let go of each other's hand.

The car left the highway and a roundabout put us on a two-lane road. We sped up the hills and sharp turns in the failing light. It was almost nine p.m. Somewhere to the west the sun was about to set. Every few minutes Madame would silence her phone, unwilling to take a call and risk missing one from her son. In this instance, no news did not feel like good news.

The car slowed around a bend lined with tall, pointy cypress trees. Then we pulled onto a white gravel driveway in front of two towering wrought iron gates between two stucco pillars. The gates silently swung open, and then we were moving again, purring through them into a manicured estate. There were forests either side of us, but the road was bordered with small hedges and every few yards a topiary tree full of white roses. They gave way to lines of lavender as the trees cleared, and cresting a small hill, there was suddenly a sweeping manor house. Low, maybe two stories with an attic, but swung extravagantly out to both sides. It was aged stucco with neatly edged plum vine and a sturdy slate roof. The car did a slow turn and crunched to a halt outside the large wooden double front door.

Outside, the evening was filled with the scent of lavender and the sound of cicadas. Astrid and Jorge went inside, turning on lights. "Xavier's housekeeper is away so Astrid will prepare our rooms," Madame said.

"I'll help," I offered. I needed something to do or go crazy. Inside, the entryway soared up two stories with stucco walls, aged wooden beams, and terra-cotta floors. Astrid jogged up the tiled stairs, and I followed. I helped her put sheets on two queen beds in side by side rooms that were prettily decorated in blue and white and yellow and white respectively. Then at the end of a hall was clearly Dauphine's room. A white canopy bed with fairy lights and covered in stuffed animals. Astrid peeled back the pale lavender coverlet and we made up the bed with fresh sheets. We worked quietly side by side, her English and my French unable to provide much conversation over the mute fear that something might go wrong, and Dauphine might not come home.

Downstairs, I could hear Madame and Jorge, and soon the smell of baking bread wound up the stairs. My stomach growled. On the side table was a picture in a frame. I stepped closer and picked it up. Dauphine was small, maybe five or six. Her mother, a slender and exotic looking stunner, her long hair falling in a silken cascade over one shoulder, knelt next to her daughter, an arm around her shoulder. They both smiled the same smile into the camera. Dauphine's was missing two front teeth, but there was no mistaking she was this woman's daughter. It must be a painful reminder for Xavier to see Arriette in his daughter every day.

Astrid cleared her throat, indicating she was waiting for me.

Following her, I entered the final bedroom. It had windows and a balcony across the back wall, but the space was dominated by a king-sized bed done in flax linen in shades of dried tobacco leaf. It was cozy and masculine and smelled of Xavier. The unique scent of his skin mixed with salt and cedar. I blinked, feeling lightheaded, a wave of sadness burning my throat.

My legs felt weak with the urge to crawl into the bed, surrounded by his scent, and wait for his return.

Realizing I was standing still, staring at the bed, I shook my head. Astrid gave me a sad and knowing smile before pointing to an empty shelf and saying something in French. I gathered there were no spare sheets in the closet, or they were already on the bed. I wasn't sure which. She straightened the bed, and then we went back downstairs.

Jorge was halfway up with Madame's valise and nodded to me. "Any news?" I asked as I passed.

"Madame is speaking with Monsieur Pascale now."

I pulled out my phone and rounded the corner into a large charming kitchen.

There was a text from a number I didn't recognize.

I have her. We will not be back until late. X.

Xavier.

I gave a gasp of relief as I locked eyes with Madame. She was smiling and nodding, her phone to her ear as she caught my eye.

Feeling dizzy with relief, I slumped into a chair at the large wooden kitchen table. I responded to several texts from Andrea asking for an update.

I was going to hug Dauphine so tight I'd have to be careful not to crack a bone in her tiny bony.

And he'd texted me. That had to mean he didn't think I was involved any more, surely?

CHAPTER FORTY-FOUR

Sounds permeated my consciousness, and I blinked my eyes open. A small lamp threw shadows up the stucco walls.

I'd fallen asleep where I sat in an armchair, waiting for news of Dauphine. My back was stiff. I sat up and stretched, rolling my neck. Looking over, I saw Madame had made her way from her armchair to the couch where she snored softly. After Madame had received word from Xavier that he had been reunited with Dauphine but that they were still dealing with the police, we had had a dinner of soup and bread at the kitchen table with Astrid and Jorge. Then we'd come in here to wait.

The sound of a heavy door opening reminded me that I'd been woken up by sounds. I hurriedly made my way to Madame's side and shook her awake gently. "Madame. I think they are home." As soon as she blinked up at me, I left her and hurried to the doorway into the entrance hall.

Evan was holding the door open and the tall figure of Xavier, his arms cradling a sleeping Dauphine, carefully negotiated through the opening.

I stifled a sob with my hand, instantly bursting into tears upon seeing her safe. Hurrying forward, eyes on her, I approached and gently touched her head, giving it a gentle kiss before stepping back.

Xavier's face, tired and grim, gave me a single nod.

Before stepping away, I squeezed his arm where he held her, pouring every emotion I had into it since I couldn't leap into his arms and hug him.

Then Madame was there, and a series of relieved and excited whispers in French and more tears caused the noise level to grow. Dauphine stirred, her forehead creasing.

Xavier shushed her and inclined his head for the stairs.

I bounded quietly ahead of him and headed for Dauphine's room but realized my mistake when Xavier headed for his own bedroom and then laid his daughter down gently on one side of his bed. Silly me. I should have realized he'd rather not let her out of his sight. Especially not knowing what she might have been through and if she'd wake up in the night. He wouldn't want her to feel alone.

Working quietly alongside him, I unbuckled her sandals, noting her bare feet were dusty and dirty. The dress she'd worn was soft enough to sleep in, but I doubted she'd want to wake up in it and be reminded of her ordeal. Madame must have had the same thought because she appeared behind us with a pale green nighty with little mermaids on it.

Dauphine's hair was tangled, and I'd have to help her brush it out in the morning. I smoothed it back before kissing her forehead gently, tears of relief burning the back of my eyes.

"Was she hurt?" I whispered to him, terrified of the answer.

He paused and met my eyes. So much seemed to flash through his—pain, yearning, apologies, and things I couldn't decipher that looked like someone who'd stared into the abyss of hell and made it out by the grace of God. Then he shook his head and went back to his task.

My breath released with gusty relief.

Stepping back and melting toward the doorway, I left Xavier and his mother tucking Dauphine in.

In the blue and white room that was supposed to be mine, I closed the door and let out a bone weary sigh. In the ensuite bathroom, simply and beautifully appointed in white marble and blue Moroccan tile, I stared at my reflection.

What a day. My hair had almost dried in its bun. My skin looked pale and blotchy despite the tan I knew should be there, and my eyes looked puffy and exhausted from crying. I opened the drawers in the vanity and found a small airline kit in the last one. Inside was a tiny toothbrush and toothpaste. Assuming it had been left here for an unprepared guest, I gratefully brushed my teeth and rinsed my face. I'd have to sleep in the t-shirt I'd thrown on in Corsica earlier today. It felt like a lifetime ago. Looking at my phone, I saw it was around three in the morning.

I wanted to sleep, but I was also wired and wanting to find out what had happened to Dauphine. Inside, I was torn. I knew Madame would probably have Xavier give her as much of a debrief as he could tonight, and I wanted to be there for it. But perhaps I should just leave them to be a family. I couldn't shake the icy way he'd looked at me earlier today when he thought I was involved and the way he'd instantly assumed my guilt. Growing up, my dad always told me that how people behaved in a crisis was the true test of their character. Today had shown me that Xavier didn't trust easily. Maybe not at all. It helped me understand why he was friends with the people he worked with. But also that he was a father before anything, and that was admirable. It was heroic, even. If only all the men of the world took their fatherly duties as seriously as Xavier, perhaps the world would feel safer.

My father had given up fatherhood through no fault of his own when he'd died suddenly. I had to acknowledge the part of me that for many years, irrationally, blamed him for leaving us. I felt betrayed. Let down. But mostly, I was angry at my father for not fighting harder to live. I'd spent several months reading everything I could find about people seeing the light and then turning back for another chance at life, convinced if only Daddy had told them how much he loved me that he'd have been allowed another chance.

Every night, I wept and argued with God. At one point, my twelve-year-old self, only a little older than Dauphine, had asked God whether if I'd been a better daughter, less willful and more loving and appreciative, if maybe, perhaps, Daddy wouldn't have died. Then, of course, I'd gotten a stepfather who didn't take his fatherly duties seriously at all, in fact had used us as a shield of respectability, leaving my mother and me almost destitute and our reputation in tatters.

No, Xavier's distrust of everyone and everything for his daughter's sake, even at my expense, only served to make me admire him more. Understand him more. Love him more.

He was the kind of man I'd choose to have a family with, I admitted to myself. And it had nothing to do with his means and everything to do with him.

Dammit. My eyes filled again, and I gripped the sink and squeezed my eyes closed. This wasn't supposed to happen. I wasn't supposed to come to France and leave my heart behind. Xavier and his daughter meant everything to me. Everything. I wanted them for my own. How could I leave them voluntarily?

I heard the soft voice of Madame and the rougher cadence of Xavier. They were probably discussing what had happened and how Dauphine had been found.

I could always find out tomorrow.

Tomorrow.

I let down my hair with a sigh, brushing my fingers through it and then braiding it loosely.

Tomorrow I would hug that dear little mermaid, then I'd have to rescue my things and try to get home. I didn't even know what

day it was. Evan had mentioned something about flight avail-
ability later in the week. But then Madame had invited me to stay.
God, I was so torn and so adrift.

There was a quiet knock on my door. My stomach tightened.

"Josie?" Madame's voice called softly, and I tried not to feel
disappointment it wasn't Xavier. "*Tu vas bien?*"

I padded to the door and opened it. "*Oui*. I'm okay."

She cocked her head to the side, assessing me. "Would you like
to come downstairs? I know it is late, but we will hear the news of
what happened. *Oui?*"

"*Merci*." I nodded and followed her downstairs.

Evan, dressed in distressed jeans and a white polo, sat in the chair
where I'd fallen asleep. He was leaning forward, resting his forearms on his elbows. Xavier was standing by the bookshelves,
leaning his fists on a table. He looked exhausted and shell-
shocked—not relieved as I'd imagined—as if everything he knew
could no longer be counted on.

Madame and I perched on the sofa.

"*Alors*," Madame began. "*Qu'est-ce qui s'est passé?*"

"We will talk in English for Josie and Evan," Xavier said.

"Yes, of course." Madame shook her head. "So what
happened? How did they get to her?"

I could tell she was still blaming herself, and I squeezed her
hand. My gesture didn't escape Xavier's notice.

"We won't know all of it until the police have been through
the surveillance tapes," Evan said, "or Dauphine can tell us. But
she isn't saying much."

Poor girl was probably in shock and exhausted.

"There isn't much surveillance footage in that part of the
marina due to the recent construction so whatever Dauphine
shares will be critical in the case against Michello."

"Maybe she will talk tomorrow," Xavier said.

"Where did you find her?" I asked.

Evan explained that he'd known about a boat Michello had been sleeping on since getting out of prison because he'd been having him followed just to keep an eye on him. "He took Dauphine there with the promise of ice cream and pictures of Arriette—that's how we think he got her to trust him. What we are piecing together is how Michello knew Dauphine was with her grandmother. Someone must have informed him of our movements."

My stomach clenched tightly. And I looked to Xavier, who dropped his eyes from mine. So this was it. I was still the suspect? Grief almost felled me.

"We think it's Rod," Evan went on.

Wait.

What?

"*Rodney?*" Madame asked, shocked.

"What?" I asked. "Rod, as in the deck hand, *oi-all-right-mate-*Rod? No." I shook my head in bewilderment. "He wouldn't hurt a fly." I swallowed. "Would he?" And here I should just be happy I wasn't the suspect anymore ... but Rod? Oh my God. Poor Xavier. We'd all trusted him. "How ... why do you think that?"

Evan pinched the bridge of his nose. He looked exhausted too, and like he realized he shouldered much of the blame. "We don't think he did it on purpose. But, when I offered him the job a few years ago, he was ... let's just say he was headed down the wrong path, with the wrong people, and his mom is a family friend. I knew he was a good kid, just needed direction and gainful employment. But I've always kept one eye open with him just in case—afraid for the right amount of money someone might get to him. I also detected a feed from the Wi-Fi on the boat a few days ago. Someone had obviously opened a bad link and well, some of Xavier's business documents were compromised. Luckily, we think they only got a fraction before it was detected. When I asked each of the staff, Rod was acting all ...

off. Not much, but enough that I pressed him. He said he'd been approached a few weeks ago by a "total ten"—his words not mine —and spent the night with her. He almost missed the boat, showed up in the wee hours. Anyway the next day, she texted him and sent a link. Thinking it was a nude, he clicked." Evan's eyes rolled. "Not a nude of course. It was a wildlife picture. And yeah, bobs-your-uncle, we got ourselves some malware on the Wi-Fi."

"What is this, bobs?" Madame asked.

"In this context it just means 'of course.' *Bien sur*," Evan added the translation for her.

God, the trap could have happened to any one of us. "But what about Dauphine?" And how did Xavier get from malware to accusing me?

Xavier paced over to the other armchair and sank into it, weariness oozing out of every molecule. "Dauphine has an uncle, I mentioned him?"

I nodded.

"Michello," Madame spat. "*C'est une racaille.*" I could surmise what that meant.

Xavier went on. "We've been watching him, and he's been down at the port keeping an eye on us. We think he even had someone at *Les Caves* the night you and Andrea were there. Were you approached?"

"No." I shook my head. "Oh. Wait. There were these two guys. Young. Gorgeous. They were all over Andrea and me. Quite insistent, actually."

Xavier tensed. "Insistent how?"

My irritation simmered. What, was he jealous now? "Persuasive. Handsy."

His eyes narrowed.

"It was nothing over the line," I added, relenting.

Evan's eyes flicked between us. "Ahem. I think we get the point. I'd just found the discrepancy in the data feed and shut it down. That's when I told Xavier I thought we had some malware."

"I remember not being able to get online or send an email that day," I said.

"We think they were trying to get another link in by approaching you and Andrea. Anyway, it took a few days to go through what was compromised. But Xavier's calendar and our itinerary definitely were. We assumed corporate espionage. Especially when the day before yesterday, while you were sailing to Corsica, I had Xavier's assistant at the office in Sofia Antipolis reach out to the older Monsieur Pascale and tell him not to invite another person to meetings with his son before clearing it with us first. That's when he said he hadn't known Morosto was coming, that the reservation had been changed to add Morosto at the last minute. He thought Xavier had done it. So Morosto had known where we were going and when. It was a hunch that Morosto had been using Michello to get to Xavier. Michello would be a natural choice given the massive chip on his shoulder. And I knew where to look for him. We think access to where Dauphine might be was his part of the bargain. That he might use her to extort money from Xavier was always a probability."

"God. Where is Michello now?" I asked, wondering about the details of how Dauphine had been found and whether Michello had put up a fight. She could have been hurt.

"In jail, arrested on kidnapping and extortion charges," Evan said.

"*Mais*, what do you possess, Xavier, that would make this evil man Morosto risk certain jail time for a chance at it?" Madame asked. "And put my granddaughter in danger?"

Xavier shook his head. "It's nothing."

"It's everything," Evan said, rolling his eyes at Xavier. "Madame, your son has invented something that almost every government and every company will need in order to secure their place in a dystopian future. Which is looking more likely every day, but that's a different story. Let's put it this way. Even Bill Gates will want to use it." He chuckled. "Especially Bill Gates."

Xavier glared. "*Tais-toi,*" he muttered to Evan.

"To be honest," Evan blithely went on, "that plebian, Morosto wouldn't know what to do with the information even if he'd found it."

Madame nodded approvingly. "Xavier. You know I'm always so proud of you."

"*Merci,*" he said uncomfortably and shot an annoyed glance at Evan before rolling his eyes.

"*Mais maintenant,*" Madame went on with a short and decisive clap. "It is very late. Tomorrow everything will be clearer."

I wasn't sure I was ready to deal with everything between Xavier and me, not after such a frightening day. Of course, I'd be ready for his apology any time, the sooner the better, but he and I needed to talk about a whole lot more than that. And I was shattered.

Madame stood, and I followed suit.

Evan nodded at me. "I'll arrange to have your belongings delivered here tomorrow," he said as he headed toward the door. "Good night, Josie."

I wanted to follow Evan out and ask him about my flight home. Looking toward Xavier, I was about to tell him goodnight too.

"Josephine, please stay a moment?" He nodded at both his mother and Evan, and they left us alone.

CHAPTER FORTY-FIVE

Xavier and I stared at each other in the dim light of the library sitting room. He seemed so far away, and so exhausted, harrowing lines of the panic he'd faced earlier today etched around his eyes and bracketing his mouth. In any other situation where someone so dear to me had been through what Xavier had been through, I'd have been up and in his arms to hold him and comfort him.

Screw it.

I seemed to fly across the room, giving in to a decision I hadn't even known I'd made, and wrapped my arms around his torso.

He stumbled as he caught me.

Maybe if I held him tight enough, all those cracks and fissures in his heart would heal back up. I sniffed his shirt. The scent of him, tired, warm skin, only a hint left of his woodsy aroma swam through my limbs like a drug.

Beneath my arms, his muscles were tense and hard and I longed to slip my hands under his shirt.

It took a moment to realize how stiff his body was, and then he was setting me away from him.

The loss of him was like a chill wind.

He opened his mouth, then closed it and swallowed heavily, his eyes flicking away for a moment.

A rock dropped in my stomach. "Um," I began, "I'm so very relieved Dauphine is home. Glad you are both home. I know you're tired." Not knowing what to do with my arms, I folded them across my chest. "We can talk tomorrow. You need to sleep."

And I wish I could curl around you in your bed, I mentally added, *or you would curl around me and take whatever comfort you need.*

He nodded, mute.

The loud sound of ticking filled the silence, and my eyes sought out the antique clock sitting on a bookcase filled with hardback books. He didn't make a move to leave so I sat back down stiffly, my hands pressed between my knees.

He turned, the low light playing with the planes of his face highlighting his exhaustion.

I didn't want to be another problem he had to solve before he slept tonight.

"Xavier."

He scrubbed his hand down his face, and then his looming form skirted the coffee table and came toward me.

Sitting back, I leaned away to look up at his face.

"I know you need my apology," he said, lowering on to the coffee table in front of me, legs spread.

I nodded. "I do."

"And you are angry."

"I was. And I was hurt." I licked my lips to find moisture, and my eyes stung with the remembered ache of his distrust.

"I'm sorry, Josephine. You will never know how much. I am normally better at controlling myself, but of course I have never faced a nightmare like someone taking my daughter."

"Of course, I know that," I said. I wasn't a parent, but even I had felt the horror of learning Dauphine was missing. With that as the touchstone emotion of the day, it now had me feeling silly for being hurt. But then the accusing words he'd hurled at me echoed in my memory, making me annoyed for letting him off the hook. "Even though I understand." I paused, trying to find the right words. "You found it so easy to blame me. Even knowing how much I love Dauphine. Even after what you and I shared. Why?"

He drew his bottom lip between his teeth. "Evan had told me about Morosto ... then when I saw the card ... I, took a jump, what is the expression?"

"Jumped to conclusions?"

"*Oui. C'est ça.* Jumped to conclusions."

"That doesn't tell me why you thought I was capable of something so horrific."

His eyes stared into mine, weary. Conflicted. Fighting, and tired of fighting. He reached his hand up and pinched a strand of my hair that had fallen out of its braid, rubbing it between his fingers.

"I want to hold you," I admitted, and I thought my chin might be wobbling. "Comfort you. I wish you'd looked to me for help instead of pushing me away. It's all right to need someone, Xavier."

He blinked slowly, looking into my eyes and searching my face but didn't respond.

And my words now felt silly and far too vulnerable bouncing off his silence. "It's late," I said, swallowing his silent rejection. "You should go and be with your daughter in case she wakes up."

He let go of my hair and rubbed the back of his neck as if to ease an ache. He took a shallow breath, then stopped. Words seemed on the tip of his tongue.

"What?" I asked.

"This thing between us ... *je sais pas* ... it was ... I am not ... I do not want you to go, but I cannot ask you to stay."

My hopeful heart leapt at his words. Though I hated how weak that made me, especially after his lackluster apology.

"I do not want to use Dauphine to try to ask you to stay," he went on. "She will miss you very much. The first question she had for me was where you were. And I hoped you would be here." His head bowed. "But I would have understood if you left after the reaction I had. After what I said. I'll understand if you leave."

I stared at the top of his head, at his glossy brown, warm and soft hair, and tried to read between the lines of his words. Was he using Dauphine as an excuse because he wanted me to stay? Or was the idea of me leaving really just that minor to him. No, I was sure it was the former. The night and day we'd spent together had been so incredible, but it had been the natural course of so many feelings building up over weeks. We'd connected in a way I'd never felt in my whole life. I knew it was the same for him. It had to be. I'd felt it. Before everything went sideways. "Xavier. You know you deserve to feel good things too." My conversation in the car with Madame came back to me. "I think you believe you do not."

"Perhaps."

"I'm certain," I insisted.

"Josephine, I am half a man, but with a whole heart devoted to my daughter." He looked up, his eyes pleading with me. "That is *all* I am capable of right now."

Oh.

Oh.

I looked down to my chest. My hand was already pressed against it as if trying to hold everything together, to stop the pain. I should say something, I thought. I should put on a strong face so he didn't know the extent of the damage. I blinked and attempted to swallow the ball of grit that had formed in my throat without success. My pulse pounded in my throat and ears. *Count to ten, Josie. Breathe.* My voice, when it came out, was a scratchy whisper. "So you want me to stay, but *only* for Dauphine's sake?"

He grabbed my hand, making me wince at the contact, relief evident on his features. "*Oui*. You are very good with her. She needs you. After the shock, she needs stability. You will stay with us for a little while longer?"

I snatched my hand away, the backs of my eyes burning. My skin flashed hot, then cold, and a chasm of aching emptiness began to yawn open inside my chest. The chasm was going to swallow whole pieces of my heart. And it was going to fucking hurt.

"Josephine ..." His head tilted sideways.

I held up a palm and pulled it down when I felt my hands shaking.

"You warned me," I said. "You warned me to protect my heart. I'm afraid it was probably too late already."

He winced, his face paling, and closed his eyes.

"It's true. You're sitting here talking as if you don't know that I'm in love with you."

"Do not say this."

"I'm in love with a man who thinks love is looking for ways to hurt him. To destroy him. But that's not love." My voice shook. "Maybe you have never truly known it."

Xavier had pulled down the iron curtain of nothingness over his expression. "Perhaps not."

Silence ensued, my ears filled with the throb of my heartbeat and the damn fucking clock ticking louder than ever.

Awkward vulnerability made my skin crawl as seconds ticked by with no response. Not that I was expecting one. I cleared my throat before the humiliation of being so raw and exposed choked me. Wasn't love supposed to make one feel invincible? I had never felt so weak. "It wasn't one-sided," I said. "I know it wasn't. I know it in my bones. But you're pretending it was. When you found yourself attracted to me, instead of looking inside yourself and rejoicing, you blamed me."

"*Non.*"

"Yes. You have had a problem with me from the start. You said it yourself, I terrified you. And I thought you weren't a coward."

His lips curled in a hiss. "You have no idea what I've been through!"

"I know I don't."

He stood and came toward me. Then he seemed to think better of it and stopped, stuffing his hands in his pockets. He then pulled a hand out and raked it through his hair. "I barely know you, and yet I let myself get distracted by you for one day and look what happened to Dauphine."

What the fuck?

Pain took my breath away, my gasp loud in the silence.

He snapped his head to look at me, remorse filling his eyes. "*Non.* I didn't mean that." He walked toward me and I held a hand up, shaking my head.

"You did," I choked out. "I've discovered you rarely say anything you don't mean, and this is no exception."

"*Merde.* I don't know how to say the right thing. I do not want to hurt you. But yes, I did mean that. In a way." His hand grasped mine, and I let him, trying to pretend touching him didn't matter. "I am a father before everything, Josephine. I let myself forget that for a moment. I am sorry for the way I have been, for what I might have led you to believe. You are correct, my head has been a mess since you arrived. And I cannot afford it. Today showed me that more than anything. There is no space for … us. For some mad, meaningless sex, when it could mean I lose my daughter."

My breath choked. "Meaningless."

He dropped his gaze, his eyes filled with regret.

I took a step back. "That's all I am. I tell you I'm in love with you, and you call me someone to have sex with? Someone you barely know?" My words hardly made it out, my voice was gone. "Call a fucking hooker then. It would have been cheaper. For both of us."

He flinched like I'd slapped him. He stepped toward me, his eyes screaming things I'd never hear him say, his mouth twisted in anger and … shame. "But even so, please stay." His hand, rough and warm, slipped around the back of my neck. His gaze flicked to my mouth and then back to my eyes. "For *her*."

My breathing grew shallow, betraying the effect he had on me. He was so close. His eyes so tortured. His mixed-messages were breaking me. It hadn't been meaningless, but he wouldn't admit it. He wanted me, but he wouldn't allow himself to.

My fingers closed around his wrist and pulled his hand from my skin because, God knew, I couldn't think clearly with him touching me, with his eyes conveying wants and needs he'd never allow himself to indulge while he ignored what it had cost me to admit my feelings.

The faint crease between his eyebrows deepened.

I took a shaking breath and lifted my shoulders as if I could ease the splintering inside me. "As I said, I love Dauphine." Dread at the idea of being around Xavier after what we'd shared was like cement in my stomach. "For her, I'll stay. For a few days at most," I added. "To make sure she is okay. But more than that, I cannot do. Please try to stay out of my way, and I will try to stay out of yours."

Somehow, I made it to the door. "Please have Evan bring my passport and my belongings as soon as possible." I turned the handle and stopped. Turning my head, I looked him dead in the eyes. The words, "You coward," danced on my tongue. "I hope one day you realize you are worth loving," I said instead. Then I slipped through and closed the door behind me.

I raced silently up the stairs to my bedroom and flung myself onto the bed.

Down the hall, I heard Dauphine murmuring in her sleep, and I waited, tense, until I heard Xavier pad quietly up the stairs. He would be with her if she woke. Only then, did I let the full weight of everything hit me.

And when the crying was done, I asked myself how I'd gotten here. Not just emotionally, but physically. So, I'd had a hiccup in my career, I should have stayed in Charleston, in my own life, and fought for what I wanted. I wasn't mad at Tabitha and Meredith, but I wondered at myself that I'd so easily gone along with this harebrained idea. My mother had been right, I'd run away.

I didn't know who I was anymore. It was as if the Josie I'd grown up with—the strong, resilient, ambitious, probably-never-going-to-fall-in-love-because-men-couldn't-be-trusted-Josie—was standing over the bed, arms folded and her foot tapping the carpet, wondering who this weak, lost, version of herself was. "You see," she said to me, "I was right. Now pull yourself together, we're going home."

Sleep when it came was fitful and tortured. In my dreams, Dauphine was still gone, and Xavier wouldn't talk to me. He'd look through me like I wasn't even there, even when I tried to pound on his chest to get his attention.

But when I awoke, I was resolved—I could lose my heart, but I couldn't and wouldn't lose my sense of pride, and that would surely happen if I stayed. He may not love me, but he'd want to sleep with me again. But come hell or hot Frenchman I was flying home before the week was done.

CHAPTER FORTY-SIX

I jerked awake, my neck aching and my eyes gritty as the plane touched down in Charleston. I took a deep inhale and tried to stretch my back, my shoulders stiff and sore. Having forgotten to close my window shade when we took off at seven this morning from New York, midmorning sun shone like a spotlight, making it hard to get my eyes open. Then the pain in my heart took over everything else, and the deep breath I'd just taken shot out of me like I'd been punched.

We taxied to the gate, and everyone around me hummed with the energy of excitement and anticipation. I rested my head against the window and let my eyes adjust, taking long, slow, breaths to ease what was happening inside me. Should I have left? Should I have stayed and fought for the father and daughter I'd fallen so hard for?

Madame had begged me.

Evan had begged me.

Dauphine had begged me.

My eyes burned as they flooded anew. I'd stayed with Dauphine five extra days, trying to give her some semblance of normalcy and joy after her traumatic experience that she still wouldn't talk about.

Xavier and I had co-existed under the same roof. Strained family meals. Avoided eye contact. Awkward silences.

And then *he* had all but begged me. And I couldn't regret the moment of weakness I'd had, allowing myself one last bittersweet goodbye.

The night before I left came back to me. Xavier, Madame, Dauphine, Evan, and I sat around the large worn wooden table under an arbor wrapped in trailing vines, eating make-your-own pizza baked in the brick oven in the garden. We'd also asked Astrid and Jorge to eat with us. Chances were it could have been the best pizza I'd ever eaten, but every bite tasted like sawdust. The evening air was thick with the leftover sunbaked scent of jasmine and lavender. The colors in the sky were fading to faint streaks of smoke and fire. The red wine had loosened my limbs, and I'd tried to laugh along and follow the conversation as it tripped back and forth between French and English.

We were clearing the table and Astrid and Jorge had just shooed Madame back to the house because it apparently upset the order of the universe to have Madame attempt to help. So she'd taken Dauphine by the hand to help her get ready for bed, and I was feeling useless. Astrid and Jorge took the plates to the kitchen, and Evan followed with a handful of glasses. Xavier went to grab the large wooden paddle that belonged to the pizza oven, and turned his back, scooping out the ashes into a metal bin. I looked away and across the yard toward the glowing blue pool. If I hadn't spent the entire afternoon with Dauphine in the pool playing everything from Marco Polo to mermaids and gymnasts, I'd have done twenty more laps just so I would maybe pass out and wake up the day I was leaving.

Xavier had spent the day working under the fans of the loggia, and I'd felt the weight of his eyes on us all day. On me.

My flip flops made no sound on the worn stone patio as I

stood and rounded the table so I could stack the remaining glasses to follow Evan.

Halfway through, I stopped to look up. Xavier's stillness had caught my attention. His back was to me but as if he knew my every move. The tension was palpable. We were alone. We'd managed not to be alone since the night in the library.

He turned.

His eyes were the deep end, and I wanted to dive in.

I was still, rooted to the spot, as he set down the wooden pizza paddle to the side and came toward me.

He glanced briefly at the house, but I couldn't let my attention go. Not for a second.

Gently he took the glasses from my hands and set them on the table with concentrated care. I flexed my hands open and closed, dropped them to my sides, and then brought them back up to cross my body.

Xavier frowned at my defensive gesture and circled my wrists, pulling them apart.

My breathing shallowed as his arms snaked around my waist and he gathered my stiff body close. He molded his frame to mine, and I tried not to breathe him in.

"I leave early for a meeting tomorrow. I will not be able to say goodbye to you, Josephine."

Oh, okay, so this was a hug goodbye.

My throat constricted as I tried to swallow and not breathe. Seconds stretched. It was okay to hug him goodbye. I should, I was being childish by resisting. I mentally counted to three and forcibly softened every muscle I could. But my will against him softened too and suddenly the feel of him holding me close broke through, sent a rush of sadness and longing head to toe. Our bodies melted together, and my pulse pounded.

His face turned into my neck and air stirred my skin. "*Joséphine*," he whispered in that musical French accent of his, turning me inside out.

My shallow breaths grew rapid for want of more oxygen and a clear head.

Then Xavier pulled back, his need-filled eyes meeting mine for a searing moment, and taking my hand, he pulled.

I stumbled to follow as he headed down into the darkness of the garden. We followed stone steps down past the terraced level of the pool to a stone gardener's hut that glowed, barely visible in the shadows, but with enough light from the landscaping above so we didn't walk right into it.

The wine I'd had with dinner was a bad idea I thought somewhere at the outer reaches of my mind as desire suddenly burned through me like a lit fuse. Because there was no other reason for him to be hauling me off into the darkness. I offered no resistance as Xavier turned, reaching for me, and pinned me against the stone-cold wall of the hut. His kiss when it came was feral, his lips sealed over mine, his tongue demanding.

I gave.

Hands skimmed up my body, shoving my t-shirt up over my breasts and slipping the cups of my bra down impatiently. I couldn't catch my breath as I clutched his head, my hands gripping his soft brown hair. His hungry mouth left mine and closed over a nipple, sucking so hard, I cried out. His lips gentled, coaxing, teeth scraping, suckling so softly then that I arched and thrust toward him, offering and needing more.

I gave.

And I took. I wanted one more memory.

He gave a groan and straightened. He rested his forehead against mine. Night air swept over my damp, exposed skin, and inside my veins was liquid fire. "Tell me to stop," he said.

I said nothing.

Suddenly he was unbuttoning my jean shorts and shoving them down my legs. He tilted my head back to look up at him. "Open your eyes, Josephine," he whispered.

I hadn't realized I'd squeezed them closed.

"Should I stop?" he asked.

My underwear followed my shorts. Which pair had I even worn? I shivered, but inside I was lava. *I should stop this.* The words rolled around my consciousness but didn't seem to make any actionable sense. He kicked my legs apart. "Open your eyes."

I didn't want to. But I obeyed, my breath seizing in my chest.

He gazed down at me full of desire and wonder and hunger. A hot hand skimmed up my inner thigh and then his long finger slid into me.

"Oh, God," I groaned, my voice low. It was too much to look into his eyes and see what I wanted to imagine. That this wasn't just his base human need, but something deeper. He slid his finger out and then back in, his palm flattened and rubbing and oh, so good.

A wave of aching pleasure rolled through me as he did it again. And again. And each time I thought, I'll stop this now.

He watched my face.

And I watched him right back.

His eyes grew glassy, his lips parted, and his nostrils flared slightly.

Then I answered him. Not in words. No, I didn't want to stop. My hands fumbled at his shorts. Urgent. When had I decided? Who was I kidding? There was never a question I'd stop. I wanted one more piece of him, even though it would be leaving another piece of my soul behind.

"*Oui,*" he rasped, and he withdrew his hand from between my legs, helping to shove down his shorts. In moments, he'd lifted me and my legs were wrapped around him. The stone wall bit into my shoulders. It hurt. It distracted from the pain in my chest. And the ache of needing him inside me was stronger. My heart pounded and my eyes burned with unshed tears.

He was hard and silky between my legs, close, but not quite there. The hand wrapped around my waist held me still while his other shoved between the tight fit between our bodies and took his length. He rubbed the tip of his cock through my wetness, sliding along my slit, and then he was there. Poised.

We stilled. My head dropped back carefully against the stone. His eyes glittered back at me in the dark. "*Joséphine*," he whispered. And then he shoved forward, and his length filled me, stretched me, completed me.

I cried out.

My back burned against the stone, but the fire between us was stronger. And the pain in my heart screamed, "Yes! You see, you cannot let him go." I'd wanted a final goodbye, and now I wondered how I could be so crazy to let him so close to my heart again.

"Xavier," I whimpered. My legs tightened around his waist. My arms clutched him close.

"*Oui*, that's it," he grunted the words, his face now against my neck, his breath hot.

He thrust again, long and hard. Then faster. Each time I thought I'd die of the pleasure.

"Xavier," I begged, deep and guttural, as the beginnings of my climax clawed its way along my spine and spread out in a sharp burning wave through my body. I thrust back, every movement pain and pleasure. I held his head, his hair, his shoulders.

His body pounded into mine. Unintelligible French words came groaning and streaming from his mouth against my skin. Every one of them choked through grunting need and staccato breaths.

We shouldn't have let this happen, but it was too late. Both of us had been taken by a tsunami of raw desperation. We didn't stand a chance. His words, though I couldn't understand them, grew harsh, begging, angry.

This wasn't making love. No, this was fighting it.

We were fighting, both of us. Fighting against our hearts being blown apart.

And then everything pulsing through me coalesced—the ache,

the need, the want, the fire, the pain, the love. My straining body bowed and snapped taut. My head crashed back against the wall and I stared upward. Stars were strewn across the black sky above me, and it was as though I flew up and out of my body, joining them.

I was still as Xavier followed soon after, like he'd been waiting. His body gave a final, brutal thrust and froze. The sound of a man in pain came from deep inside his chest.

Our breathing was loud in the silence, sawing in and out. The world around came back, soft distant music that had been playing out of the speakers on the patio. The sound of cicadas and the rustling of the wind across the fields. From the distance came the faint tinny tinkle of a cow bell.

My cheeks were wet and cold. My shoulders suddenly screamed with fire, and I gasped with it.

Xavier slipped from my body, and I winced as the jostle moved my back. Everything inside and out ached and burned. He seemed to sense my distress, and after tucking himself away, he knelt and grabbed my underwear, gently using the fabric to clean me. He tucked them into my jean shorts pocket, and then carefully directing my feet to step into the shorts, he pulled them up. He kissed my thigh and looked up at me.

I didn't realize how much I was crying until a splash of water hit his cheek. He wiped it off with his fingertips and brought them to his mouth. His hand took mine and tugged, bringing me down. My legs buckled and he moved so he was cradling me in his lap, turning his own back against the rough stone.

As if that alerted him, he pushed me forward and looked at my shoulders. "*Dieu*," he hissed, his voice rumbly with shock. "I cannot see in this light, but I have injured you. I'm so sorry. Are you in pain?"

It was nothing to what was hurting inside my chest. Instead of answering, I nestled closer to him and he held me close, careful not to squeeze too hard. I pressed my cheek against the pounding in his chest.

His mouth moved in my hair, kissing me softly.

The night sounds around us stretched out, keeping us cloaked and safe.

"Stay," he said suddenly. His voice was quiet.

I stilled my breath. Shocked. I'd expected him to withdraw emotionally.

"Please. Forget everything I said and stay with us." He swallowed, the sound audible against my cheek. "Stay with *me*."

"I can't." I turned in his arms, raising my face to meet his. "Because you don't mean it."

He gazed down at me. "I thought you said I didn't say anything I didn't mean."

"I guess you learned. Nothing has changed," I said and waited for him to refute it. "I need to return to my life. This ..." I cast a hand around us, "this is not my life." I bit back all the reasons this wasn't my life because I was worried in my state of heightened emotion it would all come out wrong.

Or maybe it would come out right, and it was a truth not worth making him face. And the truth was he'd been right. He wasn't ready. Not for the magnitude of what I believed we could be. Of the kind of love we could share. Anything less than that was me giving up my life and career for him so I could hang out with his daughter twenty-four-seven and be available for occasional sex.

I may have fallen in love with him, but I wouldn't give myself up for him. "You said it yourself, you need to be focused on Dauphine. I understand that completely. You and I, we are not ... meant to be. It's not like I came here for an architectural position, and we happened to meet where we could have a relationship based somewhere on more equal footing. No, I took a vacation from my own life to come and help you and Dauphine. And now the vacation is over. My real life is back home, waiting for me." I shifted and climbed to my feet, wincing as my back protested. I'd have bruising, there was no doubt.

He climbed to his feet too.

"I'll miss you, Xavier. I didn't know I could fall like this. It hurts." My voice shook. "And it's lonely down here. And I need to go home."

His silence was deafening, and the expressionless mask he wore, or what I could see of it in the dim light, was back. I realized now, he wore it when he was feeling things the most.

I squeezed his hand. "Goodbye, Xavier."

Then I'd turned and walked back up to the house.

CHAPTER FORTY-SEVEN

"So, are we sending Xavier Pascale a bag of dicks?" asked Meredith, eyes widening with feigned innocence as she closed her mouth over her paper straw. The Mexican restaurant in downtown Charleston was quiet for a Wednesday evening.

"Stop." I laughed thinly. Then I frowned when I thought about Dauphine accidentally coming across a bag of candy penises. No. "He didn't do anything wrong." My fingers were making confetti out of the paper coaster.

"Apart from not seeing what an awesome creature he had in his grasp and letting you go. Nay, pushing you away." Meredith set her drink down. "I'm just saying. You've been back three weeks. Stella, baby, you need your groove back."

My smile wasn't forced, but humor was just a foreign place for me. "I loved that movie. We should watch it tonight. Actually, let's go home and put on PJs right now. Taye Diggs for the win," I deflected.

She gave a saucy smile and flicked her hair off her shoulder. "He's a tasty snack. And he follows me on Instagram."

"No, he doesn't."

"Does too." She snatched her phone off the table top and swiped the screen. Then her phone came at my face so fast I ducked. "See?"

"Dude, I can't focus on the screen when you're trying to shove it up my nose." I suppressed a laugh. Grabbing her wrist, I held her phone at a respectable distance. "What am I looking at? This isn't Instagram."

"I screen-grabbed the notification of him following me obviously, duh. That's once in a lifetime shit right there."

"Let me see his profile," I teased. "Something tells me he also follows three hundred million other people."

She pouted but held her phone away from me. "No, he doesn't."

"Does too."

"Just because you're in heartbreak-loser-ville, don't drag me there too."

"Gee, thanks for the sympathy."

"I don't have sympathy." She leaned forward. "You could be boinking a smoking hot French billionaire right now, who literally asked you to stay for the hot sex by the way, and instead you came moping back home." She picked up her paper straw and swatted my hand. "You don't deserve the luck. Seriously. And we're not going home to get into PJs."

"Please?"

"No. I was by myself for weeks since you've both been gone. And then you were back with post-vacation blues, and no job, and refusing to go out. Now you have that job at the Charleston Historic Foundation, and now I have you here, we are staying out. We are having fun, dammit," she ordered.

Saluting her command, I took a small sip of my cocktail. "Okay. Also, when is Tabs coming back? I can't believe she's been gone so long." I needed to tell her what happened in person. All she knew was, after Dauphine's kidnapping, Xavier decided they didn't need to be on the boat anymore and no longer had need of someone to help since his mother was going to move in for a time.

"Between you and me, I think Tabs has hooked back up with her high school sweetheart. There's something about going home after so long for a family wedding that feels an awful lot like a cable TV happily-ever-after movie."

My jaw was hanging open, so I closed it. "No. She wouldn't." I racked my brain for all the high school stories we'd swapped over the years. "Would she?"

"And leave the big city for the one that got away ...? Yes, I believe she would."

"Are we calling Charleston the big city now?" I asked.

"Well, when you come from horse-country-Aiken, South Carolina, yes, Charleston is the big city."

"But she has a business—"

"That she can run from anywhere."

"Hmm. That's a good point. But you guys have been looking at apartments by the yacht club. Tabitha seemed into it."

"I think *I* was mostly driving that bus. I've been getting the feeling lately that she was homesick since her parents retired back to where the rest of her family is. And let's face it, *you* weren't into the idea of a move either. Anyway, you won't even be living here by the end of the year."

My eyes widened, and I choked on my drink. "Excuse me?"

She shrugged. "Just saying. You'll be living the cush-life in France."

My belly twisted, and I set my drink down, positioning it to line up perfectly straight with my water glass. "No, I won't. Don't say that."

"I give it two months tops."

"Until what?" I rolled my eyes. "Until I throw away my self-respect and beg his mother for a job just so I can be near him." I added a dramatic shudder at the ridiculousness she was suggesting. Not that it hadn't crossed my mind in my weakest moments.

She flicked her long, auburn hair behind her shoulder. "No. Until he comes for you."

My stomach dropped into free fall. The idea that he would ever do that was impossible while also intoxicating and dangerous thinking. It was a daydream. An easily crushed fantasy. An idea made worse by the fact that in the deepest, most buried part of my heart—a place where I'd stuffed my love for him under a pile of self-ridicule at being a nanny falling for her widowed billionaire boss—a little flicker of hope pulsed to life. Fuck. I'd never get over him if I couldn't stop fantasizing he missed me and couldn't live without me.

I gritted my teeth. "Just stop it, okay. It fucking hurts, Mer. I told him how I feel. He *knows*. He knows and he isn't capable of meeting me there. He's too damaged. He's untrusting. His heart is closed to me. It's not happening. And I can't afford to even entertain the idea that he's thinking about me. I can't. I'll break apart. I'm barely hanging on here. Please, as my best friend, help me forget him, help me heal, don't stick a lever in the cracks in my chest to pry them open." Tears had sprung to my eyes.

Meredith's face grew slack. Her hand covered mine where I'd pulverized what was left of the coaster. "Dammit. I'm so sorry, Josie. I'm so thoughtless sometimes. I... I didn't realize that you really and truly fell for him. Shit."

"I told you I did," I whispered and swiped a hand across my cheek.

"And I guess I just thought it was lust and a massive crush ... shit, I'm sorry."

I laid my head down on my arms.

"Okay. I'm closing us out and then we're going home to Taye Diggs. I'm sorry."

Nodding, I mumbled, "Thank you."

A few minutes later, we were walking down King Street toward home. The fall evening was still warm and balmy, but the breeze was laced with a cool undertone.

"I'm sorry," Meredith said for the fourteenth time.

I slipped my arm through hers and linked us together. "I know."

"So how was your first week at the new job," she asked.

"Great, actually. I'm definitely among my people. Half the salary, of course, but twice the satisfaction level. Also, I've dusted off my old blog I started in college. I sent out an email to my old subscriber list and they're all still there, been missing me." My chest filled again with warmth at how awesome it had been to send out those cold emails after so many years and to have the responses start pouring in.

"Wait. Your Gargoyles and Medallions blog? That's great. You really had something there, it was sad when you let it go. It was growing so fast, you could have monetized it."

"I know. I got so caught up in the soulless competition of working for the architectural firm, thinking I could make a difference that way, I forgot the passion that got me into architecture in the first place." I had Xavier to thank for waking me up to that. "I'm doubling down on doing what I love." Then I rattled off the titles of the next five niche topics I planned to write about regarding foreign influences on classic architecture by country.

"I have no idea what you just said, kinda zoned out there, but it sounds great."

"It just means I'll be focusing a lot more on my interests. And *if*, big if, I happen to visit France one day again or anywhere else in Europe, I'll be doing so for legitimate research purposes. And maybe I can even consult on building projects that are trying to conform to local architectural ordinances or aesthetics. Wherever the projects may be."

Meredith glanced at me sidelong, and I could sense her biting her tongue. Instead, she squeezed my arm to her side. "Great. I'm happy for you."

We approached the corner to our street, and I fished in my purse for the keys to the apartment. My phone vibrated, and I pulled it out. I had three missed calls and a voicemail from an unknown number. "Ugh," I said. "Someone trying to sell me a warranty on that car I don't own."

I handed Meredith my keys and swiped over to the voicemail page where a message was transcribed. *Josie, set stuffing. Silty play. Unable to transcribe remainder of message.*

"Weird," I said aloud to Meredith. Then I stopped still. Silty play? *S'il te plait?*

"What is it? Are you coming up?" Meredith stood holding the door open.

"Um. I think ... I think Dauphine just left me a message. I can't tell."

"Listen to it then. Did you give her your number?"

"I did. I told her she could call me anytime."

Meredith stared at me, her eyebrows raised expectantly. "As much as I like to stand on street corners ..."

"Sorry." I shook my head. We went inside and I pressed play and held the phone to my ear as we took the narrow carpeted stairwell up to our third floor apartment. Sure enough it was Dauphine's voice, thick with tears and whispering. "Josie. It is Dauphine. *S'il te plait*, please you call me. I am so sad. I had a very bad dream. And I am awake. *S'il te plait?*"

"Oh, God." I put my hand to my chest. "It is Dauphine. She woke up from a bad dream. I'm going to call her back."

"So no Taye Diggs for you?"

"Start without me?"

Meredith rolled her eyes with a knowing smirk. "Fine."

"What was that look for?"

"Nothing, Josie. You go and call back the daughter of the guy you're in love with."

I frowned. "Why is that bad? I—"

"It's not. Go." She shooed me into my bedroom and closed the door on me.

I stared at the wood, then walked to my bed and sat down. I looked up Dauphine's contact where I'd saved it on my phone. Then I kicked off my shoes and waited as it rang.

CHAPTER FORTY-EIGHT

My phone screen opened to darkness. "*Allo?*" a tiny voice answered.

"Dauphine? It's me, Josie, calling you back."

There was a squeal and some rustling. She was obviously in bed. "Josie!" The brightness of the tablet she held gently lit her soft features. I looked at my watch, it was around two in the morning there. "Are you okay? You said you had a bad dream."

"*Oui.* But now I do not remember." Her voice dropped to a whisper. "I must be quiet."

"Yes, um, why do you have your iPad in bed?" I knew her father didn't like her sleeping with her electronics in her room.

"I took it from Papa's room while he was sleeping."

I tutted a gentle reprimand. "So, you woke up from a bad dream and went to your father's room, but you didn't wake *him* up?" My eyebrows were raised.

"*Non.* I wanted to talk to *you.* I wish you were here, Josie. I miss you so much."

I pressed and released my lips, a hand coming to my chest. "I miss you too, sweetheart. Where are you right now? At home or on the boat? It's so dark, I can't see where you are."

"At home. Today I started school again. And the girls were so mean! I told them I had an American friend and they told me I was lying. You are my *best* friend. *Tu sais? Tu me manques.* I miss you," she said again.

"I miss you too," I repeated and bit my lip.

"*Mémé* even told Papa *he* is *irritable* because he misses you too. And he got very angry at her. But *secrétement*, I think he does."

Ah, my gut clenched, along with my teeth. "Well, I'm sure he's irritable because he's stressed with important work things."

"Josie? Why could you not stay?" Her nose scrunched up and her chin wobbled like she was trying very hard not to cry.

"Oh, sweetheart. I—I don't live there, I live here and I—"

"But you could live here. With us. I—I thought maybe you and my papa could fall in love and maybe you could be my *belle-mère*. Can you come back?"

Oh, God. "Dauphine. Honey." My voice failed me, and I blinked away the tears that pooled in my eyes. Pursing my lips, and then mashing them together, I tried to stifle the wrecking ball that was crawling up my throat. Especially when I heard the soft sniffle that told me Dauphine was now crying too. The tears in her eyes glinted in the glow of the iPad.

"Please, Josie?" Her voice was so small and shaky, it felt like my chest might crack. "Do you not love me very much?" she asked.

"Oh, Dauphine."

Fuck.

I let out a wobbly breath and sniffed since my whole head was now liquefying. And she would see I was crying. I squeezed my eyes shut and got it together with superhuman force of will. "I love you. I love you so, so much."

"Then why can you not come here?"

"It's not so simple. Just because people want to be together, doesn't mean it's always right."

"Do you love, Papa?"

I swallowed. "Sweetheart. I, that's ... that's between your father and me."

"But if you come here then maybe you can fall in love." She hiccupped.

Suddenly she disappeared from the screen in a rustle of sheets.

"Dauphine?" Xavier's gruff and sleep-infused voice thumped me in the solar plexus. He murmured to her in French, confused, questioning. It was muffled. She'd obviously hidden her device.

Shit.

Should I hang up?

I chewed my lip, debating. I should. But I didn't want her to think I'd hung up on her, or leave her to try to explain our conversation by herself. I also, God help me, wanted to hear his voice again. I wanted to hear the low rumble of his throat and soft soothing French words I would probably not understand as he calmed his daughter. My fingers hovered over the end button when all of a sudden a lamp in Dauphine's room flicked on and Xavier's face filled the screen.

My chest ballooned with the overwhelm of seeing him. I stared, drinking my fill for endless moments. He seemed equally stunned though perhaps not for the same reasons. His eyes were tired, bloodshot, and I wondered if he'd been having his midnight whiskeys again. His bed hair made my palms itch to reach through the screen and smooth it down. Warmth unraveled through my insides. "Josie," he whispered, then cleared his throat.

We stared for two long beats.

His features hardened.

"Wait," I said.

But the screen went blank.

I flung my phone on the bed next to me as I fell backward.

"Goddammit," I yelled and covered my eyes, pressing away the sting in them. The impact of seeing him kicked like an old bruise on my ribcage. And the tiny imploring voice of Dauphine who saw things so plainly, like only children could, had near ripped my damn heart out.

There was a soft knock at the door. "Josie?"

"Yeah. Come in." I scrubbed my hand down my face and sat up.

The door opened, and Meredith's face was twisted in sympathy. "Do you want to talk about it?"

I scooted over wordlessly, settling my back against the headboard and folding my legs up to squeeze them against my chest.

Meredith crawled onto the bed and lay next to me. "You know that story about the big rig that gets jammed in the tunnel and only the kid can figure out how to get it loose?"

"Um, no. I'm sorry, I thought we were talking about my heartbreak here. If we're going back to fifth grade physics, I'm out." I sat up.

She picked up a throw pillow and tossed it at my head.

"Fine. Go on." I settled back.

"So all these company executives and highway patrol come out, coz, you know, the damn rig has blocked the tunnel completely, like, really wedged in there. They organize a towing situation, but there's just not enough strength to get it out. It doesn't budge. They call the engineers, and the engineers talk about removing pieces of the tunnel ceiling. But that could cause a lot of structural damage and mean a lot of rebuilding. And at this point, the mayor of the local town is out scratching his head because this situation has blocked the road in and out of his town. People are upset."

"Did you smoke something?"

"Shh. Someone says let's get the blow torch in here and cut the roof of the truck off, and everyone thinks that's a great idea. But then someone mentions sparks, and people worry the whole thing could explode. So of course, then it's really getting out of hand because someone else is all 'let's blow up the mountain,' you know?"

"Is there a point here?"

"Hush. So with all this going on there's a bit of a traffic jam. And word is starting to travel down the lanes that there's a truck wedged into the tunnel and no way to get it out. We all have to turn around and go home because they are going to blow up the mountain and we'll be stuck in our town, cut off, isolated for years with no supplies until they can rebuild the tunnel."

"Meredith," I growled.

"Patience, grasshopper. So then this little kid—"

"Don't tell me. Fifth grade?"

"Sure. So this fifth-grader timidly raises her hand. But of course, no one's paying attention. She's small, and her voice is small, and all the grown-ups are emotional and panicked and basically having an existential crisis. The mayor is crying about the loss to the town, the engineers that they'll have to destroy everything they built, the trucking company about losing a truck. So the little girl talks louder, and eventually, goes right up to the head of the trucking company whose truck is wedged in the tunnel." Meredith winked. "I mean, it's really wedged in there, and we're only talking a difference of six inches here. Maybe seven? And that truck could get loose."

"Oh my God, only you could make this story sexual." I rolled my eyes.

"Symbolic, not sexual. *Anyway*," she exaggerated. "So the little girl gathers her courage and her loudest voice and marches up to the people in charge. The ones who are the actual decision makers. And she says '*Excusez-moi?*' She's French. Like Dauphine. This is a French town. Did I tell you that?"

"Meredith."

"So she says, '*Excusez-moi?* But why don't you just let the air out of the tires?' Everyone grows quiet and the mayor laughs and says, 'Yeah, we tried that.' And he looks to the engineers who look to the trucking company, who, in turn, look at the driver of the truck. The driver shakes his head a bit sheepishly. Actually, no one has tried that, it seems. So they all frown at the child. I mean, it's a little girl offering an opinion, you know? And all these important blustery men aren't used to that. I mean, Lord, give me the confidence of a mediocre white man, *amirite*? But they're desperate, so they try it. And lo, wouldn't you know?"

"It works."

Meredith nodded. "It works. They tow the truck free and everyone celebrates, and everyone loves everyone, and the mayor, let's call him Javier Rascale, falls in love with the mother. She's called Mosie. And the little girl, her name is—"

"I get it."

"Right, well, and everyone lives happily ever after." Meredith frowned. "Well, mostly everyone. The engineers, of course, go home and realize they're not actually that smart, and they all get super depressed. But everyone *else* is happy."

I pursed my lips, fighting a smile.

"The point is," Meredith said. "The grown-ups are making this complicated. And really it's quite simple."

Letting out a long sigh, I let my head fall back to the headboard to stare at the nineteenth century carved molding. "How does the little girl get the mayor to listen to reason?"

"I don't know."

"This was super helpful," I deadpanned. "Thank you."

She squeezed my hand. "You're welcome."

But Meredith had made me sort-of smile, and that was something.

"Can you look up what *belle-mère* means?" I asked her, spelling it out while she typed it into her phone.

"Stepmother. Did Dauphine ask you to be her stepmother?"

I nodded, mute, my eyes filling.

"It actually means beautiful mother. Trust the French to fully romanticize a replacement mother. My idea of a stepmother is Cruella De Ville."

"Same with my stepfather." I picked at a stray thread on my

pillow. "Although he wasn't exactly cruel, not to me. Just a money grubber."

"Maybe it's different when one parent dies as opposed to one of them having an affair."

"Maybe." I lifted a shoulder. Then I shivered. "The way he looked at me when he took her tablet. I feel guilty all of a sudden, even though Dauphine called *me*, and not the other way around. Maybe I shouldn't have called her back."

Meredith brought her knee up and rested her cheek on it, looking at me sideways. "It sounds like you have a good relationship with her. You guys are friends. If you hadn't called back when she was obviously upset, that would have been cruel."

I sighed. "You're right."

Suddenly my phone rang again. Another unknown number. Both Meredith and I stared at it.

"Answer it or no?" I asked quickly.

"Answer it!" Meredith practically shrieked.

I stabbed the accept button. At least it was a voice call and not a video call.

"Josephine?" Xavier's deep voice rumbled.

Meredith slapped her hand over her mouth, eyes wide.

I flapped my hand.

"What?" Meredith whispered at my gesture. "What does that mean?"

I covered the phone. "I don't know. Leave?"

"I'm leaving," she said, then stopped and pointed at me. "But you are telling me everything."

"Go," I mouthed.

"Going," she mouthed in response, backing to the door.

"Josephine?" Xavier said again with a muttered French curse.

"I—I'm here."

Silence descended as soon as I announced to Xavier I was on the line. The soft click of my bedroom door closing behind Meredith was the only sound.

Perhaps he'd hung up because I hadn't announced myself sooner. I took the phone away from my ear to check the screen. We were still connected.

"Xavier?" I asked softly, and it came out as a whisper, almost as if I was afraid to say his name. I was afraid. So afraid these feelings for him would balloon up at the sound of his voice when I'd been trying so hard to stuff them away.

"*Oui*," he said softly. When nothing else came after, I frowned, but stayed quiet, unsure of the purpose of his call. Was he angry? Did he miss me? After a few moments, I lay back against my pillows and clicked off my side lamp. Waiting. In the darkness, I became aware of the faint sound of his breathing. "Are you alone?" he suddenly asked.

"Yes. Of course." I paused. "You?"

"*Moi aussi.*" Me too.

For a moment I was tempted to fill the silence, but then I surrendered to it. There was too much between us and nothing could be resolved. Certainly not over the phone. I could ask about Dauphine, but I knew from her that she wasn't doing well. If he wanted to talk about that he would.

I shifted onto my back, letting out a sigh. "Hey, Xavier?"

"Oui?"

"You don't need to respond, and please don't end the call. I just ... I want to tell you. I miss you. I miss you both, so much." At a hitch in his breath, I went on. "Don't say anything. Let's just ... let's just fall asleep together, okay?"

"*D'accord,*" he whispered, sounding defeated. My heart squeezed.

I rolled over and curled up, still fully clothed, and closed my eyes with the sound of Xavier's breath in my ears.

CHAPTER FORTY-NINE

XAVIER
Valbonne, Provence, France

"Papa!" Dauphine bounced out of bed and into my arms in two leaps. "You're home! I already called Josie and I'm ready for my story." She grabbed my face between her palms and gave me a wet kiss on the forehead.

"What a welcome!" I looked over her shoulder as I set her down to where Martine, my housekeeper, was waiting patiently. "I'm sorry to mess up the bed time routine," I told her. "My flight was delayed." I tried not to have overnight stays, but we'd had a pitch for a massive round of investor funding in Geneva. Luckily Martine, my house keeper, was back from staying with her sister.

"*Pas de problème.*" The older lady smiled, then turned back to Josie, helping her get settled again. "*Bonne nuit,*" she told Dauphine. After I asked Martine how her sister was doing, she left Dauphine and me to it.

"What are we reading tonight?" I asked my daughter instead of asking her how Josie was and how she sounded and was she happy and did she ask about me. I couldn't believe Dauphine called Josie every day before bed. Actually, I couldn't believe I allowed it.

Every night I put Dauphine to bed and she'd call Josephine for a few minutes to say goodnight. God knew what we were disturbing Josephine from during her work day. Had she gotten a new job? Was she with a boyfriend having a late lunch? The curiosity drove me to distraction. And far luckier than I had any right to be, Josephine answered Dauphine's call every time. They talked for several minutes about Dauphine's day while I hovered, pretending to be uninterested, and then told each other they loved each other. After that Dauphine went to sleep and *stayed* asleep. It wasn't healthy, allowing Dauphine to develop a dependency to someone on the other side of the world, but whatever it was, it was working. Dauphine hadn't had a nightmare since they started talking.

After reading one chapter of a kid's version of Marie Curie's biography, I kissed my daughter and tucked her in for the night.

Walking to my room, I slipped my tie from around my neck and undid my top button. I was restless. I unpacked, then prowled the house.

One would think now that Dauphine was sleeping so well, it would mean I'd start to sleep better too. And every night after Dauphine and Josephine hung up, I'd tell myself I wouldn't call her a few hours later. But invariably, several times a week, I found myself waking up and lying in the dark staring at the ceiling and then dialing her number. I told myself it was better than getting up and drowning my thoughts in whiskey as I'd done for too many months as a single father.

Calling Josephine back that night a few weeks ago when I'd caught Dauphine calling her in the middle of the night might have been the dumbest thing I'd done in a while. As soon as she answered, I'd almost hung up. What was there to talk about? But then she gave me an out—no need to talk, just stay on the phone while we fall asleep. It seemed idiotic. Something a lovesick teenager might do. But I surrendered to her suggestion with a will that collapsed like a thirsty man in the desert. And life had truly been a desert without her here. Refusing to admit it was a losing battle. Especially when I heard about her all day, every day, from Dauphine. Even Evan wouldn't quit making digs at me. And my sleep had actually deteriorated.

Listening to Josephine breathing as she fell asleep was a meditation. It calmed my mind and soothed my soul. Unfortunately it also awakened other parts of me. Cravings I had no right to feel. And so, I battled those too before finally relaxing and drifting to sleep myself.

Tonight, though, I was antsy. Sleep was too far away. The deal I'd been working on for months had just closed. And now it was three in the morning and never mind waking up, I still hadn't fallen asleep. I wanted to call Josephine, not to lie in silence this time, but to talk.

We hadn't spoken more than our standard greeting since the first night when she told me she missed me. It was a strange ritual.

I looked over at my clock for the hundredth time. What would she be doing right now? It was nine p.m. where she was, slightly earlier than I usually called. I should feel guilt for using her as a crutch, and keeping her from her life, but when I shallowly examined my conscience, I couldn't find it. And didn't try too hard.

I rolled to my side and picked up my phone, calling her before reason and decency got the better of me.

It rang three times and connected. "Josephine?" I asked as I usually did.

"I'm here."

"Are you alone?" I asked as I did every time I called.

There was a long pause. An uncomfortable sickness slipped under my skin and curled around my stomach.

"Yes," she said at last as if it pained her to admit.

I swallowed heavily. One day, she would say no, and that would be that. "*Moi aussi*," I said, finalizing our ritual. This was where we normally ended our discourse and lapsed into silence. My mind raced through ways to open conversation. I hadn't planned what to say.

"Xavier?" she asked.

Inhaling through my nose, surprised, I braced for her telling me this was our last call. I wouldn't blame her. "*Oui?*"

"How did your meetings go?"

I shifted my head on my pillow, rolling onto my back, letting out a relieved sigh. It seemed we both felt the need to break our silence tonight. "I guess Dauphine told you? Very good. We closed the deal. Got the investments we needed. Licensed the patents we wanted to. I had to concede a little on the time. I wanted them to be renewed every year, but I agreed to every two."

"That's … good. Congratulations."

I grunted, knowing the satisfaction I used to feel at business success was nowhere to be found. "And you? Did you get a job with another firm?" It was terrible that I didn't know this yet. What if she was unemployed still? Homeless? Hungry? I was being dramatic. She was so talented and smart.

"No. I didn't look for another firm to be honest. Someone helped me realize my passion didn't lie in building the new as much as saving the old. I took a job with a preservation group."

I licked my lips. "Like my mother."

She sighed. "Without the means, and only the passion."

"Without passion, the means have no impact," I said.

She paused and gave a surprised laugh. "True."

"I'll let my mother know. She will be pleased for you."

"We … we have kept in touch," she admitted. "Not much," she hurried on. "Just a few texts here and there. So she knows of my new job."

"Ah, you keep in touch with my daughter and my mother? I should feel left out," I jested.

"And yet, here we are. Talking."

"*Oui.*" Silence strained. "So ... you love it, your new job?" I asked.

"Very much. And I like my new coworkers. No one makes comments that I'm worth having around because I'm easy on the eyes."

"And why's that?"

There was a pause. "Apart from the fact it's sexual harassment?" I could almost see her eyebrow rise from the tone of her voice.

"Of course. Apart from that," I said. "I'm sure they *think that*, but they are merely decent." What man could work alongside her and not be arrested by her natural beauty? The thought of the men who got to spend time with her every day sent that discomforting sludge through my stomach again. Jealousy. There was power in naming the emotion. I was jealous. Jealous of fictional men. So fucking jealous.

"Decent," she agreed, unaware of my mental frustration. "And most of them are women."

My muscles eased at the knowledge she wasn't working surrounded by men who wanted her. But what about her wanting someone? "Are you with anyone else? Have you—" The words just slipping out of me. My smile vanished and I pressed my lips together. Fuck.

The sound of her breath hitching came through the line. "Xavier. Don't."

But I needed to know. "Are you?"

"Xavier. Please."

"Please," I echoed back at her.

"That's not fair. This whole thing is unfair. Meredith thinks I'm a nut job, turning down offers to go out in the evenings so I can be on the phone with you. God, if she knew you and I didn't even talk, she'd have me committed. What are we doing?" Her tone turned introspective. "What am *I* doing?"

"Wait," I said quickly, sure she was about to hang up on me. "We *are* talking. Tonight at least. I … shouldn't have asked. I have no right."

"No. No, you don't."

Silence stretched. Words congregated and jostled and clogged up my throat, but every one of them were too dangerous to say aloud. They would accomplish nothing but more hurt and more confusion. The pressure built, tension coiled up my back and settled at the base of my skull. Why? Why couldn't I let go? Why couldn't I give in? Why couldn't I open myself up? What was I afraid of?

"I don't think we should talk anymore." Josephine's words cut through my turmoil. "Or not talk anymore. Or whatever the hell it is we are doing. I … I'm going to end the call now."

"Josephine, wait. *Attend. S'il te plaît* … give me a moment to get my thoughts into words?"

She blew out a long breath.

Christ. How could I do this over the phone? What was the point? What thoughts would I, could I, give voice to when I didn't want to face them myself?

I missed her. So what? She wasn't here, and I was certainly not there. Telling her would only confuse both of us.

I wanted her. But again, the geography. Telling her would only cause pain.

I was jealous. And I had no fucking right to be. Telling her would be the cruelest thing when I had no plans to do anything about it.

She deserved happiness. The kind of happiness I wasn't capable of giving.

"Please forget I asked that question. Let's begin again. Tell me about your job."

She sighed and began wearily. "Well, firstly, it's really nice to go into a job where everyone respects your opinion, and you don't have to wear hose and heels."

I tried to parse out the phrase she just said and came up blank. "What is that? Ho-sand?"

"Hose and heels. Panty-hose? Tights? Stockings? And high heeled shoes."

Des talons. A flash of Josephine in scandalous thigh high stockings and high heels hit me between the eyes and flooded down to my groin. I groaned aloud.

She stopped talking instantly.

"*Pardon. Continue,*" I said with effort. "*S'il te plaît.*"

Clearing her throat, she went on.

I did my best to focus on her words until I was legitimately caught up in her stories about the history of her current projects. "It sounds like you should have stayed on a bit longer with my mother. She's been sweet talking developers and town councils long enough that she's definitely learned some tricks. You could both learn from each other."

Josephine chuckled, huskily. "I bet. She's formidable."

"She wasn't formidable enough to get you to stay though. I wish you'd stayed." It slipped out and I cursed myself.

Josephine let out a soft breath. "I couldn't. And for what?"

"To give me time." I snapped my lips closed with a wince.

There was a pause where I guessed we both teetered on the edge. "Time for what?" she asked then, leaning over the abyss.

I leaned out precariously far too. There'd be no one to catch us if we both lost our balance. "Time ... to trust," I said.

"Me?"

"No." I licked lips. "No. In the beginning, maybe. But no. To trust myself. My own feelings." The admission blew through my lips without pause. I pinched the bridge of my nose. Suddenly the darkness, and the intimacy of our private conversation, and the lateness of the hour, all worked together to ease the ropes that held me so tightly, so safely, atop the cliff. "I ... loved once before.

Desperately. I was open. Naive." I laughed bitterly. "Loving wholly. Recklessly. Passionately. I always believed the power of that kind of love could not possibly be carried by one person. When I realized the truth, that not only was I carrying it alone, but that it was in fact an illusion, a massive deception I had bought into ... brought a child into. The pain was ... it broke me, Josephine." I paused to drag in a lungful of air. "I loved Arriette." My throat moved to close, the words ending before I was finished.

"I know."

"No. That's not ..." My hand came to my neck like I could ease away the blockage. "I had already moved into the guest bedroom. Your bedroom," I added to give context, "before she died."

"You don't have to explain."

"No. I do. I want to. I should have moved her things out. From the boat. From our house. And I did not. I've been avoiding it. But it is not for the reason you think. I loved Arriette. I loved her because I still loved the woman she was when we met. And I loved her because she was the mother of my child. A child I adore. I will always be grateful to Arriette for giving me Dauphine. I can never regret my marriage even while I regret I was unable to keep Arriette from her demons. But there was not much of a marriage at the end. I couldn't reach her. She broke my heart long before she left us. And since then, I've been ... frozen."

Josephine's soft breaths in the silence were the only indication she was still there. But she said nothing, allowing me space to find my words.

"I didn't see it coming. And I'm not talking about her death. That too. I thought I'd be able to save her and I failed. I hate that I failed. But what I really mean is I didn't see that our love was not real. *My* love was. But it was *mine,* not ours. It was like waking up from a dream into a nightmare. Waking up to realize your person, the keeper of your heart, your secrets, your fears, everything that allows you to walk this earth with the knowledge that you matter, that the earth beneath your feet is solid because someone loves you ... realizing none of it was ever real. And maybe even if it was, that you were not enough to keep it. Not enough to deserve it, perhaps. And you doubt yourself. The ground beneath your feet is gone. The weight of the hollowness inside you makes you think you'll never catch your balance again. You wonder. How did I miss this? Does everybody know that love is not permanent, and they did not tell you? Or was it just *me* that failed to keep it? The cruelty of the betrayal is everywhere, in all you do. Other couples on the street are just illusions you can see with clarity now. With sneering callousness. They'll learn, you think. They will learn the hard way." I took a deep breath. I couldn't be sure I was making sense and had a feeling I may have devolved into French every now and again when I couldn't think of the English words, but I was sure the gist was intact.

I lapsed into silence, my breathing heavy, raw. For all I knew the call had been dropped. Or she'd hung up. But I was talking now. And I couldn't stop, whether she heard it or not.

"The way Arriette died was horrible. Awful. She overdosed at a nightclub in Paris. She'd wanted me to go with her. I refused. I had a big day the next day. Every day was a big day, of course. The real reason was I didn't want that life anymore. We fought. She went without me. I got the call from someone who'd found her on the floor of the bathroom and called the ambulance. I showed up at the same time they did. I saw her." I hissed in a breath at the pain of the vision. "It was too late. It will haunt me for all of my days that I didn't go with her that night. That I could have done more to save her. And I hurt for Dauphine that her mother's sickness was stronger than her love for her daughter. That love couldn't win. But the thing that haunts *me* the most is that my marriage had died in front of my eyes, and *I* did not see it until it was too late. I did not see it! How does one, how do *I*, ever trust this emotion again when all it does is blind you and wait until you are at its mercy, and then kick away the earth beneath you? I know better now, I think to myself. I will not fall for it again. *Jamais. Jamais ... ensuite il y a eu toi*. But then you. But then ... there's *you*."

All I heard was my own breath.

She was gone. Our calls had dropped every now and again over the intervening days since our nighttime calls had begun. It was an annoyance of long distance over apps. And that was okay now. I waited and heard nothing.

I needed to do this next part alone, anyway.

It was like being in a confessional of darkness. Of forgiveness. Without judgment or repercussion. "I want ... I *want* to love you, Josephine. Maybe I do. But I don't trust that it's real. I'm sorry. *Mon dieu*. I'm so fucking sorry."

I squeezed my eyes closed against the burning behind them, my free hand coming to rest over them for a moment—a useless instinct.

The phone was pointless now too, and I slipped it from my ear to turn it off. But then I saw the call was still connected. My breath froze in my chest, and I slowly brought it back to my ear. It was milliseconds before I realized the call was now truly gone. But not before I heard the quiet sob before she ended it.

What had I done?

CHAPTER FIFTY

JOSIE
Charleston, SC, USA

Buried under my pillow, my sheet damp from my stupid tears, I heard the muffled sound of my bedroom door opening, then closing. I felt Meredith sitting on the bed beside me. She took the phone I still held in my hand and laid it on the bedside table.

"This can't go on," she said gently and removed the pillow, wincing when she saw the state of me. "You can't just put your life on hold so you can speak to Xavier Pascale every night. Especially not when it's killing you like this." She reached over and grabbed the box of tissues, ripping a handful out and pressing them into my palm. "It might be the middle of the night for him, but for you it's prime socializing time. You are young and hot and deserve a real relationship. Not to lie here crying in the dark every night over a man thousands of miles away who couldn't see what he had when he had you."

"I don't cry every night." How did I explain our normal phone calls? "I—you're right. Of course."

"So?"

"So what?"

"So what are you going to do about it?" she asked.

Tonight notwithstanding, mostly it had been comforting to lie here in silence connected to Xavier. Even though it was seriously fucked up. "Nothing. I'm not going to do anything. He needed me. I wanted to be there for him." And now we probably wouldn't speak again.

"Nothing? *I* need you. You're supposed to be my friend, yet between your new job and your nightly phone calls, I never see you."

I bit my lip. "I'm sorry."

"What does he talk about, anyway? I mean you just lie there listening. That's some weird shit."

"We don't talk. Usually. I just let him fall asleep. He-he doesn't sleep well, and—"

"You have to be kidding me. You're blowing me off so you can listen to a guy *sleep?*" She threw her arms up. "Fuck that shit. Get up." She stood.

"Meredith. No."

"Yes. I'm getting an ice pack for your eyes and we are going out. What the hell, Josie? This isn't you. You are not one to let some guy gut you of your self-esteem."

"I don't need tough love right, now, Mer. I hear you, okay? I know. I *know.* Xavier and I won't be talking anymore. I told him we're done. So just let me grieve tonight. I'll go out soon with you, I promise."

She towered over me, hands on hips. "Promise?"

"Yes."

She sank onto my bed again. "I'm sorry. I just hate to see you like this. And I really hope if you ever, *ever*, caught me in the same position, you'd kick *my* ass."

I squeezed her arm. "Pay back will be a bitch, I promise," I said sincerely.

"Fine. That was warranted. But seriously, it's killing me to see you like this. Your mom is worried, too. She called me. She also noticed how different you've been since you got back."

"I *am* different. Sure, I have a renewed sense of purpose about what I was doing with my life. But mostly, I fell in stupid, big, all-consuming love. Like I even dream of the smell of him kind of love. Of the way he spoke while we ... you know." Meredith scrunched her nose up, but I continued. "And like, I-want-to-be-a-mom-to-a-little-girl-who-isn't-mine-but-feels-like-mine-because-she's-a-part-of-him kind of love. It was as though I left Charleston like an overgrown teenager, and I came back as a woman. That's the closest explanation I can give you. And not to mention the sex ... other worldly. I mean I've always enjoyed sex, but it's never been like it was with Xavier. *Never*. So freaking intense. And I'll probably never find that again ... for the rest of my whole life."

"Well, fuck. I'd be crying too then," Meredith said, a legitimate expression of horror on her face. "Scoot over, I'm going to get ice-cream delivered, and we'll hold a wake for your sex life."

I laughed, but it morphed into a fresh round of tears. "I-ice-cream s-sounds good." I hiccupped.

"Christ, you're a mess." She sighed and pulled me in to lie on her shoulder while her other hand found the food delivery app on my phone.

I was a zombie for the next week or so.

Dauphine still called, but sometimes it was every two or three days now. It felt as though she was getting better. Finally able to move on from her grief and recent trauma. I knew Xavier had organized for her to see a therapist again after the incident with the kidnapping, so with that and having me to talk to, she'd sounded lighter and lighter. However, I hadn't heard Xavier's voice again, and my gut ached to hear it.

But then Tabitha came back and the energy in our apartment

began to slowly shift back toward the happier times we'd had pre-France. It was Friday and we'd planned a girls' night so I could fill Tabitha in sparingly about the fact I'd broken all her rules about not fraternizing with one of her families, and she could fill us in on what, or who, had kept her away from Charleston so long. The late September heat in Charleston was relentless and would continue to be for the next few months at least, and it was always jarring to see people start to decorate with fake fall foliage and real pumpkins that promptly rotted on doorsteps.

Every time I was on East Bay Street, I looked to see if the builders had broken ground on the hideously designed hotel. But today, jogging past, sweat dripping off my chin, I saw all the developer signs had been removed. I slowed and called Barbara, Donovan and Tate's assistant at my old job.

"Barbara, it's me, Josie. Don't say my name," I hastily added.

"Jo—hiii!"

"Johigh? That's a new one." I laughed.

"How *are* you?"

"Great, actually. You?"

"Mr. Donovan isn't in today. It's just Mr. Tate."

"So, pretty shitty?"

"That's exactly right," she sang.

"What can you tell me about the East Bay Street hotel job?"

"Um ... it's a doozy. Whoo boy, I'll have to check the schedule. But could you perhaps do something later in the day?"

I frowned, and then realized she must not be alone. I played along. "Today?" I asked.

"Yes, ma'am."

"Meet at King Street Tavern at five?"

"About a half hour later, and I can fit you into the schedule."

"Perfect." I grinned, though she couldn't see me. "See you then. I'm buying you your favorite Margarita, so plan on grabbing an Uber home or have Jeff come get you?"

"That'd work wonderfully. I have you on the schedule. Okay, bye now," Barbara sang and clicked off.

I chuckled as I put my phone away. It was true, every day *was* better than the last. I would come out of this broken heart stronger. I continued my jog up toward King Street. As I ran past the window of the fancy yacht company, I couldn't help thinking about Xavier. Ugh. That was why I didn't normally run this way. Then I saw the French lady I recognized from Armand's coffee shop just heading to the glass front doors and coming out. I slowed.

She came out and flicked open a silver cigarette case. Her lips were bright vermilion.

"Hey," I said. "Sylvie, right?"

"Oh. *Oui*. How are you?" She removed a cigarette and offered one to me.

"Oh, no thank you. I'm doing great. You?"

She snapped the case closed. "I don't see you at Armand's anymore."

I smoothed my damp and frizzing hair back off my forehead. "I still go, but my schedule has changed. I don't have to be in officially for an hour later, which is nice. How about you? How's ..." I laughed, because it was odd having a conversation with someone you barely knew more than to say hello to every day. "How's life? Are you French or French Canadian? I've never been sure."

"Both. I spent lots of time in Paris." She said the word exactly as a French person would, with no S. *Paree*. The sound of the accent caused my stomach to clench.

"I know *your* name, but we've never been properly introduced." I held out my hand. "Josephine Marin."

She paused in the act of putting her silver case away, her unlit cigarette dangling between two fingers. She narrowed her eyes at me.

"What?" I asked. My hand dropped between us.

She shook her head. "The strangest thing. Someone—one of my clients—mentioned your name the other day. Actually, yesterday, uh."

"Oh? Did I do some architectural design for them?"

"Him." She chuckled. "I don't think so. He asked if I knew you. Of course, I said no. I didn't realize I did." She looked closer at me, her gaze moving from my sweaty face down over my shirt sticking to me, my leggings, and my dirty running shoes. "Huh."

"Umm..." I raised my eyebrows. What a peculiar moment.

"You know the name Xavier Pascale?" she asked.

My blood drained, and I swayed. "What?" I whispered. "What did you say?" But I'd heard.

Sylvie looked past my shoulder, her eyes going round.

And I knew. "It's him, isn't it?"

She looked at the state of me again and winced. "*Desolée*. But yes."

I couldn't breathe.

"*Bonjour*, Sylvie," he said.

Oh.

My.

God.

His voice.

Right here. In real life. In my city.

His tone was jovial and friendly.

Why are you so happy? I screeched in my head. How dare he come here? He should be home, back in France, crying into his leek soup and regretting letting me go. Bitterness and pain rose up. I should keep moving. He wouldn't recognize me from behind.

Plus, I looked like shit.

And I was mad at him, dammit. I was light headed with the intensity of both shock and anger in equal measure.

"*Joséphine?*" His voice was rough. Unsure. Incredulous.

It was too late to move. I took a brief look down at my outfit, the sweat on my scalp making my head itch. There was no God. Then I turned. "Xavier," I managed, my voice feeling like sandpaper.

CHAPTER FIFTY-ONE

"It *is* you." Xavier's face was alight with wonder and relief and joy —emotions I simply didn't understand or expect.

"Why do you look like that?" My hand came up and vaguely waved at him.

His eyebrows pinched together slightly. "Like what?"

"Happy to see me."

"Because I came to America to see you, and here you are."

I looked at Sylvie, who had one perfectly plucked eyebrow arched as she took us both in. "So you didn't come to see Sylvie and check on your yacht? Because apparently you didn't just arrive today." Bitterness crept into my tone.

"No. I mean, I did, but there were some things I had to take care of." His blue eyes pinned me. "Is there somewhere we can talk?"

"Now? I—" I cut myself off. "No. I'm actually late for work." Or would be if we continued to talk. Besides, my shock was wearing off, and I was beginning to feel weak and dazed. I shook my head. "Sorry. I ... this is a shock. I have to go."

"Wait." He reached out a hand for me, and I flinched back.

Surprise and hurt flashed across his features. "Josephine ..." He lowered his voice. A lock of dark hair dropped across his brow.

Sylvie said something in French, which I belatedly understood as her going to wait for him inside. She tucked her unused cigarette back in its silver case and went back in the shop.

"Xavier," I started, shifting my weight nervously. My gaze lowered to his white shirt buttons revealed between the lapels of a dark linen blazer, anything but look at his eyes. Over the untucked tails of his shirt, his distressed jeans and pristine navy and white sneakers. God. He was so *euro*. And so fucking hot. Could he not just look like a slob for one second so I could get my bearings? "Please don't do this. I have to move on. I have to get over you. Please just sort out your fancy boat and go back to France."

"What if I say no?"

"No?"

"No, I'm not going back to France. Not right now, anyway." Both his hands came up and raked through his hair, leaving it untamed. "And no, I don't want you to move on, and I don't want you to get over me. I—*Merde!*" he bit out the curse. "This is not how I wanted to see you."

I pinched my damp exercise shirt off my chest. "Trust me, me neither."

His eyes were drawn back to me, raking over my face, my hair, down my body. "You are beautiful, Josephine. Always. But your heart, your heart inside you is the most beautiful thing about you." His hand reached out, and his palm pressed hot against my chest.

I froze. And burned. And stared.

"And I surely don't deserve it," he said and let go just as quickly, leaving me wildly bereft. "I know this. *S'il te plaît*. Please let us talk. If not now, then later. A place of your choosing. But hear me. Please hear me."

He stared at me for long moments. Around us the city

bustled, and people walked past and around us, oblivious to our moment and us to theirs. His gaze was bottomless, and I struggled not to sink into it. Into him.

Shaking my head, I took a step back.

"Josephine," he pleaded, his voice going hoarse. "Please don't—"

"Don't what?" I snapped, trying to fight the emotion crawling up my throat.

"Don't ... break me." He flinched as the admission left his lips.

My breath left my chest. My eyes were filling, my nose burning, and a golf ball increasing in size in my throat.

He swallowed, audibly, and stepped toward me, closing the distance I'd created.

Trying to breathe with him invading my senses was torture. I stepped back again and he followed, his hands coming up and cradling my face and tilting my face up. My legs weakened and I leaned against the side of the building. My hands grasped his wrists, meaning to push him away but not letting go. His lash fringed eyes roamed over my face. And behind him curious glances moved over and past us. "*Mais*, if you mean to do it, do it properly," he begged, his voice low, his eyes burning. "Destroy everything that's left of my heart. Leave nothing behind. I can't do it again. There will be no one after you. Be thorough. Merciless. Finish me."

"'Wh-what are you saying?"

"I'm in love with you, *Joséphine*." His eyes pinned mine, delivering all his secrets openly and helplessly.

The sound of my name uttered in *that* way, his accented French falling from his lips, curled into my insides.

"You have given life to a dead heart and soul. You brought me back to life. Hungry and gasping and desperate ... for *you*. My heart beating ... for *you*. No." He frowned. "It's as if it didn't *exist* before you. I'm alive now in this world that might not have you in it? No. It's impossible. I don't want the world to turn another day, the sun to burn another day without you."

"Xavier," I whispered, my voice failing me. Liquid spilled hot down my cheeks and my heart pounded.

"I'm sorry it took me so long to see. To see *you*. To feel *you*. To believe you could love me. To believe my own heart. *Mon dieu*." His forehead fell forward to rest against mine. His thumbs brushed my tears. Our breath mingled, stuttered.

My hands gripped his wrists tighter, his pulse strong and yet erratic beneath my fingertips. His mouth was so close. His tongue darted out to wet his lips.

"So please," he said, whispering now. "If you mean to break my heart, leave nothing left. I beg you. Leave nothing left. I will not survive it, otherwise. But do not break my heart, Josephine. I'm offering it to you. Completely. Take it. Take it ... or destroy it."

And then his hands slipped to the nape of my neck. His mouth, hungry and desperate, took mine. His lips opened, his tongue sweeping into my mouth, taking and tasting and begging. *"Je suis complètement amoureux de toi,"* he whispered as his mouth left mine and skated to my ear. His tongue dragged over my skin, setting me on fire. He groaned. "I love you."

I was drowning. His words and his touch overwhelmed every one of my senses. Vaguely aware we were standing in the street in full view of curious passersby and probably Sylvie, I struggled to find my common sense, or any of the bitterness or anger I'd felt moments before. But all I wanted to do was sink into his touch. My heart was on fire.

His body, held a respectable distance from mine, told me he was aware of our surroundings too. "Please. Josephine." He pulled back, his blue eyes dark eclipses. "See me later? Tell me where. Tell me when." His fingers ran over my face.

I nodded, breathless, my veins singing with his words. His confession. He loved me. But ... he'd told me himself he didn't trust his feelings. Could he really have changed?

His shoulders sank with relief at my nod.

"Um. Can I call you?" I asked. "I have ... I have work. And plans." *Cancel everything*, my heart shouted. "And I need ... I need to think. I need to think about whether I ... believe you, and what that means."

"Of course," he said, swallowing heavily and stepping back. A grimness was already creeping into his countenance, like a man who knew the blow was coming and was marshalling all his armor to withstand the force of it. His hand moved to rub the center of his chest. "Of course, I understand."

"H—how long are you here?" I asked.

He let out a humorless laugh and scrubbed a hand down his face.

"What's funny?" I asked.

He shook his head. "Nothing is funny. Ironic, maybe. I have made plans to stay for a while. An endless while. I hoped to show you I meant everything I said about how I feel. But I can see it might be too late."

"Oh." Confusion and joy and wariness all competed for my attention. His eyes grew sad, letting me see his emotions in a way I never had. I could tell him it wasn't too late. But I didn't know.

We gazed at each other, new wariness and vulnerability clashing with the realities of our situation and growing into a chasm between us. And God, not forgetting that no matter what he'd just said, words that I wanted to wallow in and savor and study and cradle, I lived *here*. He lived *there*. It was hopeless. I blinked back a fresh burn of tears.

"I will be here for as long as it takes," he said.

"But what about your business?"

He shrugged. "I own it. I feel like doing business from here now."

"Oh," I said weakly. "And what about Dauphine?" God, Dauphine, I couldn't believe I hadn't thought of her until this second.

"She's here."

My head whipped around in both directions. "Wait. Where?"

"Right now? She is with a nanny at the hotel we are staying at. The Planter's Inn. You know it?"

It was my favorite local luxury hotel because they'd worked so hard to blend in to the architectural history of the city. Low profile, high elegance, with a courtyard, just like the old Charleston houses. I nodded. "I know it."

He felt in his inner breast pocket and pulled out a card and a silver fountain pen. He scribbled a number on the back. "It's our suite number. Please come. Dauphine would like to say hello. She is desperate to see you."

"She hasn't called in a few days, I assumed it was because she was getting better at falling asleep."

"She is. Thank you for that," he added sincerely. "Your generosity with her," he licked his lips, "well, thank you."

"I did it for her. Not you."

He gave a nod. "I know that. I am thankful all the same."

"And I did it for me. I love her."

"I know that too. And I'll never forgive myself for accusing you of hurting her. I was panicked. Scared. And what I realized recently was I was not just reacting with fear for my daughter. The time we spent together, you and I ... it was like an earthquake. I felt exposed. In danger. Because I was falling in love with you. I grabbed on to a reason to push you away, to not trust you. It was wrong. So very wrong. I know I've apologized before. But, Josephine, the pain I must have caused you ..." He dragged in a deep breath through his nose and squeezed his eyes shut for a moment as if to contain his emotion.

Shit, I was going to cry again.

"I feel that pain as if it was my own now. I cannot believe I inflicted it when all you did was love and heal us."

"You're not making it easy for me to be strong."

He stepped toward me, his hand settling on my neck. Warm

and rough. "Don't be strong then. Be weak like me. Then we can be strong together."

"I need to think."

"I know. But *je suis* ... I am afraid if you think too hard you won't pick *us*. And I have so much more to say to you." His eyes left mine to swing left and right, then narrowing briefly on the window of the yacht showroom. "Things I cannot say right now."

"Sylvie is watching us, isn't she?"

"*Mais oui*." His gaze swung back to mine.

"She's wondering how a god like you is begging a sweaty, dirty, heap of a girl like me to take a chance on him."

"I love this sweaty girl." He leaned in and ran his tongue up my neck under my ear, causing goosebumps to erupt across my skin and liquid heat to settle in my belly.

"Xavier!"

"She tastes good. Her skin is flushed and damp and salty like it is after we make love. And whether she's dirty or not ..." he inhaled a hungry and breathy groan in my ear that I felt between my legs. "I would love to find out. I'm hoping she is."

I whimpered as I tried to let out a casual laugh. Jesus. I'd gone from emotional wreck to lust-crazed, weak-kneed damsel in seconds.

"Ahh, I miss your sounds, *Joséphine*. And there are things I would like to do too, and here is not the place for them." He was pulling out all the stops to get me to give him a chance.

I placed my palms on his chest and pushed him back. "Fine." I shivered. "Fine, I will see you tonight. I'm meeting friends, but I'll see you afterward, okay?"

He broke into a brilliant smile.

"Put that away," I grumbled.

He smiled wider. "I cannot." But then his face fell. "What time will you come? Dauphine might be asleep because she is on French time and she will be so disappointed. I want to see you tonight though. Maybe that is better if she is sleeping because we can talk in private. Can we see you again tomorrow?" He grabbed my hand. "Whatever happens tonight, good or bad, tell me you will keep a promise to see Dauphine tomorrow."

I swallowed. "Of course."

"*Parfait.*" He nodded, then his grin struggled to break through again.

"I didn't bring my sunglasses to deal with your smile."

His teeth flashed.

"I can't believe you recognized me from behind," I added.

"I can. You forget how much time I spent obsessed with your ass." He winked.

My heart swelled and fizzed. Letting a controlled breath out, in case I started screaming with the giddiness that was bubbling up inside me, I took a step to the side with a jerk of my thumb. "I need to go, I'm late for work."

"*D'accord, Joséphine. À ce soir.*" He pressed his lips to my wrist then let it go.

"Until tonight." I nodded and turned. Four steps later, I glanced over my shoulder to catch him looking at my butt. He winked and shrugged with his palms up as if to say "What did you expect?" I turned and jogged backward for three steps, shaking my head and fighting a smile, then with a wave I resumed my run. I didn't look back until I arrived, sweating, but driven by wings on my feet the whole way home, at the front door of our apartment.

CHAPTER FIFTY-TWO

Emergency girls' night. ASAP. I texted the group chat with Meredith and Tabitha.

Mer: We're already meeting, dumbass.

Yes. But I'm setting the tone.

Mer: Why?

It's a long story. Best not over group text.

Mer: Ooh.

Tabs: Oh, what? Never mind. I think I know why.

??

Mer: ??

Tabs: Um... It wouldn't have anything to do with me

organizing a local nanny for Xavier Pascale
would it?

Mer: What?!!!!!!

What?!!!!!!!!!!!!!!!!!!!!!

Mer: Holy shit. *(Side-eye emoji)*

You knew he was here?

Wait. Wrong response.

> *Tabs:* Yes. He called me two days ago and said he
> had business in Charleston. The question is why
> I didn't know why YOU might need to know.
> Don't you think you perhaps should have told
> me something? So I didn't have to hear it
> FROM MY CLIENT!

Mer: oof.

I'm sorry. So sorry.

Mer: This is so awkward.

You weren't here. And I know it was against the
rules. Didn't want to stress you out. But I was
going to tell you, I promise. Wait. When did
HE tell you?

> *Tabitha:* This morning. He called and told me you
> and he had had a relationship. He assumed I
> knew.

Mer: In Josie's defense she was going to tell you tonight.

I was. I promise.

Cringing, I hit send.

Mer: But anyway, back to the important shit. He's here? Like here, HERE? In Charleston. This is OMG. Josie, how did you find out?

I ran into him. Literally. Was out running.

Mer: Eek. Did he see you?

Understatement. Yes. He saw me ... drooping in the heat, sweat pooling all over me, and hair frizzing in the humidity.

Mer: Ouch.

Ouch, indeed.

Mer: Did you talk?

Yes. That's why the tone setting for girl's night is EMERGENCY. So Tabs, what did he say exactly?

Tabs: I have a meeting right now. Chat later xo

Ugh!

Mer: Ugh!

So much I need to share. And as much as it is going
to KILL ME to keep it bottled up until later,
it's better that I tell you guys in person.

Mer: Pleeeease. Just a little bit? Is he here for you?

No. His boat.

Mer: I don't believe that. Tell me just a little. Did he
say he couldn't live without you?

I'm almost at work, I gotta go.

Mer: Pleeease!!! Did he tell you he loves you?

Mer: Josie?

Mer: Josie?

Mer: JOSIE!!!!!

Yes, he did. But ...

Mer: SQUEEEEALLLL. No buts.

All the buts.

Mer: Bullshit. I'll talk you straight later.

I have no doubt you'll try. But I might not need
much convincing.

Mer: OMG. Seriously?

I bit my lip. Seriously.

> *Tabs:* Entering the chat again against my better
> judgment. Seriously?

> *Mer:* Hi Tabs. Knew you couldn't resist a good love
> story. Maybe you should open a matchmaking
> service instead? This is amazing. Do me next?

I chuckled aloud.

> *Tabs*: LOLOLOLOL. No.

> Oh, also, I asked Barb to come meet us for a
> margarita. She has some work news to share.
> Hope you all don't mind.

> *Mer:* I love Barb. The more the merrier.

> *Tabs:* Fine with me. As long as you're not
> embarrassed to be reamed out for screwing your
> boss in front of an ex-coworker.

I pursed my lips and selected the straight mouthed emoji and
hit send.

> *Mer:* oof. Again.

For the first time since I'd started my new job, the day dragged.
My mind was all over the place. The man I was in love with was in
my city. He wanted to be with me and I was dragging my feet. At
lunchtime, I only had thirty-five minutes between meetings so I

made my way to Washington Square with a smoothie, found a bench, and called my mother. It was a tiny park, one city block, if that. And not too many people knew of its existence, or at least if they did they never walked through the gate.

"Mom." The relief at hearing her voice as she answered made my throat tighten. Sometimes you just needed your mom. I didn't realize how much I'd needed her to answer.

"Darling. This is a nice surprise. To what do I owe the honor?"

"Do I really call you that infrequently?" I cleared my throat and smiled, relief loosening my whole body.

She laughed. "No, but you never call me during the work day. How's it going over there?"

"It's great. You knew me better than I knew myself, getting me the contact there. It's perfect for me. I love the people. I love the preservation projects. I do miss being creatively challenged. But I'll find a way to get back to that somehow."

"I'm thrilled. But that's not why you called me, is it?"

I blew out a breath. "No. Mom ... how did you know Dad was the one?"

There was silence. "Mom?"

"Yes, darling. Sorry. You just took me by surprise. I don't know specifically. None of it made any sense. He was 'old Charleston.' I was an immigrant outsider. You know Charleston. So progressive in so many ways, so closed and backwards in others, especially letting newcomers in. But our love was ... well, it was other-worldly. On paper, everyone's eyebrows were raised. But for us it felt bigger than anything. But what clinched it was when he said he would move and leave his friends and his family and the city where he grew up and his job. Everything. Just for a chance to be with me because I had an internship that would take me to London for six months with a chance to begin a career there."

"And you didn't go? You gave up your career for him?"

"Oh, honey. It was a different time. And no. I had the same career. Just ... different."

"But not the internationally renowned one you could have had—"

"Josephine." She let out a sigh. "The point is. It didn't matter because I had your father. The point was he *would* give up everything for me, the way I would for him. But if you're asking me for my blessing because you want to give up your job for this Frenchman, then I'm afraid I'll have to advise you to take a long moment."

"Did you feel the same way about Nicolas?"

"No."

"Then why did you marry him?"

"I was lonely. You know what it's like at my age. Well you don't, but it's always better to be a part of a couple than be a single woman. Everyone is kind at first, but then you stop getting invited to things when you're single and ready to date. And when it got to that stage, it was obvious I needed to settle down. Nicolas was ... he was kind. A bit flashy. But kind. I know now he was telling me all the things I needed to hear to trust him, but I was sad, and lonely, and you were so lonely. And I thought if we felt like a complete family again then you would be happier."

I pinched the bridge of my nose and closed my eyes.

"Not that it was your fault, at all," she hurried on. "It was me. All me. We—we had some good times, didn't we? With Nicolas?"

"Yeah. I guess. We did."

"Look, whatever is going on with you, I need you to know I want you to follow your heart. Even if it leads you to France. You know that would probably make your dad happier than anything."

"Mom—"

"It would. He always wanted to go back and see if we could trace back his history. And don't you worry about me."

"Mom. I'm not leaving. I love Charleston. My friends are here. You're here. I love my new job."

"But you love him too."

"Yes." I blew out a breath. "So much. So much my heart feels too big for my chest. And when I thought it was over, I was ... devastated. And now he's here."

"Josie? Really? He came for you?"

"Don't get carried away, he came here to check on his yacht."

"Did he bring his daughter?"

"Yes. But that doesn't mean anything."

"Maybe not. But don't you think maybe he was using the yacht as a reason to do what he really wanted to do?"

I scrunched up my face and my free hand. "Yes, Mom. Yes." I unclenched everything with the admission. "That's why I'm calling. I ... Mom, I'm scared. He's broken. God, he's so broken. I love him, and he's even admitted he doesn't trust his feelings. But now he's saying he loves me. I know if I do this I'll need to take a leap of faith, and I'm asking you, how did you know? Really, please, how did you know?" I blinked rapidly.

"That's asking how you know the full moon is round. You just know. Do you know?" she asked.

"I think I do know. I know that he's the person for me. But," I drew in a fortifying breath, "nothing is forever guaranteed, even *if* I know."

"Oh, honey." She let out a long breath. "You mean because your dad died."

I closed my eyes, squeezing out the tears that were waiting. "Yes. I—Xavier's first wife died, Mom." My voice broke. "I can't imagine that kind of pain. He's been through it. And it happened to *you*, Mom. And the next choice you made was Nicolas." *What if I am his Nicolas?* "How can I take this chance when it's not guaranteed. When he's my right choice, but I could be his wrong choice? I'm so scared. It feels too big. I don't know. Dad left us. Nicolas betrayed us. Even though I know Xavier's the one for me, how do I take this chance?" My sob broke free. "What if I'm not the one for him?"

A hitched breath, and a sniffle told me my mom was crying too.

"Oh, God. I'm sorry, Mom. I didn't want to make you cry too."

She blew out a breath. "It's okay. I'm crying because I'm happy."

"W-what?"

"I'm happy that you've found this kind of love. There's nothing, *nothing*, that if I'd known it ahead of time would have stopped me being with your father. That kind of love is the kind you'll walk through fire for. You'll die a thousand times or bear the loss again and again just to have known it. It's big and it's scary, but it's worth it. Even everything I had to go through with Nicolas. If I could do it all again, I'd do it willingly to have had those years with your father. And to have had you. Our daughter."

I swiped at my cheeks. "Oh, Mom." It came out a whisper.

"It's true. So whether or not you decide to go for this, I want you to know that I will be there for you no matter what." She paused. "And also, it would be really cool to get a head start on a granddaughter by starting with a ten-year-old."

"Mom!" I gasped a choking laugh.

"I'm just saying. I wouldn't mind being the American grandmother who spoils her rotten. I'm ready."

"She'll be lucky to have you."

"She'll be lucky to have *you*, Josephine."

A strange whining sound came from my chest and throat as I fought back more crying. I tried to purse my lips and blow like I was blowing into a paper bag. "Whoo."

"What else is it?"

"Well, you know he's like really well known in France. If I do this … people are going to want to know who I am. Who my family is. And I'm worried."

There was a pause. "For who?"

"You. Mostly you. Me. Maybe even Xavier. I don't know."

"Well, don't worry about me. One good thing I've accomplished is growing a thicker skin. But you know, darling, Nicolas has taken so much from us already. Don't let him take this from you too. You're going to be okay. You're going to be happy. I know you are."

"I'm a fucking mess, is what I am."

"Josephine!"

"Sorry, Ma." I laughed then, feeling as though something inside my chest had broken free. "Thank you."

We said our goodbyes, and I tilted my head up to the sun, willing it to fade the mess my face must look like.

I walked back to work and ducked into the bathroom to wash my face and reapply my makeup with my small emergency kit. The mascara was two years old and caked, but the concealer and lip gloss were adequate. After I saw my girls, I would have to maybe run home for a shower and proper touch up before seeing Xavier.

At five thirty p.m. I'd never been more ready for girl's night. I was approaching the King Street Tavern when my phone rang. *Donovan & Tate.* I frowned. Barbara must need to cancel, and frankly with everything that had happened today, I could totally wait on hearing the latest news on what had happened to the deal on East Bay Street.

"Hey, Barb," I answered.

There was silence. And then, "This is Ravenel Tate. Is this Josie Marin?"

I swallowed. "It is."

"Right. Okay. Well, I'll get right to it. Uh. I was wondering if I could, um, possibly, uh..."

My eyes widened, my eyebrows rising, and my steps slowing. "Yes?"

"Well, uh, the thing is, we, Jason, and of course Donovan, and I, definitely me, well, we were wondering if we could offer you your old job back."

I came to a complete stop. "Excuse me?"

"We wanted to know if you wanted your old, no, I'm sorry, we wanted to know if you would, if we could perhaps offer you a job here again at the position of Senior Associate."

Frowning, I turned in a circle, the phone to my ear and my eyes unseeing. I stepped back out of the flow of tourists on King Street and stared blindly into the display of new and estate jewelry in Crogan's. "And why would you want to do that?" I asked, genuinely curious.

"Oh. Well, uh, there's a new developer for the East Bay Street Hotel Project. He bought out the old developer. And, uh, we'd obviously like to keep the business. But ... he doesn't like Jason's design. Wanted something more ..." I heard Tate clearing his voice and pictured him sticking a finger into his collar like it was choking him.

I smirked. "Go on."

"He wanted something more historic. Given the history of the land."

"I see."

"So you'll do it?"

"No."

"No?"

"You can hire someone to consult. You can even use my designs since you took them from me. But if you think I'd work for you again after what you did, you must be out of your mind." My heart pounded with the boldness and brashness of speaking my mind. My inner feminist cheered, even as my well-behaved, lady-like inner me that took a multitude of micro-aggressions in order not to rock the boat at work, cringed and hushed and clutched her pearls. My cheeks throbbed and my face grew hot.

"I see. I understand. Could we, ah, perhaps hire *you* to consult?"

I barked out a laugh. There was no answering laugh. "Wait. You're serious?"

"Very much. We'd pay you hourly the same amount, if you broke it down, that you were earning hourly—"

"No."

"We'll double it. Just for consulting."

"No. And don't insult me by offering more money. You see, the problem isn't the job."

"Oh? But what about the history?" he asked, his voice getting a bit superior and mocking, clearly unused to dealing with rejection. He was resorting to goading and ridicule.

I frowned.

"You have a chance to save it," he went on as if he was doing me a favor. "To do it *your* way."

Mistake, buddy. I took a deep breath. "The problem, I'm afraid, is you. While you are still in charge of the project, or anywhere near it, I won't be working on it." I bit my lip, astounded at myself. I knew I'd always been taught not to burn bridges. At least not in Charleston. But right now, I had no fucks left to give.

There was silence.

"If there's nothing else ..." I tested. "Friday evening is calling my name."

"Ah, no. No. That's all right. H-have a good evening."

"You too." I hung up.

Wow. This day. I shook my head.

Entering the bar, I saw Barb, Tabs, and Meredith were already there.

"Boo!" they all chorused upon seeing me.

I stopped and held my hand to my chest. "What?"

"Why are you here and not going after your one true love?" Meredith asked, clearly speaking for the group when they all nodded.

I glared.

Tabs kicked out a bar stool at the high top for me, and Barb slid a drink in a martini glass over to me. "Gin, right?" she asked. "For the record I agree with Meredith, but you might need some Dutch courage."

"Thanks." I raised the drink as I sat. "Tabs." I looked her in the eye before turning to Meredith. "Mer." Then I took a huge sip.

"So?" Meredith asked. "Don't keep us waiting."

I looked at Tabs. "I'm sorry. I fell in love with my boss, your client. We had a relationship. We didn't mean for it to happen. If it helps, I resigned before—"

"You resigned?" she screeched. "In the middle of a job, without telling me? What did you do wrong?"

"Shhh." Meredith laid a hand on Tabitha's and looked around.

"Sorry. But, um, what?" Tabitha asked.

"Not because I did anything wrong, I promise. After I found out he'd wanted to replace me, things got uncomfortable. I was hurt. I was going to resign, but then I found out he only wanted me gone because he was so attracted to me. He couldn't handle it, apparently."

"God knows why." Meredith mock grunted, and I narrowed my eyes. "Kidding, just kidding," she said.

To my left, Barbara practically melted on the spot, a hand on her chest. "Oh my God, that is the most romantic thing I've ever heard."

Tabitha seemed to be mulling it over, her mouth practically inverted with the way she was chewing her lip.

"I promise it wasn't anything untoward. I did in fact resign before anything could happen. Dauphine didn't get—" Shit. I'd been about to say Dauphine didn't get hurt by it. But she'd been freaking kidnapped while her father and I had been hours away having a sexy escape. My stomach flipped over into utter nausea. God. My gaze dropped to my drink.

"I need the restroom," Tabitha said, her voice subdued and disappointed. She hopped off the stool.

"Yikes," I said. "I feel like shit." I was going to have to give Tabs way more than the brief outline I'd just given her. And many, many apologies.

"There's never an easy path to true love," Meredith said sagely. "I'll go check she's okay." She slipped off her stool and followed.

"Is she okay?" Barb asked.

"It's—it's too much to go into right now." I sighed heavily. So much for a healing girls' night and getting advice on talking to Xavier. "But, hey, guess who called me on my way in?"

"Tate?" Barbara guessed.

"Wait. How did you know?"

"That's what I needed to tell you. So, you saw the signs were down? Well, apparently the developer sold his entire position to a new guy. And the new guy hates the plans Jason had approved. And even though they warned him it will slow the project down another twelve months at least, he wants different plans. Doesn't care he has to hold it longer. Clearly the guy is rich as Croesus. And apparently Donovan showed him *your* plans. He loves them. He especially loves the little footnotes you had about why you made certain choices and the history of the land and what not. He wants an archeological dig first, and then wants to build in a display room to outline the history of the land on which the hotel is built."

I blinked, moved. And a little astounded that the new developer wanted all the same things I did. "That's ..."

"I know! Amazing, right?"

"That explains why Tate was begging to have me back then. I'm probably the only person who's been championing the historical element. But they have my plans, why don't they just use them?"

"Because Mr. Pascale," she dropped her voice, "that's the new owner who bought the project, told them if they can't get the original person who designed those plans back on board then he's going with a different architectural firm."

My drink was suspended two inches off the table where I'd been frozen in mid-flight when she mentioned Mr. Pascale, and now it slipped back to the table with a loud crack.

The sound jerked me to attention, and liquid sloshed down the sides onto my hand.

"Oh, dear! Here," Barb said and pressed her napkin onto the spill. She fussed and mopped and blotted.

"What did we miss?" Meredith sang as she sat back down. Tabs trailed in behind her.

My mouth opened then closed.

"Oh," Barb said. "I just told Josie she was offered her job back because the new guy—"

I stood abruptly. "I'm sorry. I, uh, have to go. Thanks, Barb. Sorry I have to run."

Meredith tilted her head.

"Mer, fill Barb in on Xavier Pascale?" I turned to Barb. "Fill Tabs and Mer in on what you just told me?"

Barb nodded. "Sure. Wait. Xavier ... Pascale?"

"Yeah," I said. I tipped back my gin drink and almost choked.

"Go get him!" Meredith clapped.

Tabs stared at me, a mix of emotions in her eyes. And Barb, piecing everything together, just whispered. "Go get your man."

Seconds later, I was running out the door.

I was already so late.

CHAPTER FIFTY-THREE

I flew through the door of the Planters' Inn and came to an abrupt stop on the walnut stained wide plank floor. *Shit*. Had I left the card with his room number at home when I went to shower before work? I opened my purse and half-heartedly checked the inner pockets even while I remembered laying the card down on my bedside table thinking I'd get it when I popped home to refresh my outfit and make up after girl's night. Should I go home and get it or have a drink in the Peninsula Grill, the hotel restaurant, and call him?

"May I help you, miss?"

A uniformed bellhop or footman or whatever they called them here, appeared at my elbow.

My shoulders sagged. "No. I'm good. Thanks. I forgot my friend's room number. I was hoping to surprise him."

There was a squeal and running feet. "Josie!"

I turned just in time to catch Dauphine as she launched herself into my arms. "Whoa!" I laughed in surprise as I caught her and gathered her into a tight hug, lifting her off her feet. She clung and tried to wrap herself around me, and I staggered under her weight. "Whoa. Wow. You're heavy!"

"Dauphine. *Arrête. Descend!*"

She slid down, but her arms didn't let go. Over her head, Xavier stood in his blue jeans and white button down, his forefingers stuffed into his front pockets. "We came down for dinner," he said. His teeth bit into his bottom lip. My heart swelled.

"You look nice," he said, eyes sliding down my silky green top and white jeans. "Not that I don't like your jogging outfit too."

Under my hands, I felt a tremor. "Dauphine?" I looked down.

She shook her head and pressed her face into my belly, her shoulders shaking.

"Oh, honey." I ran my hands over her hair and her shoulders. "I'm here." Sinking down, I crouched and looked up at her, gently brushing her hair back from her wet cheeks. "Mermaid tears?" I asked with a smile.

"You came." Her voice was tremulous, her lip quivering. "Papa said I couldn't see you until tomorrow."

I glanced behind her. "I was missing you both so much," I said, looking right at him. "I couldn't wait."

Xavier's eyes flickered and his throat bobbed, his chin dipping slightly.

I dragged my eyes from him and smiled back up at Dauphine. "Any chance I can join you both for dinner?"

"*Oui! Papa, s'il te plait?*" She turned to her father.

"*Bien sûr, ma petite.*" Then he caught my eye and held out his hand to me. "I would love nothing more."

I dropped my gaze from his deep, warm eyes to his outstretched hand. With a deep breath, I took it. His fingers, warm and dry, closed around mine. Inside, my soul seemed to levitate and I wasn't sure it would come back down. Dauphine grabbed my other hand, and with a laugh, I let myself be dragged toward the Peninsula Grill.

Dauphine's tears were forgotten as she caught a second wind and chattered nonstop until her eyes grew droopy.

Xavier signaled for the check as soon as we finished eating some appetizers and salads.

As we left the restaurant, Xavier picked Dauphine up effortlessly, and she tucked her head on his shoulder. There was no discussion of whether I should go with them, but Xavier strode away and opened the door to the courtyard for me. I slipped through, my heart getting louder in my ears.

We walked across the courtyard, the landscaping gently lit by lights even though it wasn't dark yet. The tinkling from the central fountain made me think about peeing. I was nervous.

Xavier swiped a key card, and we entered a foyer that had stairs going up. He waved me ahead of him, and even though he had Dauphine in his arms I couldn't help think of him following me up the stairs in Calvi. On the first level was a living room and kitchen, elegantly decorated in earth tones with modern lines and sumptuous finishes. There was another stair well going up but Xavier headed through a door to another bedroom with Dauphine. I quickly used the bathroom while Xavier helped her get her pajamas on.

"Josie," she said sleepily when I came out.

"I'm here, love. Let's go to the bathroom and clean your teeth. Papa will hold you up."

She sleepily did her business, and then leaned against Xavier as I gently brushed her teeth while she slept standing up. Then he carried her to bed and kissed her forehead. I kissed her too, and then heart in my throat, I followed Xavier out to the living area.

He strolled to the kitchen. "Would you like a glass of wine? Or something else?"

"Wine would be great." From across the counter, I watched him take down two glasses and reach into the fridge for a chilled bottle. "This is a nice hotel. One of my favorites."

"Why's that?" he asked, twisting the corkscrew into the top of the bottle and then popping it free with ease. His forearms, the tendons flexed, the scattering of dark hair over tanned skin, were mesmerizing. "You okay?" he asked, amused.

"I'm sorry, what?"

He shook his head and pressed his lips together to hide a smile. Then he poured two glasses and held one out to me. "I asked why it was one of your favorite hotels."

Taking the wine, I clinked against his glass softly, then took a small sip. The tart chill slipped over my tongue. "How about you tell me about *your* latest hotel project?"

"Ah. Hard to keep a secret in this town, eh?"

I leaned forward, resting my elbows on the concrete kitchen counter. "About as hard as keeping a secret on a boat."

He chuckled and nodded.

Setting my wine aside, I clasped my hands. "I don't want to work for Tate ever again. I would have thought you'd known that."

"I did."

My eyebrows pinched together. "So why ask him to give me my job back or risk losing the business entirely?"

"So you could have the pleasure of telling him to fuck off."

Inhaling deeply through my nose, I reveled in the ballooning joy and love that was filling my chest. "Ah," I said. "And why would that be?"

"I figured that was the best gift I could give a woman who doesn't need anything."

"You bought an entire hotel project worth millions just so I could tell someone to stuff it?"

"I wanted him to recognize how talented you were, how much he'd lost, how short-sighted he was, and I wanted him to beg. Did he beg?"

"For him, I think it was begging." I shrugged, trying to fight the smile that was desperate to break out.

"Some men don't know how to beg," he said quietly, rounding the counter top. He stopped when we were face to face. His eyes roamed all over me, leaving sparks in their wake. Taking a lock of my hair, he twisted it around his finger.

"Is that so?" I asked, my breath choppy. "Are you one of those men?"

He bit his lip as if deep in thought, then looked me square in the eyes and slowly got down on his knees.

I laughed nervously. "Xavier, get up. I was joking."

His fingers wandered up my thighs and hips to my waist and then encircled me, his forehead coming forward to rest against my belly.

I swallowed, my mouth dry and my heart racing. My fingers danced through his soft hair.

His lips found my skin under my shirt.

I hissed in a breath.

"Please," he begged against my skin, peppering soft kisses and taking small tastes. "Will you be with me? Will you be with Dauphine and me? Will you let me love you? Will you love this broken heart of mine? And forgive me for hurting you? Let me wake up every morning to your smile, to the smell of your skin, to the sound of your love?"

"I don't—ouch!" I hissed. "Did you just *bite* me?"

"*Mais, oui.* You said something that did not sound like *yes.*"

"Maybe you aren't that good at begging."

He raised an eyebrow in challenge, mischief dancing in his darkening eyes.

"Also, I actually do want to consult on that project."

He laughed as his fingers made quick work of the button and zipper for my white jeans.

"This is unfair." I gasped as his mouth followed my jeans down over my hips, his breath hot against my fast dampening core.

"Is it?" he asked, pausing to slip my heels off. At his prompting, I stepped out of my jeans. His hungry gaze on the tiny pair of panties I was wearing was going to burn them right off me, showering us in floating sparks of burned silk. His hand ran up my inner thigh and then a single finger ran over the center of me.

"Oh, God," I moaned. "Yes. Yes, it's unfair. How can I think straight?"

He hooked into the side of my underwear and peeled them down my legs. "I don't hear you asking me to stop."

"Just don't bite me again."

"I can't promise that," he said with a dark chuckle.

He stood then, and his mouth took mine. I surrendered to the kiss, winding my hands around his neck and sliding into his hair. His lips moved over mine, urgently, nipping and tasting. I parted my lips, sneaking a taste with my tongue against his.

A guttural groan came from his throat, and his tongue came back for mine, hungry and demanding. He tasted of tart wine, sweet sin, and lifelong promises.

"*Joséphine*," he uttered in that unique way of his.

If my heart were a ribbon, it would be swirling up and up and wrapping around his. "You were wrong, you know," I managed between kisses.

"What about?" An arm locked around my waist, and his other hand tilted my head so he could take more. He drank and sucked and licked into me. I was being devoured, and I loved it.

"That I'm a woman who doesn't need anything," I said into his kiss. "I need *you*."

Then suddenly I was airborne and deposited on the ice-cold kitchen counter. I squealed in shock.

He drew back, breath sawing in and out of his chest, lips glistening. "*Mon dieu*. You make me lose my mind! I'm sorry. I was ready to taste you right here. And we'll wake Dauphine." He pulled me off the counter as quickly as I'd landed on it and scrubbed a hand down his face. His hair was tousled and sticking up in five directions.

My heart squeezed and my body throbbed. "Go put the fan on

in her bathroom. Let's ... let's take this to your room?" My cheeks heated.

"Yes. *Mon dieu*, yes." He backed up and then hurried to her room. I took a second to gather myself, then I gathered my shoes, underwear and jeans and tiptoed up the stairs. I knew we still needed to talk. And me sleeping with him right now didn't mean we didn't still have a lot to work out. I mean, was he *moving* here? Did he really buy out the developer just for me to teach my old boss a lesson? Did he mean to actually build a hotel? I thought, due to his father, that he didn't dabble in construction. Or was he expecting me to go back to France with him? My mind tumbled around, and I felt weird and exposed standing by his bed waiting for him while naked on the bottom half.

The second level of the suite was an open loft with a half wall hiding us from below, and the bed was king-sized and sumptuous. But there was no door, nor walls, and should we really be having sex when his daughter could come up here any time she woke up?

Feeling utterly self-conscious, I slipped my underwear back on, and then sat to pull my jeans on. We should be talking realities not tumbling into bed.

Xavier jogged up the stairs. He got to the top bare foot, took one look at me, and growled.

"*Non*." He shook his head and prowled toward me. Leaning down he grabbed my face and covered my mouth with a hungry kiss, then he slipped my shirt over my head and undid my bra. He pushed me back on the bed and grabbed my jeans, yanking them off the one ankle I'd managed to slip on and sent them sailing over the loft wall to the level below. "*Je veux te baiser, Joséphine*," he whispered.

"W-What does that mean?" I asked.

"You've already heard it. It means I want to fuck you, Josephine."

"Xavier!" Heat flashed through me.

"*Oui?*" he asked, then with one hand tore my underwear off.

I gasped in shock. "Did you seriously just rip my underwear off?"

"I think I have finally run out of patience," he said, and standing up, and with one hand behind his head, pulled his shirt over and off.

My eyes devoured this strong, beautiful, loving father of a man. My gaze trailed down his defined chest, sprinkled lightly with dark hair, and moved down over his flat stomach to the vee that disappeared into the tops of dark blue low-slung jeans. I looked back up at his face, but his eyes roamed over my nakedness and ended pinned between my legs.

He knelt down at the end of the bed and with a hand on each ankle, pulled me down toward him. "Still want to get dressed?" he asked.

My breath was fast and shallow. I shook my head. I wanted to be naked with this man more than I wanted to breathe.

"Say it."

"No." God, no. He'd just fucked me with his eyes and his words, and I felt on the verge of an orgasm and he'd barely touched me.

"*Bon*," he said and spread me open, his face coming within inches of me. His breath was hot and cool at the same time. I squirmed. "Please," I begged.

"What is it, *mon ange*. What do you need?"

"Please kiss me there."

He hummed. "Mmm," he said and then pressed a small closed mouth kiss right on my clit.

I bucked.

"Just a kiss?" he asked and did it again.

"No." I sobbed a breath. "More."

"Tell me."

I gasped as his hands pressed my legs farther apart. My body was weeping and quaking for him, sparks shooting all over my skin like it was too tight for my bones.

"Tell me."

"I-I want your tongue."

"Ah, a *French* kiss? *Oui?*" He chuckled, and then licked me long and slow.

"Yes!" My back bowed up. "Oh, God." The words dragged out of me in a deep and guttural sound I barely recognized I was capable of making. Every slow swipe of his tongue had my body chasing his mouth, arching my hips toward him. My hands came to his hair, grabbing. His tongue kept coming, repeatedly, maddeningly slow, like he knew I was close, but winding and winding until I couldn't breathe. "Please." This may have started with him begging me to be with him, but I was the one begging now.

Especially when suddenly he paused.

I looked down, blinking, and watched him suck two of his fingers into his mouth and then slip them just inside me. "Oh, shit." My head dropped back. "Xavier. Please."

"*Comme ça?*" He slid them in farther and pressed upward, and his hot mouth closed over me again.

I whimpered and arched, fire licking and flaring through my body with increasing speed, a hungry ache growing stronger.

"*Oui,*" he muttered against me.

The ache grew, dark, fierce, and aching, from deeper and deeper within me. I wanted this man, his body, his heart, his passion, his fears, his hurts, his temper, his frustrations. I would take it all.

"I need you inside me," I managed, using my grip in his hair to lift his head. "Please, I need you. I'm so close. And I want, I need you with me. Don't let me fall alone."

He didn't argue. He stood and undid his jean and pulled them and his underwear off. His erection bobbed stiff and huge and then he was leaning over me and crawling up my body. Hooking under my arms, he hauled me farther up the bed, and without stopping, he was suddenly over me and entering me in a long, slow, and deep thrust.

A sound ripped from his chest, joining mine, and his head flew back, exposing his throat. "*Joséphine.*"

I slipped my hands up his hard arms and over his shoulders and wrapped around his neck.

His eyes blinked open, and he focused on me as if through a haze.

"I'm here," I whispered, my hand curving on his cheek. "Make love to me."

"Always," he said and withdrew agonizingly slowly before sliding back in. The pressure and fullness of him had me gasping. He did it again, his eyes having trouble focusing. "I love you, Josephine." His forehead creased, sweat beading. He thrust into me again, slower, harder. And dragged out. "I love you so much. My heart began beating again from the moment I met you. Even before you knew. But this will kill me, I know it."

My eyes burned with tears, and I stroked my thumb down toward his lips, brushing across them. "No. No it won't. I won't hurt you."

"Love me, Josephine. Please." He thrust and withdrew and thrust again. "This is me begging. Love me." He shifted his weight to one arm and used the other to slip down my side and bring my leg up, pressing me even farther open.

I groaned. "I do. I do love you." In seconds I was back at the edge. My muscles strained tight, my breath caught in my chest and prickles racing across my skin. "God, Xavier. You feel so good."

He picked up speed, his arm trembling, his jaw tensed tight, his eyes flashing. Words in French I didn't understand fell fast and desperate from his lips.

Then his body was on mine, his hips moving, his mouth devouring my lips, my chest. Somehow in my arching up, he managed to suck a nipple hard into his mouth as his pubic bone ground into me.

That was it. I snapped and soared.

His hand was across my mouth, and I screamed into it, my body convulsing and dissolving.

His hips slammed into me, taking the movement of my hips bucking involuntarily and using it to his advantage. It was brutal, almost violent. Then he froze, buried so deep, I was pinned, immobile, and probably bruised but quaking with the beauty of it. I blinked my eyes open. The hand across my mouth fell away to support him and leaving me gasping. I watched as the agony of his ecstasy ripped across his face, his head thrown back, teeth bared and tendons in his neck straining as he poured himself into me. I'd never seen anything so arousing or more beautiful. This man was mine. Mine to keep and hold and love and protect. I'd never hurt him or allow anyone to either. I'd protect his heart no matter what. Forever.

Temples wet with sweat or tears, and heart thundering, my fingers soothed up the damp skin of his throat and around to the back of his neck, pulling him down to me. "Come here," I whispered. He offered no resistance, his arms weak and trembling, folding down until his body covered mine, his face turning into my neck.

CHAPTER FIFTY-FOUR

I became slowly aware of daylight behind my eyelids and the tickle of small finger pads walking slowly up my arm. The bitter and delicious aroma of coffee hit me next. Then the sound of a soft rustle of paper turning over as if someone was reading the paper.

Then a whisper. "When will she wake, Papa?"

"Dauphine, let her sleep." Xavier's low voice came from behind me. I was still in his bed. Oh my God, and Dauphine had found me here!

I inhaled sharply. I'd slept so deeply it was an effort to open my eyes. They focused slowly on Dauphine's face not three inches from mine and bearing a huge smile.

It was impossible not to return that smile, even if my body felt boneless and heavy like a sack of potatoes.

"Dauphine, leave her."

"She's awake." She clapped her hands together. Then she leaned closer and whispered to me. "You fell asleep in Papa's bed."

"Mmm," I managed, then stiffened. Was I naked? Was I covered? I took stock and concluded that though my arm and one foot was exposed, the rest of me was warm. I rolled onto my back, careful not to dislodge my modesty and turning my head to see the other side of the bed. Xavier, shirtless in just his jeans, leaned up against the headboard, a newspaper open and hiding his head. He folded a side down and peered at me, his blue eyes ringed with a pair of black reading glasses.

"*Bonjour,* you *are* awake." He gave a small smile.

"And you wear glasses?"

"I don't like to travel with my contacts." He lifted a shoulder.

"I didn't even know you wore contacts."

"Is it going to be a problem?"

"God, no, you look inc—" I bit my lip, glancing toward Dauphine who was watching my every move and word. "Um. You look lovely." I cleared my throat. "Very distinguished. Hot and nerdy. Um, it, ah, does it for me."

He smirked. "Is that right?"

I nodded. "You should, you know, wear them a lot." I bit my lip.

He inhaled noisily.

"Papa. Now that Josie is awake, what about the plan—"

"Dauphine." He dragged his eyes from mine. "Not now."

"What plan?" I looked back to Dauphine.

She scrunched up her face and worked her lips between her teeth, like she was busting with a secret she was dying to share. "Are you hungry?" I asked, taking pity on her misery and trying to distract her. I'd have to ask Xavier what that was about later. "I'm starving." On cue, my belly growled.

"We have been up since very early," she said. "It is lunchtime already in France. But we saved a little bit for you, in case you were hungry. But just a little bit because we have a plan today to—"

"Dauphine, why don't you go down and make sure everything is ready for Josie," her father said. "We will come down in two minutes."

She gave a long sigh and nodded and stomped down the stairs.

"Hey, I wanted to ask you. Last night, when we were ..."

"Making love?"

"Yeah. You said your heart started beating again when you met me, and then you said even before I knew. What did you mean?"

"You were able to have a coherent thought during that? I must not have been doing a very good job."

My cheeks heated. "Trust me. You did a great, *great* job."

He preened, and then folded the paper away and took off his glasses, more was the pity. "The day I called Tabitha—the day you quit your job—I was on screen. Tabitha had stepped away for a moment, but you came home, crazy, mad, spitting fire and throwing your high heels. Undressing. Seeing you ... it was like someone suddenly plugged me in. And then you arrived, and we met. And I ... I fought it. I fought it so hard, but I was drawn to everything about you. Your spirit. The way you were with Dauphine. The way you could make me laugh at something absurd. Even the way you knew how seeing my father affected me. I wanted to share everything with you. It was terrifying and addictive. And I know I was harsh sometimes. Pretending you didn't affect me. Making sure you couldn't see how much."

"Oh, Xavier. And here I thought you hated me half the time."

"No. Hated the way you made me feel like I could lose control. I pride myself on my control in every arena. And then suddenly it all meant nothing."

Xavier folded the paper away, and then scooped his linen button down off the floor and held it out to me.

Holding the sheet to my chest, I sat up and took it gratefully. "Thank you."

"Pleasure will be all mine, I can assure you. Come on. Dauphine waits." He chuckled then leaned forward and pressed a lingering kiss to my forehead before jogging down the stairs. To my left, my jeans, shirt, underwear, and purse were all neatly on a chair.

I saw what he meant two seconds later when I went to the

bathroom and saw that you could see my nipples through the shirt. I shook my head and took it off. After a quick rinse, I slipped on my bra before buttoning up the shirt again and then pulling my jeans on. I opened a small hotel toothbrush and toothpaste package. I wondered when Xavier and I were going to talk about our relationship. It was one thing admitting you loved each other and having amazing sex, but logistically what did that mean? Was there any permanence in that? I wanted to be with him, but there was no way I could see him living here anymore than I could see myself living in the South of France—

I spat the toothpaste out and rinsed my mouth out with water several times so as not to ruin the taste of breakfast. Me, living in the South of France?

All that gorgeous architecture. Amazing food. A wonderful man. A wonderful *family*. A vision of my mother and Mrs. Pascale sipping wine on her patio and discussing art flashed through my head. But what if we broke up and I'd moved to the other side of the world? My chest grew tight. I'd be alone and I'd feel so dumb.

I grabbed my phone that was tucked into the back pocket of my jeans and sent a group text.

> *If I moved to France, you would visit right?*

> *Or if I had to come back because it didn't work out, you wouldn't think I was an idiot?*

> *Am I crazy to move to France to date a guy?*

> *Not that he's asked me to go.*

> *I'm freaking out.*

I chewed on a piece of skin next to my thumb nail as I waited for an answer to any of the five rapid fire texts I'd sent. There was a knock at the door.

"Josephine? Are you okay?" Xavier asked, concern and something else in his tone.

"I-I'm okay."

"Are you sure?"

"Yes. I'll be right down."

IS ANYONE AWAKE???? I texted.

> *Mer*: Bitch. Seriously? Is it not enough that you get a hot French billionaire to fall in love with you, but now you have to wake us up at the crack of dawn to crow about it?

> Sorry. I'll wake up for you when you need relationship advice. Please help.

> *Mer*: Go to France and fuck his brains out, and ask him to marry you, and have lots more little Frogs. Yes, we'll miss you, and yes, we'll visit. Good night.

> *Tabs*: ditto.

"Ugh!" I muttered. I splashed cool water on my face and finger combed my hair and then opened the bathroom door.

Xavier sat on the end of the bed, elbows resting on his knees, dread on his face.

"Are you okay?" he asked, his face morphing to slight disappointment when he saw I was fully dressed. "Are you sick?"

"No."

A flush spread across his cheeks, his lips were pale. "Do you want to leave?"

I swallowed and shook my head. "No."

"Do you ... regret anything between us?"

"No. Never. Never," I repeated with a frown.

"So you still want us, Dauphine and me?"

I blinked and nodded. "Yes. But logistically, I—"

"So what happened in the bathroom? I get the sense you were freaking out?"

"I was. Well, a bit. I asked Meredith and Tabitha what I should do."

"About what?"

I licked my lips. "Whether I should move to France." I winced. "So we can date. Not that you've asked, and I'd never—"

"And what did they say?"

"What?"

"What did your friends say?"

"Um ..." I slipped my phone out my back pocket and unlocked it, then handed it to him.

His eyes grew wide as he read Meredith's response, and a smirk curved his mouth. When he looked back at me, his eyes were burning. He gave my phone back. "Does anything about your friend's suggestion freak you out?"

I took a deep breath and looked him in the eyes. "No."

He pressed his lips together, as if containing a reaction. "Not even the 'more little frogs' part?" He raised his fingers in air quotes. "Which I have to say is mildly insulting."

"No," I whispered after a short pause and tilted my head. "You?"

His eyes dropped to my mouth as he contemplated my question. "No," he said at last. His eyes flicked back up to mine. And the gravity of what we'd both just admitted was like a silent explosion. Promises and hope and a future filled with love and laughter and a bigger family suddenly bloomed in the ether between us.

I exhaled, a giddy smile splitting my face even while I tried to bite it back.

He stood. "Good, then come. Dauphine has a question she'd like to ask you." He held out his hand and I placed mine in his. He kissed my wrist and then led me down the stairs.

Halfway down, I looked up from following my feet and saw the dining room table with food and flowers and champagne. "I-I thought you said you'd eaten and saved me some. Not—" I glanced to Xavier, only to see him looking toward Dauphine. She was waiting, holding an envelope out in her hands.

My name was etched in her chicken scratch across the front. I let go of Xavier's hand and stepped toward her. "What is this?" I asked.

She covered her mouth and jumped up and down twice.

I took it and carefully tore it open and removed the card. It was written by her in French.

Josie,
  S'il te plaît, veux-tu être ma belle-mère?
  Je t'aime,
  Dauphine.

I was frozen.

"You can turn it over. It is in English on the back," she pleaded and turned my hands.

"Josie," I read aloud. "Please will you be my stepmother, I love you, Dauphine." I choked out the last word. "Oh, honey." Did Xavier know that his daughter had done this? What if he wasn't quite ready despite our understanding upstairs? I whipped around to look at him. "Oh," I gasped.

My eyes landed on Xavier, down on one knee, and my hand came up and covered my mouth.

He held out an open box, a crooked smile on his face, and inside was nestled a brilliant single diamond ring.

Next to me Dauphine jumped up and down.

"*Joséphine*," Xavier began, his voice rough. He cleared it. "*Joséphine*, you are the empress of my heart. You own me. I know it's been fast. But I have never been more sure. You have made me believe in love again, and I cannot imagine a world in which you are not by my side—"

"Et moi," Dauphine interrupted.

I laughed, tears rolling down my cheeks.

"*Desolé, mon chou.* Ahem, I cannot imagine a world in which you are not by *our* side as part of our family." His blue eyes gazed at me and into me, fathomless and earnest and full of more love and trust and hope than I could ever have thought myself worthy. "I love you, Josephine Marin. *We* love you. I know it seems fast, but I have never been more sure of anything in my whole life than how I feel about you. Please will you marry me and make my heart whole again and make our family whole again? I promise I will take care of you. You and your mother. We can live here, or there, or anywhere. On a boat, on land, I don't care as long as we are together. And you can work, or don't work. Build ugly buildings or save old ones. Whatever makes you happy. But I will always respect the importance of what you choose to do—"

"Yes," I cried. I grabbed Dauphine into a tight hug, then released her and fell to my knees in front of Xavier. "Yes. Yes. Yes, I will marry you. I don't care where we live as long as it's not a boat. But anywhere else, as long as I am with you." I took his face in my hands and only this close could I see the glistening emotion in his eyes. I wiped my thumbs across his cheekbones and then leaned in to kiss him, crushing the box with the ring between us just so I could hold him.

I heard him snap it closed and his arms came around me and held me tight.

"*Hourra! Hourra!*" Dauphine squealed, and then burst into tears.

"Oh no." I reached for her. Xavier and I folded her between us. "It's okay, darling. Don't be sad."

She sniffed and wiped her face back and forth on my shirt. Xavier's shirt. "I-I'm not sad." She pushed us apart and squeezed out. "I am going to call *Mémé*!"

She ran into her bedroom to call Madame and left Xavier and me alone. We pulled apart, and he kissed me softly one more time, and then brushed my hair back from my face. "You have made me happier than I ever thought possible. I thank God every day that asshole Tate made you quit so you could come to France. That's the only reason I haven't fired his firm already."

I laughed and shook my head. "Donovan is very nice. And Barbara and a bunch of drafters, engineers, and junior associates. It would horrible for them to lose that project."

"Eh." He shrugged. "Okay."

"You're crazy," I said.

"Almost certainly." He kissed me again, then pulled away and lifted my hand. Fumbling with the box, he managed to get the ring out one handed, letting the now empty box fall to the ground. "Is that ... a Crogan's box?" I asked, recognizing the local family and estate jeweler on King Street's logo. "When—?"

"Yesterday. In fact, I almost thought you saw Dauphine and me. You were on the phone at the window. She helped me pick it out. I don't know how she kept it a secret at dinner last night. I would have brought a ring from France because I already knew I was going to ask you. But then I thought if we needed it resized, or you wanted to change it—"

"Shut up and put it on my finger, you beast."

"A beast? You have no idea." He chuckled and slipped it on my finger.

"God, are you trying to show me how rich you are or something?" I teased, holding it up where the solitaire in an elegant, antique setting of small filigree sent a million light points beaming around the room. "Hmm, though actually," I brought it close to my face, squinted my eyes, and scrunched up my nose. "There's no helipad on it. Maybe you aren't that rich after all."

He barked out a laugh.

My God, we were both so giddy and sickeningly filled with love and joy. It was a good thing Meredith and Tabs weren't here. They'd barf. Meredith especially.

Xavier sobered. "Could you love me if I gave it all up tomorrow? The boats, the money, everything, except for you and Dauphine? Because I'd do it. There are a thousand worthy causes. You could pick who we gave my money to. I would retire tomorrow."

"Yes," I said, matching him with the same amount of seriousness.

He swallowed. "*Je sais,*" he said, his eyes growing half-lidded. "I know you would. We would live a simple and happy life on your salary."

"Let's not get too hasty. Do you not have a retirement account? Surely, you are not that irresponsible?"

Laughing, he kissed me on the nose. "Yes, we'd be comfortable. But I might get bored not working. But perhaps I can get rid of just the boats."

"And what would you do with all those amazing people who work for you? I miss them. Besides, I have fallen in love with the Mediterranean. I could learn to tolerate the boats. And what about Sylvie, are you not completing the new boat purchase from her?"

He laughed. "I've already paid for it and approved all the designs. I had no reason to come here really, except to come for you. Visiting Sylvie was just a courtesy." He stood and helped me to my feet. "Come on," he said. "Let's eat, and then I want you to show me your city and all the history, the good, the bad, and the ugly. And for dinner, you must take me for ... *qu'est-ce que c'est que la* ... ah, shrimp and gits?"

"Grits. Soft polenta."

His mouth twisted. "Soft polenta ..."

"You'll love it, I prom—actually, you might not."

He shuddered. "Can you invite your mother?" he asked. "I have spoken to her on the phone, but I would like to meet her in person."

"You have?"

"Of course! I had to ask for her blessing. I have asked Meredith and Tabitha too. We should invite them to dinner too."

I pressed my hands together and stared at him in wonder. "Wow, you really were serious."

"I have asked you to marry me, how is this not serious? Wait, you know this is serious, *oui*?"

"*Oui*," I whispered. "It was just an expression."

Dauphine flung open her door. "*Mémé* wants to wish you congratulations. Can my bridesmaid dress be like a mermaid? Please, please, please?"

I locked eyes with Xavier and we both laughed, and he squeezed my hand. "Thank you," he said, sincerely. "For making our family whole. For making *me* whole."

The End.

If you would like to know more about my romances and not miss my next release or sale, let's keep in touch by visiting my website www.natashaboyd.com and signing up for an infrequent newsletter

Or text 31996 to NATASHABOYD

Read on for a word from me, and my other books. Also there were some characters in this book that feature in my *Charleston Series*. If you like steamy romantic comedy, you will love **ACCIDENTAL TRYST** and ***IRRESISTIBLE BEAU***! And if you loved the angsty romantic hero of Xavier, you will adore Jack in my movie star romance series ***EVERSEA*** .

ACKNOWLEDGMENTS

From the bottom of my heart, thank you so much for reading Broken French. You can check out my writing playlist on Spotify (see my website). I'd like to particularly note with appreciation the music of Ursine Vulpine (Frederick Lloyd).

It's been three years since I published a romance, and if you were still here waiting for my next one, there are no words left to convey my deep and humbling appreciation. I have to thank my husband (thanks for all the tea in bed and G&T's at 6pm) and my kids for still championing me and still seeing me as an author on days/weeks/months that I thought I'd never write again. Same for all my dear friends and followers on Social Media.

Thank you to Brenna Aubrey for nine plus pages of single spaced typed notes on how to make this a better book. (in addition to French corrections). I was so far in the mud and weeds, I couldn't see. You put your boots on and came to find me and dig me out, and I will forever be in your debt. Anyone who enjoyed this book, should thank her too :) she writes great romances. Check her out at www.brennaaubrey.net

Thank you also to beta readers Lisa Wilhelm, Julie Burke,

Brenna Rattai, Caroline Benton, and Karina Asti. And as always Al Chaput and Dave MacDonald, thank you for slogging through 54 chapters rewritten 17 times while I found my footing again! And then massive appreciation to Judy (www.judy-roth.com) for editing, and Karina (Kainaasti.com) for the proofread. *Merci*, Rose Griot, for the additional French corrections and fun Skype chat!

Thanks to my mom for making sure my kids, husband, and I, were fed during the creation of this book and even on days I just sat like dead jelly fish in front of my laptop. I'm so glad the pandemic caused you to get stuck with us! Thank you also for reading my book. I'm glad Josie and Xavier's story gave you the giddy feels. And I'm really sorry about all the sex lol.

I used to travel to Southern France as a kid (we lived in England), and I recently returned in the summer of 2019. I knew instantly I wanted to set a book there. I particularly want to thank Minky Gray for her hospitality in Valbonne, FR and hope beyond hope we can visit you again soon. You are owed so, so, many hugs.

Thanks to *Le Club 55* for unwittingly being a character in the book. And also the Historic Charleston Foundation who do incredible work to save the cultural heritage of Charleston.

Special mention goes to the color of the Mediterranean. It's hard to find a picture that does it justice, but my dearest friend Erin Gianni had recently been on a yacht (before Covid times), in the Mediterranean *et voilà*! This is her original, unfiltered picture. Doesn't it make you just want to dive right in? Thanks Julie of hearttocover.com for using it to make such an awesome cover.

This book is a homage to the big beautiful world out there, waiting for us all to get well and safely start exploring again. Until then, we can still dream about oceans, yachts, true love and happily ever afters.

Any nonsensical geographical issues, transit times, and French mistakes are mine and mine alone. And yes, Xavier says *Merde* a lot, but I would have had to include a dictionary for all the many colorful curse words the French actually use lol!

Thanks for being here, and your support,

With all my love,

Tasha x

Tasha xo

ALSO BY TASHA BOYD

The Butler Cove Novels
Eversea (Eversea #1)
Forever, Jack (Eversea #2)
My Star, My Love (An Eversea Christmas Novella)
All That Jazz
Beach Wedding (Eversea #3)

Deep Blue Eternity / *The Recluse*
(A standalone contemporary romance)

The Charleston Series
Accidental Tryst
(A Romantic Comedy)
Irresistible Beau
Sunshine Suzy *(TBA 2021)*

ALSO: Ever wished your favorite romance author would write a "bookclub" type book? Well, I did! ***The Indigo Girl*** a historical fiction (or should I say, *herstorical* fiction?) novel is available now in hardcover, ebook and audio. It's based on a true story and it's a woman's story you don't want to miss. I am so incredibly proud of this book, and the honor of being able to tell this incredible young woman's story. I do give talks about it at libraries, museums and schools and bookclubs via zoom. So contact me via my Website www.natashaboyd.com

ABOUT THE AUTHOR

Natasha Boyd (writing romance as TASHA BOYD) is a USA
Today and Wall Street Journal bestselling and award-winning
author of both historical fiction and contemporary romance. Her
historical fiction novel THE INDIGO GIRL was long-listed for
the Southern Book Prize and was a Southern Independent
Booksellers' Association OKRA PICK. She holds a Bachelor of
Science in Psychology, and lives with her husband, two sons, and
her dog in Atlanta, GA.
Text NATASHABOYD to 31996